The N the Warak Shu

MW00390386

in which

Camille, a Humble Nash Metropolitan,
Saves the Earth From
the Threat of Extraterrestrial Domination
and
Maisie Finds a New Friend

By Rhyscary Wade
UFO Sex Comedy - Book 2

The Night of the Warak Shu

Dedication
I have a feeling that all my dedications will wind up being the same.

With love to my wife, Lee,
Proofreader extraordinaire and perfect life companion,

And my mother, Joyce,
The start of a lifelong love affair with words
and my first inspiration to write.

Also by Rhyscary Wade
Currently available on Amazon as Kindle eBooks - Print editions coming soon
Attack of the 50-Foot Labradoodle - *Print edition available on Amazon*
Enki Goes to Hollywood
A Goblin in the Moonshine
Invasion of the Incredible Transparent Shrinking Zombie Thingys
The Prescient Wisdom of Nancy Drew
One Night in Tombstone

Table of Contents

Chapter 1 - Christmas in July

The knock on the door was as unexpected as it was unwelcome, arriving at virtually the same moment as Jakob's orgasm. The door in question was at the base of a steep flight of carpeted steps leading up to the attic room that Rita Mae Marshaux rented from Mrs Agatha Kelley. She rented the room whenever the Project Stall team's presence was required in Washington DC.

The attic room had never been intended as a full-time residence, but it was cheap, convenient, and rarely occupied. The room itself, with its peaked ceiling and dormer window, was barely large enough to contain a single bed along one wall and a three-drawer bureau beside it, but it was usually available due to the dwarfish height of its ceilings.

Jakob's withdrawal, timed as neatly as any tactical retreat, came just in the nick of time, as the repressed semen of their five-year courtship shot up her torso as if propelled from the barrel of a cannon. Spewing forth a straight line that ran from the furry forest of Rita Mae's pudendum, Jakob's jizz left a draftsman's line of spunk all the way up her sternum before pooling in her clavicular notch.

Her landlady's voice came up the perilous stairs, clearly ignorant of both her little man's presence and the damage done to the sheets she'd be laundering.

"You have a gentleman caller who wishes to see you, Miss Marshaux," Mrs Kelley called up in the cracked voice one might expect of a retired fishwife.

Horrified at the prospect of being caught *in flagrante delicto*, Rita pushed free of the tiny man who would soon be her husband. Yanking the towel from under her buttocks, she used it to wipe the excess jizz from her spunky torso. Meanwhile, displaying the native agility of a crippled house cat, Jakob Kleinemann rolled to the floor with a loud thump, a beat out of time with Rita's descent.

"I'll be down in a second!" Rita called before thinking to ask. "Who is it?"

She heard a murmur of voices from the bottom of the stair, followed by the appalling creak of the door opening a crack. Rita tossed the towel aside as she reached for her housecoat.

"He says you'll be expecting him. If you don't mind my saying so, this one looks like a much better catch than that little Jew fella you've been seeing."

Jakob Kleinemann, that little Jew fella, growled a bit too loudly, "It is only Ångström. But I told him to come by at nine o'clock and it is only..." Jakob paused to glance at the bedside clock, "... nine o'clock."

Rita Mae's eyes went wide in alarm. Other than being mostly naked, her appearance had changed little in the five years since joining Project Stall. Her carriage was still upright and ramrod straight from her duties as an Army typist, her body as firm and taut as a teenage gymnast's.

The only change of any real significance involved her hairdo. In its current configuration, Rita Mae's hair was considerably longer than the helmet of tight curls CeCe Villiers had tricked her into back in 1947. The old perm made her look like a Greek boy only recently absent from the Mediterranean fishing village he called home.

Her new do was a shoulder length bob, tucked in at the ends, with a straight line of bangs hanging down over her forehead. The new do was as awful as the old, but in a different way. This one, in concert with her easily obscured bust, made her look like a page boy from a medieval drama starring Errol Flynn.

"What were you thinking?" Rita hissed. "The two of you should have met somewhere and then come here."

"I was," Jakob insisted. "I was going to meet him outside and we were going to fetch you together."

"He's a very nice looking man," Mrs Kelley reported, her voice redolent with the dreamy quality that seemed to afflict a large segment of the female gender in Lars Ångström's presence.

"Shall I have him wait in the parlor while you dress?"

There was an almost greedy quality to the landlady's voice. Though Miss Agatha was still legally married to the absent Mr Kelley, gone missing in South America these seventeen years, the septuagenarian Mrs K cooed like a lovestruck adolescent entranced by the arrival of an older sister's beau.

Rita knew, from her own experience, that once Mrs K had Lars seated in the best of her precarious chairs, she would offer him tea, then proceed to coax information out of him as efficiently as a Gestapo interrogator.

"That'll be fine, Mrs K! Tell him I'll be down in a minute!" Rita called back, frantically searching her drawers for a clean pair of panties. She scratched at the unfamiliar itch of semen drying under her housecoat.

Jakob, trying and failing to get both legs into his pants at the same time, tripped and landed heavily on the single mattress that made up her bed, his weight balanced precariously on the brink of another precipitous fall.

"Quiet!" Rita hissed. "Are you trying to get me evicted?"

Jakob looked up at his fiancee, struck again by his good fortune in winning the hand of such an unattainably normal girl. She wasn't tall by any measure, but she towered over him by half a foot. She wasn't Jewish either, but even his aunts would concede that she wasn't half bad for a *shiksa*.

"Why should it matter?" He responded with an initiate's smile. "By the end of the week, we will be married."

Having wiped away as much of his spunk as she could find, Rita Mae discarded the towel. The modest depression between her breasts still glinted in the reflected light streaming through the window. Downstairs, the old Queen Anne creaked with the retreating footsteps of Lars Ångström and Mrs K.

Jakob listened as he pulled on his socks. "What are we going to do now? I can't very well follow you down the stairs."

He paused for a goofy smile, imagining how their superiors at Wright-Patterson might view the news that the physically unprepossessing Professor Jakob Kleinemann had been caught with his pants down in the room of an unmarried woman.

Her mind occupied with finding clothes, Rita Mae ignored his question, clawing her way through the bureau in search of an appropriate outfit.

Since her breasts weren't really large enough to require a brassiere, the wire-framed torture device was often an afterthought. In her rush to get downstairs, it was one she now forgot. Selecting a knee-length skirt from the drawer, she wrapped it around her waist and buttoned it into place. The girdle she didn't need and hadn't brought was discarded as a concession to the heat, as were the stockings and garters that would take far too long to locate. Finding a stain on her favorite blouse, she discarded it in favor of a light sweater of loose weave that usually required wearing a slip underneath. She checked her hair in the mirror and shook it out, relieved that it could once again reach her shoulders.

"You better get going," she reminded Jakob, bringing a concerned rise to his bushy eyebrows.

"Yes, but how?" He asked again, reminding her a second time that, "Mrs Kelley will surely notice if I leave by the stairs."

Rita pulled the sweater over her head, shoving her arms into the sleeves. For the first time since their aborted exploit into coital maturity, she smiled.

"How are you at climbing trees?"

Jakob Kleinemann was shocked by the suggestion.

"I have never climbed a tree in my life."

Rita's smile grew mischievous, her eyes sparkling with a dangerous mixture of glee and anticipation. Jakob recoiled slightly, when he realized she really was going to put him through this rite of passage.

"Well, my daddy always said there's no time like the present to learn. If you just open the window, and crawl across the roof, you'll find a big elm with a branch even you should be able to reach."

Jakob's discomfort grew with mounting horror.

"I can't climb a tree! It's...it's...undignified. I am a professor of"

"I know, I know," Rita smiled, quelling his protest with a stroke of her index finger under his bearded jaw. "You have many doctorates and I will concede that you are a very smart man. But at the moment, nothing in your education is of the slightest use to you. This is a situation where all of your scholarship and book learning won't help you a lick."

"For once in your life, you need to think like a man of action. You're trapped in the room of an unmarried woman whose reputation will be besmirched by your presence. If you don't want her to face disgrace and dishonor, you'll have to climb out that window and shimmy down that tree."

Rita Mae fluttered her hand as if waving away an attack of vapors. In truth, she wasn't really a Southern belle, but she'd observed more than a few belles in action, and picked up enough to play the part when necessary. As a *coup de grace*, she tweaked the little bulb at the end of his nose, reminding him, "I love you, furry bunny," as she twisted his heart a little tighter around her pinky.

Doctor Jakob Kleinemann, recipient of those many doctorates, sighed on his way to the window.

"Try to be quiet," Rita Mae cooed encouragingly as she helped him through the window. "Maybe she'll think you're a squirrel."

***

As the day was going to be hot and having already eschewed both stockings and garters, Rita Mae also decided to forgo the formality of heels and makeup for a pair of lightweight casual slippers and nothing respectively. She made this decision on her way down to the second floor, but opted for a compromise just outside the parlor, pausing to draw a thin line of lipstick across her mouth. A loud thump came from the roof above, followed by the satisfying creak of the elm as it took Jakob's weight.

Lars Ångström rose as she entered, a full cup of Mrs Kelley's lethally sugary tea sitting untouched on the table by his chair. Mrs K's eyes grew full and wide as Ångström rose to his full height, the crown of his head towering a good fifteen inches above her own.

"I must apologize, Miss Marshaux," Lars said with the formality of a recent acquaintance. "It appears that I am early. The Major asked me to pick up you and Doctor Kleinemann on the way to the hearing. We should go at once. The Major has heard rumors that they may want us to testify."

"Testify?" Rita Mae reared back like a started horse.

"Yes, some congressional committee on Un-American affairs or activities, I've forgotten the exact title."

Now it was Mrs Kelley who was startled, but a good hostess knew when to keep her mouth shut, and Mrs K considered herself to be such.

"The McAfee committee?" Rita goggled, even more shocked.

"Yes," Lars replied affably. "Have you heard of it?"

Rita Mae wanted to swear, but knew she couldn't do so in front of Mrs K. He was toying with her, playing his idea of a joke. Lars Ångström was too well versed in public affairs to be unaware of the effect the McAfee committee was having on the country.

"We really should be going," Lars continued. "We still have to pick up Dr Kleinemann. Also, the Major asked if you might pick up some bicarbonate of soda on your way. He said his breakfast didn't agree with him."

Rita looked down at the clothes she was wearing, realizing at once they were more suited for a picnic than a Senate hearing. She wanted to ask what the hearing was about, but she couldn't do so in front of Mrs Kelley if she wanted to keep her head on her shoulders when Arthur Ecks found out.

"I can't go to a government hearing in this," she complained, noting Mrs K's nod of approval at her discretion. "I'll need five minutes to change into something nicer."

Lars shook his head, enjoying himself immensely at her expense.

"I'm afraid there just isn't time. Don't worry, though. I'm sure that no one will be looking at you."

Turning to the landlady, Lars made their goodbyes.

"Thank you for an enchanting cup of tea, Mrs Kelley. I don't believe I've ever tasted its equal."

***

They found Jakob Kleinemann outside, clinging to the lowest branch of the elm, a heretofore unidentified fear of heights, as well as his own lack of experience, preventing further descent. The drop was no more than five feet, but as this gap was greater than Kleinemann's height, it might just as well be the Grand Canyon. Jakob blushed as Lars reached up to help him down, ignoring the jeers of the two neighborhood boys who stopped to watch.

The jeers died when Rita tweaked his nose a second time, delivering a very public kiss that was seen by the boys, but obscured from Mrs Kelley by the trunk of the elm and Lars Ångström.

"I love you, furry bunny," she whispered, making Jakob's toes curl inside his shoes. Straightening up, she sent him off to Lars' Chrysler.

"Can we drop you anywhere?" Lars asked. "We don't have much time."

"Where are we going?" Jakob complained, aggrieved at always being the last to know.

"You tell him, I need to find a cab" Rita called back as she headed down to the corner where flagging a taxi would be easier. "I need to get Arthur his bicarbonate and it's probably best that only one of us is late."

"Do you know where the hearings are being held?" Lars called out as she walked away.

"No, but this is Washington. I'm pretty sure the cabbie will."

***

Twenty minutes later, Rita Mae Marshaux exited the yellow cab with a small box of bicarbonate stashed in her purse. She looked up as a growl of thunder rolled off the mass of choppy clouds forming over the Senate building. A second later, the first drops struck the pavement to sizzle and die in the burgeoning heat.

At just past ten o'clock, it was already over ninety degrees on what was looking more and more like a normal DC summer day. The air was redolent with the cloying thickness reminiscent of her childhood in Louisiana.

Rita quickened her pace, sliding her purse strap up to her shoulder in what was sure to be a futile effort to protect the calfskin. Always a worrier, she wondered if there was a penalty for being late, muttering an insincere and silent prayer that she'd be able to get inside before the downpour started in earnest.

A slender man in a tan summer suit ran past on her right. At first, he seemed to be headed in the same direction, but suddenly he leapt off the sidewalk into the oncoming traffic, dodging cars until he found a gap that allowed him to reach the other side. A moment later, he was followed by a pair of men in dark suits who prudently chose to wait for the light. Rita Mae hurried on, taking no interest in the motivations behind this obscure drama.

The rain came suddenly and it came down in sheets, pelting the sidewalk with heavy drops that turned to mist as soon as they hit the hot cement. Rita ran the last twenty yards only to be stymied by the crowd queuing outside the doors. She hadn't expected the rain, and now realized she should've brought an umbrella. She paid for her lapse with a good drenching.

Once inside, she slithered through the crowd blocking the entrance, then dashed down the hallway, anxiously unaware of the attention she was drawing as she scanned the throng of milling men for some sign of Jakob. Lars had told her to meet them outside the hearing chambers, but no one, not even Major Ecks, could've predicted the size of the crowd.

She checked the number on the nearest door and started down the hall, fighting against a river of gray-suited men who paused at her approach, but lacked the etiquette to move aside. One after another, she saw the bland or bored expressions on their faces turn to interest or delight. Sensing she really was late, she ignored these looks and was grateful when the number on the next room told her she was headed in the right direction.

Lars saw her first and his features lit up with the same delight she'd seen from every other man. She looked around for Jakob, finding her Project Stall colleagues in his shade, Dexter Wye, Arthur Ecks, and finally, Jakob. She skipped through the final gap in the mob as if that could make up for her tardiness. Jakob heaved a sigh of exasperation as she approached, too soft to hear. As soon as she came close, he removed his homburg, only to immediately clap it across her chest. One newshound, trapped well back in the pack, actively voiced his displeasure with the little man's action.

"Spoilsport."

Rita thrust the bicarbonate into Ecks' outstretched hand. Ecks took one look at her and without further greeting, led them into the crush of reporters blocking the entrance. Somehow, Jakob found her hand and squeezed, but she was blinded as a dozen flashbulbs exploded around her. Once again, she had to fight her way upstream against a torrent of men.

***

1952 was a bad time to be working on any government-funded project, and Project Stall was at the height of both its importance and its need for secrecy. With HUAC busily working its way through the whispered gossip of low-level civil servants, it was also an awkward time to be keeping those secrets.

In theory, the committee was charged with ferreting out persons involved in what were broadly described as un-American activities. In practice, this was narrowed down to anyone in an official capacity with either communist or homosexual sympathies. But this wasn't why the committee was meeting this day, while most of Congress was out on summer recess.

But on this day, in an odd reversal of direction, word had trickled out that the committee had decided to look into the flying saucer phenomenon. Fortunately, unlike the State Department effort, the saucer review wasn't expected to last more than a day or two.

The story making the rounds amongst the reporters was, that in the process of lining up witnesses for testimony into other matters, the committee had come across references to the ongoing investigations being conducted by the Air Force and other agencies. In tracking down those references, the committee had run across an organization whose security clearance was well above top secret. These were no more than rumors, at least until they were brought to the attention of Senator Joseph McAfee, the committee's chair. Through further investigation, McAfee had managed to connect the dots that led to Project Stall.

If there was ever any significance to the name of Project Stall, it'd been forgotten over the years of its existence. But to Arthur Ecks' ongoing disgust, enough had surfaced to confirm certain facts about the project's personnel and purpose. Those facts were enough to persuade the Senator that other items of interest might exist as well.

In pursuit of this research, the Committee's investigators were unable to discover virtually nothing about two of the men who were rumored to be involved with the team. The same was true of its lone woman.

But if these were mysteries, the same could not be said for the other two members of the team. Though the two academics performed their Project Stall duties in secret, both were publicly notorious, albeit for reasons having nothing to do with UFOs or flying saucers.

Two years prior, Dr Lars Ångström had published the most exhaustive research on human sexual practices the world had ever seen, an encyclopedic volume that made the *Kama Sutra* seem like a connect-the-dots coloring book. Despite its audacious subject matter, the book was a guilty pleasure that'd topped the bestseller lists for two years. Its success was surprising as it was the kind of book that everyone knew of, but no one admitted having read.

The study was the culmination of years of research cataloging sexual behavior based on a wide range of factors. Ångström wanted to call the book *Human Sexual Response in 20th Century Society*, but his publisher, perhaps sensing the book's bombshell potential, nixed that idea, insisting that it simply be called *Sex!*

Ångström was a striking figure, tall with blond curls and the sculpted physique of a Johnny Weissmuller. Since the publication of *Sex!*, Ångström had appeared on the covers of *Look* and *Life*, as well as several lesser magazines. For some, he was easily identifiable as a public figure, being one of those rare persons who possess the kind of celebrity where his face was known even though the reasons behind his fame remained obscure. Perhaps it was an indictment of how closed the world of government reporting had become, because while many of the fourth estate recognized his face, only three were able to recall his name.

Even with this anonymous celebrity, Ångström had the kind of personal presence that set flash bulbs flashing and reporters scurrying for phone booths before anyone stopped to ask why he was there, or more importantly, who he was. By the time they came running back, Ångström had absconded with his imperfect fame, climbing the narrow stair to the observation lounge where he would to await the call to testify with the other, less identifiable, faces.

But though Lars Ångström was easily the most notorious, he wasn't the only public figure of note with connections to Project Stall. As the tall Swede followed Arthur Ecks and Dexter Wye up to the lounge, he was shadowed by a tiny man in the dark conservative clothes of an itinerant rabbi. Only one reporter knew this man's name, and that was only because he was the kind of man who took a special interest in the accomplishments of his fellow Jews. The tiny man's book hadn't caused the general furor that Ångström's had, but it'd certainly stirred up the academic community, arousing the ire of several unconnected disciplines that were all prepared to go on record denouncing its findings without having so much as perused the biography on the book jacket.

Schrödinger's Catastrophe was an exhaustive tome of historical research that purported to prove that the solar system wasn't always the nice stable neighborhood uniformly portrayed by mainstream science. The book was groundbreaking in that it pioneered the use of myth to reconstruct present conditions, calling into question the roles of Mars and Venus by suggesting that our nearest neighbors had engaged in a game of cosmic chicken with each other as well as the Earth. It told of the many catastrophes that'd almost wiped out humanity, of comets passing close to the Earth, creating fear and havoc in their passage. The book debuted a radical new method of research, giving credence to stories long dismissed as the fanciful imaginings of primitive cultures.

Professor Jakob Kleinemann was physically incapable of making the kind of entrance that nature granted Lars Ångström. However, there were a few reporters in the group who liked to read something other than their own bylines, and one of this group recognized the diminutive Jew in the rabbi's togs.

Bertie Stein of the *Times* and John Haste of the *Post* made furtive eye contact at the collective lack of reaction to the little professor's presence, and with a complicit nod, agreed not to spill the beans to their more ignorant competition. Haste hadn't recognized Kleinemann, but he'd seen the unmistakable signs that Bertie had, and if there was one thing Haste had learned in his time on the Washington beat, it was that Bertie Stein was one smart cookie.

There was another reason Professor Kleinemann went unnoticed and her name, which would remain unknown to all in attendance, was Rita Mae Marshaux. Of average height and minimal bust, the auburn-haired Cajun had arrived dressed in a thin white sweater and a gray wool skirt that almost managed to disguise an extraordinarily attractive derriere. But on this day, it wasn't her hindquarters that drew the attention of the newshounds.

While there was a charisma to her face, with its elevated cheekbones and the faint spray of freckles, the kind of dusting one might find across the pert nose of a French peasant girl, there was something else about this young woman that had aroused the keen interest of the veteran newshounds.

With her hair lank and dripping from the rain, in concert with the fact that her thin sweater wasn't designed to repel water, the sheer half-slip beneath it did nothing to conceal her objects of attraction. Her nipples, brought into stark relief by the air-conditioned chill of the Senate, stood out like twin reproductions of Rudolph's nose on Christmas Eve.

Chapter 2 - The Search for Fire

The chamber was still filling as the five members of Project Stall were led up the stairs to the observation lounge. Enclosed by a high ceiling that rose more than thirty feet above the Senate floor, the chamber spread out from the stage like the Greek amphitheater it was modeled on. Twelve rows of terraced seats lined the clamshell floor as it rose away from the podium. Serving as the focal point for every seat in the room, a long oaken table ran about half the length of the low stage.

The table was the most prominent piece of furniture in the room. With its ponderous majesty, it gave the impression that it had arrived first and everything else had been built around it. The table commanded such presence that the rest of the chamber, with its high-paneled walls and sloping floor, was diminished enough to be dismissed as a mere accessory. On its far side, six mahogany chairs were set at regular intervals, with four already occupied. The chairman's seat, set to dead center, was currently empty, as was the seat at the far right.

Opposing the stage, a shorter table with seats grouped closely together, had been set up facing the one on the stage. These chairs were less impressive than those behind the main table. Set at a lower altitude, the positioning alone gave anyone seated there the not-so-subtle impression that their lives and their desires were of less importance than those of the men above them.

Each station at both tables was home to a single microphone, each with its own cable that ran into a hole in the floor. Each hole was a signal that an unseen world lay beneath the floorboards. As the hearing had yet to begin, the microphones weren't turned on.

Few of those who entered had taken their seats, leaving the aisles congested with reporters and onlookers, all curious to see what Senator Joseph McAfee, the committee's infamous chair, was up to during what was supposed to be his summer break. July in Washington DC was muggy and miserable, and by tradition, the month was a time when members of Congress returned home to visit their constituencies. The reporters gathered in clusters, each group sprinkled with the crude conversation of their profession, their veiled eyes scrutinizing any who weren't known members of the fourth estate.

Despite this heightened awareness, everyone managed to miss McAfee's entrance, most only realizing he'd arrived when the gavel came down, calling the session to order. As if on cue, the other empty seat was taken by the young man who served as the committee's secretary, his fingers flying in a rapid blur over the keys of a stenographic machine, like a sprinter stretching before getting into the blocks.

McAfee seemed to appear out of nowhere. Standing, he was a bulky man with unshaven jowls, wearing a suit that seemed tailored for someone else. There was speculation that his personal appearance might cost him a chunk of the women's vote in the next election, but McAfee seemed inclined to wait for the campaign before making any changes. With a better suit, he might be able to mitigate the impression of a plumber who'd risen above his class.

Despite his overall bulk, his head still appeared to be too large for his body. In addition to the heaviness of his jowls, his face had a lumpen quality that made it seem that too much skin had been used in its manufacture. Most of his hair was gone, but in this first postwar decade, politicians weren't expected to maintain their appearance the way they would once Jack Kennedy came on the scene.

The greater part of the hair McAfee had retained took the form of two enormous caterpillar eyebrows facing off like rivals preparing to battle over a prospective mate. His other dominant features were a pair of enormous ears with high arcing helixes and dangling lobes. Veterans of previous sessions had reported that these appendages glowed lobster red when the Senator was aroused, usually by signs of vacillation in a witness' testimony. Some even said it was as if his ears were able to smell blood.

At the sound of the gavel, a name was called, and without further ceremony, Dr Lincoln La Paz took the center seat at the witness table. He took a moment to settle in, speaking test phrases into the microphone until the sound engineer signaled that he had a good level.

Dr La Paz was a fit, stocky man in his mid-fifties, standing just under six feet in height. His short black hair drew away from an intelligent forehead, while extending the tentative finger of a reluctant widow's peak. His face was mild and inexpressive, the face of a man who played his cards close to the vest, revealing nothing before its time. He wore a thick mustache, also black, which trimmed to a manageable length, served to disguise the fullness of his upper lip. His face was a rich tan, an indication that he'd spent considerable time outdoors. He wore a conservative charcoal suit with a thin black tie over a white dress shirt.

McAfee waited until La Paz had made himself comfortable before beginning.

"If my notes are correct," McAfee said with a self-deprecating smile, "you are Dr Lincoln La Paz, currently chair of the astronomy department at the University of New Mexico?"

La Paz had to lean forward to speak into the mic. "Yes."

"Thank you for coming to speak with us today, doctor."

"I am always glad to help my country, Senator. How can I be of service?"

A grin creased McAfee's lumpy face.

"Thank you, Doctor. I wish everyone who testified before this committee had your attitude."

Recalling the experiences of previous witnesses, La Paz's expression was bland.

"I've done a bit of government work over the last decade. Passing information on to elected officials has always been part of my job, though this is the first time I've had the honor of addressing the Senate."

McAfee cocked his head in a folksy way.

"Well, doctor, this hearing will fall somewhat outside the committee's normal purview. I've been asked by my fellow members of Congress to make use of the summer session by looking into this flying saucer business. My hope in doing so is that we can flush out a few commies and queers in the process."

McAfee paused, waiting for a laugh that never came, then proceeded to stare at his witness until realizing he hadn't said anything requiring a response.

"We've requested your presence here today to ask if there's anything you might be able to tell us about these flying saucers that have been plaguing our air space for the last five years."

Dr La Paz remained his impassive self.

After a brief pause, he said, "I know absolutely nothing about flying saucers. My specialty is astronomy, although I've achieved some notoriety for devising a method of locating meteorite crash sites."

McAfee appeared to be stunned by the denial.

"You know nothing about flying saucers? My understanding is that you're considered an expert in the field."

"I've never seen a flying saucer in my life," said La Paz firmly. "Nor have I ever been asked to look into them."

McAfee rifled through his notes to find a page he wanted.

"That doesn't sound right. My records show that, back in 1949, you were brought in to investigate a phenomena commonly described as green fireballs."

La Paz nodded. "Then I understand the confusion, but the green fireballs were never shown to be flying saucers and I don't believe anyone has ever suggested such a thing."

"Then what were the green fireballs, doctor? Perhaps you could give us a history of the phenomena."

La Paz's right eyebrow rose ever so slightly.

"I can provide some history, but I have no answer for the question. I can only tell you what the green fireballs were not. I cannot advance any theory as to what they actually were."

"This committee will accept whatever you can give," McAfee replied amicably.

La Paz slid closer to the table, and resting his elbows on that surface, folded his hands. He paused to gather his thoughts before beginning.

"The fireballs were first reported in November of 1948. The first sightings were reported in the area around Albuquerque. Witnesses described what they saw as green streaks in the sky, usually low on the horizon. When these were first reported, the Air Force determined that they were only flares. At the time, there were thousands of GI's who'd been recently discharged from the service, and many had acquired various pistols and flare guns during the war."

McAfee came forward, lowering his great head to speak into his mic.

"So, to paraphrase, these reports were initially dismissed as being something quite ordinary? Was there any actual investigation done?"

La Paz shook his head.

"To my knowledge, not at that time. But this was before I was brought in to investigate the matter. At that point, the military didn't see any way to approach such an investigation. I believe their hope was that the fireballs would simply go away. In the meantime, the flare guns served as a reasonable explanation for the phenomenon."

"I see. What happened to change their minds?"

La Paz took a sip from his glass of water.

"Well, I suppose what happened is that the sightings continued, but the reports got better, too. The fireballs in these later reports were larger, and judged to be far too powerful to have come from flare guns."

"Could that be because people had heard about them? I think we've all seen how a story can grow in the telling."

La Paz rocked his head a little side-to-side. "There wasn't any publicity being given to the phenomena in those early days. I don't think the sightings reached the papers, but I suppose it is possible, even likely, that the sightings were discussed with friends and neighbors. All I can say is that the Air Force credited these new reports and began to reconsider the flare gun explanation."

"What other explanations did they consider?"

A small smile flickered across La Paz's otherwise implacable face.

"Why don't I just continue with the history? I think we'll get to that question soon enough."

"Of course, please go on."

"The turning point came on the night of December 5th-"

"So the sightings had only been going on for a few weeks then?"

"That is correct. Just before nine-thirty in the evening, the crew of an Air Force transport flying ten miles south of Albuquerque was startled by a green fireball streaking across the sky. The fireball flew right across the nose of the plane and the pilots reported that it looked like a meteor. That would have been a likely explanation if not for a couple of factors."

"And what were those?"

"First, the fireball was glowing bright green. Some metals do glow green when superheated, but that green is generally more muted. Second, meteors will

13

usually arc downward, even if they might first appear to be moving parallel to the ground. This fireball started low, just above the ridge of a nearby mountain range, then arced upward before leveling out. Needless to say, that isn't typical meteor behavior. In addition, this meteor was very large, larger than any member of the crew had ever seen. After a quick discussion, the crew decided to radio in a report on the object. The final factor in that decision was that they had seen an identical object twenty minutes earlier, near Las Vegas, New Mexico."

A burst of discussion spread through the room, a general hubbub that forced McAfee to make liberal use of his gavel. When the conversation died back to a more respectful level, the Senator motioned La Paz to continue.

"I find it interesting that the crew didn't report the first sighting."

"Indeed, but this wasn't the end of the story. Minutes later, the captain of a commercial airliner radioed the tower that he'd also seen a green fireball near Las Vegas."

Once again the hearing chamber erupted, prompting another smacking of the gavel and a caution from McAfee.

"Please, gentlemen, I know this is an incendiary topic, but this is the Senate and a sense of decorum is expected. Please continue, Dr La Paz."

La Paz scratched an itch at the center of his mustache.

"There isn't much more to this story. The Air Force had intelligence officers waiting for the pilots when they landed. The pilots reported that what they'd seen was too low and had too flat a trajectory to be a meteor. Additionally, they'd witnessed the object change color, going from orange to red to green. The object approached the plane, coming close enough that the pilot veered away rather than risk a collision. As the object drew alongside, it began to fall, growing dimmer until it disappeared from sight. Before the pilot swerved, the fireball appeared to be as large as a full moon."

Unlike the previous revelations, this one caused a stunned hush to fall over the chamber. La Paz used the silence to conclude his story.

"These sightings were enough for the Air Force to dismiss the idea that the fireballs were flares or meteorites, but since they bore some resemblance to the latter, I was called in to consult on the matter."

"Why you, Dr La Paz?"

"Well, as I said, I've had some success tracking meteorite trajectories. Through mathematical analysis, I've often been able to find the crash sites. I believe the hope was that I might be able to do the same for the fireballs. I think another reason was that for the first time, we had real data to work with. This fireball was seen by dozens of people, and the planes were tracked on radar. This allowed us to make use of their flight paths in calculating the trajectory, as well as calculating an approximate speed for the object. We never found one, though given the size of the object, it should've attracted some attention when it touched down."

"Don't you mean 'if' it touched down, doctor?"

"Yes, that would be more accurate, but, if true, it would also open up a real can of worms."

A ripple of laughter went through the room.

"And did you draw any conclusions from your investigation?"

La Paz fell silent as he considered whether to answer the question or not. Though it wasn't obvious from his testimony, he had his academic reputation to consider. Finally, he said.

"Yes, for the first time I seriously doubted that the fireballs were meteorites. There were many similar incidents that followed, but we were never able to find out if or where they crashed. The green fireball sightings went on all through December and January. Finally, in mid-February, a conference was called to decide what to do."

"Did you attend that conference?"

"Yes, I spoke extensively at it. The conference included experts from the Air Force, Project Sign, which was then the group responsible for investigating UFOs, and the intelligence group from Kirkland Air Force Base. There were also prominent scientists from Los Alamos and a number of universities in attendance. It was an interesting meeting because due to the number of incidents, virtually everyone had personally seen at least one fireball."

"Extraordinary! And what was the outcome of that conference?"

Dr La Paz brought his palms together in a gesture of reluctant patience.

"At the outset, we had hoped to resolve the issue of whether the fireballs were natural or an artificial phenomena. As I've said, I was of the opinion that they were certainly not meteors or meteorites."

"So then, in your opinion, the fireballs were manmade?"

"That seems highly unlikely, Senator. There is currently nothing within the scope of our knowledge capable of achieving the incredible speeds we observed from the fireballs. Not even our jets or our rockets could match the speed of the fireballs. And to still be able to maneuver while traveling at such speeds? We had people familiar with virtually all of the government's current projects at the conference and those men denied any suggestion that the United States has anything even close to possessing the abilities displayed by the fireballs."

McAfee's eyes narrowed shrewdly, flicking around the chamber as if gauging the interest level of each reporter. Most were on the edge of their seats, with pencils poised to take down whatever La Paz said next.

"So," the Senator said slowly, drawing the moment out, "the fireballs weren't meteors, and they weren't manmade. What else might account for them?"

La Paz looked down at his hands, as if wishing there was another answer than the one he was about to give. "The reported trajectories overwhelmingly suggest that the fireballs were under intelligent control."

Lincoln La Paz sighed before completing his answer, knowing that in doing so, he was symbolically kicking his academic reputation to the curb.

"It's nearly impossible to avoid the conclusion that the fireballs were anything but extraterrestrial in nature. Despite this, no one at the conference was willing to go on record as saying so."

The room fell so still that one could hear the shifting of a hundred butts on a hundred wooden chairs.

Joseph McAfee again broke the silence.

"So...was anything actually accomplished at this conference?"

Lincoln La Paz took another sip of water before answering.

"The conference resulted in a renewed determination to track the fireballs. That effort was code-named Project Twinkle. Project Twinkle went on for several months before giving up."

"Why did they give up?"

La Paz sighed. "We were unable to gather any more detailed information due to logistical problems."

McAfee's beetle brow rose sharply. "Logistical problems?"

La Paz shrugged.

"We had no control over where the fireballs chose to appear. By the time we moved the equipment into place, the fireball was long gone."

McAfee nodded, able to see some truth in the statement.

"So what did the conference decide? What were the green fireballs?"

There was no humor in La Paz's reply.

The conclusion was clearly not one he shared.

"The conference concluded that, despite the preponderance of evidence to the contrary, the fireballs were a natural phenomenon."

Chapter 3 - The Search for Answers

The observation lounge was situated at the top of a steep but short stairway. Set twenty feet above the floor of the chamber, it provided the occupants an unimpeded view of the proceedings. Sound from the witness and committee microphones was piped in through a speaker mounted on the wall at the back of the room. The view of the chamber came through a smoked glass window that obscured the occupants from the audience below.

For four of the Project Stall's members, the room was slightly reminiscent of a similar one at Roswell Army Air Field. While inside that other room, they'd witnessed what was probably the strangest and least conclusive autopsy in human history. That event had occurred on the first day of their acquaintance. Now, five years later, having added a fifth in the person of Dexter Wye, the quintet was a well-honed team that'd dealt with over three dozen incidents, most of which had failed to attract any attention from the wire services. As a result of those involvements, they knew more about green fireballs than even Lincoln La Paz, the man providing expert testimony on the subject.

But even given what they knew, there were still unavoidable factors preventing public disclosure of the fact that the green fireballs had been escape pods from a disabled Nemertean expeditionary ship. The Nemertean ship had been torn apart by the Earth's gravitational forces upon its exit from something that both science and science fiction would one day describe as a wormhole. The irony of that description was as lost on the survivors as it was on its human audience.

The breakup of the ship had forced its passengers into the escape pods. Since the individuals in question were pencil-thin worms up to three meters in length, most pods could easily hold a hundred without feeling crowded.

In the course of their investigations, Project Stall had learned that the pods had fallen to Earth at different times. Depending on each individual pod's rate of orbital decay, the pods could circle the Earth for years before coming down. A few pods had descended in the aftermath of the ship's breakup, but others were still stuck up there.

The worm leaders might claim that the pods still in orbit were waiting to hear it was safe to descend, but the truth was the pods had no ability to maneuver. As a result, the pods were entirely reliant on gravity taking its course in order to descend. And given the haphazard trajectories of most, gravity was going to take her own sweet time before drawing the pods into her bosom.

Nonetheless, a significant group did descend during the latter months of 1948. Like an extended meteor shower, the pods continued to randomly fall throughout most of 1949. The pods, when descending, glowed with an aurora of green fire, a result of the metal shell being superheated by contact with the atmosphere. From the ground, the pods were visible as green fireballs.

Upon concluding his testimony, Dr La Paz was returned to the observation room where he would remain throughout the rest of the hearing. His continued presence was a precaution should any clarification of his testimony be required. Upon entering the loft, La Paz took a seat with three other men, all of whom were familiar to him.

For the second man called, this reacquaintance was a short one.

***

Donald Keyhoe was a retired Marine pilot. He was already an established author by the time the modern fascination with flying saucers struck in the late '40s, having published a number of science fiction stories in *Weird Tales* during the '20s and '30s, as well as a stream of investigative news articles for more mainstream magazines. A thin, lightly fleshed man, he had a bony skull accentuated by a hairline that had retreated well past the crown of his head. Keyhoe had a narrow face with prominent ears and a hatchet blade for a nose. Upon making his way through the mass of reporters, he took the seat recently vacated by Dr La Paz.

As before, the chairman gaveled the hearing back to order. When everyone had returned to their seats, Joe McAfee began.

" Mr Keyhoe, the committee would like to thank you for coming to speak on such short notice."

Keyhoe approached the mic slowly.

"Glad to help, Senator. It was probably easier for me to come here than Dr La Paz. My home is in Virginia. He had to come all the way from New Mexico."

If McAfee's cold smile was any indicator, he didn't like being upstaged in his own chambers. As with any thin-skinned comic, Joe McAfee liked to be the one making the jokes.

"I'll get right to the point. For the past five years, you've done more to actively investigate the flying saucer phenomenon than anyone outside the Air Force. You've written several articles on flying saucers, mostly for *True* magazine. You've also published a book called *Flying Saucers Are Real*, based on your experiences trying to track down the source of these mysterious objects. I trust that, in your case, you will have no difficulty speaking on the subject."

A wry smile creased Keyhoe's stoic face.

"You are correct in that regard, Senator."

McAfee leaned forward with an easy grin, now all folksy warmth.

"So what can you tell us about these flying saucers, Mr Keyhoe? Why are we seeing so many of them now? And why were they never seen before?"

Keyhoe cocked his head to one side.

"I'm afraid your last statement isn't quite true, Senator. I've collected reports of strange aerial phenomena going back a hundred years and more. Sometimes these were only lights in the sky. Those were unexplainable because no one knew how to fly back then. Another thing limiting the early reports was the lack of modern communications. There was no telephone or radio. Even the telegraph was new. As a result, stories of these sightings didn't travel very far."

"How far back are you talking?"

"Well, when I began my investigations, the editor of *True* provided me with background material dating as far back as 1762. The reports weren't just from the United States, either. Sky-borne phenomena have been observed all over the world. Now, that's not to say that there weren't sightings earlier than 1762, only that none were provided to me. Those early reports were generally pretty sketchy, but that started to change about 1870. In that year, there was a report in the London *Times* of an elliptical object sporting a comet-like tail that crossed the face of the moon. The next year, there was a report from Marseilles of a large round body that some people mistook for a second moon."

"I could go on listing such incidents, but all I want to point out is that they came from all over the world. And the surprising thing is that the reports clearly aren't describing the same kind of object. The UFOs came in a multitude of sizes and shapes. There were sightings at sea as well, where ships reported seeing lights at high altitude moving very fast."

Another senator, a man with white hair and a weathered face from South Dakota, leaned forward to interrupt. "Pardon me, but you just said these early reports didn't describe the same kind of objects? Are you saying these weren't flying saucers?"

Keyhoe nodded. "The reports don't always describe the shape of the objects, but quite a few are described as being shaped like torpedos or cigars. Some are lights without any shape at all. Dr La Paz told you about the green fireballs, and those were roughly spherical."

The Senator from South Dakota tried again. "Could these objects just be balloons or dirigibles? That's what a lot of 'em sound like to me."

Keyhoe nodded at this most common of objections.

"If all we had to go on were the shapes, then that might be true. But there's a problem with balloon theories. Balloons tend to be very slow. They're sluggish and at the mercy of the wind. I worked with balloons during my time in service. Frankly, I'm surprised to hear them so often proposed as an explanation. Under certain conditions, a balloon can move very fast, but they can't change direction because they can't fly against the wind. Once we get to the modern sightings, a balloon can't outrun an airplane, much less a jet-"

Another Senator, a short dapper man from Missouri interrupted using the mechanism of a polite cough.

"This history is all very interesting, I'm sure, but maybe we should move on to the modern sightings. That's what we're all here for after all."

Keyhoe shrugged. "Of course. Shall we start during the war, or go straight to Kenneth Arnold's sighting in June of 1947?"

The Senator from Missouri scowled.

"During the war? What are you talking about? I never heard of any flying saucers during the war."

Keyhoe did a good job of hiding his amusement at the man's crankiness.

"That's probably because they didn't call them flying saucers. They were most frequently seen in the skies over Germany, during Allied bomber attacks. These were lights that flew alongside the bombers as they made their runs. I've never heard of any interference, but quite a large number of pilots and crews on our planes reported seeing these lights. Naturally, the thought at the time was that the lights were some kind of Nazi super-weapon, but there was never any real evidence to support the idea. I don't know if the general public ever heard much about them, but within the ranks they were known as foo fighters."

The cranky Senator scowled again.

"Foo fighters? Stupid name. So what were they?"

Keyhoe rested an elbow on the table and leaned into it.

"I couldn't tell you, Senator. No one ever found out what they were. The only thing we did learn is that they weren't something the Germans had come up with. We know this because these foo fighters were later spotted over Japan. I've heard they were even tracking the *Enola Gay* on the Hiroshima run. But I have no proof and I've never found anyone directly involved who was willing to talk about it. So that one will just have to stay a rumor."

"So what do these foo fighters have to do with flying saucers?"

"Maybe nothing. As I said, we never found out what they were, but many men who saw them believed they might be some kind of probe. Those who saw them all reported feeling like they were being watched."

The Senator dismissed the notion with a wave of his hand.

"Probably just war nerves. Some kind of shared hysteria."

Keyhoe visibly bridled at this suggestion.

"You can dismiss these experiences if you want, Senator, but many of these reports came from good men who risked their lives to save this country from fascism. Personally, I find it a little hard to dismiss them so easily."

The Senator, belatedly sensing he'd said something that might cost him votes, visibly subsided. McAfee intervened to get the hearing back on track.

"Maybe we should move on. This committee is more concerned with the recent sightings than these historical events. You mentioned the Mount Rainier sighting by Kenneth Arnold. Why don't you start there?"

Keyhoe took a sip of water before beginning.

"Very well, the Arnold sighting, as it's come to be known, took place on

June 24, 1947. Kenneth Arnold was a businessman and pilot, operating out of Boise. He was flying near Mount Rainier on his way from Chehalis to Yakima when he saw a bright flash off his starboard wing. Looking toward the mountain, he saw nine shiny disks, each about the size of a C-54 military transport. The disks seemed to be flying in a kind of chain, like they were linked together, though Arnold was specific in reporting that there was no physical connection between the disks. It was a clear day and the mountain made it easy to gauge distance. They appeared to be twenty to twenty-five miles away. Arnold estimated that their speed approached twelve hundred miles per hour."

"That's preposterous!"

The man from Missouri backed away from his mic, startled by his outburst. Keyhoe didn't bother to hide his smile this time.

"I understand the Senator's disbelief, but Arnold is an experienced pilot and he did have the luxury of observing these objects for over three minutes in good visibility. It was a cloudless day, and he had Mount Rainier as a backdrop. Knowing his own position and his distance from the mountain, he was able to calculate the speed of the saucers with reasonable accuracy. When he reported what he saw after landing, the story made the wire services."

"What isn't as well known," Keyhoe continued, before anyone could interrupt, "is that on that same day, a prospector from Portland spotted a half dozen of these disks from his camp site in the Cascades. After observing the disks for a few seconds, he chanced to look down at his compass. He noticed that the pointer was wildly rocking side-to-side, as if the disks were having some kind of magnetic effect on it. And, in case you were wondering, the prospector couldn't have heard about the Arnold sighting because news of it wasn't broadcast until later in the evening."

McAfee scribbled a note on a sheet of paper, and paused to nibble at the eraser on his pencil. "So this was the first of the modern reports?"

Keyhoe shook his head emphatically.

"At first, I thought so, too. But it turns out the Pentagon had been receiving reports since January. As we discovered after the Arnold report, a lot of other incidents surfaced as well. It turned out that a lot of sightings were being kept quiet because the witnesses were afraid of being ridiculed. Within days of the Arnold sighting, other incidents surfaced all over the western United States. The Air Force announced that they would be investigating and a few days later, issued an official report that said it was all hallucinations."

Keyhoe took another sip from his glass.

"Guess there must have been something in the water, because after that, the number of sightings skyrocketed. Many were seen by large numbers of people. Saucers were seen by commercial airliners, military pilots, police, you name it, everybody was seeing flying saucers. Even people who were once profoundly skeptical have come forward, claiming to have seen these objects. One pilot made a statement denying the existence of the saucers just before taking off. On that very flight, he saw a group of nine over Idaho, all of which he estimated to be larger than the plane he was flying."

"Could these be something that our own Air Force has?" McAfee asked. "Something they've neglected to tell the public about."

"Or Congress," muttered the cranky Missourian, again too close to his mic.

Keyhoe chuckled along with everyone else.

"I'm actually glad you brought that up, Senator. I have good contacts within the Air Force, quite a few in fact, and they all say no. The Air Force doesn't have anything like these saucers, and apparently they don't even have anything like them in development."

A hubbub ran through the reporters. McAfee silenced it with his gavel.

"So, if the saucers aren't something the Air Force developed-"

"And failed to inform the taxpayers," Missouri muttered.

"Then what are they?"

Keyhoe's smile returned, but disappeared as quickly as it came.

"I have a story from July 7th that you might find interesting. I don't know who said this, except that he was described as being with the Air Force. In this story, the writer proposes that flying saucers are solar reflections off low-hanging clouds, essentially small meteors carrying crystalline ice that reflect the sun when they break up in the atmosphere. I've discussed this with competent scientists and they've all agreed this is a ridiculous idea that fails to account for any aspect of the sightings."

"Frankly, every explanation I've heard is ludicrous. The only one that makes any sense at all is the weather balloon, and no experienced pilot would ever mistake a balloon for a flying saucer. Weather balloons don't move the way flying saucers are purported to move, but a number of these incidents try to use weather balloons as supposedly rational explanations for the observed phenomena. A weather balloon might have the vertical lift to perform the ascents some witnesses have described, but balloons are at the mercy of the wind for horizontal movement and no one would ever claim they show signs of intelligent control."

McAfee frowned, pensively transferring the gavel from one hand to the other and back. "Then why are balloons used to explain so many sightings?"

Keyhoe leaned forward, feeling more in his element now.

"Before I address that, I'd like to talk about one more case. This one might be the most important so far because it actually forced the Air Force to admit there might be a problem."

McAfee tapped his pencil against his jaw, looking like a man who really wanted to nibble on the eraser, but didn't want to get caught doing so.

"Go ahead, but I'd like to come back to this."

Keyhoe nodded. "Of course. The case I'm referring to, was dubbed the Mantell case, and I wanted to mention it because it changed the way flying saucers were investigated. Before the Mantell incident, flying saucers were being dismissed as hoaxes, hallucinations, or products of mass hysteria. The Mantell case forced the Air Force to treat the investigations more seriously, and it was instrumental in creating the organization I call Project Saucer in my book."

"Though I'm sure everyone is reasonably familiar with this incident, I'd like to review the events of January 7th, 1948. Captain Thomas Mantell was a pilot in the Kentucky Air National Guard. On the date in question, he was out on a routine training flight in a P-51. The P-51 was a new plane then, and while Captain Mantell was an experienced flyer, he was still in the process of getting familiar with the plane. He was flying with two other pilots under his command when he caught sight of a strange object."

Keyhoe paused for a sip of water before continuing.

"Curious as to what the object might be, Mantell radioed the field and was told that it couldn't be identified. As it had also failed to respond to all attempts to contact it by radio, Mantell decided to give chase. That chase lasted almost half an hour and took place within sight of dozens of observers. Those observers included the other pilots in the air, the men in the control tower, and several more on the ground."

"During the chase, the object maneuvered rapidly enough that it was able to maintain a sizable distance from all pursuers. When the object started to climb, Captain Mantell left his wingmen to follow. He was still in radio contact when he drew close enough to report on it. At that time, he said, and I quote, 'I've sighted the thing. It's metallic and it's tremendous in size.'"

"He also reported that the object was only moving at half his speed, but when he started to close on it, the object kept pace, even when he increased his speed to 360 miles per hour. Mantell continued to climb and was soon lost in the clouds. Several minutes dragged by before Mantell again made contact, reporting 'It's still above me, making my speed or better. I'm going up to twenty thousand feet. If I'm no closer, I'll abandon the chase.'"

Keyhoe fell silent, and the room followed suit. When he began again, his voice was more somber.

"Those were Captain Mantell's last words. A few minutes later, Mantell's P-51 disintegrated. For reasons that are still unknown, Mantell was unable to bailout. As a result, both plane and pilot plummeted to the ground. Naturally, Captain Mantell was killed. To this day, the Air Force has kept a tight lid on the investigation, releasing no information about either the plane or the condition of Mantell's body."

McAfee and the rest of the committee had been listening to the story with rapt fascination. Fearing that Keyhoe had come to the end, McAfee leaned into his mic. "So, what was used to explain the object that Captain Mantell chased to his death?"

Keyhoe's smile was incapable of being any wryer.

"Well, the initial explanation...," Keyhoe paused for emphasis, "was that Captain Mantell had died chasing the planet Venus."

After the hubbub died down, Keyhoe continued.

"That particular idea comes to us courtesy of Professor J. Allen Hynek who will be speaking later today. I mention this because it's something you might want to discuss with him."

Keyhoe paused again, steepling his fingertips as he stared off into space. His voice lost much of its harsh quality as he continued.

"There are a number of problems with the Venus explanation, not the least of which being that Venus, when seen from the Earth, could hardly be described as tremendous in size. Nor could a planet, especially one close to the same size as the Earth, maneuver in the way described by both Mantell and the witnesses on the ground. Realizing that there was something wanting in this explanation, the investigators from Project Saucer quickly changed their story."

"Let me guess," McAfee interrupted. "They said it was a weather balloon."

Keyhoe nodded, a satisfied smile widening his narrow mouth.

"Specifically, they announced that the balloon was from Project Skyhook. The reason for their secrecy, or so they claim, is that Skyhook was still classified at the time. But I hardly think the Air Force, or any other agency, would allow a pilot to chase a balloon to his death even when the existence of that balloon was top secret. The problem with this explanation is that Mantell had been flying for several years and was quite familiar with balloons. It is highly unlikely he would mistake a balloon for a spaceship. Personally, I believe the balloon explanation is a disservice to all involved. It's an insult to any experienced pilot."

McAfee frowned again, running the eraser across his lower lip.

"So I guess that leaves us back where we started. Why does the Air Force use balloons as an excuse for so many sightings?"

Keyhoe shifted his weight to lean against the back of the chair.

"If you want my opinion, and I'm afraid that's all I can give you, it's because of the way flying saucer sightings are being investigated."

A puzzled expression appeared on McAfee's rumpled face.

"What do you mean?"

Sensing he was nearing the end of his testimony, Keyhoe took a deep breath.

"Well, as you know, the job of investigating flying saucer sightings has fallen to the Air Force. I know from my own experience that military organizations aren't the most patient in the world. You're expected to get results fast, and its frowned upon when you're unable to provide solid answers. This is exactly the pressure these investigators work under. As far as their superiors are concerned, it is imperative that a plausible answer be found for each event. This mandate, which I find profoundly unscientific, has halted many investigations in their tracks. But even with this willingness to compromise scientific integrity, there are still a number of sightings that remain unexplained."

"The problem is, having an explanation for every sighting has become more important than determining what actually happened. There have been hundreds of good sightings in the last five years. Many aren't investigated at all, but many are, and of those, a significant percentage remain unexplained. I've met Captain Ruppelt, the current head of Project Saucer, and he's a good man doing good work, but he's also the first in his position to put any serious effort into the job."

"Based on my talks with him, he's not dismissing anything without good reason. I think that's the right attitude. His predecessors didn't share his zeal for the truth nor did they value the objective approach required for these investigations. This is the heart of the problem."

"The Air Force has been looking for explanations rather than seeking the truth. Unfortunately, the one thing no one wants to suggest is the one thing that may well provide the answer."

Keyhoe paused to fix his unblinking eyes on the men on the stage.

"Flying saucers are real, gentlemen. They are spaceships from other planets, visiting and observing our world. I've investigated these incidents for four years and, from everything I've been able to learn, that's my inescapable conclusion. Nothing else fits the facts and nothing else makes sense."

Chapter 4 - The Search for Explanations

"That sonuvabitch is going to be trouble," Arthur Ecks muttered.

The remark was made in what Ecks believed to be *sotto voce*, low enough not to be overheard by the men at the other table. It was with some chagrin that he realized he was mistaken. Ecks forced an embarrassed smile onto his features, apologizing to the men who'd clearly overheard him.

"Easy, Artie," murmured Dexter Wye. "Remember, we're out in public."

Lars Ångström took a more proactive approach, laughing heartily as if Ecks had delivered a clever *bon mot*. Responding to a raised eyebrow from the Swede, Jakob Kleinemann and Rita Mae Marshaux joined in on yet another coverup, albeit one of an entirely trivial nature.

The men at the other table were clearly acquainted with each another. All three had made observations during Keyhoe's testimony, though none as forceful as Ecks' comment. Dr La Paz had his back to Project Stall and didn't bother to turn, but the other two, the spade-bearded professor with the wire-rim glasses and the Air Force captain with the buzzcut looked up. Both lost interest in the wake of Ångström's theatrics.

Minutes later, Keyhoe rejoined the group, cordially greeting the three men before taking a seat. At the end of Keyhoe's testimony, Senator McAfee called the lunch break, that announcement triggering a mass exodus. Most left the building at once, heading off to queue at the hot dog stands around the Plaza Fountain.

Asked to stick around, the witnesses in the observation lounge were treated to corned beef sandwiches on the government dime. The groups ate separately and talked separately, at least until Ruppelt's curiosity drew the two tables into conversation.

"Hey, I know the fellas over here, but I don't know any of you. I'm Ed Ruppelt."

Keyhoe put his corned beef down, his eyes widening in sudden recognition.

"Well, I'll be darned. I recognize one of 'em. That's Jake Kleinemann, isn't it?"

Obviously familiar with Kleinemann's notorious academic reputation, Hynek and La Paz stiffened while Captain Ruppelt shook his head.

"I'm sorry, but the name doesn't mean anything to me."

Keyhoe laughed dryly as he turned to rest an elbow on the back of his chair.

"This is the fella that wrote *Schrödinger's Catastrophe*. I used some of his stuff about Venus in my book. How ya doing, Jake?"

Jakob Kleinemann rose to execute a short bow. As always, standing up made little difference to his height.

"It was a pleasure to hear you speak, Mr Keyhoe. I should like to introduce my fiancée, Miss Rita Mae Marshaux."

All four men expressed their own version of appreciation at the little man's good fortune. Someone whistled, but it was unclear who until the catcall was traced back to Lars Ångström.

Ruppelt, the youngest by a decade, spoke for all four.

"Yes, you may. I can see you're lucky as well as brilliant, doctor. It's a pleasure to meet you, Miss Marshaux."

Rita Mae smiled more easily than might be expected given the trials of her morning. She felt more comfortable now that her sweater had dried and her nipples had relaxed. Nonetheless, she'd learnt her lesson. Rita resolved to make sure she wore a bra if she ever had the misfortune of being invited to another Senate hearing.

Reading the bars on Ruppelt's shoulders, she cooed in pure Southern belle, "It's a pleasure to meet you too, Captain. What brings you to this little soirée?"

The three older men looked up at their young colleague with a measure of almost paternal pride. La Paz cracked a smile, his first real one of the day. "I guess there's no reason you'd be familiar with our young friend. Most of his work is handled in secret. Ed here is heading up Project Blue Book-"

"Which used to be Project Grudge," Keyhoe added.

"And Project Sign before that," concluded La Paz. "Blue Book is the Air Force's official attempt to get a handle on UFOs. Under Ed, I think they're finally making some progress."

"Helps to have an open mind," Keyhoe remarked.

"Well, then it's a very special pleasure to meet you, Captain Ruppelt."

Rita Mae did a little dip that landed somewhere between a curtsey and a bow, and somehow avoided being either. She turned from the beaming young captain to the youngish professor with the goatee and glasses.

"I've been introduced to Mr Keyhoe and Dr La Paz through their testimony, but I don't know this gentleman."

Dr La Paz rose with mock gravity, executing a bow of his own as he extended a hand toward the fourth man.

"Miss Marshaux, I'd like to present Dr Josef Allen Hynek. Dr Hynek is an astronomer of the first water. He currently teaches at Ohio State, but probably the most interesting part of his *curriculum vitae* is that he's the man tasked with finding rational explanations for the strange aerial phenomena we've seeing."

"Yeah," Keyhoe joked, in a needling tone. "The doc here's the genius who came up with the idea that Tommy Mantell died chasing Venus."

"Ease off, Don," Ruppelt scolded. Hynek blushed, bridling at the dig. "Allen's just doing what the Air Force wants him to do."

27

"It's a pleasure to meet you," Allen Hynek stammered, rising to bow and sitting back down just as quickly.

Keyhoe accepted the admonishment good-naturedly, choosing to turn his attention back to Jakob Kleinemann.

"So what brings you here, Jake? I never pegged you for a saucer man."

Jakob Kleinemann inclined his head to avoid the warning look from Ecks.

"As you might suspect, I have many interests."

Keyhoe barked out a short laugh.

"As do we all, eh, doc? Who are your friends?"

Lars Ångström, peeved at being left out of the conversation, wasn't one to waste an opening. Rising from his chair to tower over everyone in the room, Ångström extended his hand for whoever was willing to take it. As the other men remained seated, this duty fell to Captain Ruppelt.

"I am Dr Lars Ångström. It is a pleasure to meet all of you."

It took Ed Ruppelt a few moments to place the name, and when he did, he was startled enough to retrieve his hand.

"Ångström? The sex doctor?"

With the publication of Sex!, Lars Ångström had become an odd kind of household name. Though its size alone clearly advertised it as an academic tome of considerable depth, the title suggested by the publisher was so provocative that sales had skyrocketed. Even so, it was the kind of book that few Americans would admit owning. Among the population at large, its primary criticism was a regret bemoaning its paucity of pictures. With its publication, Ångström became a *cause célèbre* overnight, and blessed by his movie star looks, had since graced the covers of several national magazines.

Ruppelt took a step back, confusion spreading over his young face. The other three men shared looks of incomprehension. The consensus was that the infamous sex doctor must surely be out of place at a hearing on UFOs. Ruppelt stared at his hand as if it'd become infected with some kind of communicable virus, then back at the still-beaming Ångström. It took a while to shape what he wanted to say.

"Please excuse my awkwardness," the captain stammered, "I'm just baffled to find a man so far out of his discipline."

Ångström laughed heartily. "I assure you, Captain, that both my studies and the reasons for my being here are well within my purview. My specialty is communication, and sexual communication, though of an abstract nature, is something we will have to consider when we inevitably come into contact with extraterrestrial civilizations-"

"That's enough," Arthur Ecks said grumpily, effectively trying to shut down the conversation before it got out of hand.

Ångström nodded. "Of course, I was only-"

"I said, that's enough."

Concluding that there'd been enough socializing and concerned that his was the next logical introduction, Ecks rose from his seat, tapping Dexter Wye on the shoulder. Without uttering another word, Arthur Ecks led his protege down the stairs, thereby avoiding that delicate denial.

Hynek watched Ecks depart, only to be overcome by a powerful premonition. Something about the man made him suspect that the answers he'd sought over the course of the last few years were walking out of the room. Acting on impulse, Hynek rose to follow, but by the time he reached the bottom of the stairs, Arthur Ecks and Dexter Wye had vanished into the crowd.

Hynek stopped there, his eyes searching the milling reporters for some sign of the two men. Not being tall enough to see very far, he climbed back onto the bottom step for a better view, his heart thumping with the fear that he might never see them again. Hynek was right about the answers Ecks could provide. But while years would pass before they met again, this wasn't the last Allen Hynek would see of Arthur Ecks.

His search was curtailed by a Senate page, who summoned him into the hearing chamber to begin his testimony. Hynek continued to scan the crowd on his way to the witness stand, but the mystery men weren't among those who followed the reporters inside when the session resumed.

***

It was after one o'clock by the time Joseph McAfee gaveled the hearing back to order. Hynek seemed dazed as he took his seat, but was startled back to the moment when McAfee announced him by name.

"Thank you for joining us today, Dr Hynek. The committee thanks you for coming on such short notice."

McAfee shuffled his papers until he found the one he wanted.

"For those who aren't familiar with Dr Hynek, he's a tenured professor of the Department of Physics and Astronomy at Ohio State. Tough luck for your football team last season, doctor. I'm a Badger myself."

Hynek came out of his fog, but took too long to work out McAfee's football reference. After far too lengthy a pause, he managed a weak smile murmuring, "Maybe next year."

McAfee favored the professor with a suspicious glance, disturbed by his apparent lack of enthusiasm for football, even though he worked for one of the nation's gridiron powerhouses. The senator checked his information sheet on the professor, learning with a quick glance, that Hynek's parents were from Czechoslovakia.

The senator stroked his chin in contemplation, wondering if maybe the professor might be worthy of interest when the full committee reconvened after the break. He didn't like Hynek's beard either. It made the man look like an anarchist. McAfee made a note to have the professor checked for Communist sympathies, then continued his introduction.

"In addition to his academic duties, Dr Hynek has assisted the Air Force's efforts to get a handle on the UFO problem. He's worked with the Air Force since 1947, and is currently the primary scientific authority consulting with Project Blue Book on aerial phenomena. It's my understanding, doctor, that you're responsible for the explanations given to some of the more interesting sightings. How would you characterize your work with Project Blue Book?"

Hynek cleared his throat before beginning, but his voice still squeaked a bit.

"It's been my contention from the start that most UFO sightings are due to natural phenomena being misinterpreted. I feel that my contribution has been to apply a trained scientific viewpoint to details the untrained observer might miss in the rush to explain what he's seen. These incidents, extraordinary though they may appear, will usually have rational explanations without," Hynek paused to scoff, "the necessity of resorting to extraterrestrial interpretations."

Joseph McAfee's head bobbed up and down throughout this discourse, and continued to bob after Hynek finished.

"So, if I may paraphrase, are you saying that you approach each investigation with the goal of debunking the idea that flying saucers are flown by little green men from Mars?"

Hynek cocked his head if unwilling to accept this characterization. He worked his way through a series of possible objections before deciding to accept it at face value.

"That would be a less academic way of describing my contributions."

Based on this answer alone, Joseph McAfee abruptly decided that he didn't much like this astronomy professor from Ohio State.

"So, were you able to follow the testimony of the man who preceded you, Major Donald Keyhoe, the author of the book, *Flying Saucers are Real?*"

Hynek nodded a bit too smugly.

"I'm familiar with Mr Keyhoe's arguments, though I can't say I agree with him. I still maintain that these events are explainable, though admittedly, some take more time than others."

"How do you feel about his assertion that you go into each investigation trying to find an explanation rather than doing any real research?"

McAfee's tone was casual, even if the question wasn't.

Nevertheless, Hynek didn't miss the implication.

"I would argue that finding rational explanations is doing real investigation. Aerial phenomena are notoriously difficult to categorize, especially so from the distances prevalent in most sightings. Please understand, Senator, in most cases, I don't dispute the reports of the witnesses, even when I dispute what they actually see. These men are often competent pilots, quite used to seeing unusual things in the sky. But with all the reported sightings over that last few years, I believe a kind of hysteria has crept into our culture, and this hysteria has brought with it a certain willingness to entertain extraordinary explanations for very ordinary events. In the end, it's simply a matter of perception."

McAfee gnawed the end of his eraser.

"Would that interpretation pertain to the Mantell case?"

"Absolutely."

"So, it makes sense to you that the object Captain Mantell chased to his death was the planet Venus."

A slight blush formed at the base of Hynek's throat, rising to his cheeks as he framed his answer. "Venus was only one of a number of suggestions."

Sensing blood in the water, McAfee moved in for the kill.

"Isn't it true that Venus is rarely visible in broad daylight?"

A casual observer might have missed the rosy blush that appeared on Hynek's throat. As the blush rose, the senator continued his assault.

"Isn't it true that Venus is entirely incapable of the movements reported by both Captain Mantell and the observers on the ground?"

"I-" Hynek began, but McAfee ran over him like a train.

"Isn't it true that the Air Force subsequently retracted that explanation and chose to claim that Captain Mantell was chasing another one of these weather balloons we hear so much about?"

Allen Hynek had worked hard to master his stammer, but not hard enough to fend off McAfee's question.

"All those things are true, but it is also true that the Venus explanation was subsequently reinstated, as Mr Keyhoe is well aware."

McAfee's caterpillar brows rose theatrically.

"Despite Captain Mantell clearly describing the object he chased as being of tremendous size? I fail to see how the Venus' relative size could grow appreciably when it never comes closer than 24 million miles to Earth. Isn't it also true that Venus was much further away on the day of Mantell's death?"

Allen Hynek looked shellshocked as he stared back up at the senator. Clearly, he hadn't expected to be answering questions about Venus' position in the sky, on a date four years in the past. McAfee continued without giving him time to answer.

"Leaving, for the moment, the idea than Captain Mantell was chasing Venus, did you hear Mr Keyhoe propose that the object might've been a balloon from Project Skyhook?"

Professor Hynek sighed as he glanced around at the reporters who were scribbling furious notes on their pads.

"At the time of the Mantell incident, Project Skyhook was classified as top secret. The Venus explanation was initially proposed due to the heightened security around Skyhook."

McAfee shook his papers at Allen Hynek in much the same way he'd done to Alger Hiss.

"You would have saved your country both concern and hysteria if you'd simply told us we were seeing weather balloons. Balloons have been used so often as explanations for these sightings that I fail to see how any balloon could justify such secrecy when it was visible in plain sight of thousands of civilian observers! What made the Skyhook balloons so different?"

Hynek took a less than satisfactory breath. His response came out sounding more like a question than an answer. "They were bigger?"

McAfee ignored Hynek's response, referring again to his notes.

"I'd like to examine another one of Mr Keyhoe's remarks, specifically this idea that the objects being sighted are products of our own technology. There has been speculation that the flying saucers, especially those described as being cigar-shaped, are products of our rocket programs. Mr Keyhoe has gone on record saying that if anyone had told him the saucers were our own technology, he never would have written his articles or his book. Instead, he was told repeatedly that we have nothing of the sort."

In the aftermath of this rant, his chest heaving with theatrical outrage, McAfee waited for the professor from Ohio State to respond.

After considerable wait, all Allen Hynek could manage was, "Orson Welles." Even this was delivered in a tone of voice that could only be characterized as timid.

Stalling for time, the professor took a sip of water, letting it linger on his tongue before swallowing. When his thoughts were in order, he responded with the only argument he had left, the one he kept in reserve for such a need.

"Please try to understand, Senator, we were worried about a national panic. Can you imagine the effect it would have on the country if the general public was told, as Major Keyhoe would have us do, that flying saucers really are from outer space? How would the country react if our citizens no longer believed we were able to protect our borders? Our air space?"

"Look at what Mister Welles accomplished with a few false news broadcasts. Can you imagine what the country would do if we really were under attack by aliens from outer space?"

Chapter 5 - The Search for Truth

Dr Josef Allen Hynek was a beaten man by the time he climbed the stairs back to the observation room. His ascent was ponderous, the heavy-footed slog of a man who'd gone down to defeat in a contest where he'd clearly expected no opposition. He paused as he reached the top, experiencing a brief moment of optimism. There remained the possibility of unraveling the mystery of the departed men. But upon opening the door, he was to be disappointed in this as well.

Neither Arthur Ecks nor Dexter Wye had returned to the observation lounge. It would be years before he would even learn their names.

Having witnessed Hynek's all too public evisceration, the room's remaining occupants fell silent at his return. Even Major Keyhoe, the closest he had to an adversary, was conciliatory in his welcome. Ruppelt, with whom he'd worked closely on several occasions, was so neutral that Hynek suspected he was fighting an impulse to shun him. La Paz, who'd faced his own share of public criticism for not solving the riddle of the green fireballs, simply pulled back the chair next to him and motioned Hynek to take a seat.

"Tough session," Keyhoe remarked.

Hynek ignored the table of his peers to stare at the table of unknowns, and the empty seats that represented Ecks and Wye.

"They haven't come back then?"

Jakob Kleinemann looked back at Hynek with innocent eyes.

"Who?"

Hynek pointed to the empty chairs vacated by Ecks and Wye.

"The man, the two men who were sitting with you before I left."

Jakob Kleinemann looked to Lars Ångström, then to Rita Mae Marshaux.

"I do not know who you are referring to, Dr Hynek. Dr Ångström has been with us the entire time, and Miss Marshaux, I am reasonably sure, could never be mistaken for a man."

Hynek scowled. "Not them, I can see Dr Ångström and Miss Marshaux as well as anyone. I'm talking about the other two men in your group, the ones who left just before I was called to testify."

Hynek turned to his table of peers.

"You know who I'm referring to. Certainly, you saw them!"

La Paz turned away as Ruppelt shared a glance with Keyhoe. Ruppelt and Keyhoe were military and ex-military respectively. Both had experienced coming across government projects that were meant to be kept secret at all costs. The missing men were clear evidence that another project, one of a more secretive nature, was involved in the search for the truth regarding UFOs. That in itself was a revelation for Ed Ruppelt, and only slightly less so for Don Keyhoe.

When neither man could come up with a response, Rita supplied an answer. "We're only human, doctor," Rita said with a conciliatory smile. "Sometimes our perceptions are just plain wrong."

The budding conversation was interrupted by a sudden hubbub down on the floor. The murmurs of the audience grew louder and louder, coming up to the observation lounge through the speakers on the wall. Hynek took his seat, then suddenly froze as he sorted out the scene below.

"Oh my god," the astronomer exclaimed as the remaining color drained from his face. "It's Menzel!"

***

But in spite of the disturbance creating havoc in the media circus below, the next man called to the stand was Captain Edward Ruppelt. At a summons from a young page, Ruppelt rose to follow the young man down the stairs.

The Ruppelt testimony began just after two o'clock, a fact that struck Hynek like a slap in the face. The professor's testimony had seemed like hours, but had lasted only twenty-five minutes. As with previous witnesses, McAfee read through the captain's biography, finally introducing him as the current head of Project Blue Book, the Air Force's ongoing effort to get to the bottom of the UFO mystery. With the preliminaries complete, Senator McAfee began in earnest.

"Captain Ruppelt, since UFOs are an airborne phenomenon, the Air Force was tasked with investigating them. But it's been five years since this started and, so far at least, we've seen very little in the way of results. Our hope is that you can bring us up to date on what's been done so far."

A veteran of long-winded presentations, Ruppelt rose with the intention of addressing the hearing from a standing position, but the committee chair quickly waved him back to his seat. Once seated, Captain Ruppelt began.

"As has been pointed out, the effort to explain flying saucers began in 1947, originally under the code name Project Sign. Project Sign actively investigated sightings through 1948 before delivering its final report in early 1949. In that report, which was never made available to the public, it was concluded that some UFOs represented actual aircraft. The report also stated that there wasn't enough data to determine where the UFOs came from. However, most of the personnel working on the project believed that the saucers were of extraterrestrial origin. Despite the academic weight behind this evaluation, this conclusion was rejected-"

The crabby Senator from Missouri held up a hand to interrupt.

"Wait a minute, captain. What do you mean the conclusion was rejected?"

As he'd been expecting it, this interruption did little to shake the captain's reserve. Suppressing a smile, Ruppelt leaned into the detour.

"When the report was turned in, it was approved all the way up the chain of command until it reached Air Force Chief of Staff, General Hoyt Vandenberg. Citing its lack of supporting physical evidence, General Vandenberg rejected the report and all copies of it were ordered destroyed."

"That's ridiculous," said the man from Missouri. "You can't just order an investigation and destroy the report because you don't like what it says."

Ruppelt continued without comment.

"When the Sign personnel who supported the extraterrestrial hypothesis continued to push their ideas, Project Sign was reorganized and renamed Project Grudge. Under Project Grudge, the personnel favoring the ET hypothesis were purged from the team. The name given to Grudge was no accident."

"Project Grudge was given a different goal. Rather than searching for the origin of the flying saucers, Project Grudge was tasked with finding normal explanations for the phenomena, that is, to explain rather than investigate. This prejudice continued to dominate UFO investigations until late last year. By that time, many of our higher-ups at the Pentagon had grown so disenchanted with the reports that Grudge was dismantled. A new effort was subsequently established under the name Project Blue Book."

McAfee pointed his pencil at the young captain. "And this Blue Book project is currently under your command?"

"Yes, sir."

"And how does Blue Book differ from its predecessors?"

Ruppelt paused to take a sip of water.

"Our primary effort now is to develop a methodology for investigation of unidentified aerial phenomena. Project Sign could be accused of prejudice in favor of the extraterrestrial hypothesis while Project Grudge held an even stronger prejudice against. Blue Book intends to remove the prejudice from these investigations, to view these events objectively, and to make judgments based on our findings, rather than immediately writing them off as natural phenomena. Those explanations still have a place, but I believe we are doing a better job of evaluation now than was done by those prior efforts."

The cranky Missourian loudly cleared his throat and scowled.

"What about the possibility that these flying saucers are Russian products?"

This query came from a corpulent Texas oilman who hadn't made a peep up until then. Ruppelt nodded, evidently having expected that the question would arise earlier than it had.

"The performance capabilities we've observed in flying saucers tend to argue against them being the product of any human engineering. If you've flown at all, you might remember the resistance your body feels when the plane takes off. That tug is the force of gravity working against your body."

"When an airplane takes evasive maneuvers, your body will feel this force at work. It will make you feel heavy, as it presses down with the force of multiple gravities. In extreme situations of ascent, descent, or simply banking too fast, pilots have even lost consciousness. This same force works against the structure of the plane as well. Trying to bank too sharply creates extra stress on the rivets, and in extreme cases, can actually tear a plane apart."

"The performance we've observed in many UFOs would tear any craft of human design to pieces. This is the one thing we can say definitively, that flying saucers are clearly the product of a superior technology. That is, in fact, the primary argument for the extraterrestrial hypothesis. So no, Senator, we have very little reason to think the UFOs are Russian."

The five Senators at the tables shared a look, before McAfee returned to an earlier subject. "You mentioned a methodology for the study of UFOs."

"Yes, obviously getting UFOs on film or in photographs would be ideal, but doing so is often difficult due to altitude, weather conditions, and more often than I care to say, inappropriate or missing equipment. The average consumer camera doesn't have the telephoto lens required to shoot objects at long distance. Add to this the difficulty of catching an object traveling at a high rate of speed and you have the answer to why photographs of UFOs are generally of poor quality."

Ruppelt paused to collect his thoughts before continuing.

"Still, we have to work with what we're given. Though visual sightings are considered poor evidence, their value goes up when the sighting is confirmed by radar. But there are problems with radar sightings as well. False readings due to particular weather conditions are a constant problem so we tend to downgrade reports from less-experienced operators. But, imperfect though it might be, even witness testimony can give us valuable information such as the direction in which a UFO is traveling or its perceived speed. Since so many sightings come from reliable sources, we've learned a great deal about UFOs over the past five years. Even so, the science is in its infancy and needs more time to grow."

The oilman, now that he'd started, wouldn't readily surrender the floor or an idea he'd gotten his teeth into. A voluble man by nature, most of his Senate colleagues could attest to his intransigence on a variety of subjects.

"So if it isn't the Russians, where the heck are these things coming from?"

Ruppelt face split into a small smile.

"It's an excellent question, Senator, and one I have no ready answer for. At this point, we can't even find many similarities between the craft being reported. We're all familiar with the flying saucer reports, but Blue Book has reports of UFOs shaped like cigars, rockets with small wings, elliptical discs, and even pear-shaped craft. We've heard today about the green fireballs, glowing lights, metallic spheres, and one in particular where the observer claimed that the object was shaped like his hat."

"There was a very interesting report back around the time this all began, of several ships shaped like clamshells. We even had a report of a ship that was shaped like a triangle, a V-shaped wedge of lights-"

McAfee let go of his pencil, letting it fall to the floor where it rolled away to be lost under the table. "Wait a minute. You say someone saw a triangle?"

"Yes, sir. But it was only that one sighting."

A murmur rippled through the men seated at the table. The ripple spread to the room at large, leaving the reporters confused by whatever had disconcerted the Senators. The hubbub went on until McAfee gaveled it into silence.

"I think we're best served by moving forward rather than focusing too much on any one detail. We've heard a lot of testimony today, but I'd like to request a more personal evaluation. Captain Ruppelt, in your opinion, what has been the most significant sighting to date?"

Ed Ruppelt, in a lighter situation, might have chuckled at the question. But this was a formal Senate hearing and a serious question had been asked.

"Well, Senator, I am still attached to the Air Force and we're discussing issues that affect the security of the nation. So, given those limitations, I will edit my comments accordingly."

McAfee chuckled knowingly at the young captain's disclaimer.

"Of course, captain. I was in the military myself. But what can you tell us that hasn't been covered up to now?"

Ruppelt showed no sign of hesitation in answering.

"Well, first I'd have to make clear the sheer number of incidents that have been reported since the flying saucer phenomenon came into the public eye. The modern beginning of these incidents may date back to the Arnold sighting, but we've averaged at least three dozen reports for every month since. Some months have been higher. Based on these numbers, the UFO phenomenon isn't going away any time soon."

"Are there any particular incidents that were harder to explain than others?"

Again, Ruppelt didn't hesitate.

"St. Patrick's Day, 1950. Farmington, New Mexico, is one hundred-seventy miles northwest of Albuquerque. Farmington is know for its oil deposits and its proximity to the Four Corners Indian reservations. On that date, this little town was invaded by flying saucers and the story was carried in every major paper."

"Yeah, I recall something about that," McAfee mused, rubbing his jaw.

"St. Patrick's Day was one of those extraordinary events. Several people had reported sightings on the two days prior, but all hell broke loose on the 17th. Every flying saucer in the galaxy must have put in an appearance that day, and most of the town's citizens, thirty-six hundred in all, saw the invasion fleet. The first reports came in at a quarter after ten in the morning. For the next hour, the sky was full of flying saucers."

"Estimates ranged from 500 to thousands. Most witnesses said the ships were saucer-shaped and traveled at unbelievable speeds. More interesting was that none of the saucers seemed to have any set flight path. The individual ships were reported to be darting in and out of the swarm, often avoiding collisions by a matter of inches."

"These ships were clearly not hallucinations. The witnesses were made up of every type of person imaginable. They were seen by the mayor, ex-pilots, the highway patrol, every kind of person you might expect to find in a community that size. I've heard dozens of explanations, cotton blowing in the wind, bugs' wings reflecting sunlight, a hoax to put Farmington on the map. On person in particular even suggested that they were real honest-to-goodness flying saucers."

A ripple of laughter went through the room. Captain Ruppelt let it die out before continuing.

"One explanation was never publicized. If there was a reasonable way to explain what these people saw, I think this one maybe best. It seems that, under conditions of extreme cold, the plastic bag of a skyhook balloon can become brittle. While in this state, the balloon takes on the character of an enormous light bulb. If a gust hits a balloon while it is in this condition, it will shatter into a thousand pieces. As these pieces of plastic are carried along by the wind, they might look like thousands of flying saucers."

McAfee cleared his throat and, after a bit of hemming and hawing, got to the heart of the matter.

"Now I hate to pour more cold water on a respected scientist like Dr Hynek, but that balloon explanation? It wasn't one of Dr Hynek's by any chance?"

Ruppelt reddened slightly before he shook his head.

"No, sir, the idea actually came from one of my superior officers in the Air Force. Though I do believe it was corroborated by Dr Hynek or one of the other scientists we consult with."

"I'd like to ask a few questions if you don't mind," the crabby Senator from Missouri interrupted. "For the moment, I'm going to ignore the sightings from the previous days. My first question is this. Was a Skyhook balloon launched in the area on that day?"

Ruppelt winced, sensing the direction of the questions to follow.

"There was a Skyhook balloon launched from Holloman Air Base."

"How far is Holloman from Farmington?"

"Just under three hundred miles."

The crabby Senator nodded before observing, "That's quite a long way off. What time was that balloon launched?"

"Balloons are usually launched just after dawn. For that time of year, that would be somewhere between 6:30 and 7:00 in the morning."

The crabby Senator from Missouri nodded pointedly, as if considering the math to follow.

"So we'll assume it was launched around 7:00. That leaves our balloon about three hours to travel three hundred miles. I will allow that the wind at altitude can be fierce that time of year, but that still means our balloon had to be traveling at almost a hundred miles per hour to reach Farmington by ten o'clock. Was the temperature on that day conducive to the scenario you've presented? Was it cold enough at that altitude to shatter the balloon?"

Ruppelt nodded, now reasonably certain that he was about to be torn apart in much the same way Hynek had been.

"Yes, our experts have gone on record as saying that at sixty-thousand feet, that's almost eight miles high, it would've been cold enough to shatter the plastic the balloon was made of."

"Have you ever seen a balloon shatter in the manner you've described?"

Ruppelt shook his head.

"Not personally, but my experience in this area is limited."

"Have you ever spent any time in southern New Mexico?"

"Yes."

"Which way does the wind usually blow in New Mexico?"

From his hiding place against the back wall, Arthur Ecks let out a low whistle of admiration at the lack of hesitation shown by Captain Ruppelt.

"When there are strong winds, they almost always come from the north, off the slopes of the Rockies. On March 17th, there were no strong winds, but the winds at Holloman were coming from the north."

Though he clearly expected more resistance, the Senator from Missouri crowed his triumph anyway.

"So, I don't know about you, but it seems unlikely to me that this balloon from Holloman would be able to travel three hundred miles against the wind to shatter in the sky over Farmington, doesn't it?"

Even if he didn't share the same opinion, Captain Ruppelt would've been hard pressed to disagree.

"Yes, Senator, that's one of many reasons why we've listed the Farmington sightings unexplained. If you'll recall, I only said that the Holloman balloon was the best explanation we've been able to come up with. I didn't say it was correct. We had other explanations proposed that were even more unlikely. For reasons I've been unable to uncover, the Air Force closed its investigation of this event within a day of its report. Speaking personally, this is one I would like to know more about."

McAfee looked down the table, then back to his witness.

"Well, we would like to thank Captain Ruppelt for his appearance here today. It has been most enlightening. Is there anything more you'd like to say before ending your testimony, captain?"

Again, Ecks was impressed by the preparation of the young captain. Ruppelt sat up a straighter and his response was immediate.

"Yes, Senator. First, I would like to add a note regarding Dr Hynek's proposal of Venus as the object Captain Mantell chased to his death. Dr Hynek himself rejected Venus as an explanation a few days after proposing it. The continued use of Venus for this purpose comes from the anti-saucer faction that dominated Project Grudge. Dr Hynek has apologized for his remark long ago and shouldn't be blamed any further."

"Second, I cannot share my source for this information, but it has been brought to my attention by a certain person at ATIC, the Advanced Technical Intelligence Center in Dayton, Ohio, that there will likely be a sharp increase in the number of UFO sightings for the rest of this month. I don't know how they arrived at this conclusion, but I feel compelled to report it."

A loud and prolonged murmur went through the room, but this time McAfee let it run its course rather than gaveling it down. There were amused smiles on the faces of all five Senators, but this anomaly was noted by only one man, and Arthur Ecks had no idea what could possibly be the reason behind it.

Chapter 6 - The Search for Sanity

When the gavel brought the chamber back to order, it was because a new man was taking his place on the witness stand. Surprising those who were still up there, this new man hadn't joined the earlier witnesses in the observation room.

The new man was in his early fifties and conservatively dressed in a gray worsted suit. His hair was a wavy blond well into the process of fading to white. He wore glasses that were a combination of horn rim and wire frame and his plump lips were set in a peeved pout, as if he'd canceled something enjoyable to come to the hearing. This was, in fact, the case.

As he took his seat behind the table, Donald Menzel turned to stare up at the hidden observation window. As his eyes burned through the obscuring glass, he seemed to be staring straight at Allen Hynek with undisguised malice.

For the fifth time that day, Joseph McAfee called the session to order.

"Well, gentlemen," the senator from Wisconsin drawled, "it seems our little get-together has attracted some notice in the halls of academia. Our next witness comes to us from the astronomy department at Harvard where he's professor of astrophysics and associate director of solar research. We must thank Professor Donald Menzel for taking time out of his schedule to address these proceedings."

"You're quite welcome, Senator," Menzel replied, his plump lips pursing in disapproval. "When I heard what was going on here, as well as who you were interviewing, I felt it might be of some benefit for someone to inject a modicum of sanity. We've been hearing a lot of speculation regarding UFOs in the last few years, and frankly, most of it is wild-eyed nonsense."

An amused smile crossed McAfee's lips. "Then I trust you are familiar with the testimony of the men who have already spoken today."

"I am aware of Major Keyhoe's opinion from his articles in *True* magazine, and I have consulted with Dr Hynek, as well as Dr La Paz on some of the more interesting sightings. I know Captain Ruppelt by reputation, though I've heard enough to suspect he may be keeping too open a mind in respect to his findings. In any case, most of these sightings are easily explainable as natural phenomena occurring in unexpected places."

McAfee lifted one heavy eyebrow.

"Natural phenomena? Perhaps if you could elaborate."

"Gladly, Senator, but first I'd like to go into some history of this phenomena if the committee hasn't grown too weary of the subject."

"The committee has no objection," McAfee replied agreeably.

Warming to his topic, Menzel began.

"For as long as human beings have looked up into the night sky, we've seen things, phenomena, if you will, that are unexplainable given the knowledge of the times. It may surprise the committee to learn that objects, similar to what we now call flying saucers, have been observed since the dawn of recorded history."

"As an example, in mid-April of the year 1561 the citizens of Nuremberg, Bavaria were witness to an appearance by a large black triangular object."

As with the previous mention of black triangular objects, a murmur of alarm rippled through the men seated at the table. Unaware of the effect his words were having, Menzel went on unperturbed.

"In addition to the triangle, hundreds of spheres, cylinders and other odd-shaped objects were observed moving erratically across the sky. A being that looked like a man was seen at the controls of the triangular object. The sighting lasted hours and was observed by thousands. It was even recorded in a famous painting of the time."

"What explanation was given?" The Missouri senator asked.

"Naturally, given the times, the explanation was religious in nature, angels and that sort of thing. Some latter-day scholars are now claiming that these were extraterrestrial visitors. Such conclusions strike me as the worst kind of revisionist history, explaining historical events with the latest fads."

"How would you explain such an event?"

Menzel shook his head.

"Therein lies the problem, Senator. Without any means of investigation, it's impossible to arrive at any rational conclusion. I mentioned the Nuremberg incident as an example of revisionist history. This is the worst kind of science, fabricating an explanation without any means of verifying its accuracy."

"Captain Ruppelt and Dr La Paz have already alluded to this problem. Since we can't know when or where a flying saucer will appear, it's impossible to have the proper equipment in place to analyze a sighting. Base on some conversations I've had, the Air Force wants nothing to do with investigating the saucers. It's hard to blame them when they have little more than eyewitness testimony to go on. Fortunately, it's easy to explain most of these events as natural phenomena."

"You mentioned natural phenomena when you began," McAfee pointed out. "Are you ready to go into more detail yet?"

Menzel nodded emphatically. "Yes, Senator, I believe I am. In doing so, I will reference an article I wrote for *Look* magazine last month."

"First of all, when I speak of natural phenomena, I should make it clear that I am referring to things we perceive through our sense of sight. Any good stage magician knows how shockingly easy it is to deceive this particular sense through sleight of hand or misdirection. Nature has its own techniques for accomplishing the same purpose."

"Now, before we delve too deeply into this, I feel compelled to share that the reason *Look* magazine asked me to write this article was because I am one of the lucky few to actually observe a saucer in flight."

A ripple of scattered commentary washed through the room and died.

"My astronomical studies often take me to Colorado and New Mexico where the majority of these sightings have been observed. I was at Holloman Base near Alamogordo at the height of the scare. One morning, I spied what appeared to be several flying saucers. I have to admit that even I was fooled until I realized that what I was seeing were a group of weather balloons that had just been released for high altitude testing. This was a signal moment for me, realizing that if I could be fooled, even momentarily, how easily an untrained observer might be deceived into mistaking something so ordinary for a flying saucer."

"This was an epiphany for me. Later that same day, I shared my belief that most saucer sightings could be explained along similar lines. This isn't to say that my opinion was shared by everyone. There were others in our group, several prominent scientists among them, who expressed the belief that there had to be more to the saucer stories than mistaken identifications of weather balloons."

"Later that same day, I had a second experience. At that time, I was driving into Alamogordo, admiring a beautiful full moon as it rose over Sacramento Peak. A few degrees north of that orb, I spied what seemed to be a bright star, and then a second not far from the first. Without thinking about it, I assumed that I was seeing Castor and Pollux in the constellation of Gemini. But then I realized that Gemini was only observable in the northern hemisphere during the winter. This meant my two stars had to be something else, so I stopped the car to take a closer look."

"I saw that both of my stars were hazy disks that shone with a slightly bluish tint. Realizing that I was seeing something extraordinary, I got out of the car. Unfortunately, I was too late. My saucers suddenly faded away, as mysteriously as they'd appeared."

"Now you may be expecting me to provide an explanation for what I saw, but here I must admit I don't have one. Since then I've located references to such phenomena, specifically one by the English meteorologist, Edmund Lowe in 1838, that offer far better descriptions of what I saw. As to my own sighting, I have some ideas, but hardly anything concrete."

"But based on that experience, I *can* say what I do not believe I saw, and I believe this pertains to the observations of others as well."

"I did not see an unearthly missiles or extraterrestrial craft. I did not see anything that might have originated from Russia or, for that matter, from our own technology. I did not see, as our ancient ancestors believed, the aerial aspect of a godlike creature."

"Then, what *did* you see, Doctor?"

Senator Joseph McAfee seemed almost somber now.

Menzel lifted his hands and shrugged theatrically.

"The simple answer is I don't know. But speaking as a scientist, it doesn't worry me in the slightest if I'm unable to provide an iron-clad explanation for everything I observe. The work of science is far from complete, and I take joy in the fact that it will never be complete in my lifetime. The world remains full of problems we have yet to solve and I have no desire to invent any causation that makes reasonable explanation either unnecessary or impossible."

McAfee scratched an itch on his temple.

"So why are we hearing so many of theses reports now? Surely there must be some reason that the number of sightings has gone up so dramatically since Mr Arnold's Mt. Rainier sighting."

For the first time since beginning his testimony, Menzel cracked a smile.

"I believe there are, at the core, two reasons. First, the idea of flying saucers is out of the ordinary and we are all fascinated by mysterious things. Second, when the world didn't return to normal at the end of the war, it made people nervous. I don't think any of us expected this post-war world to be so hostile."

"We're filled with uncertainty about what might happen with Russia. We fear that in discovering the secrets of the atomic bomb, we may have released forces that will grow beyond our control, forces that may even destroy civilization as we know it."

A silence fell over the room to be interrupted when the Texas oilman belched, then followed it up with an observation.

"You know, Dr Menzel, we've heard you talk a lot about natural phenomena, but we have yet to hear anything specific as to what those might be."

"Well, Senator," Menzel replied, adjusting his glasses. "I believe it's time to examine that question. I'll start by pointing out that most sightings can be attributed to one very simple cause."

"And what might that be?"

"They're caused by a phenomenon we've all heard about for centuries, an optical phenomenon known as the mirage."

The oilman snorted, "You mean like in the cartoons?"

This bizarre nature of this comment knocked Menzel off his game, but he recovered quickly. "I'm more familiar with the desert phenomena where one sees an oasis miles from its actual location. These mirages are caused by layers of hot air creating reflections, but the same might be said for any observation where it is difficult to identify the object in question. In such situations, observers often settle for the mostly likely explanation. Once upon a time, these were seen as manifestations of God. Now they are seen as flying saucers."

"Such reflections can be created by many conditions, but are most likely due to temperature inversion layers in the atmosphere. Inversion layers are especially prevalent in desert climates, which is where we see most of our saucer sightings.

Inversion layers can make relatively tiny objects, such as light reflecting off the backs of high-flying birds, or odd cloud formations, seem significant."

"As cloud formations can be pushed along by winds that aren't felt at ground level, they can often make aerial objects such as Venus appear to be moving faster or further they actually are. Few realize that Venus is sometimes bright enough to be see in broad daylight, and I believe that for many of the light-in-the-sky type sightings, the need for explanations goes no further than this. Weather balloons have only recently become a common sight, and are still far enough out of the ordinary that most people can't identify them on sight."

"Even so, while these things account for a majority of the sightings, there are still a significant number that defy such explanation. Many sightings refer to some great distance or speed, an unusual ability to maneuver that appears impossible in light of what we know of manned flight and gravitational forces. They move without the sound of engines. These are all attributes outside the capabilities of what we know as human flight, and the ships that perform these maneuvers bear little resemblance to anything built on Earth."

"So, incorporating all these reasons into our argument, are we justified in saying that these ships are of extraterrestrial design? This is a big step and while admitting that such a solution solves many of our problems, there's still some doubt as to whether such a capitulation is necessary. Fortunately, there is another solution."

Menzel paused to let his words sink in. His speech had been so long that it took his audience some time to realize he'd stopped. Menzel used this pause to take a sip of water before beginning again.

"Has it occurred to anyone that there is one phenomenon in the universe that is capable of all these things, something that can move instantaneously, reverse direction without penalty, that can be seen in many places at once, and that can distort and reform without harming the original manifestation?"

Menzel paused a second time, scanning the chamber in the manner of a professor quizzing his students on an arcane topic that wasn't going to be on the final, but might be included in a snap quiz. Failing to get any kind of response, Menzel provided the answer.

"Light, gentlemen. Light is capable of all those things."

Having supplied this answer, Menzel paused a third time. When he began this time, his tone was gentler, as if he was talking to children who were a bit on the slow side.

"Has anyone noticed how little of what we hear reported in these sightings is actually material in nature? Don't these objects react more as if they're made of light being reflected from one location to another?"

"As it happens, I've been able to reproduce the look and behavior of many of these mysterious objects in a laboratory setting. It is surprisingly easy to do. Using reflected light, I can make our supposed flying saucer change directions on a dime at high speed. I can make it ascend at speeds greater than the escape velocity required to leave the planet. I can split my single ship into many, and finally, I can make each ship dance to its own trajectory before bringing them all back together to reform the original vessel."

"Ships have been reported in many sizes and shapes, some with portholes or visible figures aboard. Most, if not all, of these can be put down to our desire to see something unique. As this UFO phenomenon has grown, so too has the imagination that gave it birth. I believe that many of our citizens have reached a point where the testimony of their senses is no longer reliable."

"As might also be expected, there are valid reasons to explain what we see. During the war, I was a member of the Wave Propagation Committee, which conducted a series of tests out in the desert. Our primary focus was on radar images, but we discovered that, in many ways, light behaves like radar, and what we learned about the desert applies as much to light as it does to radar."

"We learned that temperature inversions were extremely common in desert climates. During the day, the desert is extremely hot. At night, the ground cools rapidly, but air cools at a slower rate. The air cools more quickly where it is in contact with the ground, but for some distance continues to get warmer with altitude. Then, when it is well away from the ground, it becomes cooler again. We have known for quite a while of regions of the upper atmosphere where the temperature changes rapidly. We've also learned that height can create a mirage."

"Mirages are the key to the problem with the saucers, and working on that assumption, I've been able to reproduce the most essential features of the saucers in the laboratory. More study will be necessary before we fully understand this problem, but I'm confident that we'll eventually be able to produce and observe everything related to the phenomenon in a laboratory setting."

"So what is a mirage?" The Texas oilman asked.

Menzel nodded approvingly at the question.

"At its core, a mirage is an image caused by a lens of air. Since air lenses are never perfect, what we see through them is distorted and unreal. The world we see is like seeing through spectacles that don't match our prescription, or looking into a funhouse mirror."

"Though we may not be aware of what they are, we see mirages every day. As you drive along a highway on a hot day, the dark asphalt in the distance seems to be covered with a film that evaporates as your car approaches. This is the most common type of mirage, the one we associate with the desert. Like the Senator's cartoons, we imagine a thirsty traveler seeing a vision of a receding lake that he'll never reach. The water he sees is an image projected on the sky, drawn from a distant point on the landscape. The light rays that produce the illusion traverse a path that bends upward."

"But give us a cool layer of air at ground level, as is found in the desert at night, and light rays will curve in the other direction, to follow the surface of the earth. What do we have then?"

Menzel waited a length of time he considered appropriate for his brighter students, but this was a consideration wasted on Senators.

"Like any mirage, the inversion layer will reflect what it finds on the ground for a distance of some miles. Most likely, our lights in the sky are the streetlights of a distant town or city, bent, propagated, and distorted by the curvature of the earth. These lights are extremely unstable, of course, only appearing to move as the cooling earth and air shift against each other."

"And that, gentlemen," Menzel concluded, with an air of satisfaction, "is the source of the natural phenomena that produces flying saucers."

Chapter 7 - The Infamous Chair

Arthur Ecks watched the testimony of the last three witnesses from the back wall of the chamber, huddling with Dex behind two magazine reporters from *Yank* and *Girl Watcher*, respectively. He was especially impressed by the poise of Captain Ruppelt and Dr Menzel, the only witnesses he felt to have shown the proper gravity for the proceedings. When Menzel was dismissed, he nudged Dex, whispered two quick instructions into his ear, and leaned back against the wall as his protege made his way down to the table where the senators were seated.

As chair of the committee, Joseph McAfee, the notorious junior senator from Wisconsin, held the center position. He was flanked by the crabby senator from Missouri and the somnolent lion from South Dakota on his left and the corpulent Texas oilman in his second term on his right. The last seat, where a three-term real estate man from Arizona usually sat, was currently vacant, its occupant having vacated as he went in search of the mens room.

Ecks watched as Dex explained the situation to McAfee. When Dex had finished delivering his message, Ecks smiled openly as he watched McAfee's face purple in indignation. Buried by all the concurrent conversations in the room, he was unable to hear the chairman's response, but his reaction was easy to read. Dex let McAfee have his say before repeating and clarifying his instructions. There would be no further negotiation, at least not if McAfee wanted anyone from Project Stall to testify.

The gist of the chairman's anger was easy to understand. He was being asked to turn his public hearing into a private session, out of the fawning eyes and ears of the press. Ecks understood the objection. Limiting the press was the last thing the grandstanding senator wanted. When the senator capitulated, Dex nodded and moved on to his second task, making his way through the crowd as the chairman gaveled the room to silence to request the removal of the audience. The good men and women of the press were initially caught by surprise, then outraged at being singled out. But the few who protested soon found a Senate page at their elbow, firmly escorting them from the chamber.

Arthur Ecks continued to linger while the newshounds queued at the exits. With his first task complete, Dex ascended the stairs to the observation room where he would carry out his second. When he appeared in the doorway at the top of the stairs, Josef Hynek jumped out of his seat in his excitement. It was with some difficulty that he was restrained by Keyhoe and Ruppelt.

"But that's one of them!" Hynek protested. "That's one of the men I was talking about!"

Dex ignored the commotion and hurried over to where Lars, Jakob, and Rita Mae still sat. He leaned in close, speaking so quietly that only the members of Project Stall could hear.

"Artie says he's got this. No one'll have to testify."

As if to punctuate Dex's statement, the blinds over the observation window rolled down and the monitor that had broadcast the previous testimony shut off with an electric click. A moment later, a page arrived at the top of the stairs to inform both groups that their presence would no longer be required.

The Project Stall table declined the invitation, but the other witnesses, with the exception of Allen Hynek, were all too happy to go.

***

Arthur Ecks took his time ambling down the aisle to take the seat at the witness table. When he had composed himself, he signaled the apoplectic chairman that he was ready to begin.

McAfee glowered across the divide at the mystery man. Ecks returned the stare without flinching. It was a talent he acquired long ago as well as one he still practiced. When McAfee broke away, he turned to speak his colleagues. After a short whispered conversation, the rest of the committee rose and exited through a door at the back of the room.

McAfee disconnected the cable from his microphone, then did the same with the other microphones on the stage. By the time he looked back to Arthur Ecks, his face was already colored by an angry scowl.

"I trust this is to your satisfaction." His one-handed gesture encompassed the empty room. "For the record, who the hell are you?"

Ecks shook his head. "There will be no record of this conversation, Senator. If you feel the need to call me something, I'll answer to Mister X. I don't know how you got wind of my organization, but this hearing goes no further. You have blundered into a subject you aren't authorized to pursue."

Somewhat surprisingly, as he wasn't a man known for holding his temper, Joseph McAfee did not go ballistic.

"You do realize that you're addressing a member of the United States Senate. I hold one of the highest offices in this country, and I don't like being told what to do by anyone. I could have you arrested for contempt of Congress and you would simply disappear. Now who the devil are you and what is about Project Stall that makes it so goddamn secret?"

Arthur Ecks slightly raised one eyebrow, surprised to hear the name of his project mentioned so openly.

"I'm curious to hear how you came across that name, Senator."

McAfee broke into a wide smile that was replete with sarcasm.

"You're asking me for information? You got balls, I'll grant you that. Tell me your real name and I'll consider answering that question."

Ecks remained impassive, his posture unaffected by McAfee's contempt.

"It has been determined for reasons of national security that the identities of those on my team be kept secret. It is why I insisted no photographs be allowed during this interview. It's why I insisted that the press and the other members of the committee be removed. I am unofficially here to warn you against taking this any further. The UFO investigation is being handled by people who understand the implications and it's too important to be debated in the arena of public opinion. From this day forward, you will consider the subject of UFOs outside the jurisdiction of both your committee and the American people."

McAfee's throat crimsoned, and that color soon rose into his cheeks.

"Let me get this straight. Are you saying that the American people have no right to know who their tax dollars are being paid to?"

Ecks' features remained carven in stone.

"In this case, that's exactly what I'm saying. If it's any consolation, we don't receive any funding from public sources, which is also why you won't find us in any budget."

McAfee drew back, a crafty look creeping into his eyes.

"What gives you the authority to decline to speak before this office?"

"If you need to ask, Senator, I must assume you're not authorized to know."

McAfee cracked his first smile.

"Are you going to stand here, before a fully authorized subcommittee of the United States Senate, and tell me I don't have the power to question your activities?"

Ecks returned the smile, answering without any trace of ambiguity.

"Yes, Senator, I am."

"Are you aware you can be found in contempt of Congress for simply failing to answer my questions? I can send you straight from these chambers to a jail cell."

Ecks shook his head as if this threat was childish and pathetic.

"Really? You're wasting time now. That sounds like something they'd do in Moscow. In this country, we have values like freedom of speech and due process of law. It's also the reason I can ask you the same question you've asked everyone else. Tell me, Senator, have you or anyone in your family ever been affiliated with known members of the Communist Party, past or present?"

McAfee lost his smile. "I'm not the one on trial here..."

Arthur Ecks let his smirk go away.

"I'm not on trial either, Senator. There isn't a single man who has spoken in these chambers whose been on trial."

All traces of the Senator's prior affability disappeared.

"I don't want this to become controversial, but I'll ask the questions if you don't mind. Let's start again with your name."

Arthur Ecks shook his head in mock dismay.

"We're going around in circles. You can address me as Mr X or not at all. Have you ever been a member of the Communist Party, Senator?"

"No, I have not," McAfee snapped. "Who do you work for, Mr X?"

"That information is given on a need to know. I'm still waiting for you to tell me how you discovered our existence."

"Who determines who needs to know?"

"My superiors are responsible for making that determination."

"Who are your superiors? I'd like to contact them to get permission for you to speak publicly before this body."

Arthur Ecks crossed his arms and leaned back into his seat.

"That's unfortunate, because I wouldn't be at liberty to divulge their names, even if I knew who they were."

Both of McAfee's palms slapped the table at once, a sharp sound that sent echoes through the empty chamber.

"You can't even tell me the names of your superiors?"

"That is correct, Senator. You have my apologies."

McAfee went quiet for a moment before trying a different tactic.

"Then perhaps you can discuss the focus of your organization. The Air Force has responsibility for conducting investigations into UFO activity, and it's been under their purview since 1947. Under Sign, Grudge, and now Blue Book, those investigations have yielded reports that never see the light of day."

"It's the nation's misfortune that those reports aren't being released to the public or to the legislative wing of the government. My understanding is that your group was also assembled in 1947. That's about the same time as Project Sign, and apparently for the same purpose. Both groups seem to be responsible for research into the nature of UFOs. I would very much like to know how Blue Book's purpose differs from your own, and maybe then you can tell me why the country needs two projects doing essentially the same work?"

Arthur Ecks recrossed his arms, an action the chairman judged belligerent and obstructionist. "I can only respond in the most general terms, Senator, but your statement is accurate in only the broadest sense, though not so much in the details you've provided."

McAfee straightened his spine, adding inches to his height.

"I don't believe I have any details to mention. What part do you dispute?"

Arthur Ecks ticked off his objections one by one.

"Organization, 1947, purpose, activities, length of existence. The purpose of our organization might be like that of Project Grudge, that is, to create plausible deniability. I'm not at liberty to say. We might have formed in 1947, but we just as well might not have. Either way, the length of time since our formation must be called into question. We might have formed before the war or we might be strangers who met in the waiting room adjoining these chambers. Whatever any of those answers might be, they aren't any of your business."

51

McAfee's weight eased up against the back of his chair.

"Can I assume that you've known your associates longer than the time you've spent waiting to testify?"

"You may assume anything you wish, Senator. As an American citizen, you're entirely free to draw your own conclusions."

"But you will not confirm those assumptions?"

"That is correct, sir. It is not my place to contradict or correct a member of the United States Senate."

McAfee shook his head slowly from side to side.

"I have never been presented with such a clear case of obfuscation in all my years in public service. As a fellow public servant, I commend you. You should consider a career in politics."

The smirk returned to Arthur Ecks' features.

"Thank you, sir. I'll take that as a compliment."

The smirk irritated the senator and he resolved to wipe it off Ecks's face.

"This is the last time I will ask these questions. You are testifying before the highest legislative body in this nation. I'm going to give you one final chance to answer before I find you in contempt of Congress. I should like the following questions answered. What is your real name and who are your superiors? What is the purpose of your organization? And finally, what are the names and specialities of your subordinates?"

The door at the top of the aisle opened, and a slender man in a tan summer suit entered to stand at the back of the room. Though his sandy hair was cut in the same brush cut worn by both Senator McAfee and Arthur Ecks, it lacked the intestinal fortitude to stand erect on its own, laying flat over his scalp in direct contradiction of his barber's intent. His freckled features reminded one of a midwestern schoolboy, incapable of disguising his purpose.

Joseph McAfee leaned forward into the dead microphone, his voice cold with repressed anger.

"The man behind you is a bailiff. I have summoned him to escort you away should you still continue to refuse to answer. You've heard the questions several times now. Consider your answer carefully. This is your last chance."

Arthur Ecks didn't bother to look at the new arrival.

"As previously stated, you are requesting classified information that may only be provided with a specific clearance. That clearance is granted only to those with a need to know, a need which you don't possess."

Joseph McAfee found his gavel, and taking some comfort from the solid heft of its handle, hammered it down on its wooden anvil.

"Mister X, I find you in contempt of Congress. Clarence, please escort this man to a cell where he will remain until he sees fit to answer my questions."

The sandy-haired bailiff folded his hands in front of his crotch, but made no move to arrest Arthur Ecks.

"Bailiff?"

Clarence coughed into his fist, then cleared his throat in the manner of one embarrassed to bring up a delicate subject.

"I'm sorry, Senator, but I can't do that. This gentleman has been put under the protection of the President of the United States. I'm afraid you don't have the authority to place him under arrest."

Joseph McAfee, junior senator from the great state of Wisconsin, and head of his very own Senate subcommittee, dropped his gavel and covered his face with his hands. The little wooden hammer clattered to the floor.

"Fine, then just get him the fuck out of my sight."

Chapter 8 - The Fourth Estate

Arthur Ecks waited patiently for the bailiff to retrieve the absent members of Project Stall from the observation lounge. Leaning against the witness table with his hands folded in his lap, he stared at the empty chamber, watching the pages as they cleaned. It wasn't long before Jakob Kleinemann, Lars Ångström, and Rita Mae Marshaux joined him there. When Dex returned from the restroom, the bailiff named Clarence led them out of the chamber, departing through the same exit the senators had used. Arthur Ecks was pleased that when they left, it was with their anonymity largely intact.

While it was true that photos had been taken of their arrival, most would later prove to be obstructed images of raised hands, shoulders lost in a sea of gray suits, and blurred images of heads and bodies that might belong to anyone. The photographers who took the pictures knew better than to turn in anything of such poor quality. It was easier to admit they weren't able to get the shot.

A small segment of the audience left as soon as they were expelled from the closed-door session, opting to file what they already had. Others hung back in the hope of getting another chance to identify the mystery men, but most of these had given up by the time the doors reopened. A select few remained until the end, their curiosity aroused by the unprecedented dismissal. When the doors opened, these last dozen or so rushed inside to find an empty chamber.

The only stragglers who didn't bite on this fake were Bertie Stein of the *Times* and John Haste of the *Post*. There were easy explanations for the presence of both. Bertie had recognized Lars Ångström and knew Jakob Kleinemann by reputation and description. John Haste recalled both the name and notoriety of Lars Ångström. So, while the frantic newshounds pushed and shoved their way back into the empty room, Haste and Stein held back, one caught up in evaluating whether the infamous sex doctor was an element worthy of pursuit while the other casually wondered why no one ever recognized famous Jews.

Considering these questions, the two men slipped out of the current, each finding a spot on opposite sides of the chamber doors, Stein to the left, Haste to the right. This subterfuge went unnoticed by the general mass, their defections going undetected until the doors had closed.

When the corridor cleared, Bertie Stein could be found leaning against the wall, staring into the rafters as an idea took shape. John Haste searched the tiled floor for similar epiphanies as he gnawed at the raw skin of a ragged cuticle.

The doors, being products of excellent craftsmanship, made only a modest thump as they fell shut. The corridor, now devoid of foot traffic, was so quiet that the footfalls of a sandy-haired man in a tan summer suit were the only audible sound. Once around the corner, the sandy-haired man vanished into the mens room, his chocolate cap toes making only faint ticks on the marble tiles.

In the void of the vacant corridor, both reporters broke out of their respective reveries, each having arrived at the same conclusion. As Stein's gaze fell and Haste's rose, each became abruptly aware of his rival. Bertie Stein blinked up at the tall man from the *Post*, feeling for the half-smoked cigar he'd slid into his breast pocket an hour ago. John Haste froze like a predator caught in mid-sneak. Observers by nature and profession, both men were inclined to wait to see what happened next rather than precipitate any overt action.

Bertie found his cigar, sliding the damp end between his molars as prelude to greeting the younger man with Swiss neutrality.

"John."

John Haste was caught in an awkward position, half-risen from his normal slouch, but well short of full verticality. He wanted desperately to continue to a standing posture, but was restrained by an irrational fear that doing so might somehow expose his speculations regarding Lars Ångström. Haste could remain neutral. If Bertie was Switzerland, Haste was Sweden.

"Bertie."

Bertie Stein was a short fat man who knew his limitations. As a reporter, he'd never been one to race about chasing leads. Lacking the long legs and foot speed of a John Haste, he'd become adept at assembling cogent accounts based on the facts at hand. He was sixty-four years old, and while he prayed he'd never have to retire, he also harbored the fear that someone might make the decision for him. He was five feet four inches tall, weighed one-eighty-five after his morning dump, and generally looked like someone had put a gray suit on a large toad and never had it cleaned. He had a round head with thick lips and fleshy cheeks, not much hair, and a mind as sharp as a safety razor.

He remembered the look he'd shared with Haste before the session started, then shrugged as if there wasn't much to hide. If Haste recognized Kleinemann, the Texan would rise considerably in his esteem. Bertie sucked the bitter end of his foul cigar, sharpening his mind with the taste of damp tobacco.

"You saw him, didn't ya?"

John Haste was thirty-five, just more than half Bertie's age and a foot taller. He had recognized Ångström, just as he'd successfully resisted the urge to call out a question that would force the infamous sex doctor to identify himself. But in noting the blank looks on the faces around him, Haste realized he might have exclusive information. So, as the prurient eyes of his fellow newshounds focused on nipples, Haste held his tongue and was shocked that his colleagues could fail to recognize a man who'd graced the covers of both *Life* and *Look*.

"S'pose I did. Think there's anything to it?"

Bertie nodded his approval. The response was well played. Haste had given away nothing and invited Bertie to share more. That wouldn't do, of course, but Bertie Stein admired a well-played hand.

"Hard to say. The man's a giant in certain circles. You can run with it if you like. I think I'll hit the john, then head home. Frankly, there wasn't as much here as I was hoping there'd be."

Bertie's peanut bladder and balky bowels were a well-travelled talking point amongst the members of the capital press corps.

Upon hearing the word giant, John Haste naturally assumed the New Yorker was referring to Lars Ångström. Haste did a good job of masking his thrill of confirmation, but he was sure that Bertie had given up the goods. The man *was* Dr Lars Ångström, infamous doctor of sex, so there had to be a story in there somewhere, even if his connection to the UFO question remained obscure. Bertie Stein's career may have stalled in the backwaters of the capital press corps, but his nose for news was legendary. Haste fought down his excitement, striving for a dismissive response.

"It's probably nothing. I'm heading outside for a smoke if you wanna join me."

Haste nodded toward the doors at the front of the building.

Bertie knew as well as anyone that there weren't any restrictions on smoking. He hid a smile as he moved away to complete his own ruse.

"Yeah, you take it easy, Haste. See you in the funny papers."

Haste watched Bertie go, admiring his lack of urgency. The funny papers gag was old in the thirties, but he still waited until Bertie had entered the restroom before breaking for the exit.

Once inside, Bertie left the door open a crack, his ears keen for sounds of Haste's departure. He was distracted momentarily by a man in a tan suit, who gestured to move him out of the doorway. As the door closed, Bertie Stein finally released the smile he'd been holding back, exulting in having kept his secret. Haste had recognized Lars Ångström, but not the tiny man with the cupcake in the see-through sweater.

Maybe there was something in all this.

***

It had been seven years since John Haste graduated from the outhouse of Texas politics to the open cesspool of the federal model. He'd found similarities between the two, but the language was different, even if the tactics were often the same. He did find more variety at the federal level, but that was to be expected with the wider range of influences and the greater diversity of issues.

Haste was a tall man with rounded shoulders and a scoliotic question mark of a spine, a flaw exacerbated by years of bending over typewriters on tables too low to accommodate his frame. Fully extended, his height might reach six-five, but with his compromised spine, he was no more than six-one on a good day. He

56

had an equine face with long-lobed ears and a mouth that drooped as much as the flesh under his eyes.

He'd developed careless habits during the war, those years having been spent as a war correspondent, sharing foxholes with filthy men. That lack of care was easiest to spot in his shaving, which lacked both accuracy and finality, the result being that the long slopes of his cheeks and neck were marred by dark patches of missed stubble or dotted with snow-capped islands of sticking plaster.

As promised, he paused for a cigarette outside, but it was a quick one, and only half-smoked as he ran through his options. When his mind was made up, he ground the smoke under his heel and started down the steps, only to be passed by a sandy-haired man who took the stairs two at a time.

***

Bertie Stein knew about Jakob Kleinemann because he pretty much knew about every Jew who'd done anything important. That was a long impressive list, but Bertie had a head for facts and faces. It was one of many things that made him a good reporter. Jakob Kleinemann, while admittedly not as well known, was every bit as controversial in academic circles as Lars Ångström was to the public at large.

So, given the tiny man's presence, Bertie had to ask, what could possibly involve both Jakob Kleinemann, Lars Ångström, and flying saucers? Neither man was known for any research into UFOs. This question was still puzzling him as he left the sanctuary of the mens room.

But as Bertie Stein poked his head out to see if John Haste was gone, a young woman with a sensible haircut poked her head through the doors at the end of the corridor. Her timing was fortuitous as she caught sight of the man she was seeking just as his shabby suit was swallowed up by the revolving door. The young woman wasted no effort on stealth, hurtling across the tiles at a run and arriving at the revolving door before Bertie Stein reached the bottom of the steps outside.

Janie Gently was neither young nor old, neither thin nor fat. Judging her with unfair honesty, she hid the bland features of a librarian behind the sartorial style of the lunch counter lady at a local Woolworth's. She wasn't beautiful in any conventional sense, but, to be fair, she wasn't a real uggo either.

As a reporter, Janie combined a keen eye for detail with the tenacity of a rabid wolverine. It was because of her keen eye that, earlier in the day, while her male colleagues were getting worked up over a flash of veiled nipple, Janie was scanning the faces of her fellow newshounds. It was something she did often, but even so, she didn't realize she'd found something that excited her curiosity until late in the afternoon, after the reporters were evicted.

Unlike Haste and Bertie, Janie had no idea who any of the five people in the mystery group might be. Though it was shocking for a woman of her time, she didn't even recognize Lars Ångström, and while she'd seen few men as short as

57

Jakob Kleinemann, Janie wasn't as well versed in academic heretics or prominent Jewry as Bertie Stein.

So though she hadn't picked up on the importance of either man, Janie had caught the look of recognition that passed between Haste and Stein, and she knew from her own well-honed instincts that there had to be some significance behind it. Bertie and John had seen something or recognized someone. As she followed the newsmen back inside, that look came back to haunt her.

Once inside, Janie was vaguely disturbed to find that neither Bertie or John were anywhere to be found. She unwrapped a stick of gum, slipped it between lips that barely parted, and began chewing on the anomaly. She was sure she'd seen them in the corridor, and she was just as sure that neither were among the defectors who left early.

The gum still had most of its flavor when she worked it out.

At least one of the witnesses was someone they recognized.

Like Haste, she pondered the value of following the lead at once or waiting until the hearing was over. When that decision proved unnecessary, she beat the crush back to the entrance, arriving back in the corridor outside just in time to spot Bertie Stein exiting through the revolving doors.

Chapter 9 - The Secret Passage

The bailiff's name was Clarence, a fact advertised by the name tag above his right breast pocket. Upon exiting the chamber, Clarence led the team down a deserted corridor to the rear of the building. They stopped where the hallway terminated at an L, as the main branch continued on to the left. Rather than follow this established path, Clarence laid restive palms to the section of paneling where the hall would continue had it not terminated in a wall.

Displaying a remarkable facility for complex polyrhythms, the bailiff slapped out an intricate *bossa nova* pattern on the panel. In response, the wall slid back to reveal a well-lit tunnel that was a yard wide, and so long they couldn't see its end. Clarence ushered them inside, waiting until everyone was in before closing the wall with a more prosaic shave and a haircut. As the panel slid shut, the lights came on.

No one said anything until Dex had the bad manners to ask where they were headed. Arthur Ecks shushed him as soon as the question left his lips.

"It's just a different way to the parking lot," Ecks explained. "Gets us past those goddamned reporters. If I ever find out who leaked us to McAfee..."

Ecks let the threat die without a defined punishment.

"Rest assured, major," Clarence assured him from the front of the line, "we have our best people looking into the problem."

"Your what? Damn it," Ecks swore, "who else knows about us?"

Clarence's smile was formal, thin, and utterly without humor.

"As I said, sir. Only our best people. Now, if you'll just follow me, we have to go down before we come back up."

The tunnel ended at a flight of stairs that left the bright lights of the passage fading behind them as it descended into a murky darkness.

"Do we really need to go this way?" Ångström asked, staring down the gloomy descent. "I have a plane to catch. I'm supposed to meet Maisie and the girls at the airport by four o'clock."

"Really?" Rita Mae asked, a bit surprised to be hearing this now, only a week before the wedding. "We were hoping you'd be able to come to the wedding. We were hoping to finally meet your family."

Ångström's anguish seemed genuine, but he was a skilled emotional mimic.

"I do apologize. I would love to be there, of course, but our trip to Sweden was planned long before we received your invitation."

"You're going to Sweden?" Jakob asked. "I thought your family was all here in the States."

Ångström nodded. "Most are, but I still have some cousins back in the old country and I think it's important for the girls to know where their family came from. Besides, the Olympics are being held in Helsinki this year, only a hop, skip, and a jump away, across the Gulf of Finland."

Turning a corner, they entered an unlit portion of the stair and, for a time, everyone disappeared into the dark.

"You'll have to follow the wall here," Clarence called, "but only for a little way."

"Jesus," Ecks growled, "I hope we don't have to walk this far to get back to the surface."

"No, sir," Clarence said as an overhead light appeared like a halo. "There's an elevator to take you back up. The stairs end just ahead."

A minute later, they reached the bottom, passing through an imposing set of double doors into yet another long dark corridor.

As their route already seemed far more convoluted than necessary, Jakob Kleinemann caught up to the bailiff, tugging at his elbow because it was too big a stretch to tap him on the shoulder.

"You will pardon my saying," Kleinemann said, "but it seems to be taking quite a long time if our goal is to simply reach the parking lot."

Clarence turned to the little professor, producing the disarming smile he'd been practicing diligently in his bathroom mirror. The smile was the primary technique promoted through a mail order self-improvement program called *Smile for Success*. The bailiff's hope was that it would improve his prospects at work. Most of his co-workers thought the new smile was creepy, though no one had yet found the nerve to tell him so.

"There's no problem, sir. This route allows us to exit the building undetected. We're over seven hundred feet underground, but after taking the elevator, you'll emerge just across the street from the parking lot."

Jakob Kleinemann didn't find the smile the slightest bit disarming. If asked, he would have agreed it was creepy.

This new corridor was wider than the tunnel at the top of the stairs and better lit. But like its predecessor, it was also devoid of distinguishing features. The air was cooler, and while the drop in temperature was a welcome relief from the heat and humidity, for some it created a new set of problems. Rita Mae shivered in the chill, now wishing she'd worn a heavier sweater.

The walls were painted cinderblock, coated with a shade of industrial beige that'd recently become far more popular than it deserved. The floor, tiled in a noir checkerboard of modern pseudo-plastic, had been simply glued down over the naked concrete. The corridor also showed signs of abandonment. The edges where the cinderblock walls met the tiled floor were lined with a border of dust and detritus that appeared to go back decades.

As another question had come to him, Jakob Kleinemann tapped on the bailiff's elbow a second time.

"This may be nothing, so I beg your indulgence, but I noticed that you said 'you will come out across from the parking lot' rather than 'we'. Aren't you going to accompany us to wherever this corridor leads?"

There might've been a rational answer to this question, but Clarence was already in motion by the time Jakob finished asking it. With a surprising display of agility, Clarence danced back into the stairwell, arriving before anyone could stop him. The double doors immediately slammed shut behind him.

Dex was the first to react, but lacking knob or latch, the door was shut fast against them. It also proved impervious to the pounding and yelling Dex applied to the problem. Giving up, he turned back to the others.

"What the hell just happened here?"

Four men and one woman looked at each other for several seconds before all eyes landed on Arthur Ecks. Ecks didn't answer, his ears still tracking the footsteps of the departing bailiff. Finally, he admitted.

"I suspect we may have been double-crossed."

***

Neither Lars Ångström nor Jakob Kleinemann were known to be particularly confrontational outside the subject areas of their respective academic circles.

Within those circles, Jakob Kleinemann was still an infamous figure, known for the intellectual savagery of his attacks on his detractors, but by and large, this was a legacy dating from the years prior to his involvement with Project Stall.

Lars Ångström, on the other hand, was famously amiable in both public and private settings.

Dexter Wye remembered his military service too well to kick up a fuss with a superior, and besides, he liked Artie.

The same should've been true of Rita Mae Marshaux, but wasn't.

"Who would do such a thing?" Ångström asked in all innocence.

"And why?" Kleinemann added.

Ecks shrugged. "Hard to say who, and even harder to say why. The most obvious answer is McAfee. He clearly didn't like my telling him to butt out. But this Clarence—"

"Who's Clarence?" Dex asked.

"The bailiff who brought us here. McAfee wanted to toss me in a cell for contempt of Congress, but Clarence wouldn't enforce the order. He said we had the protection of the president."

"Why would President Truman want to help us? Hasn't he already decided not to run for another term?"

Ecks shook his head. "Beats the devil out of me. I'm not sure Truman even knows about us, but I'm damn sure he wouldn't go out of his way to help us. At the same time, I don't think he has any reason to trap us underground."

"Then...who?" Lars wanted to know.

"Well," Jakob mused, "we have made a few enemies over the years. Perhaps it was one of them..."

Arthur Ecks perked up at this thought. "Who do you have in mind?"

Lars tapped a perfect tooth with a perfectly manicured nail.

"Washington has become a political cesspool over the last year or so, and it is in no small part due to the influence of Senator McAfee and his committee. Perhaps a faction within the Pentagon-"

"Son of a bitch," Ecks breathed, his voice barely a whisper.

"What is it, Artie?" Dex asked.

Ecks regarded the massive door blocking their exit.

"You guys weren't around to meet them, but back in Roswell-"

"Do you mean when we first met, or later?" Rita Mae asked.

"When we first met," Ecks replied, staring at the tiled floor. "The rest of you never had contact with them, but Dex and I had a run-in with...well, another group like ours."

"Like ours? You mean they were-"

"-investigating flying saucers. In fact, they were the ones who were supposed to meet that ship you three were taken to by mistake."

"Ulayee?" Lars Ångström was a hard man to surprise, but there was a note of incredulity in his response that sounded out of place on his patrician lips.

"Exactly," Ecks nodded. "Dex and I ran into them while we were searching for you. We walked in while they were interrogating Lieutenant Grady. Their leader was a man named Corbett and he was very unhappy with Grady for giving you those flight suits. He didn't want Grady to talk to us, and he was pretty adamant about it."

"I'll say," Dex snorted. "He shot Grady right in front of us."

A gasp went through the three who hadn't been there to see it.

"Why didn't you ever tell us about this, Arthur?" Rita asked.

Rita Mae's voice was about as cold as it could get. Jakob Kleinemann took the tiniest of steps away from his fiancé. The dreaded code word 'Arthur' rarely fell from her lips, but he knew it meant about the same thing as when she called him Jakob instead of furry bunny.

Feeding the need for diversion, Kleinemann asked, "What makes you think of this other group now, major? That was five years ago."

Ecks winced at the memory. "Do you remember hearing about three men who died in a helicopter crash during the storm?" He didn't wait for an answer. "I found out later that those three same men were on that chopper. They were led by Major Corbett, the man who shot Lieutenant Grady."

"Karma," Kleinemann suggested.

"It would be," Dex said, "except Artie and me saw all three outside Colonel Mazer's office on the day we left Roswell. And they were all alive and well."

***

Rita Mae's attitude had changed markedly in her five years with Project Stall. In the initial giddiness of her release from the typing pool, she was willing to do whatever Arthur Ecks ordered. In those early days, she gave Ecks the same trust she would give her own father. More often than not, her trust was rewarded.

But the magnitude of Ecks' occasional failures had worn on her, leading to the expression of a temper that military protocol no longer had any power to check. As he hadn't responded to her question, Rita prodded again.

"Forget about five years ago. I want to know about here and now. Because, you know, Arthur, these things affect all of us. So let's start with what the hell was *supposed* to happen?"

Arthur Ecks shrugged, still a bit confused by the turn of events.

"Well, I guess Clarence was supposed to escort us out of the building. My understanding was that he'd take us to where a car would be waiting."

The tapping sound everyone heard could be traced to Rita Mae's impatient right foot. "And it appears that didn't happen. Who set up this little exit?"

Ecks' expression hardened, dragged down by a deepening frown.

"Someone I thought I could trust. I was afraid McAfee might try something and we needed to get out of there without facing the press."

Dex tried to change the subject.

"Well, I don't know about the rest of you, but I was pretty surprised that President Truman endorsed us so openly."

Rita Mae slid a cigarette from her purse and lit it with a kitchen match and her thumb. She delivered the bad news through a cloud of first toke smoke.

"Come on, Dex, use your head. He didn't. It's like Arthur said. Harry doesn't even know we exist. Clarence only said that so we'd trust him."

"Well, then... ?" Dex cocked his head to one side, running back all he'd heard. "The bailiff wasn't one of ours?"

Arthur Ecks thought about joining the future Mrs Kleinemann in a smoke, but decided against it.

"He was supposed to be working with us, though technically he's from another agency. I thought they were doing us a favor. The idea was for us to be out of reach by the time McAsshole found out he'd been conned. That," he said, turning back to Rita, "was what was supposed to happen."

Dex stifled a giggle. But again, Rita Mae ruined the moment.

"But he isn't one of ours. Whoever he is, he belongs to someone else."

There was a somber silence as each contemplated the mystery in their own way. It ended when Dex reminded them where they were.

"Are we going to hang around here until someone comes for us? Doesn't Dr Ångström have a plane to catch?"

"That's right," Lars exclaimed, checking his watch. "Maisie should be at the airport by now."

Jakob Kleinemann brushed a wisp of steel-wool hair from his forehead and smiled at the thought of Europe. "I haven't been back to Europe since I was a boy. It is a shame that Poland is behind the Iron Curtain now," he said, looking up at his fiancée. "I would love to show you the village where I was born."

Rita found the place under his chin that made his knees go weak and drew his face close to hers. "And why would you want to do that? Do you have family you want to show your sexy American bride to?"

An instant later, she realized what she'd said.

"I'm sorry, Jakob. That was thoughtless of me."

Jakob lost his smile, though a ghost of it struggled to remain on his lips. Even now, seven years after the war's end, he had no idea if any part of the vast network of aunts, uncles, and cousins that sent him to America was still alive.

"No, it is fine because yes, I would very much like for them to meet you. They would say, 'Jakob, you married a *shiksa!*' And I would say yes, I did, but oh, what a *shiksa!*"

Rita Mae laughed in spite of her embarrassment, and was joined by Ångström, who shared Jakob's high opinion of Rita and also didn't like seeing conflict in the ranks. "You're quite right, Jakob. She would create quite a stir!"

Rita blushed at their praise, but was still alert enough to dodge Ångström's bald attempt to cop a feel. Arthur Ecks put an end to the fun and games.

"Quit clowning around, you two. Dex is right. We need to get Lars to the airport which means we need to get the hell out of here."

Jakob scanned the empty corridor in both directions.

"I suspect he may need to re-schedule his flight."

"I think this may be inconvenient for all of us," added Lars.

"That's right," Rita said. "Jakob and I have a reservation at Niagara Falls next weekend. Of course, when we scheduled our wedding, we didn't know we'd be testifying in front of HUAC."

Ecks' protest had an injured quality. "I said it would take an hour, and I got us out in half that. Not my fault the bailiff was a double agent."

"Yes," Lars interrupted, "but you didn't tell us five men would be testifying before we got our turn. Now, let's stop this bickering. It doesn't matter whose fault it was. If we don't get going, it will ruin all of our plans. So," he concluded, looking at each in turn, "which way do we go to get out of here?"

Ångström crossed his arms over his chest, pointing simultaneously in both directions, a gesture stolen from a famous movie scarecrow.

Arthur Ecks considered their options.

"I think we can safely assume that either way might lead to an exit."

Jakob Kleinemann shook his head with infinite sadness.

"This from a man who warned a US Senator not to make assumptions."

Chapter 10 - Post-Mortem

Donald Menzel was waiting at the bottom of the stairs when Josef Hynek finally descended. In the hope of avoiding one of the many bosses he reported to, Hynek delayed his departure when Keyhoe, Ruppelt, and La Paz descended from the observation lounge. He made the excuse that his delay was intended as a mechanism for dodging the press. While La Paz and Ruppelt accepted this falsehood at face value, Keyhoe's doubt hid behind a sour smile that seemed to know more than it was willing to say.

The snapping newshounds of the capitol press corps were being hustled out of the building by the time Hynek emerged, poking his head out of the stairwell like a wary turtle. He was only exposed for a moment, but it was long enough for Menzel to spot him. Known as a man who abhorred physical contact, Menzel wasn't given to actions so gauche as the furtive tap on the shoulder. Lacking this method of introduction, he had to be content with watching the younger man jump at the murmured mention of his own name.

"Doctor Hynek," he said, "I'd like a word if you can spare a moment."

As intended, Hynek jumped, which Menzel found enormously satisfying in both the height and rapidity of response. Accepting his fate, Hynek stepped out into the foyer, achingly aware of the flop-sweat staining the inside of his jacket.

"Doctor Menzel!" Hynek cried, pointing out the obvious. "I didn't see you there."

A door slammed shut somewhere down the corridor just as the door to the observation lounge closed behind Hynek. In shutting but a split second apart, one thump sounded like an echo of the other.

"I'd like a word with you," Donald Menzel said, pushing away from the wall, "in private."

The older man scanned the corridor in both directions. The doors to the hearing chamber had been propped open to allow egress, but with the press gone, there was no longer a need. Menzel kick-released the doorstops, leaving the chamber to the pages who were still cleaning up.

"Of course, sir," Hynek concurred, clearly wishing he had a forelock to tug or some better way to show obeisance. Lacking such, he followed Menzel into the corridor.

"I was hoping we could discuss my testimony," Hynek began. "You see, there were a few things I think they misunder-"

"We are discussing your testimony," Menzel said, cutting him off.

Hynek shrank visibly. Menzel continued without noticing or caring.

"You made a complete hash of it in there. I thought I made it pretty clear that you were to simply stick to the original story, no matter how ridiculous it might sound. Instead, I must remind you again that you're working in an official capacity now. No one, at least no one who matters, is interested in your doubts or personal opinions. When you give an explanation, you are to stick to that explanation, no matter how idiotic it may seem. People expect solid answers from the government, not the kind of wishy-washy crap you peddled in there. Captain Mantell died pursing the planet Venus, end of story."

"But, sir-"

Menzel turned on the younger man, speaking with considerable heat.

"As scientists and astronomers, we both know how harebrained that sounds. We both know that Venus was over a hundred-sixty million miles away from Earth at the time, and we both know it had already set by the time Mantell died chasing it. We both know that, even from high up in the atmosphere, Venus appears no larger than a pea seen from across the average-sized living room."

"I've told you repeatedly that none of that matters. The public doesn't know enough to know you're wrong. Your job is to satisfy public inquiry, which will buy time for other men to sort out the problem. It took time to get that across to Ruppelt, too. Now, though he may need a refresher himself, most of the time he can manage to keep from stepping on his feet and ours. You, on the other hand, appear unable to do even that."

Hynek's hand went to his forehead, but still failed to find the missing forelock.

"But, sir, it was never my intention to use Venus as an official explanation. I only said it was a possibility, and even that was based on preliminary analysis. There was this reporter-"

Menzel stopped in the middle of the corridor, the click of his last footstep ringing off the tiles. He almost spat the word.

"Reporters?! When the hell will you learn you can't trust reporters to get things right. They're not scientists! They don't understand! They'll take what you tell them, understanding only a small fraction, then write it up for an audience that understands even less. Even then, they get most of what we tell them completely wrong. In the future, just say the simplest thing possible and stick to it!"

"Sir-" Hynek started to protest before breaking off at the older man's fury.

"Your job is to provide explanations, Doctor Hynek. Whether or not those explanations make any kind of sense is entirely up to you. If you want to play your hand cautiously, give it a little more thought before you commit yourself. Just don't take too much time. If you start taking too much time, those reporters you're so concerned about will start doing your thinking for you and I don't think either of us want that. If you can't do this very simple job, then let me know now and I'll find someone else who can. Are we clear?"

"Yes, sir," Hynek said, visibly cowed. "But what about Ruppelt? You said-"

"I know what I said," Menzel growled, "but as it happens, I don't have any authority over Captain Ruppelt. But don't worry, his superiors are going to read him the same riot act. Now if you'll excuse me, my wife has insisted on dragging me to one of those infernal cocktail parties tonight. If you think I've been hard on you, you should hear what she'll say if I'm late."

***

While Allen Hynek was busy having his already plummeting self-esteem further punctured by Donald Menzel, Captain Ed Ruppelt was being called on the carpet by Hoyt Vandenberg, one of the Air Force's highest ranking generals. If this seemed odd, given the disparity in their ranks and that Ruppelt had only seen the man from a distance prior to that, he wasn't given much time to think about the anomaly.

"Goddamnit Captain," Vandenberg shouted as soon as the door closed behind them, "your job is to look like you're doing a good job! You're not actually supposed to do a good job!"

Ruppelt stifled his shock, but knew better than to drop his salute.

"Sorry, sir!" The young captain said, trying to explain. "I mistakenly thought the two were the same thing."

Vandenberg's puffy features, already crimson with rage, deepened a shade. "The same thing?", he fumed incredulously, "You were assigned to your position because one of your superiors, who shall remain nameless, considers you publicity savvy. You were told to make it appear that you were looking into the flying saucer problem. You were told to do this because your predecessors in Project Sign tried to go public with their conclusions and their successors in Project Grudge didn't do a goddamn thing! You were supposed to make it look like you were getting close to the answer, but no one ever suggested that you were actually supposed to do it!"

"But sir," Ruppelt protested, still holding his salute even as his arm grew weary, "I haven't come close to finding the answer."

Vandenberg slapped a hard palm against the sturdy oak of his desk.

"I know that," Vandenberg said in quieter tones, "and God help us if you ever do. But the way you run around the country, gathering information... Well, son, it's just a matter of time before you discover something of actual value."

Ruppelt's arm started to quiver. He concentrated on keeping the shaking from reaching his voice. "I promise you, sir. To date, I've learned nothing of any value whatsoever."

"Then why the hell didn't you just say that to that goddamned McAfee! How the hell did that bastard even find out you exist? I thought Project Blue Book was supposed to be Top Secret! What kind of secret is it if some busybody Senator can pull you in off the street to testify?"

Ruppelt's elbow was starting to visibly bob up and down.

"I don't know how he found out, sir. Shall I investigate the leak?"

Vandenberg took a heavy seat behind the desk, easing his weight back into the chair.

"No, damnit, with your luck, you'd probably find out who it was and blab it to the wrong person in the command chain. Clearly, we can't trust our own men any more, at least some of them. I'll have someone else look into it. From now on, just keep your mouth shut about this meeting and flying saucers in general. Those reporters know who you are now, so they're going to start pestering you for information. From now on, I want you to only answer in the most general terms. If you must answer, stress the extreme sensitivity of the investigation. Most of those bastards went through the war, so they understand the concept of loose lips. And from now on, you'll let me know if you run into any newshound who won't take no for an answer. At ease, captain."

Edward Ruppelt dropped his arm to his side, feeling a little twinge in his chest as he did so. "Thank you, sir. But how will I contact you if I can't go through my superiors?"

"I was getting to that," Vandenberg said. "Who do you report to now?"

"I'm currently reporting to Colonel Wilhelm, sir."

Vandenberg scowled as he pressed a button on his desk.

"We'll set up a way for you to get in touch that bypasses him."

The button made a beep. A reedy voice came through the intercom.

"Sir?"

Turning to the intercom, Vandenberg issued a command to the man on the other end. "Clarence, get in here and don't bring your pad."

A tall sandy-haired man with lieutenant's bars poked his head through the door, saluting as soon as he entered the room.

"Lieutenant Clarence, this is Captain Ruppelt. We need to devise a way for him to contact me without going through his superior officer. Can you handle that for me?"

"Yes, sir," the lieutenant replied at once. "I believe I can."

"I'm not sure I'm comfortable with this, sir," Ruppelt said.

"At-ten-SHUN!"

Vandenberg's bellow wiped out every other sound in the room. Both men responded at once, Ruppelt raising his flattened hand to his temple while Clarence lifted his elbow just a little higher. Vandenberg paused, forcing the younger men into still greater expressions of vigilance until he finally relented.

"At ease, now you were saying, captain?"

"Nothing, sir," Ruppelt gulped.

Vandenberg nodded.

"That's what I thought. Now go with Lieutenant Clarence. I'm sure you two can work out a way to stay in touch without alerting every blessed soul in the chain of command."

***

It took almost half an hour for Donald Keyhoe to shed the dozen reporters who followed him out of the hearing. He found a measure of revenge by drawing them out into the swelter of the DC afternoon, then leading them on a brisk walk across the wide lawns adjoining the Senate building. The hike left nine of them panting to keep up, and the other three peeling off to file what they had. By the time he descended into the underground garage to get his car, he'd lost another four and the ones still following only wanted to get out of the heat.

He drove away with a smile on his face, returning to the Ambassador where there was a message for him at the front desk. He returned to his room, packed, and went down to the lobby to check out. As instructed in the message, he went out onto the curb to wait. He was still wondering at the six words in the message when a black Lincoln pulled up beside him. The rear passenger door opened and when the hand waved him inside, Keyhoe got in.

He took his seat in the back, sized up the tall sandy-haired man inside, and asked. "Okay, I'm here. Now what the hell is this all about?"

He never got to hear the answer.

***

Dr Lincoln La Paz was also staying at the Ambassador. He'd just returned when a call was patched through to his room.

"Dr La Paz?"

La Paz didn't recognize the voice, but it sounded tinny, as if it was coming from a great distance. "Yes, this is La Paz."

"Dr La Paz, my name is Detlev Bronk. I work, in an administrative capacity, for the National Academy of Science."

La Paz took a seat at the edge of the bed, a position that perfectly framed his body in the mirror over the dresser. Even in the mirror, he had a baffled look.

"What can I do for you, Mister Bronk?"

Something shifted on the other end of the line. The rustling sound that came back to him sounded like a piece of paper being crumpled.

"I must apologize for the late notice," said Bronk. "I just heard you were in town from one of my subordinates. He was at the hearing today. He was very interested in your work and gave us a good report on your testimony. There are some of us at the Academy who are very interested in the issues you brought up. We'd like to discuss these matters at your earliest convenience."

La Paz looked back at the mirror, now finding that his image seemed a bit blurry. "Well, Mr Bronk, that may be a problem. I have a full schedule tomorrow and I'm leaving on the afternoon train. I just don't see how there'll be time."

A hand covered the receiver on the other end. La Paz heard the murmur of a whispered exchange. Bronk came back on the line.

"We don't want to disturb your plans, but we were hoping you might be available for dinner tonight. Truthfully, we've already arranged a car for you."

La Paz felt his head swimming. The image in the mirror grew fuzzy.

69

"I was..." He struggled to remember what he was going to do, only retrieving the appointment with great effort.

"I was planning to have dinner here at the hotel, then meet some colleagues for drinks. They're old friends and I haven't seen them in quite a while."

Bronk sounded peeved.

"Would it be possible to cancel? It's very important that we speak. We would like to discuss an opportunity within our organization. We think you'd be perfect for the post."

"I don't know-" La Paz started to say before the phone cut out. He heard a hiss of escaping gas, followed by the too-sweet smell of lilac.

Lincoln La Paz was barely aware of the knock at the door, but it sent a shiver through the image in the mirror. La Paz regarded himself dubiously, wondering when he had become so shaky. He'd alway prided himself on being a solid person, but the man in the mirror seemed more liquid than solid. He let out an uncharacteristic giggle, remembering just in time to cover the mouthpiece.

More liquid than solid, more plasma than liquid, more gas than air, Lincoln La Paz giggled again at his little joke, then slumped unconscious onto the bed.

The knob turned and the door opened to admit a tall sandy-haired man. The sandy-aired man crossed the room to pick up and replace the fallen receiver.

Without identifying himself or checking to see if there was anyone at the other end of the line, he lifted the receiver and broadcast a series of sounds that resembled the skittering speech of crickets.

When he was done, he set the receiver down, lifted the stocky La Paz with surprising ease, and left.

Chapter 11 - Sands Down Under

Wally Sands had never liked waiting, even during his first life, back when he was completely human. Now, in a resurrected body, with a seven foot Nemertean worm coiled inside his frontal lobe, Wally was still the same impatient little son of a bitch he'd always been. If one were to analyze his psyche in further detail, it would become clear that the worm had only exacerbated these tendencies. The worm, whose name was Shff, said this was because of the sympathetic resonance between them, and that resonance was what made Sands such a perfect host. As far as Sands was concerned, this was just a long winded way of saying the worm was a mean little shit, too.

Wally's task, the reason he was currently stuck in this ten by six closet eight hundred sixty feet under ground, was to wait until something happened. The room, whose only feature of note was a circular vent in its ceiling that led God knew where, was off an unused corridor deep under the Library of Congress.

There was nothing to see down here and precious little to hear, with only the phlegmy wheeze of the ancient ventilation for aural stimulation. The only entertainment was watching dust motes drift out of the vent to spiral around his head. The dust made him sneeze, as it fell in slow whorls to collect on the tiles. It made one wonder when the ducts were last flushed and it sickened the human part of him to know he was breathing that shit.

It was a crappy assignment, one that should've gone to Russell or Grady. After all, he was Corbett's, and by that logic, Kraall's, second in command. Wally Sands wasn't some flunky to plop down in an isolated room on unspecified guard duty. Back before the worm, when they were all part of Project Nemesis, he never would've stood for this shit.

Project Nemesis was a top secret Pentagon effort to negotiate with the extraterrestrials who'd started cropping up back in 1947. Now, with the worm in his head, the aims of Project Nemesis were compromised, but Wally Sands was still second in command, albeit for a different army.

He heard a door slam in the distance, that reverberation echoing down the long halls like a stone dropped in a well. Relieved that something had finally happened, Wally tiptoed to the door where, rather unnecessarily, he placed one ear to the door while the worm extended its senses into the corridor outside. When Shff gave the all clear, Sands moved out into the corridor, kicking away a spiderweb of dust and hair that'd grown overly attached to his left shoe.

Now he could hear the voices as they funneled down to him through other vents. His quarries were arguing, and both the worm and human parts of him shared a smile over that. A little dissension in the ranks made any job easier.

Sands crossed the aisle, opening the door of what looked like another closet, but was actually a transit shaft to the lower levels. As Shff relayed the news of the arrival of the targets to their *thang*, Sands stepped into what looked like an empty elevator shaft, paused to adjust his airspeed, corrected for crosscurrents, then plummeted down into the Stygian depths of the underworld.

***

Wally Sands hadn't always had a worm in his head. He acquired the worm in much the same way a renter might acquire a brownstone flat through the death of the previous tenant. The only difference, in his case, was that Wally was the flat.

Sands was still part of the military when he got his worm, though even then he was more beholden to Allen Dulles' vision of what would one day become the CIA. Like Abel Corbett, Wally was one of many men whose loyalty would be coopted by the budding spymaster. At the time of their deaths, Corbett and Sands, and for that matter, Russell, were all assigned to Project Nemesis, the Pentagon's top secret effort to contact and negotiate with extraterrestrial visitors.

Their superiors at the Pentagon would never know how good a job they'd done, though their closest connection wasn't with the aliens they'd been assigned. At the time, the Nemerteans were a race the Pentagon still hadn't made contact with. Playing on their supposed loyalty to Dulles, they'd also found an in with the spymaster, all the while keeping the existence of the worms secret from both the Pentagon and the CIA. From the worms' point of view, things were going swimmingly.

Project Nemesis had also benefited from earlier contacts with the visitors. The earlier visitors, the diminutive Greys, had grown irritated by the American military's ability to shoot down their ships by disrupting the planet's magnetic field. Rather than going to the expense of redesigning the ships, the Greys had negotiated a truce that made Project Nemesis the recipient of some very interesting technology.

That technology could be used to track down anomalies in the dimensional ether that separated the universe into manageable parts. It was interesting stuff, to be sure, but with Shff in his head, Wally Sands no longer needed that crap. Shff always seemed to know when something or someone from another world was around.

It was funny how he still remembered things that had happened while he was still alive. He still remembered his surprise when Corbett first told him about the alien visitors. Corbett got his information from higher up the food chain. Corbett had learned that the only reason the Earth hadn't fallen under the thrall of aliens was because there were so many competing for the honor.

Sands had since figured out that a fragile balance of power existed between their many potential overlords, and maintaining that balance was the only way to protect humanity. For history buffs, which Wally Sands was not, it was a bit like Europe just prior to the First World War, but with stars and spaceships instead of cannons and Maginot Lines.

Wally was surprised to learn that his government was on friendly terms with more than one species, and that one of those friends had provided the US with several tools derived from various alien technology. The Inter-Dimensional Threat Detector (internally dubbed the IDTD) was one such device.

Wally was captain in the Army back then, before the accident that killed him and Russell. They'd died following an IDTD alert across southeastern New Mexico in a requisitioned helicopter. Russell was piloting when the storm hit.

The storm was a real haboob, the mother of all windstorms. No chopper pilot in his right mind would fly in that kind of weather, but Abel Corbett wasn't really in his right mind. Making matters worse, he didn't much care for the opinions of Ivy League college boys in general, and Winthrop Walton Russell III in particular. As anyone who'd served under him was well aware, Abel Corbett had a habit of ignoring advice from anyone who knew more than he did.

Once airborne, they'd followed the IDTD to the point of the disturbance, with Russell doing his best to keep the chopper in the air. But, as soon became apparent, nobody alive could have flown against that wind. Helicopters were relatively new technology then, and they certainly hadn't reached the level of stability where it would be sane to venture out into such a storm.

They were right above the disturbance when a sudden gust had caught hold of the chopper, tossing it about like a toy in the hands of a temperamental child. As a plaything, the chopper didn't last long before the wind smashed it into the ground with an authority that could only come from Mother Nature herself. Sands smiled at the memory, and the lesson Corbett had never really learned.

You don't mess around with Mother Nature.

Winthrop Walton Russell was as useless as the day was long, but he was dead right on this occasion. It was almost karmic that Russell, who'd warned them to turn back, was the one to get cut in half when the windshield shattered. Karma, if there were any logic to her actions, should have reserved that honor for Abel Corbett.

When the chopper crashed, Corbett and Sands were thrown about like Ken dolls inexcusably tardy for a date with Barbie. Wally Sands broke his left leg in the initial impact, and his right leg when Corbett landed on it. The human part of Wally Sands died minutes later without regaining consciousness.

Even so, Wally had a reasonably clear memory of his death. Always a great subject for speculation among the living, Sands had a few things he could tell those know-know-it-all yogis and fakirs. Wally recalled Death as a release from his broken body, followed by a floating sensation that accompanied his astral self as it rose up to an ethereal heaven. It was actually pretty nice, enough to make him regret being such a shit of a human being while he was alive. He remembered a few folks he'd known in life, reaching down to pull him up, extending their long insubstantial limbs through the ether.

But that was when the worm showed up. The disturbance being tracked by the IDTD turned out to be a cluster of Nemertean escape pods falling to earth. The pods were released when the Nemertean ship, commanded by Kraall, broke up in the ionosphere. Scattered hundreds of miles apart in some cases, the pods orbited the planet for long periods of time before falling to Earth in the form of green fireballs.

For the next three years, the fireballs came down intermittently, mostly over the vast mid-section of the United States, though many landed in Asia, Africa, and the oceans as well. Once on the ground, the pods burrowed into the earth where the only course of action lay in being discovered by an indigenous species with the right natural resonance to host the worm.

Natural resonance was very important to the worms, as the wrong mix of personalities could result in a worm being rejected by the host. Rejection left the worm homeless and the host dead, which was a no win situation for every one. One trait the worms always insisted on when selecting a host, was that the host be dead. Live hosts tended to have stronger personalities that gave them more of a say in whether they really wanted a worm in their head. A live host made taking over more of a challenge. As far as the worms were concerned, dead was good.

Sands would learn, as would Russell, Corbett, Grady, and all the hundreds of others killed in the attack on Roswell Army Air Field, that the worms could repair any damage done to a human body, all the way down to the cellular level. If there was even the tiniest smidgen of viable DNA, the worms could reconstruct a dead human being back to a functioning whole. The resurrected human was under the control of the worm, but that was still better than being coyote shit, which was all that was left of Abel Corbett when Kraall found him. Russell's worm, Mudduk, reclaimed the halves of the pilot's bisected body and knit him back together so well you couldn't find a scar with a microscope.

Corbett was bounced around pretty good in the crash, suffering multiple fractures before the fall that finally killed him. As he was immediately eaten by a giant coyote, Corbett was in a pretty receptive frame of mind when Kraall found him. Since their resonances were a good match, Kraall brought him back to life in a matter of minutes. Making him physically whole took about a day.

Five years later, the tradeoff still seemed like a good one. Where someone else might wonder what happened after death, Wally Sands wasn't one to think that far ahead. The only down side as far as he could see was not having any free will. He always had to do exactly what the worm wanted. But even this wasn't much of a problem as it might sound because Sands and Shff generally wanted the same thing, which was to create pain for all living things.

Maybe there was something to this idea of resonance.

The fact that Corbett's group now had a dual allegiance was one of the few significant bits of information lost on Allen Dulles. It just showed that even the great spies miss one occasionally. But even here, the worms and the spymaster were so rarely at cross purposes that Kraall would sometimes stare at a framed picture of Dulles for hours, imagining what a wonderful host he would've made if Kraall had found him before Corbett.

Relationships are like that. Few of us are satisfied with the ones we have.

Between the Pentagon and Dulles' protection, Nemesis was given a freedom they might otherwise never obtain. These connections, though excellent, were soon augmented by Dulles' fawning pursuit of a membership in the shadowy group known as Majestic. Five years after crashing empty-handed on an untamed world, the worms were sitting pretty.

***

Sands landed in a crouch at the bottom of the shaft, his descent slowed by a rising column of hot air that exploded into a cloud of fine particles the moment he touched down.

"Jesus," he swore. "This place is filthy! You'd think someone might consider using some of that high-powered alien technology to clean out these vents."

Seated on the other side of the room, Abel Corbett smirked.

"Yeah, it's a crying shame that Nemertean vacuum cleaner technology is so primitive. It isn't anywhere near as advanced as ours."

As always, Kraall bridled at the dig. Like his host, he was thin-skinned and irritable. He projected his thoughts at such a high volume that everyone could hear. He was even loud enough to disturb the other men in the room.

Winthrop Walton Russell III looked up from the device he was working on, the failure of which being what forced Sands into sentry duty. Perseus Grady was wearing a helmet over his head that amplified his thoughts and made it possible to communicate remotely with the dozens of worms still stuck in their pods.

Other than indulging in this worm version of social media, Grady wasn't doing anything particularly important. This wasn't at all unusual. Grady never did anything particularly important. Not caring about so trivial a subject as vacuum cleaner technology, neither man nor worm said a word in protest.

This wasn't true of Kraall.

"Your statement is incorrect," said the *thang*. "Our vacuum cleaners are much more powerful and clean far deeper than anything humans possess."

Telepathically deafened by the volume of Kraall's thoughts, Grady removed the helmet and set it down on the table.

Corbett and Kraall were well matched. Despite being the unchallenged top dogs in their respective hierarchies, both were petty creatures, thin-skinned enough to respond to any slight. Sands interrupted before they lost a whole day to the petty bickering inside Corbett's head.

"Anyhow, they're on their way. Is everything ready?"

Abel Corbett felt a chill, but this was only a punishment meted out by his long gummy master. He rubbed his hands together as a villainous worm-driven laugh forced its way past his thin lips.

"Oh yes," Kraall said, using the mouth of Abel Corbett like a ventriloquist's dummy, "everything is ready."

Chapter 12 - Nothing Done in Haste

John Haste was out of sight by the time Janie Gently made it through the revolving doors, but Bertie Stein was only halfway down the stairs. In her loose skirt and sensible shoes, Janie was easily able to run him down.

"Hey, Bertie! Where ya headed?"

Bertie hesitated only a second, but that second cost him. He took the cigar from between his teeth, preparing a smile before turning to greet the competition.

"Why, if it isn't little Janie Gently!" Bertie said, as if pleased to see her. "How's *Woman's Week Daily*'s answer to my sister Gertrude?"

"She's not your sister, Bertie. You were an only child."

Janie adjusted her glasses, which had gone askew in her flight down the steps.

"I saw you leaving and I was worried," she lied. "You feeling okay?"

Bertie took the bait far too easily.

"Ah, you're a sweet child for asking, Janie. Yeah, my gut's giving me a bit of trouble, so I thought I'd head home and have a lie down."

Janie took the bold step of taking Bertie's arm in the kind of grip lampreys could only wish for.

"That's a good idea, Bertie, cause you look awful. Hey, I got an idea. Howzabout you let me give you a ride? I'm parked just down the street."

Bertie tried to shake her off, but barnacles were easier to dislodge.

"Aw, that's sweet of you, child, but it's no trouble. There's a bus stop at the end of the block."

"Nonsense, always glad to help a fellow member of the fourth estate."

She guided him away from the bus stop, helping him up when his efforts to pull away made him stumble.

"And maybe on the way," Janie said as if it were the most natural thing in the world, "you can tell me where you're really going. I know I'm just a girl and all, but the Bertie Stein I know would never walk out on a Senate hearing without a good reason to be somewhere else."

Bertie tried to dig his heels in, but the girl from *Woman's Week Daily* was shockingly strong.

"That is," Janie continued, "unless he had a better story in mind. So what is it? This girl smells a good one."

"I got no idea what you're talking about," Bertie claimed.

Janie simply shook her head.

"Yeah, you do. You're not a dumb guy. I even think you're kind of smart, at least some of the time."

She knew she had him when his body slumped, so she let go, knowing he'd never be able to outrun her.

Bertie found the stump of the cigar in his pocket and took it out, pinching its filthy end between his thumb and middle finger.

"Aw, Janie, listen, you got me, but it's not much at all. Really, it's nothing worth your time and trouble."

The concerned tone in Janie's voice abruptly departed.

"Cut the crap, Bertie. You saw something in there and Fast Johnny saw it, too. You recognized one of the people who didn't testify. Now who was it?"

Bertie Stein's face split in a wide froggy smile.

"Aw, is that all you want? Fer crying out loud, Janie, the guy's been on the cover of *Life* and *Look*. Johnny and me can't be the only ones to figure that out. But if that's all you want, well there it is. It's that Swede sex doctor, Engstrom or Ångström, something like that. Go to the library and check the back issues. I think it was sometime last year, October maybe."

Janie Gently froze, the face in question now clicking with the face on a back issue of *Life*. She remembered now, though it was September, not October. Lars Ångström. They were calling him 'The Sex Doctor' and his book had risen up the nonfiction bestseller lists, with enough sales enough to challenge the middle rungs of fiction. Now that the face had clicked, she wondered how she ever could have missed it.

Sex! That was the name of the book. How could she forget a title like that?

"I get it now, Bertie, but what would a guy like that be doing testifying in front of McAfee? He's not part of the government, and I know for a fact he doesn't get any government funding."

For anyone taking notes, Bertie's beetle brows rose slightly at this juicy piece of unsolicited information.

"That a fact? Ångström doesn't get any federal money?"

Janie shook her head back and forth, as if she was scolding him.

"Didn't you read the article? He's completely self-funded, his wife has money, but his research is done on a shoestring, mostly using student interns and volunteers. I don't think he even gets anything from his college 'cause they're afraid of what people might think. It's some school in Wisconsin, I forget which one. He moves around a lot. He's interviewed thousands of people about how they like it in the sack."

Suddenly realizing what she'd said, Janie blushed.

"I never read it myself, of course, but I hear it's pretty raw stuff."

This wasn't exactly true. Janie's copy was kept under lock and key in the bottom drawer of her nightstand, where she believed it safe from the prying eyes of her Vassar roommate.

It wasn't.

Bertie rested his butt against a big concrete thing with flowers in it.

"So why does McAfee want him to testify? He a commie?"

Janie laughed at Bertie's ignorance.

"Hardly! His wife's old man used to be a Senator! You remember Stanford Neill, the man who lost his seat to Joe McAfee?"

Bertie was thinking that this was too easy. In exchange for one little thing, this little girl had already spilled three times the information he was hiding. He wondered if there was more to be had. Bertie wagged his hand, extending the thumb and pinkie finger.

"So, is he, you know, a little *faygeleh*? He's a very pretty man."

Janie scoffed at the suggestion.

"Boy, you don't know this Johnny at all! It's like I told you, he married a Senator's daughter from Wisconsin, the Senator is from Wisconsin, not the daughter, though I guess she is too. Anyway, Dr Ångström has three of the most adorable little girls, they had a picture in the article, and he's been fired more than once for getting a little too familiar with the student body, if you catch my drift. So, no I don't think he's even a little..."

Janie stopped, suddenly realizing she'd been had.

"You dirty chiseler! You've been milking me like a cow with swollen udders!"

Bertie laughed and thrusting the cigar back between his teeth.

"Hey, don't stop now, doll. You just saved me two hours of legwork, maybe five 'cause I bet that stuff about why he gets fired ain't exactly common knowledge."

Bertie shook his head in wonder.

"You got a lot to learn about talking to the press, little girl. We eat our own."

Bertie Stein started back toward the bus stop, but he'd only gone three steps when Janie called him back.

"Wait a minute, buster."

Bertie turned to look at her, his caterpillar brows lifting in a quizzical arc.

Janie closed the distance with an easy stroll. When she got close enough, she looked into his eyes with a look unlike any woman Bertie Stein had ever known. Even his wife Sadie had never looked so stern.

"I offered you a ride, mister, and you're going to take it."

Again, she caught his arm in her lamprey grip.

This time she didn't let go until they reached the car.

***

John Haste would've been mortified to know that his colleagues referred to him as Fast Johnny behind his back. The sobriquet, no more than a play on his surname, had nothing to do with his manner of approaching a story. Haste was a bit slow for the most part, more concerned with getting his facts right than making his deadlines. It was a strategy that paid off for him time and time again, as he was regularly scooped by the competition, but nearly always got them back the second day, either by finding something that invalidated the previous day's story, or adding a depth of detail that had the city editors screaming bloody murder at their own men for not doing the legwork that came naturally to Haste.

With only the one lead to pursue, Haste's first stop was a library and the Library of Congress was the best the country had to offer, even if the service was on the slow side. He even liked the delay in some ways because it gave him time to think. So, figuring he was destined to wait, that was what he did, sitting on a hard wooden chair and twirling his hat in one hand while scratching a mosquito bite with the other.

He tried to recall what he knew about Ångström on his own. He liked to do this with anyone in the public eye, reckoning that he didn't know any more about most folks than the average citizen. But that was why he'd recognized Ångström in the first place. Haste was the kind of man who had a subscription to *Life*, but didn't turn his nose up at *Look*. The details about Ångström's life were coming back now, married to a Senator's daughter, three girls, and the scandals and sex research that kept him moving from school to school.

After twenty minutes, the desk clerk returned with a stack of periodicals, newspaper back issues, and a copy of Ångström's bestseller. Haste took the stack and found a table he didn't have to share.

For the next two hours, he immersed himself in the life and accomplishments of Dr Lars Ångström. When he was finished, he returned the stack to the desk and left feeling better informed, but no closer to understanding why the man was at a Senate hearing on UFOs, or why he hadn't been called to testify.

Haste also wondered why the committee had turned to that issue in the first place when it'd never done anything that didn't involve communists, homosexuals, or both.

Lars Ångström made no sense. Sex and communication were the subjects he seemed to know the most about, but what did either have to do with UFOs?

Chapter 13 - The Long Dark Hall

Dex set off down the corridor, leaving the others to follow at their own pace. They were deep underground now and well beyond the footprint of the Capitol Building. The bare bulbs set in the middle of the ceiling were no more than low-watt concessions to the need for visibility. Set at hundred foot intervals, the lights made vague reflections on the dusty tiles, but were so far apart that one didn't see the next bulb until well after the previous one was in the rear view mirror.

These ventures into darkness were repeated at every station, and made Dex feel like he was taking a conscious leap of faith every time he passed one of those islands of light. They saw no doors, and the corridor hadn't branched since they'd first established their direction. Rita Mae, bringing up the rear with Jakob, had the disturbing thought that if they were to turn back now, the door they entered through might no longer be there.

Adding to the gloom, there was the silence. There was some talk at first, but the darkness was oppressive, and as the tunnel continued without feature or interruption, their spirits fell, making it more difficult to keep any real dialogue going.

There was no sound that wasn't of their own making, and even their own scrapes and shuffles were dampened somehow. There was none of the echo one would expect, despite the vast expanse of tile over concrete. When they stopped, there were no sounds of ventilation, or even rats. Even so, the air smelled clean if a bit stale. After what seemed like an hour, Lars Ångström suggested they turn back, but was outvoted. After another twenty minutes, he was certain he'd miss his flight even if they did. The lights ended ten minutes later, leaving absolute darkness and signaling an end to the weak faith that had sustained them.

Arthur Ecks disturbed an uncomfortable memory, a *déjà vu* of a place much like this in his past. He hoped this venture underground wouldn't meet the same fate the first one had. Dex reached out to find the wall, just to have an anchor. The others, acting on their own, did the same, blind to his action.

"I can't see anything at all," said Ecks.

Dex tried closing his eyes to see if it made a difference and was surprised to find he could actually see better. But before he could say anything, someone said, "Uh-oh," but didn't follow up on it. Rita Mae finally broke the silence.

"Uh-oh, what?"

"Look back behind you, the way we came."

Rita turned, they all did, but finding the way back was impossible.

"What is it, Artie?"

Dex slid his hand back toward Ecks, pleased when it found a full set of knuckles rather than one of the dark hairy fears of his imagination. Artie's hand flipped onto its back as his fingers intertwined with his, giving him a firm squeeze before releasing it.

"The last light. We should still be able to see it."

"We haven't gone very far."

"We must have changed direction."

"Which direction was it?"

"I can't see in any direction."

Artie ended the conversation with the only logical answer.

"The light went out. Somebody or something turned it off."

This news was greeted with a long silence.

"Would it be wrong to turn back?" Dex suggested.

When there was no answer, he asked again, only to hear the same silent response. He shuffled back a few steps, expecting to find Artie, but this time he found nothing. He felt a stirring in the air, as if something large had passed close by, but then that was gone, and for several seconds there was nothing.

Frantically, he flailed for the wall, his panic ending when his hand slapped concrete. He paused to catch his breath, to get his bearings in a place where the only usable sense was touch. In the absolute dark, he was truly blind. To find a way out, he would have to rely on other senses.

In waiting, he sensed a faint breeze moving past, but it wasn't coming from the direction he'd been heading. He turned around in a circle, trying to find the source and his heart soared when he saw a dim glow far off to his left. He waited a moment, just to be sure his mind wasn't playing tricks on him. When the glow didn't fade, Dex felt a surge of hope. Suddenly, the long dark hall felt like a test. Reaching that light would give him a passing grade.

He moved forward again, leaving the wall behind. Again, he called for the others to follow, letting his voice be their guide. He talked about the light ahead, describing its advance and the changes in it as he drew closer. He could see it growing slightly larger with each shuffling step. He had to go slow because the floor was no longer a smooth tiled floor. He suspected that in leaving the tiled area, he'd also left the civilized part of the maze.

He confirmed his suspicion by reaching down to touch the floor. The surface was no longer tile, or even concrete. There was a new texture, unlike any stone he'd ever known. If he had to put a name to it, it reminded him of limestone worn smooth by running water.

He felt the breeze gust again, then something brushing against his hand. Dex jerked back, and rose to standing, his heart pounding in his ears. Again, he waited, but there were no more gusts. After a time, he decided it was probably just one of the dust bunnies he'd seen lining the tunnel higher up. It was odd that so much dust had penetrated so far underground.

He started moving and found the light, though it now seemed to be coming from a different direction. This made him wonder if he'd gotten turned around. He decided that it didn't matter. The important thing was that the light was still there, and he had no other alternative.

He'd run out of words by then, so he called out nonsense syllables, praying that somewhere behind him, someone could still hear and was still following. But the dark was empty, and the further he walked, the more it grated on him. He really didn't want to be alone down here.

When the light moved right, he debated following it, but the path seemed inevitable, and his choice of direction, all ways being equally black, was less choice than capitulation. His anxiety was at a fever pitch, as he strode cluelessly into the black with only the strange light as guide.

A dusty smell rose to his nostrils, and he could feel the tiny motes of it attacking his sinuses as his feet stirred the dormant specks into flight. He had a weird thought that real bunnies, formed from this civilized detritus, were following him.

The light continued to grow and take on sharper lines. First it was no bigger than a keyhole, but gradually it grew larger until it was taller than he was, and wider. The outline of something began to take shape, and again he feared his eyes were playing tricks on him. He continued to call out, cycling through the familiar names, even as the associated faces started to fade in his memory. He ached for something familiar, for anything that wasn't this dingy unswept floor.

The light finally resolved into the shape of a high arch that seemed neither crafted nor entirely natural. The shape was regular, even symmetrical, but wasn't in any known style. After so much time straining in the dark, his eyes narrowed in the relative brilliance of the opening before him.

When he emerged from the tunnel, he found himself on a dimly lit platform that extended about fifty feet to his left and right, but only ten feet in front of him. There, its terminus was delineated by a sharp ledge which, despite the light around him, was as black as anything he'd seen on the way down.

Dex explored his new surroundings, walking from one end of the platform to the other. Both directions ended in high steep walls that rose out of sight. He touched the walls and the floor, finding both were made of a material similar to what he'd touched on the way down.

He returned to the arch, to listen for his companions, but nothing came down to him. He tried calling again.

"Hey, Artie! You back there?"

His voice died, having gone nowhere.

"Professor Kleinemann? Rita? Doctor Ångström!"

"Yes, Dexter," a familiar voice replied, "I am here."

Dex almost jumped out of his skin at the unexpected response.

The shadowy form of Lars Ångström came out of the arch in pieces, a hand here, the left side of his face, his right foot stepping into the light. It was eerie watching him appear this way, as if the pieces were being created, then assembled right before his eyes. Dex felt an odd thrill rise up his spine.

"Where is everybody?" Ångström asked, looking around.

Dex shook his head. "I don't know, doc. I thought everyone was behind me, but there was no one following when I got here. You're the first person I've seen in an hour. Where've you been?"

A completely formed Lars Ångström stepped out onto the platform. To Dex's eye, he appeared to be as fresh as if he'd just left his house. There were no signs of stress or exertion, his forehead was smooth and dry, his suit so perfect it looked like it had just been pressed.

Ångström was, as always, immaculate.

"How do you manage to stay looking like that, doc?" Dex asked, not expecting an answer. Now that he was back in the light, Dex compared Ångström's pristine appearance to the sweat-soaked and filthy suit he was wearing.

Ångström did as Dex had done on arrival, walking from one end of the platform to the other. He made no comment as he inspected the site, nor did he do anything out of the ordinary, the only exception being a few kicks to clear the dust and detritus drifting through the arch in a steady stream.

"Where the hell is this stuff coming from?" Dex complained, kicking away a clump that'd glommed onto his shoe. The stuff was getting sticky and more difficult to dislodge. I've seen dust bunnies before, but never so many at once.

Ångström looked over at him, an amused smile gracing his lips.

"Dust bunnies?"

Dex blushed, "That's what Artie calls them. I never saw anything like them growing up, but our apartment gets them from time to time. Artie says they're just dust and hair that blows out of the ventilation ducts when the heater comes on."

Ångström's smile grew a little broader. "I never heard them called that. But in any case, that's not what these things are."

Dex stared back at the linguist. "They're not?"

"Oh, my, no," Ångström said, shaking his head. He turned toward the far end of the platform, then, for reasons Dex couldn't imagine, up into the dark heights above.

"But I forget, you can't see the world the way I can."

Dex looked up the taller man, curious to know what he was talking about. "What do you mean?"

Ångström turned to him, revealing the change.

It looked unbelievably creepy.

"Jesus!" Dex swore, jumping back into the stream of dust.

He had good reason to be startled. Lars Ångström's eyes were rimmed in a golden glow that reminded Dex of fluorescent mascara. He ran three steps back toward the arch before he could make himself stop.

"Doc! What's happened to your eyes?"

Ångström hadn't moved. The glow was only around the edges, leaving the globe and pupil in darkness. Ångström was staring at him as if he was unable to understand Dex's reaction, but that soon proved not to be the case.

"I don't believe we ever told you or the Major," Lars said as calmly as if they were discussing something they'd had for breakfast. "It was a gift of the Ffaeyn."

Dex reached the wall and pressed his body into it. The wall was very cold. Dex eyed Ångström's new optics warily.

"No, I think I'd remember something like this."

Ångström nodded. "We owe you an apology then."

"What happened to you?"

"Oh, it wasn't a bad thing. You see, when Jakob, Rita, and I made contact with the Ffaeyn, our bodies were inhabited by millions, perhaps billions of them. They used us for transport partly, though they are quite capable of independent movement. I think their real purpose was to get an idea of how human beings experience their world. In doing so, they discovered the limitations of our senses. For them, inhabiting our bodies was like this tunnel we just came down. Most of what they would normally perceive was obscured by a lack of sensory input."

Dex held up a hand to stop this flood of information.

"Before you say more, you should know that I went to a very poor grammar school and never graduated."

Ångström fixed his golden eyes on Dex's blue ones.

"At first, they could see only what we saw, feel what we felt, hear what we heard, you get the idea. This was too great a limitation so they made some changes that added a few capabilities to our sensory apparatus. Actually, that isn't right. I should've said they gave us access to potential we didn't know we had."

Dex mulled this information over and came up with an explanation that seemed to fit what he was being told. "You mean, like superpowers?"

Ångström scoffed at the notion.

"Hardly, to get to the top of a tall building, I take the elevator like anyone else. But they did enhance the three of us in significant ways. I don't think you met Jakob until after our experience with the Ffaeyn. He was a different man. When I met him at Wright-Patterson, he was almost blind. He wore lenses as thick as the bottom of a soda bottle. And he was in a great deal of pain."

"So what happened?"

"The Ffaeyn happened. When they took control of our bodies, they repaired anything they regarded as flawed. In Rita's case, they made her feel empowered, more sure of herself both socially and sexually."

Dex's ears burned at the mention of sex and Rita.

"In Jakob's case, there was much more to do. They repaired his sight. They fixed some problems with his spine. Jakob had a dreadful scoliosis, but they straightened him out. You might not believe it, but he is four inches taller now than when I met him."

Dex smirked. "He's still a shrimp."

Ångström smiled oddly, his golden eyes winking.

"Yes, but he's a very happy shrimp. They didn't do anything to repair me because I'm already perfect and they couldn't find anything physically wrong."

Dex wanted to dismiss this claim, but the doc was right. There really wasn't anything wrong with him. Ångström continued while Dex followed his thought, so he missed whatever came before.

"-but they did something much more interesting to all of us."

Dex snapped back to attention.

"What was that, doc?"

"They made changes to our neural networks, opening channels that have been dormant since human beings were created. While they were doing this, they also expanded the range and capabilities of our existing senses."

"We can, if we wish, see a wider spectrum of light. We can see the flow of electricity through the air. We can see the fields of magnetism that bind the planet. Our sense of smell is on par with that of the most sensitive bloodhound. And when the Ffaeyn departed, they left these changes intact."

Dex's jaw dropped open in awe. "Wow."

Ångström shrugged. "Yes, it sounds wonderful, but it's pretty much useless in everyday life. We've had these abilities for five years, but I doubt that any of us ever put them to any use. One needs to be faced with a particular situation to use them, for example, to have a need to see in the dark."

"You can see in the dark?"

"Technically, no, but I can see a wider range of the visible spectrum than humans are accustomed to. It's an ability that we all have the potential for, but it's been switched off."

"But to speak the heart of your question, yes, I can see in the dark, though I must say it's a mixed blessing. There are things here I hope you never see, things we never notice and are probably better off for it. For example, I now understand how some can claim to see ghosts."

Dex shivered as a sickly stripe of fear crawled up his back.

"Can you see ghosts now?"

Ångström's smile was odd and unsettling.

"I'm not sure they are ghosts in the conventional sense, but we're sharing this platform with someone who hasn't properly introduced himself."

Dex whirled around, brushing against something that was gone before he could guess what it was.

"Where?"

Ångström shook his head as if it was of no consequence.

"I suspect he'll make himself known in his own good time, but he's standing right next to you."

Dex's heart jumped a full foot, and the rest of him was quick to follow.

Chapter 14 - A Walk in the Dark

Despite the golden-eyed evidence of the Ffaeyn's gifts, there were a few things Lars Ångström neglected to tell Dex about the extended senses gifted to him. Chief among these omissions were what could be thought of as the penalty for using them. Their first experiences with the senses came under the influence of the billion or so Ffaeyn who guided them from the infirmary to the hangars at Roswell Army Air Field back in 1947.

On that occasion, they suffered no ill effects. It was only later, upon realizing that the Ffaeyn had left those senses operational when they departed, that Jakob, Lars, and Rita tried to use them on their own.

And ran up against some very good reasons for not doing so.

This penalty was comparable in manifestation and severity to a truly nasty migraine headache. Once Lars and Jakob realized that every time they used those powers, they'd be treated to twelve hours of hellish crippling pain, both decided separately that he could get along just fine without being able to see lines of magnetism or the flow of electricity.

The same wasn't true for Rita Mae Marshaux. Unlike Jakob and Lars, Rita continued to use her abilities, explaining the penalty as a bad case of menstrual cramps. As a result, she learned that with practice, the migraines subsided and she could go about her day in a mental state she could easily pass off as just a grumpy mood. Naturally, she kept this information to herself. One never knew when a grumpy mood might come in handy.

She didn't know how she and Jakob had become separated from the others. By the time they noticed, conversation had since ceased. She didn't question why everyone had gone silent, though it was strange given the situation and their need to stay connected. The problem was, there were so many other thing to think about, not the least of which was that so much of the nation's capital was hidden underground.

Even the clearly manmade parts made one wonder why they'd been constructed. None of what she'd seen on the way down appeared older than ten to twenty years. Everything was built from common building materials, available from supply contractors. It wasn't until the lights petered out that she began to suspect they were being led somewhere for a particular purpose.

This thought, when it struck had an energizing effect.

Rita shook her fiancé's sleeve to get his attention. They'd been holding hands since passing the last of the lights and both were now grateful for this contact.

"Jakob?"

As might be expected from a career academic, Jakob Kleinemann was entirely unaccustomed to strenuous physical exercise. He'd grown sweaty on the way down and now, as the temperature fell, he felt the perspiration cooling against his skin like a wet blanket in a refrigerator.

"Yes?"

"Is there anyone else behind you?"

Jakob's mind surfaced from a deep fog.

"I don't think so. We were the last I think."

"I don't hear anyone else in front of me either."

"You don't?"

"I heard Arthur for a while, but Dex and Lars were further ahead."

Jakob was quiet for a time, listening for sounds of their companions. Finally, he acknowledged defeat. "Then...we are alone?"

"Looks that way."

"Do you suppose it is time to panic?"

The question was asked in such a serious analytical way that she laughed in spite of her tension. "I'm not sure," she said finally, "do you want to go first?"

"It would be a terrible breach of etiquette. I believe it should be ladies first."

"We could panic together," she offered.

"Or not at all," he replied.

"All right," she said, now reassured, "let's not panic then. But what can we do? It's too dark to see a thing unless..."

Rita Mae trailed off, inspired by a random memory of her extended senses. She hadn't accessed any of them in quite a while and, for that matter, wasn't even sure one existed for seeing in the dark. Adding to her reluctance was the lie of omission she'd told in not sharing her semi-regular practice with the others.

"Would you promise not to be mad if I told you something?"

"How can I know until you tell me?"

She had to allow that this was only logical.

"You know how we all stopped using the parts of our brains the Ffaeyn opened up for us?"

She felt Jakob's shrug as a tug on her hand.

"Well, I didn't."

"You didn't what?"

"Stop using them. It really hurt at first, using them I mean, but it gets less painful the more you do it."

She felt him pull away a bit, and not wanting to let go, she pulled right back.

"Are you angry?"

"Why should I be angry? Tell me what you see."

This brought up the other lesson learned as a result of her practice.

Another reason not to use the extended sight was what you saw when you did. Disturbing things became visible when one shifted into what Rita liked to think of as the spectral range of visible light. This was where the ghosts lived.

She suspected these ghosts were things that were always there, but she also hoped that, just as humans couldn't see ghosts, the ghosts couldn't see humans.

The problem was, there was no way to be sure

Her heart always jumped at the first sight of an Object of Questionable Reality, but she was quick to remind herself that OQRs were always there, lurking in cupboards and dark corners. These were the things that floated through from other dimensions, the things that haunted old houses and occasionally, when the mood struck them, went bump in the night.

Rita Mae sighed. A career in government service where acronyms had been created for everything under the sun and this was her contribution.

She gasped at the sight of a particularly creepy tentacled creature and clutched wildly for Jakob's hand.

She knew as soon as she found him that Jakob hadn't been using his sight, but he turned it on to share her revulsion.

"Oy! That is a nasty one!"

"Watch your step!" Rita warned.

A pool of iridescent green slime, visible only using the spectral sight, oozed toward them. Rita felt a chill, unrelated to the declining temperature, crawl up her leg. It made her wish she'd worn pants. Nylons made legs feel naked, but offered scant protection against pools of green slime.

...pools of green slime...

Rita slid her hand up Jakob's shoulder to stop him from going forward.

"Do you see that pool of green slime?"

Jakob cocked his head, a hint of curiosity creeping into his voice. "Yes."

Rita approached the slime, going down on one knee to probe it with her finger. The slime came at her in a rush, then stopped just short of her fingertip. Rita paused, leaving her finger extended as if trying to pet a wary cat.

"I think it's intelligent," she said.

"I think it's more than that," Jakob replied. "I think it's Ffaeyn!"

It had been five years since they'd had any contact with the infinitesimally small beings. The Ffaeyn had saved them then, returning things to normal after the devastating attack on the air field. But they'd also made it clear they wouldn't be around to bail humanity out every time a situation got weird. Jakob thought this was why the Ffaeyn had given them the extra senses in the first place.

The Ffaeyn were subatomic intelligences with only a fragile toehold in the physical world. In some interpretations, they were a vast shared consciousness that lived within virtually every particle of matter in existence. Being so small, their interactions with humans could occur in one of two ways.

First, they were capable of merging their physical presence to create aggregate bodies. Some were large enough to mimic human or extraterrestrial races. To do this required trillions or quadrillions of Ffaeyn, any exact number being of a scale difficult to conceive.

But if their numbers were few, something difficult to grasp given how pervasive their presence was, they could also use the bodies of existing species as vehicles, their omnipotent minds sharing space with the consciousness of the host. Rita, Lars, and Jakob had since learned that the cowboy method, as they'd come to think of it, was considered a bit rude by the Ffaeyn, not that being rude stopped them from doing it.

The slime paused on the cusp of touching Rita's finger, clearly considering which method of communication to use. Making its decision, the slime drew back as it began to swirl, rotating slowly like a galaxy spinning around its core. As it gained speed, it became a tornado, and inside that tornado, a shape took form. First came the bones of its skeletal structure, then its muscles and ligaments, and finally an epidermal outer layer.

When it was all done, Jakob and Rita were looking at a tall slender Negro wearing a skintight silvery garment. The man's face was ageless, with the kind of features that might find a home on anyone between twenty and fifty years old. His hair was very long, though rather than falling to his shoulders, it radiated outward like the rays of the sun, partially obscuring the somewhat elephantine nature of his ears. Neither Jakob nor Rita had ever seen him before. The man raised his palm in greeting, creating a wide V between the middle and ring fingers.

"Hey there, meat sacks! Long time, no see!"

Jakob groaned.

There was a lot to like about the Ffaeyn, but the way they combined the superiority of a vast universal intelligence with a decidedly juvenile sense of humor wasn't one of them. Having had the tiny beings inside them, Jakob and Rita had a better understanding of how the little buggers thought, but the attitude and childish taunting had nearly driven Arthur Ecks mad with frustration.

Jakob had once matched wits with a Ffaeyn and managed to come out even. But it was easy to forget you weren't dealing with a single mind. The Ffaeyn were uncountable, and while each individual had its own personality, every one of them was a goddamned know-it-all.

"Oh, good," Jakob scowled, his retort rich with sarcasm. "Are you back for another pony ride?"

The Ffaeyn put a grin on the faux man's face.

"Good one, little man. It took you long enough to notice us. We've been following you since the hearing."

Jakob looked up at the grinning man, assessing his height and length, and his decidedly futuristic mode of dress.

"I don't recognize the form you've taken. What on earth are you wearing?"

The grinning man's smile grew wider. "Do you like it? It's what Michael Rennie wore in *The Day the Earth Stood Still*."

Jakob nodded. "One of Simon's better ideas, though I don't think he got any credit."

The Ffaeyn's faux fingers went to its faux face.

"You haven't met the man with this face, but he was in New Mexico when you were. If you ever meet him, you should be able to work together. Your goals are much the same."

Rita frowned as she stepped in for a closer look.

"Our goals? What are our goals? Who is he?"

The faux grin went away.

"Someone of unimaginable importance."

Jakob shrugged, rocking his head side to side as if evaluating a melon.

"So he is a real Mr Big Shot?"

Instead of answering, the chocolate man thrust his hand forward, producing a wispy blue globe that quickly grew to the size of a grapefruit.

"There are many paths to the future. In some, he will save the world."

"We need saving again?" Jakob's response held the kind of irritation one got when faced with an unpleasant, but unavoidable task.

The tall man nodded sadly. "Time after time after time."

He drew his palm back, the globe disappearing.

"The future looks bleak?" Jakob queried.

"It's always darkest before the dawn." Rita offered, not wanting to be entirely left out of the festival of clichés.

Jakob scratched an itch behind his ear before deciding it was his imagination.

"Who is it this time?" He pointed up, toward an occluded sky. "More from up there?"

The faux man nodded.

"It's a rough neighborhood. But we have more to tell."

"More?"

The faux man mimicked the human state of embarrassment.

"We may have made a mistake when we cleaned up your mess in 1947."

"Oh? How so?"

"Um..well, we were able to repair the physical damage..."

"...and we were able to resurrect all the dead people..."

Jakob took his fiancé's hand, only to have it crushed. He tried to pull away, but years of typing had given Rita's hands the strength of an upright bass player.

"...we found another problem while dealing with yours..."

Other voices emerged from the construct.

"There was a ship that crashed..."

"They were completely helpless."

"They could live for a long time in their escape pods..."

"But what kind of life is that?"

"Stuck on a planet where you can't go-"

"-more than a few feet without dying of oxygen poisoning?"

The first voice returned.

"Then there was the problem of our own people. We weren't about to stick around in human form. We needed a control mechanism for each resurrected human and no one wants to be human for an entire lifetime. We exist in a state beyond time and space, but we're easily bored."

"Human lives are very limiting."

Jakob pulled free, as soon as Rita released her grip.

The faux man spread his hands wide, protesting his innocence.

"They seemed very nice at the time."

Rita's voice was steely with suspicion. "What did you do?"

"Well, like we said, the resurrected humans needed someone to control them, and the Nemerteans..."

"Nemerteans?"

"The worms in the escape pods come from a planet called Nemertea."

"Oy," Jakob muttered, recalling what Arthur Ecks told them about the worms. He experienced a sudden premonition of where this was going.

"The Nemerteans have a very interesting method of colonization, but your oxygen atmosphere is poisonous to them."

"So, Earth isn't such a great place for them to colonize?"

"Normally no, but like we said, they have a way of adapting."

"And what is that?"

"Well, their normal environment is a warm liquid..."

The voice changed again.

"Let's not pussyfoot around. The worms can colonize planets where they can't normally survive because they're able to adapt their neural connections to control native creatures..."

"This allows them to survive on worlds that aren't normally conducive to their form of life..."

"If they can find the right host."

"Host?" Jakob asked, not liking where this was going.

"The body of a native whose sentience has been vacated by death."

"The worms can repair the damage to dead tissue."

"Essentially bringing the organism back to life."

"Of course, when they come back they're subservient to the worm."

"Right, that's kind of important."

Jakob Kleinemann had been listening to the rapid-fire explanation, mostly confused, mostly wondering where the conversation was heading. Now the fragments suddenly came together with a chilling shock.

"You gave the Nemerteans the bodies of the people killed at Roswell!"

"Well, in so many words..."

"They liked your frontal lobes."

"Roomy living quarters, they said."

"Not much to get in the way."

The faux man looked from Jakob's horror to the anger radiating from Rita.

"They seemed friendly..."

"...and so happy to get out of those pods."

"It seemed like a win-win."

Jakob's voice shook as he summarized the situation.

"So there are, what? Several dozen Nemertean worms now controlling the minds of resurrected human bodies, bodies that look human, indistinguishable in every way..."

The faux man shook his head.

"Not indistinguishable, no."

"You can always crack open the skull..."

"A prize inside every one..."

Jakob concluded his summary with a single question.

"These Nemerteans, can we peacefully co-exist with them?"

"Well, of course..."

"They just need a new home..."

"Their planet was dying..."

"A nice warm frontal lobe..."

"No, probably not."

"They're total control freaks."

Chapter 15 - Counsel & Commiseration

Normally, Captain Edward Ruppelt wasn't the kind of man who indulged in daytime drinking. So sitting on a stool in the bar of the Ambassador Hotel wasn't one of the places he imagined landing when he started his day. He was even feeling a bit pleased with himself. His testimony had gone remarkably well, especially so when compared to how the other witnesses fared.

With it being so early in the afternoon, the population density inside the bar was predictably sparse. If one took a closer look, a practitioner of the budding science of demographics might find the makeup of that population fascinating. Excluding the bartender and the cocktail waitress he was hitting on, the clientele was entirely made up of men who'd testified before HUAC.

After the cloying heat of the city outside, the hotel bar was an oasis of cool. The lights were kept low to preserve this impression, and the dark woods of its paneling and furniture served to further enhance the effect. The only sounds were the steady hum of an air conditioner and the occasional clink of glass. There were seven tables, booths along two of the walls, and a row of a dozen stools along the long slab of mahogany that separated the bartender from his clients.

Ed Ruppelt entered through the open arch and made his way down the line of stools to take the next to last. The broken man on the final stool looked in serious need of some cheering up. He sat with his back bent by the day's labors, his forearms resting on the bar. His head hung forward like a piece of ripe fruit that'd grown too large for the branch that held it.

The broken man cradled a half-filled glass of diluted amber fluid, staring at it like a crystal ball he was having trouble getting a straight answer from.

"I really don't feel like company right now," the broken man said as Ruppelt took his seat. "It's just been a bad day all around."

"You got that right, brother," Ruppelt said, calling the bartender away from his waitress to order a scotch straight up. "Don't feel bad, Allen," he said to the broken man, "I just got chewed out, too."

The broken man was Allen Hynek, of course. Hynek had to blink twice before looking up to find a friendly face. He blinked two more times before he recognized Ruppelt. His reaction time was slow enough to convince Ruppelt that the glass in front of him wasn't his first.

"Ed," Hynek said at last. "What the devil are you doing here?"

Ruppelt looked around the empty bar, holding his reply until the waitress set his drink down and departed.

"Probably the same as you, I imagine. I got called in for a chat with General Vandenberg as soon as I got out of chambers."

Hynek shifted around to face him, relieved to have someone else's misery to consider. "Got a good dressing down, huh?"

Ruppelt took his first sip and let it lie on his tongue.

"First rate," Ruppelt said, "and then some. He kept me at attention the whole damned time. I probably shouldn't call a four-star general a son of a bitch, but he's got me drinking left-handed."

"I tried to slip out," Hynek confided, "but Menzel was waiting."

Ruppelt drew back in mild confusion. "Menzel?"

It took a moment for the relationship to resolve.

"I didn't know you reported to him."

"Him and who knows how many others," Hynek replied, slurring his words.

Ruppelt took a second sip that was less of a shock.

"What'd Menzel want? For what it's worth, I didn't think you did that bad a job up there."

The expression of sympathy went over well.

"He said I shouldn't change my mind."

Ruppelt turned his head to stare at the professor, but Hynek's attention had returned to his glass. "What?"

Hynek nodded again. "He said that once I assigned an explanation for a particular sighting, I wasn't supposed to change my mind. Stay the course, he said, no matter how ridiculous it sounds."

"So if the explanation was Venus, it has to stay Venus?"

"Uh-huh."

Ruppelt took a bigger nip this time.

"So I guess it won't be Venus in the future."

Hynek shook his head almost sadly.

"Nope."

They drank in companionable silence. Ruppelt finished his drink and ordered a second. Hynek seemed content to stare at the one he had.

"How about you?" Hynek finally asked. "What did Vandenberg want?"

Normally, Ruppelt wouldn't have breathed a word of what'd happened with Vandenberg, especially to a man so far outside his chain of command. But the scotch had relaxed him, and besides, they were talking shop.

Ruppelt sighed.

"He chewed me out for doing a good job."

Then it was Hynek's turn to be confused.

"What the hell? Why would he do that?"

"Yeah," the captain said, swirling the glass in his right hand. Feeling had returned to his shoulder. "He said my job wasn't to research the sightings, only to make it look like the Air Force was doing its job."

Hynek sighed. "That's too bad. I had high hopes for Blue Book."

"The way I see it, researching the sightings is the only way I can do a good job. Doesn't make a lick of sense to just pretend. That's what Grudge was doing and look where it got them."

Hynek shook his head in commiseration.

"Menzel says the reporters will just get it wrong, so why worry about the explanation. They're going to write it the way they see it anyway."

Ruppelt, having fallen into his own woes, wasn't listening.

"I don't know why they bother if all they want...I don't even know what they want."

The same was pretty much true for Hynek.

"They only want us to look like we're doing our jobs. At least, we try. I wish I was a reporter. That guy Keyhoe's got it made. Writes whatever the hell he wants and gets paid for it."

The mention of Keyhoe snapped Ruppelt out of his funk.

"Actually, Keyhoe does a pretty good job. I wish to hell I knew where he gets his information...who his sources are. I think he's got the best handle on what's going on of all of us."

Hynek released his glass about half an inch above the bar. The amber fluid splashed up against the side but didn't crest the rim.

"You gotta be kidding."

Feeling that he was venturing into dangerous territory, Ruppelt took another sip, and shook his head.

"I'm not. Look at it this way. Out of all of us, he's the only one who can talk openly about the extraterrestrial hypothesis. Project Sign got shut down because they reached that conclusion. They shut down Grudge because they weren't doing any work at all."

"Blue Book does some good work, but we're handcuffed because the one thing we can't say is that flying saucers might come from another world. Despite what Menzel says, there's a good chance they do."

Hynek shivered at the invocation of Menzel. A tall man passed by the open entrance, briefly halving the light from the lobby.

"That man gives me the-," Hynek admitted, cutting himself off before committing to specifics.

Ruppelt shook his head, swirling his whisky in a clockwise direction.

"Hey, Menzel did a credible job up there. He had me half-believing the saucers were mirages by the time he finished."

Hynek nodded in agreement.

"You're right. It's just a damn shame that he's so very wrong. It's not like him to be so completely off-base..." Hynek trailed off as if he'd just realized what he was saying.

Ed Ruppelt was staring back at him, open-mouthed. His comments, though tinged with excitement, were almost whispered.

"You think he's wrong! You think the saucers are real!"

Hynek blinked back at him, but didn't deny the statement.

"I...have suspicions," he said finally.

Ruppelt put his drink down, surprised by the other man's admission.

"You think maybe Menzel knows more than he's telling?"

Stunned by the heretofore unspoken conclusion, Hynek nodded again, finishing with the words of a solemn bride.

"I do."

Ruppelt pushed his drink away as he rose from his stool.

"I think Vandenberg knows more than he's letting on, too."

Hynek looked up at him. "Where are you going?"

Captain Edward Ruppelt straightened his cap, squaring his shoulders as he did so.

"I'm not entirely sure, but I'm going to see if I can find some answers."

Ruppelt was already through the arch by the time Hynek got off his stool.

"Hey," the astronomer called, "do you mind if I tag along."

***

Captain Ed Ruppelt might not be the most politically astute officer in the US Air Force, but he was right about one thing. Hoyt Vandenberg knew a hell of a lot more than he was letting on. As the meeting was urgent, it was called without notice. As no notice was given, no one was surprised when only four of Majestic's twelve members were able to make it.

As they couldn't hold a meeting in so public a location as the Pentagon, the others accepted Dulles' offer of a conference room in the CIA's headquarters at 2430 E Street NW. They accepted his offer even though it meant that Dulles, whose status was still provisional, would be joining them.

Dulles was waiting when they arrived. To avoid the suspicion his uniform would arouse, General Hoyt Vandenberg stopped by his house to change into civilian clothes. He was encouraged in this bit of deception by Dulles, though one had to call into question the effectiveness of his disguise.

Vandenberg's checkered slacks were so loud that letting them off the golf course they were intended for should be grounds for federal charges. Open to the third button, the beige summer shirt was an odd choice, entirely too casual to be supported by the general's military bearing. While few would recognize him, the ensemble made Vandenberg look like a tourist who couldn't relax, never mind the suspicion created by a golfer showing up at CIA headquarters.

Vandenberg nodded to Dulles as he entered. Dulles had only recently been appointed to the position. In getting the appointment, Dulles had outmaneuvered Walter Bedell Smith who, as director of the CIA, was the more natural replacement. Among the current twelve, Dulles was the only one who hadn't been a founding member.

If Dulles had anything to say about the way Vandenberg was dressed, he diplomatically refrained from saying it. Vandenberg took a seat, waved off the perfunctory offer of coffee and leaned so far back in his chair that the front legs left the floor. He saved himself from toppling over by catching his knees under the lip of the table. Dulles thought it was ridiculous behavior for a man in the general's position, but wasn't prepared to face his wrath by saying so.

Next to arrive was Detlev Bronk. Bronk was a refined, white-haired man in a Brooks Brothers suit. Once seated at the table, he gave the impression of a kindly humanities professor. Bronk looked around the nearly empty room, a bit discomfited by his status as the only true civilian.

"Oh dear," he said, adjusting his tie. "Where's Donald? Is this all we have?"

Dulles scowled, "We don't have the time. Besides, it'd just spoil their summer vacations. In any case, I believe there are enough of us here to deal with the situation at hand, at least there will be once Doctor Menzel arrives. I propose that we see what we can accomplish before alerting the others."

"I quite agree, Director," Donald Menzel said, entering the room and closing the door behind him. Nodding to Dulles, he added, "I shall trust your judgment as to the security of this room."

"You're in CIA headquarters, gentlemen," Dulles said, a trifle unctuously. "I can't imagine a more secure place in the free world."

"Then, let's get started," Vandenberg growled. "We're waiting valuable time."

"Just so," Bronk said. "Why don't you brief us, Donald, since you were the one who alerted us to the problem?"

Menzel took the seat opposite Dulles.

"I trust that everyone is familiar with HUAC's abrupt change of direction. I'm at a loss as to how Senator McAfee's UFO hearing managed to slip through the cracks. The first I heard about it was this morning and even then it was only because a former student of mine is interning as a Senate page. I believe this falls under your purview, Allen. Why weren't we notified?"

There was no smile on Dulles's face now.

"I'm sorry to have to contest that assertion. I thought everyone was aware that the CIA has no jurisdiction within the territorial boundaries of the United States. The last I checked, the District of Columbia fell within that realm."

"So, what are you saying?" Vandenberg snarled. "Do we need to invite Mr Hoover to join our ranks? He certainly has no problem with sticking his nose into other people's business."

"I strongly object to-" Dulles began.

"Gentlemen, gentlemen," Bronk interrupted. "We're getting quite off topic. We've discovered a gap in our network and we must take steps to correct it. I don't think anyone thought we'd have to-"

"It's that damned McAfee!" Vandenberg stormed.

"Senator McAfee has been quite useful up until now," Menzel reminded them. "He's drawn a great deal of attention to our friends in State. I understand that many have even seen the error of their ways."

"Error, schmerror," Vandenberg continued. "What the hell gave him the right to look into UFOs? And how did we get so blind-sided by all this? It must have taken time to set this up, call in witnesses and such. Hell, if Don hadn't sniffed this out, some of our own people might be up there testifying! Fortunately, I think our boys would be able to stand up to the test."

"One of our boys did testify," Menzel said quietly, "that is, one of mine did. And he did not do well at all."

"You're referring to Professor Hynek, of course" Bronk said. "Yes, that was unfortunate, but thankfully he doesn't know enough to give anything away."

"I think you're underestimating the damage." Menzel came forward to lean his elbows on the table, steepling his fingers in open-palmed prayer.

"By displaying his uncertainty regarding the explanations that he provided, he undermines our public assertion that UFOs are a lot of nonsense. He makes it appear that the government itself is unsure about their existence, their intent, and our ability to combat them. If his testimony gets into tomorrow's papers, which I have no doubt it will given the slow news cycle, it could bring all of our work crashing down on our heads. It might even expose the existence of our allies. Clearly, we cannot allow that."

"And just as clearly, I believe we will have to do something about it."

Vandenberg came forward, bring the chair back to earth.

"The question is what are we going to do. I've already chewed out Ruppelt and I've ordered him to get in touch with me before making any other stupid decisions. There's a problem though. Because he doesn't report to me, we'll have to circumvent the normal chain of command-"

"Isn't that taking an enormous chance, general?" Dulles hissed. "If he's caught-"

Vandenberg snorted. "You're goddamned right I'm taking a chance! But what choice do we have? Ruppelt is doing what he considers a good job, which means doing real investigative work. If he gets lucky, and our friends get careless, we've got real trouble. I can't fire him because he doesn't report to me and his direct superior is sharp enough to smell a rat if I try. The only thing I can do is insist that he contact me first, then figure out a way to defuse the situation."

Dulles subsided moodily. "I see your point, general, even if I don't like it."

"What about Dr Hynek?" Detlev Bronk asked, interrupting the silence that followed. "What shall we do about him?"

"Academics are a bit easier to deal with," Menzel mused. "I just reminded him that he works for the government now and that the government has certain expectations. If he veers off course again, I can threaten his tenure. That usually brings them back in line."

Dulles rested an elbow on the arm of his chair, his eyes growing dreamy.

"What about these other men who testified, La Paz and Keyhoe?"

Detlev Bronk roused himself to answer.

"I don't think we need to worry about La Paz. From the reports I've had, I don't think he's given much thought to flying saucers. I haven't spoken to the man personally, but I'm told he's having dinner with friends tonight, then flying back to New Mexico in the morning. He hasn't displayed the slightest curiosity, so my recommendation is that we simply leave him alone."

"And what about Keyhoe?" Dulles purred.

"Him, we bring in for a chat." Vandenberg growled. "That man is a bulldog."

"Keyhoe won't let go unless we give him a damned good reason," Menzel pointed out.

Dulles nodded, his gaze focused on some distant ideal.

"Then maybe that's what we need to do."

Menzel looked over at the director, now curious.

"What are you suggesting?"

Dulles came out of his reverie.

"We've seen that Mr Keyhoe has quite a nose for ferreting out information. I suppose we could kill him, but that might draw unwanted attention and I don't believe we can afford that option, at least not at this juncture."

"That's quite generous of you, Allen," Bronk commented, his sarcasm going right over Dulles' head. "What do you propose then?"

Allen Dulles prodded the ash in his pipe with a probing finger.

"I propose that we ask Mr Keyhoe to join Majestic."

Vandenberg was only the first to break the silence. His chair slid back as his feet came back to earth. "Have you lost your mind?"

Dulles shook his head.

"Not at all, general, I've simply discovered over the course of my years in espionage that certain men bridle at not being in on the secret. It doesn't matter what that secret is, they simply despise the feeling of being excluded. I believe that Major Keyhoe may be one of those men and I've found that the best way to enlist their cooperation is to let them in on the secret, albeit with the caveat that they will not be able to share what they've learned. A great majority will fall right in line once you let them attend the party. It's a simple matter of character, and satisfying their needs."

Vandenberg chewed his lower lip, then shook his head.

"Well, Allen, I don't know if Keyhoe is one of those men you're talking about, but I guess it's worth a shot."

Dulles nodded smugly.

"I should also make it clear that we won't be telling him everything, just enough to ensure his cooperation."

"Then it's decided?" Bronk intervened, looking from one man to the other. "We'll invite Donald Keyhoe to join us? Personally, I should be more comfortable if we cleared this with the others."

"I don't think we have time," Menzel pointed out. "Is it agreed then?"

The others nodded their agreement.

"And," Bronk continued, "we'll leave it to Allen to make the approach?"

"Actually, Doctor," Allen Dulles objected, "I've found that I enjoy a rather poor reputation with certain members of the press. I think we might have more success if you or General Vandenberg did it."

"I've already got Captain Ruppelt to deal with," Vandenberg pointed out. "Besides, Keyhoe knows me by sight. We might be able to be more discreet if Dr Bronk handles it. Keyhoe would have more difficulty locating him if this doesn't pan out."

"Very well," sighed Detlev Bronk, "I will try to catch up with him."

"All the witnesses were booked into the Ambassador," said Allen Dulles in an effort to be helpful.

"Then I'll find him there," said Bronk, "since it's where I'm staying as well."

"Which brings us to our last loose end," said Donald Menzel.

Dulles's eyes narrowed. "What else is there? Five men testified, one of those was you and we've established dispositions for the other four."

"Someone else talked to McAfee after I left," Menzel informed him, "and whoever it was, he got McAfee to clear the room. They kicked out the reporters and the observers. Even the rest of the committee was dismissed. This person spoke only to McAfee."

Dulles laid his palm on the table the way another man might pound a fist.

"Well, who was this person? What did he say?"

"The answer to both questions is the same. I don't know," Menzel said.

"That's what we have to find out."

Chapter 16 - Chilidogs and a Clown Car

It was almost three o'clock when John Haste left the Library of Congress, and having skipped lunch to do his research on Lars Ångström, he was ravenously hungry. One problem with the area around the Capitol was its distinct lack of eateries. This was true in the best of times, but with Congress on break, most of the lunch counters closed early, leaving few alternatives.

As it was still hours too early for dinner, the easiest solution to his problem lay just across the street. Haste's forehead was swimming in sweat by the time he crossed the teardrop lawn separating the Library from the Capitol. With his back to the street, he failed to notice the creamsicle Metropolitan speeding through the intersection. Haste paused there to buy three chilidogs and a Pepsi Cola from a street vendor.

Recrossing the lawn, Haste took his purchases to a seat against the trunk of a shady elm. He set his back to the tree, and with the Pepsi by his hip, balanced the chilidogs on his thighs to keep the ants away. The afternoon was ridiculously hot and humid, the kind of day that made a man wonder why Joe McAfee hadn't simply waited until fall to hold his UFO hearing. Brushing away the leaves and twigs that had accumulated under the tree, Haste removed his jacket, loosened his tie, and opened the top three buttons on his shirt before starting on the dogs.

With the exception of one hardy tourist who soon high-tailed it back inside, the teardrop lawn was empty. Haste heard the traffic going by on Independence Avenue, but it was no more than a murmur from where he sat. Washington natives generally used the summer recess to beat the heat by getting the hell out of town, flocking to their summer houses in droves. Haste was halfway through the second chilidog when he saw a man in a tan suit step out of the trees on the far side of the lawn.

At first, it seemed like the man was coming straight toward him, but a few steps removed from the shade, his gait turned crablike, listing to the right like a cat chasing its tail. He paused to look behind him as if someone had called his name. Haste imagined he heard something, but he was too far away to be sure. When the man turned toward him again, he increased both the length of his stride and his pace, his arms swinging in a pumping rhythm that seemed designed to get the maximum amount of speed out of his legs without breaking into a run.

But even with this effort, it took the better part of two minutes for the man to cross the wide lawn. With little else to draw his attention, this gave John Haste plenty of time to observe the stranger. From his spot under the elm, Haste was hidden by a low sweep of branches that forced him to duck down if he wanted to see beyond the canopy.

When the man stopped at the very center of the lawn, Haste started to take real notice. The man was almost as tall as he was, with sandy brown hair and something that discolored his skin in a stripe that ran from one cheekbone to the other.

Upon stopping, the man brought his legs together and his arms to his sides with his palms resting on his thighs. He turned his face up toward the sky, letting the afternoon sun shine bright on his features. Haste saw that he had the plain freckled countenance of Midwestern Boy Scout grown to adulthood. He stood this way for a time, in devotional silence.

Haste had a fleeting thought that he looked like a daisy opening its petals to the sun. He'd just started to lose interest when the man's arms came up over his head, both hands pointing into the sky, like Superman preparing for takeoff. Haste was somewhat disappointed when he didn't leap into the air and fly away, but what did happen was far more interesting.

While Haste watched, those fingers began to curl and darken, turning into something that resembled the lichen-dappled twigs at the end of an oak branch. Something changed in the light around him, a shadow that made him appear darker than the rest of the lawn. Haste leaned forward in his curiosity, the third dog rolling off his thigh, leaving a trail of beans and chili running down his leg. Fixated on finding the object throwing the shadow, Haste didn't notice the mishap until well after the damage was done.

Haste rolled over onto hands and knees. The shadow fell in a column just wide enough to envelope the man. Now low enough to see under the branches, Haste looked up to find that a circular door had opened in the sky above the man. The door wasn't attached to anything, it was just a black spot in the sky that hovered a dozen feet over the man's head. The shadow came from the door and light seemed to bend around it. It reminded Haste of waves of heat rising off the desert floor in his native Texas.

With his eyes still in the sky, Haste missed part of the transformation, the process by which the man became something utterly unrecognizable. From Haste's vantage, he looked like the twisted branch of an impossible tree. Haste saw that branch clearly for only an instant. Then, in little more than the blink of an eye, it rose under its own power to disappear inside the door in the air. Its object achieved, the door closed and vanished.

John Haste dropped onto his belly, peering out from under his canopy. He felt the squish of the final chilidog under his knee, but he couldn't find any sign of the strange door, or the odd insect-like thing that passed through it.

***

Janie Gently had the distinction of being the first Gently to ever own a car. Growing up in New York City, where the nearest subway station was never more than a few blocks away, cars were luxuries at best and parking liabilities at worst. Using the subway, everything one needed could be found within a few stops, and if not, she could always take a cab.

But when *Woman's Week Daily* assigned her to the Washington beat, Janie knew she was going to need a car, and that need had prompted her purchase of a brand new orange and white Nash Metropolitan.

The Metro was in its first model year and it was the sweetest thing Janie had ever seen. It was barely half the size of the great steel juggernauts clogging the interstates. She saw her first Metro through a window on the train ride down from New York. The driver was a young woman, no older than she was, and there was something, in her joyous expression, in the way her hands were set at ten and two o'clock, that made Janie want to be that woman.

The perfection of the car was in its size which was too small to comfortably allow a man inside. It was a car designed for a new breed of woman, a woman who would drive herself wherever she wanted to go, without any help from men.

Her first task upon reaching Washington was locating an apartment, but her second involved a visit to the Nash dealer where the salesman told her they could get other color combinations if she didn't mind waiting a few months.

But the creamsicle Metro was too perfect to resist. Janie emptied her savings, and signed loan papers for the balance. After a fifteen-minute driving lesson from the salesman, she lurched out into the Beltway gridlock to find her way back to her new apartment.

***

As another native New Yorker, Bertie Stein didn't like cars in general. But if he had to ride in one, he preferred something that didn't remind him of a clown car from a traveling circus.

Like Janie, he'd grown up with cabs, subways, and buses, all vehicles where someone else was responsible for his safety. Bertie preferred to keep his mind focused on bigger things, disconnected from the mundane process of going from one place to the next. He also preferred riding in vehicles that afforded more protection in the event of an accident. He knew on first sight that he wanted no part of the creamsicle tinker toy Janie Gently had slipped inside while he was trying to figure out which Ford, Chevy, or Buick belonged to her.

"You gotta be fucking kidding me."

"Language, Bertie. You don't want you should hurt Camille's feelings."

Janie hadn't had many men inside her car, but the few who'd taken the plunge had reacted just like Bertie. Bertie's hand slid into the pocket that held his stogie, pinching the end of the disgusting thing like a used tampon.

"Camille? Who the hell is Camille?"

105

Janie gave Camille's dashboard a loving stroke and reached over to pop the lock on the passenger side. Bertie stepped away as if she'd offered him pork on Passover.

"Who the hell names their car?"

"Get in, Bertie."

"I ain't riding in that thing!"

"Get in, we ain't got all day. You want Fast Johnny should scoop you?" Bertie shook his big froggy head. "Not in that."

Janie slipped the key into the ignition. Camille started on the first try.

"Well, that's fine, Bertie. Walk if you want, but I already know more about Ångström than you do and it'll take you ten minutes to find a phone the way you walk."

Janie released the parking brake. She'd already shifted into reverse when Bertie Stein ended his protest to climb into the passenger seat, ducking his head in humiliation as his ample butt spilled off to either side. Janie reversed out of the parking spot and put the transmission into first. The stick on the steering column reminded Bertie of a fat knitting needle.

Then, before he could think of anything else to complain about, Janie pulled out into traffic, accelerating smoothly into the no man's land known as Constitution Avenue. Gunning the engine, she pulled within inches of a new Hudson four times the Metro's size, before darting into the left lane to pass. Bertie's hand went to his heart and stayed, even after she pulled back into the slow lane with the Hudson in her rear view mirror.

The driver of the Hudson was a jowly man who honked and shook his fist, angry at being passed by such an insignificant vehicle, but likely more peeved at being outdriven by a girl. Camille had to run a red light to do it, but she finally shook the Hudson two blocks later. As Constitution turned into Maryland, Bertie started to relax. When they passed Stanton Park, Camille took C Street before bearing right on Massachusetts.

Bertie let go of his heart long enough to ask the question he should've asked before getting in. "Say, where the hell are we going, anyway?"

Janie, though a relatively new driver, had already found she did her best thinking behind Camille's steering wheel. It was as if the little car had a mind of its own, and that mind was able to add its own intelligence to Janie's ample stock. Janie started her thinking process the moment she got behind the wheel and it didn't take long to figure out that Bertie was still holding something back.

First of all, he may have known who Lars Ångström was, but he clearly didn't know a thing about him. Second, he wasn't at all reluctant to give Janie that information. The Bertie she knew wouldn't give away the '0' it took to call the operator on a pay phone. There had to be something else, another card hidden up another sleeve. As she merged back onto Constitution, most of what Janie discussed with Camille involved getting Bertie to play that card.

106

"I don't know, Bertie. How about **you** tell **me** where we're going?"

Bertie leaned sulkily against the passenger door, discomfort growing in both mind and bowel. "Why ask me? You're the driver."

Janie shifted up a gear, sending the speedometer up to forty miles per hour.

"Let me put it to you this way, Bertie. Where would you be going if I wasn't giving you a ride?"

A flatbed truck, stacked to the rails with the bedroom furniture of a first term congressman who'd just lost a recall election, pulled out in front of them. Janie downshifted and passed with the insouciant ease of a reckless driver. The congressman, who'd been found guilty of taking bribes, shook an angry fist at her from the truck's passenger seat.

Bertie regarded the girl reporter in disbelief.

"I got no idea what you're talking about."

Janie briefly shifted back into third, then dropped to second as she took a right at the next corner.

"Oh, ya don't? Well, let me spell it out for you. I may be new to this beat, but I've been around the block enough to know you got another card up your sleeve. Fast Johnny thought he knew what you knew, so he couldn't wait to get away. But you let him go without a fight, and the only way I see you doing that is if you still have something he hasn't figured out."

"And then I come along and even though I'm nice enough to give you all the background you could want on that sex doctor, for some reason you're still holding out on me. So, I'll ask one more time, Bertie, and then I'm going to drive you to someplace way the hell outta town and dump you by the Potomac. So, what's it gonna be? Where are we going?"

Bertie Stein looked over at the girl behind the wheel, noting the joy that seemed to radiate out of her every time the little car whipped around a corner or overtook one of the great steel monsters from Detroit. He considered his remaining store of knowledge and decided it wasn't so much.

Bertie took the rancid cigar out of his pocket and jammed it between his molars, sucking a trickle of the awful juice onto his tongue.

"Fine," he growled, "Turn around and head for the Library of Congress. We need a copy of *Schrödinger's Catastrophe* and a pay phone."

Chapter 17 - The Way Out

Lars Ångström didn't realize he'd become separated from the others until well after it was too late to do anything about it. Like everyone else, he wandered around for a while, lost in the dark. But unlike his friends, Lars possessed a reservoir of good luck he'd barely begun to tap into. It was this luck that led him through the void of the lower levels back into a lighted tunnel.

His finding this tunnel was due to the most fortuitous of circumstances. At some point, he turned the wrong way, or rather the right way, considering what happened to the others. Following this false path, he wandered into an area of tiled flooring that soon gave way to the tunnel in question.

Like the tunnel they'd come through, this new corridor was little more than a yard wide. The walls were of the same cinderblock construction and coated with the same industrial beige paint. In the bare bulb light of the overheads, the tiles proved to be the same black and white checkerboard pattern he'd left so long ago. The only difference he could see was the ceiling being lower.

Also like that prior corridor, this one was filthy with the same combination of dust, hair, and detritus. Unlike it, this one was well lit, and as he proceeded along this path, he passed several junctions that, given the law of averages, had to lead somewhere. Even so, he wasn't tempted to try these alternatives, as the one thing they lacked was any kind of lighting. Every alternate path was as black as the gloomy cavern he'd left behind.

After a time, he came to a flight of stairs and, buoyed by his luck, he flew up the steps two at a time. The lights resumed at the top, but only in one direction, essentially making his decision for him. He'd ascended two more flights and walked down another corridor when he started to hear voices.

Someone laughed, and it wasn't a normal laugh. There was neither humor in it nor joy. It wasn't the kind of laugh that invited approach, but it sounded human, and after so long in the dark, that was enough. Lars sighed with relief as he hurried toward it.

It took longer to reach the voices than he expected, but he finally found an open doorway with a brilliant throbbing light spilling out into the hall. Again, he hurried forward, then stopped when one voice said, "Hey, you hear that?"

At that, Lars threw caution to the wind. There was no point in disguising his presence. He needed help and this dungeon room with its many voices was the only source of that commodity available.

"Excuse me," he called out. "I seem to be lost. Is there anyone in there who might show me the way out?"

The silhouette of a short bald man appeared in the doorway.

"Well, well, well," said Wally Sands. "Look what the cat drug in."

***

In addition to Sands, there were three more men inside the room. At one end of the room, was a laboratory worthy of a mid-grade mad scientist, where three large tables were littered with various examples of arcane technologies. A pulsing generator, that was clearly no product of human invention, dominated one wall, venting the light he'd seen from the corridor.

Lars followed Wally Sands inside, though he was a trifle nonplussed when Sands declined his offer to shake hands. Nonetheless, his smile remained affable and, as he was the beggar here, he was prepared to accept whatever conditions these men required in order to enlist their help.

He looked the men over, searching for the friendliest face. The youngest man was obsessively bent over some device he was working on. He displayed no curiosity about Lars whatsoever. He was so focused on what he was doing that Lars assumed he must be up against a deadline.

The second man was almost as tall as Lars, though of a less powerful build. He was balding but not bald, with sharp features and eyes that glinted with an animal cruelty. Lars took him for the leader, an impression that would prove correct. Abel Corbett also declined his offer to shake hands.

The third man was the short mean one, and the atmosphere in the room grew ominous when Wally Sands closed the door.

The fourth man was pure trouble.

The second he laid eyes on the big Swede, Perseus Grady's jaw dropped and his eyes got huge. Grady accepted Lars' hand, and continued to hold it long after etiquette would dictate its release.

"Oh my stars!" Perseus Grady exclaimed, "I can't believe my eyes!"

"What is it?" Abel Corbett asked.

"You remember those flight suits? The ones you were so upset about."

"What flight suits?" Corbett growled.

"You remember," said Grady, still pumping Ångström's hand. "The ones I gave away the night we met."

"What about them?" Corbett asked, still without interest.

"Well," Grady said slowly, now teasing Corbett, "this man got yours."

Corbett's attention perked up. Grady let go of Ångström's hand.

"You don't say."

Abel Corbett pushed away from the wall, approaching Ångström with slow menace. He stopped just short of the Swede to extend his hand, now willing to indulge the greeting. As Lars reluctantly gave custody of his palm to Corbett, the man with the worm in his head smiled his movie villain smile.

109

"Please join us, Dr Ångström. You can't imagine how much I've wanted to meet you in person."

Lars was surprised to hear his name spoken before he could introduce himself. Still holding his hand, Corbett retreated, drawing him deeper into the room. Grady and Sands separated to surround him, leaving him at the center of a hostile triangle. An ominous shroud fell over the room, only to be shattered by a cry of triumph.

"I did it!"

Everyone turned at the cry. It had come from the long table by the far wall, where the young technician was celebrating his success. Behind him, a section of the wall lit up, turned black, then settled into a hazy gray. Two figures took shape. Lars had just enough time to identify the figures as Jakob Kleinemann and Rita Mae Marshaux before they vanished.

"I have it now," the young man said, "just need to reconfigure the power supply and button it up."

"It's about time," Corbett snapped at the technician. Turning back to Ångström, he continued in an off hand way, as if the technology that made the wall screen possible was of trivial importance.

"We have so much to discuss, doctor. We've been watching your friends and you won't believe the mischief they've gotten into."

***

Lars Ångström tried to remember what Arthur Ecks had told him about these men. These were only a few of the men who were resurrected after the Roswell debacle. There were supposed to be dozens of others, but no exact count because no one knew how many had died that day.

But these men were known to him because, Major Ecks and Lieutenant Dexter Wye had surprised these same four in a locker room. As both were unarmed, they could only watch when Perseus Grady was shot through the head by the same man Lars had just shaken hands with. Arthur Ecks had described these men in detail.

Their leader was Abel Corbett. Corbett had provided Ångström with his first flight suit, the one that was too tight in the crotch. He remembered Perseus Grady well enough, and he remembered Ecks saying that the short bald man was Wally Sands. That meant the technician must be the one named Russell, that coming from Dex, who'd read it off of Russell's uniform.

Now five years after those events, despite Grady's death by gun shot and the other fatalities from a helicopter crash, all four men appeared to be the picture of good health. As near as Lars could tell, Perseus Grady hadn't aged a day. And Russell, though Lars had never seen him, didn't look old enough to have enlisted more than five years ago.

"My name is Ångström," he said, trying again.

Corbett's reply started with a sneer and ended with a snotty reply.

"We know who you are, Dr Ångström. Your name is of no importance. I would tell you ours, but they would mean nothing to you, and besides, you won't be living long enough to make use of them."

Lars ignored the threat to walk over behind the young man at the tables. The youth didn't look up, as he continued fiddling with the insides of an open metal case. Ångström didn't recognize the tools or the device, but as he watched, a lavender flicker came to life on the wall behind the table. Again, he was looking at Jakob and Rita.

"What's this?" Lars asked, hoping to get the conversation moving in a different direction, one that didn't involve his murder. No one answered because the wall suddenly burst into sharp detail. He was shocked to see a room not unlike the one he now occupied. In that room, he saw Arthur Ecks, bound to a chair. There was another figure he could only see from behind. As a result, Lars didn't recognize the man until he turned around.

Lars Ångström suppressed his gasp with an effort of will.

The man holding Arthur Ecks hostage looked remarkably like Senator Joseph McAfee.

***

By the time Donald Keyhoe opened his eyes, he was no longer in the back seat of the car. At first glance, it was hard to tell exactly where he was. Slow to come out of whatever drug had put him under, he knew only that he was lying in a cramped position on an uneven surface and that it was dark. But once the engine started, he realized he was still in the car, just no longer in the back seat.

The trunk, a deduction he made upon recognizing by touch the slim length of the jack, was spacious enough to hold two, an estimate he was able to confirm when he encountered the rough fabric of a man's sport coat. His head was too foggy to question this discovery, or find significance in it. Only one thing seemed clear, and that was that he'd been drugged with something strong enough to make him forget an undetermined amount of time.

Soon, the car started to move. The first roads, products of Roosevelt's New Deal investment in infrastructure, were relatively smooth. After a time, Keyhoe recovered enough to realize that he, along with whoever the other man was, had been kidnapped. Even if his head was clear, Keyhoe couldn't imagine who might do it or why. He'd clearly been kidnapped, but his hands and feet had been left unbound. That could only mean his kidnappers didn't see any reason to fear him.

He tried to remember how he'd come to be in this fix, and slowly, the events came back. He'd been given a note. Someone had wanted to talk to him. There was a time and place on the note, and in following up on it, he was drugged and taken hostage. Since the engine was off when he woke, he wondered if there was any chance they hadn't left the Ambassador parking lot.

Realizing that it might be valuable to know how far he was being taken, he started counting seconds, assigning five minutes to the time since leaving the hotel. He continued to count, pausing whenever the car stopped, for the next twenty-five minutes. There wasn't any way to know if his measurement was even remotely accurate, but it gave him something to do other than fearing for his life.

Several times, he caught himself nodding off and had to fight to stay awake. The air in the trunk was hot and stuffy, and it made him sleepy. Making matters worse, he could smell the noxious scent of carbon monoxide.

About thirty-three minutes out, the car finally stopped. As the engine died, he wondered why there wasn't any sound to fill the vacuum. He'd expected to hear voices discussing what to do with him. Clearly, they'd reached a destination, which meant there should be further steps to enact. Yet he heard nothing until the doors started opening. He counted doors, and was mildly surprised when the count reached four.

Keyhoe had only seen one man. With the second man driving, that was still only two, which meant they must have picked up two more along the way.

He felt a sudden urge for a cigarette.

He fumbled in his coat, found the pack, then went in search of a lighter.

His lighter.

If he could have kicked himself in the cramped quarters of the trunk, Don Keyhoe would have done so. Here he'd been wasting time counting seconds when he could have fired his lighter up to have a look around. Careful not to burn his fingers, he flicked the lighter and sparked it into life.

He let the flame breathe for a few seconds before letting it die. In that brief interval, he saw enough to get a good idea of what was going on and why he'd been abducted. He wasn't any closer to understanding, but at least he now had something to work with.

The other man in the trunk was Lincoln La Paz.

Chapter 18 - A Benevolent Brand of Torture

Arthur Ecks wasn't sure exactly when he realized he was alone, only that it was well after they'd passed the last of the lights. He heard the steady fall of Ångström's oxfords for a while, but he'd lost touch with Kleinemann and Marshaux long before Ångström's footfalls faded in the distance. Dex, leading the group, was somewhere ahead of Ångström. Musing on how this could have happened, he kicked something solid that skittered away into the dark.

Sound behaved oddly down here. He was deep underground now and still descending. Even after he lost contact with the walls, Ecks could still tell he was in an enclosed space with hard, albeit distant surfaces on all sides. But knowing that, there was surprisingly little echo. The shuffling of his own feet was so faint and muffled that he felt like he was walking on a thick carpet in fuzzy slippers. The only thing that didn't fit was the object he'd kicked. Wondering what it was, he decided to see if he could find it.

Ecks dropped to his hands and knees, immediately discovering something as unexpected as it was unpleasant. It took a moment to realize he'd plunged his hands into a very thick layer of dust. Cursing the filth, he brushed his hands against his trousers, then started toward the kicked object, estimating its trajectory from his present position. It was strange the way it had rattled across the floor, then, before it had time to slow, simply stopped making any sound.

He had only a second to wonder why that might be. In the end, he could only think of one reason. Given time, he might come up with a second, but he wasn't given that luxury. He barely had time to notice the dust shifting under his knees when the floor beneath him gave way. Then he was falling.

After several seconds of freefall, he understood why the kicked object had stopped rolling.

It was a very long way down.

He was still gaining speed when he stopped. His landing was much softer than he had any right to expect. He'd presumed that his landing would be the final act of his life, and that it would involve striking a rock or some other hard object. This would end his life, freeing him to move on to wherever it was that dead men went.

To his eternal consternation, he didn't really land at all.

He didn't strike a rocky outcropping or pancake into a stony floor.

He simply stopped.

As he lay in the dark, catching his breath and trying to process the surprise he felt at being alive, strong hands lifted him up, carried him a short distance, then deposited him in a chair. He tried to struggle, but he was so unaccountably weak that he stopped resisting and let the hands take him.

A light came on over his head, blinding in its intensity after so long in the dark. He felt his arms and legs held immobile as leather straps were tightened, binding him to the chair. He struggled with kittenish impotence, blinking furiously to clear his eyes to get a glimpse of his captors.

He heard movement around him, the sounds of many bodies in a confined space. But when he could see again, only a single man stood before him, his face and most of his body obscured by shadow. Ecks tried to fight his way through the glare, but couldn't see beyond the cone of light over his head.

The conclusion that he'd fallen into a trap was inescapable. He wondered who his captors might be and started listing possibilities, comparing the results to the gray trousers and black shoes of the man before him.

When the face came out of the shadows, it only served to confirm the most obvious of his guesses. It wasn't a surprise to see the smiling face of Joe McAfee.

McAfee's smile faded as he strolled around the back of the chair. Ecks heard a whispered communication, then the sound of a closing door as three sets of feet exited the room. With his subordinates out of the way, McAfee continued his slow perambulation until he was back where he'd started.

"I tried, you know."

He didn't wait for a response.

"I tried, but you stubbornly refused to answer my few simple questions."

He sighed, as if this great shame could easily have been avoided.

"I guess it's all water under the bridge now. Now we're here and now things have to get...," McAfee paused to select the right word and landed on, "...serious."

"Now it looks like we'll have time for our chat after all. So, why don't we start by you telling me a little more about your little club."

Ecks felt his face turn hard.

"You're wasting your breath, Senator. I'll stand by my answers. I won't tell you any more now than I did in chambers."

McAfee leaned into the light, resting his hands on his knees. His smile was the unfriendly one reserved for evasive witnesses.

"Oh, I do hope that's not the case. There's no one to help you down here. You could scream for days. If someone did hear you, it'd be one of my people."

When Ecks still didn't answer, McAfee laid a gentle hand on his shoulder, the act of a trusted friend offering sage counsel.

"If it helps, you have my word that anything you say will stay between us."

McAfee raised his hand, with two fingers extended and the others folded under the thumb. "I won't tell a soul, scout's honor."

Ecks thought about spitting in his face, but decided against the idea.

"That knowledge is on a need to know, Senator, and it's well beyond your security clearance. You won't get another word out of me."

McAfee didn't appear particularly fazed by his refusal.

"It's a small thing, I suppose, but it'll let me know you're willing to cooperate, and I value your cooperation."

"You won't get it," Ecks snarled.

McAfee didn't bother to acknowledge his defiance.

"I'm also very curious about the others on your team, especially the ones who never got a chance to testify. I know who your academics are, of course, it's the other two that have me stumped. It's a shame, the hearing was going so well, but with Menzel showing up to put a patch on Dr Hynek's testimony, then you flat out refusing to talk..."

McAfee sighed and shook his head with feigned sadness.

"That isn't how I imagined the day ending. There's so much left to learn."

Ecks bared his teeth in feral defiance.

"Are you trying to make me feel bad about disappointing you, senator?"

McAfee stopped his pacing to lean back against a high solid table.

"I doubt that you'll disappoint me for long. I don't know if you realize this, but you're quite a catch. Frankly, I was surprised to see you show up. After all, you weren't invited."

It took a moment to process the last sentence. Ecks found he could only repeat it. "I wasn't invited?"

McAfee laughed, and held up his hand.

"Not in the normal sense, no. You see, the witnesses, and here I must exclude Professor Menzel, all received invitations. But the men and the young lady at your table, let's just say your presence was a bit of a surprise."

"I was thinking we might've cast too wide a net until you all chose to sit together. That was revealing because it meant you knew each other. You really had Clarence scrambling for extra chairs, as well as finding out who you are. You're quite the odd bunch."

Ecks shook the only part of his body he could move.

"I knew that damned bailiff was one of yours. I'll grant you it was a nice piece of work though. I didn't question that bit about the president until it was too late. That should've given you away, but I figured it was something Clarence invented to get you off my back."

Ecks started to say more, then stopped. The significance of the lack of invitation nagged at him. He tried to remember back. Surely, there had been a summons. Why would they all show up unless they were summoned?

"I don't get it," he said finally. "Why did we-"

McAfee interrupted his puzzling.

"Your confusion is understandable, but there is an explanation. We've recently acquired some new technology that's made our HUAC work a hell of a lot easier. This UFO thing was a dry run, just to see what we could pull out of the woodwork. I must say, it did not disappoint."

"Technology?" Ecks asked, now thoroughly confused.

"Yes, it's really quite interesting," McAfee confided, leaning closer as if to speak more confidentially.

"All you do is define what you're looking for, activate the transmitter, and poof! Just like that, it summons everyone who meets the criteria within a limited range. That's all there is to it. The people who are summoned come right to you, without any need for subpoenas or investigation."

"So it's what?" Ecks pondered. "Some kind of search engine?"

"I suppose that's as good a description as any," McAfee agreed. "There's a downside to it, of course, because if your specifications are too broad, the results will bury you. Clarence was screening witnesses all week as it was."

Ecks' brow furrowed in thought. "What's the range of this thing?"

"The range?" McAfee shook his head, puzzled momentarily by the question. His confusion cleared an instant later. "Oh, I see what you mean. You're wondering how we were able to get men like Keyhoe and La Paz to appear, when they live so far away."

"That's right," Ecks confirmed.

"Oh, that's simple enough," McAfee replied. "The first four witnesses were window dressing. Their presence was intended to give the hearing a legitimacy it would have otherwise lacked. Major Keyhoe, La Paz, Hynek, and Captain Ruppelt were sent printed invitations. They were summoned through what you would call normal channels. The actual summons was for people who were directly involved in UFO research. I must say, we really hit the jackpot with you."

"Wait," Ecks said, now catching up, "are you saying you just broadcast a request for anyone who knew anything about UFOs to show up and testify?"

"Yup," said the senator, looking extremely pleased with himself.

"Where the hell did you get this...technology from? I've never heard a damn thing about anything like it."

"I believe I'm the one asking the questions," McAfee said, "and I think it's time we get back on track. I was quite surprised to see Drs Ångström and Kleinemann, and I was very disappointed that you didn't let them testify. I'd love to hear what they might tell us about UFOs."

"You could just read their damn books," Ecks growled.

"I have and you should too." McAfee said, "Each is quite interesting in its own way, but neither says a thing about UFOs. Your young people are more of a surprise because their roles are less clear. In due time, I'll be able to track down the identities of the young man and woman, but you didn't give us much time. And speaking of time, we're wasting a lot of it with all this chit chat."

"How about you tell me what I want to know? Tell me about your work."

Ecks tested his restraints and found they were top notch, thick leather bands that barely moved when he challenged them. Steeling his nerves with a bravado that was completely unwarranted given the situation, Ecks snarled.

"You'll have to torture me."

To his everlasting dismay, McAfee lit up at the suggestion.

Ecks realized too late that, at least if he went by appearances, this idea wasn't anything McAfee would have entertained on his own. His delight was unfeigned and genuine. His eyes shining with an almost gleeful brightness, he radiated joy in its purest form.

"Okay!"

***

Joe McAfee withdrew the needle from Arthur Ecks' upper arm, wiping it on a soft cloth before consulting a plain steel wristwatch. He patiently watched the sweep of the second hand as Ecks' eyes rolled up into white marbles. Sixty-three seconds later, Ecks blinked his eyes open, the signal that he was ready for business.

McAfee bit his lip, delighting in the brief frisson of pain it sent into his gums. He considered possibilities, trying to determine the best place to start. The decision made, he found the point where he could make the beam of the overhead lamp flick off of the blade in his hand into the eyes of his subject. When Ecks blinked again, he was ready.

Arthur Ecks watched the blade descend. Despite his earlier intransigence, he now found himself asking if his secrets were really worth all this trouble.

He shuddered at the effect of some new influence flooding his bloodstream. He heard a new voice in his head, a soothing voice that radiated rational thought. For a moment, he felt the way a king must feel when presented with a new advisor, one of a more conciliatory nature than his predecessor. Ecks looked up at the shiny blade and decided he liked this way of thinking.

Finding his voice, Ecks suggested, "Perhaps we could consider some alternatives."

Joe McAfee paused to look at the scalpel, cocking his head this way and that as if giving his suggestion serious consideration. He looked away, subconsciously directing Ecks' gaze toward the tray of exotic instruments, with its thumbscrews and bamboo shoots, its vials of potions and acids. McAfee repeated the gesture, drawing his stare to the wall and its wide selection of blunt cudgels and razor sharp blades.

Displaying an unexpected degree of patience, McAfee set the scalpel back on the tray, giving Ecks a quizzical look that seemed out of place given the situation.

"Are you sure? I mean, I'll admit I'd rather not get into all this. I'm not a bad guy, and I'm not asking hard questions. Truthfully, this seems like a bit like overkill to me. Frankly, you'd be letting me off the hook."

Ecks eyed the discarded scalpel with bald relief.

"You'd never be sure I was telling the truth. Torture's kind of a waste of time."

McAfee rocked his head side to side as if unprepared to admit the truth of Ecks' statement. Coming back to center, he decided to go along with it.

"You're right, of course. It's fun in a way, but if you feel ready to talk, I have no objection. There won't be as much mess to clean up."

McAfee peeled off the rubber glove and set it on the tray.

"Okay, let's start with your name."

Ecks sighed. "My name is Ecks."

McAfee shook his head, and reached for the scalpel.

Arthur Ecks hurried to clarify.

"My name is Arthur Ecks. E-C-K-S."

McAfee's brow furrowed and unfurrowed until the name made sense.

"You sonuvabitch!" He laughed, "You weren't kidding. That's funny because it sounds just like the letter X, though speaking frankly, Mister X sounds like something out of a spy movie. I was going to say I thought you could do better. I really thought you were lying."

McAfee's smile was wide and genuine. Ecks was surprised to find that he rather liked making the man happy.

"Okay, that's a good start. I'm guessing you must be military or ex-military. That's just an impression, mind you, but you do give the impression of being rather obstinate. I hope that doesn't offend you. So tell me, which branch of the service were you in and what was your rank when you left?"

Ecks pondered not answering this, but like his name, it didn't seem like much to give up. "I was Army originally, then went with the Air Force when it broke away. When I left the service, I was a major."

Ecks flinched as McAfee's hand went to his breast pocket, only relaxing when the Senator removed a silver flask. He rested his palm on the screw top while pondering his next question.

"That's interesting, I was a captain when I got out. Heck, I would've had to salute you when we were in uniform. It's funny how things change. Now I'm a senator."

McAfee removed the top and took just enough to wet his lips.

"All right, I've met a few of your ilk before, both when I was in the service and after I got out. I'm guessing that if I have Clarence check into you, he won't find any record of a Major Arthur Ecks. Am I right?"

Ecks didn't feel he needed to do more than nod.

McAfee held out the flask and gave it a little shake.

Ecks shook his head, declining the offer.

"You know," he said, "there's one thing about the military in this country that really impresses me. When they want to keep a secret, they do a pretty good job. Frankly, I don't see how it's possible. You'd have to find and destroy every scrap of correspondence where the man was named. That's quite a job."

Ecks couldn't help but agree.

"I think you already have your answer. The men who work in national security are very good at hiding our tracks when the need arises. For my team, that need is paramount. It's vitally important that we don't report to any organization subject to political influence, just as it's important that our identities be kept anonymous to avoid compromising our actions."

McAfee screwed the top back on the flask and set it down on the tray next to an array of sharpened bamboo shoots in various sizes, but away from the vials to avoid confusion. He nodded, as if appreciating what Ecks had confirmed.

"Yeah, well, I guess I can see that, but, I've run into national security issues before and I've always been able to find something. With you there's simply nothing to find, no file, no birth date or birthplace. It's like you disappeared from your own life. Do you have a wife?"

Ecks shook his head. "No. I never married."

"Any family?"

"All deceased."

"Friends?"

"Not as such."

"Are you a homosexual, Major?"

The question, breaking the rhythm of easy dismissals, caught Ecks by surprise.

"No, of course not."

McAfee let his hesitation pass without comment.

"And are you willing to tell me the name of your project yet? I hope I'm not assuming too much. It does have a name, I trust?"

Ecks hesitated, but couldn't find the will to keep it up.

"We're known as Project Stall. I worked alone for the first seven years."

"And when was this?"

It was hard to believe he could reveal this so easily, but he didn't seem to have any will left. "I started in 1940, everyone else joined in '47."

McAfee nodded. Ecks felt relief when he moved on to other issues.

"Your academics, Ångström and Kleinemann, have been in the news enough that I think it'll be relatively easy to learn more about them, but I'm still curious about your group's other members."

McAfee held up a hand, forestalling any denial.

"No, I know they're your people. As I said, you were all too comfortable with each other to make me believe anything else. Let's start with the blond kid. Who is he and what does he do?"

Ecks hesitated. He'd done everything he could to protect his subordinates. He couldn't give them up now without putting up a fight.

"Is that necessary? They don't know anything close to what I know."

McAfee scratched his chin where he'd missed a spot shaving.

"We can always do it the other way."

Ecks sighed before giving his reply. "His name is Wye."

119

Ecks held up his hand, bent his wrist really, when he saw signs of disbelief on the senator's face. "His name is Dexter Wye. W-Y-E."

McAfee seemed suspicious.

"That is a rather extraordinary coincidence. Ecks and Wye. What does Mr Wye do for you?"

Arthur Ecks thought the question oddly worded, but spoke to what he hoped was the heart of the matter.

"He does whatever is needed whenever it is needed."

"How did he come to be involved with Project Stall?"

"I met Dex when he was a private serving at Roswell Army Air Field. I'll only say that the circumstances were extraordinary and he handled himself very well. I had need of an assistant and he'd already learned too much by helping me. So I requisitioned him for the project. He's performed well, and I've come to rely on both his judgment and his talents."

"You say the circumstances were extraordinary. What were the circumstances?"

Arthur Ecks didn't answer for a long moment.

McAfee reluctantly reached for the scalpel.

"May I remind you that I am a legally elected member of the highest branch of legislative power in this country? I'm having a difficult time understanding your reluctance to speak to me."

"Senator, we don't even tell the president what we do."

McAfee scraped the wide face of the scalpel against his thumb.

"So I guess we've finally reached the real questions. Tell me, Major. What exactly does Project Stall do? You say you're involved in national security, but you have a remarkably small staff for dealing with whatever you deal with. You don't appear to be involved with UFOs, at least not in the way the other witnesses are. You have funding, but I'm pretty sure I won't find it in the defense appropriation."

"We've started hearing about black projects, stuff that's not in the budget, but I suspect I'd find little there either. You have two well-known academics on staff, but I can't see any relationship between their disciplines. You're so secretive that even presidents aren't briefed on your activities. Have I missed anything?"

McAfee paused, giving Ecks the distinct impression that the interrogation was building to its zenith. "So tell me, Major, I'm only going to give you this one last chance before I start slicing, what does Project Stall do?"

Arthur Ecks told the truth.

"Project Stall was created to investigate interactions between American citizens and extraterrestrial entities. We look into UFO sightings, contacts, interactions between aircraft, you name it."

McAfee smiled as if Stall's purpose was something trivial.

"Like Project Blue Book? We've known about Blue Book since it started."

"We're not like Blue Book. We're different."

McAfee pursed his lips before tucking the lower one between his teeth.

"Really?" He said dubiously. "Exactly how are you different?"

Ecks fixed McAfee with a cold-eyed stare. The stare was to make sure there weren't any misunderstandings.

"Blue Book is in place so the Air Force can claim they're looking into the UFO problem. They aren't given much in the way of resources and, in truth, they don't do much actual work. The men above Blue Book know enough not to take their reports seriously."

Ecks paused for a breath, wishing he could have a sip of water.

"The stuff we get is real. We make actual contact with extraterrestrials and we negotiate any issues we encounter."

Ecks had expected any number of ways McAfee might react to this revelation, but the senator still managed to surprise him.

McAfee turned slightly as he scraped the scalpel's blade across an unshaven patch on his chin. He winced as the blade took a shallow divot out of his flesh, then covered the cut with two fingers as he showed the blade to Ecks.

"Well, that wasn't so hard after all. I thank you for your honesty, major, though I have to say this would've been so much easier if you'd simply answered my questions in chambers like everyone else."

"Now that we have that out of the way, perhaps this will help you understand my interest."

Suddenly, Ecks did understand.

Along the scalpel's edge, Ecks could see a thin trace of green that was already pooling toward the blade's lowest point. When enough had accumulated, the little drop plopped to the floor, sending up a spray of dust.

Ecks flinched, his lip curling into an involuntary sneer.

Suddenly, it all made sense.

"You're a bug."

Chapter 19 - Things That Go Bump

Dex landed like a spooked cat, whirling about as he scanned the platform for signs of the person or thing that Lars Ångström had described as standing right behind him. When he found nothing, he continued to turn until arriving back where he started. The Swede, with his glowing golden eyes, stared back, entirely unaffected by his reaction.

Dex felt a mild surge of anger at being made the butt of a joke when the situation seemed so serious.

"What's the big idea? There ain't nothing there."

"Oh, but I assure you there is."

Dex looked around again, arriving at the same result.

"Then how come I don't see him?"

"I'm not entirely sure it's a him."

This comment didn't help much.

"Are you saying it's a woman?"

"I'm saying I'm not sure it has a gender."

"Then what the hell is it?"

Ångström pursed his perfect lips, mildly puzzled by the mystery before him.

"I haven't the foggiest idea."

Dex fought back another surge of anger.

"Why can't I see it? And while we're at it, can you stop doing that thing with your eyes? It's really creepy."

Ångström made the glow diminish, though it didn't entirely go away.

"You can't see the apparition because you've never learned how to use your extra senses. The only reason I can is because the Ffaeyn showed us."

Dex's vocabulary had expanded during the years he'd spent with men like Lars Ångström and Jakob Kleinemann. In spite of his growth, there were still times when words, or the way they were used, eluded him.

"Do you think you could give that to me in plain English?"

Ångström considered the matter, "All right, do you remember earlier when you compared my abilities to superpowers?"

Dex nodded, "Right, like in the comic books."

Ångström nodded once. "Yes, well the reason I can see these things is that I've had a part of my brain turned on. You have it, too, but you've never been shown how to find it or use it."

Dex frowned, still not sure that he was getting it.

"Like some kind of switch."

To his relief, Ångström nodded again. "Exactly, and once this switch is turned on, once I see where it is, I can turn it on or off whenever I need it."

"Why don't you just leave it on all the time?"

There was a hint of embarrassment in the way Ångström looked away.

"Because if I do, it gives me a splitting headache."

Dex pondered this, then decided that being able to see things no one else could see was just one more thing that made Lars Ångström different from anyone else he knew.

"So," he said finally, "this thing you see. What does it look like?"

Lars turned up the glow again as he surveyed the platform.

"Sorry, it moved while we were talking. As to what it looks like, it's roughly human-shaped, though its arms and legs are much longer. It is rather gray to look at, but it has a head, a body, and limbs, much like our own, though of different proportions. Its face is hard to make out. It shifts constantly from one set of features to another. It's like seeing a series of faces rather than just one. Also, it has wings coming out of its back."

"Like an angel?"

"More like a bat."

Dex stared up at the Swede. "That sounds scary as hell."

Ångström shook his head.

"It isn't half as scary as some of the things I've seen."

"Does it look like it wants anything?"

"Not particularly...oh, now it's doing something, pointing to the edge."

"The edge? The edge of what?"

Angstrom looked down at the flat expanse of polished stone they were standing on, searching for the right word to describe it.

"This lip, this ledge..., what would you call it?"

Dex looked back at the arch they'd arrived through, then down the long expanse in both directions.

"Well, if I had to put a name on it, I'd say it reminds me of a railway platform. You know, where you go to wait for a train."

Angstrom blinked, "A railway platform...yes, that could work."

Dex walked over to the edge of the platform, peering over the edge into the inky black depths below.

"That's weird," he said, mostly to himself.

"What's that?" Ångström came over to join him.

"Well," Dex said, picking through his thoughts, "if I look down there," he pointed into the blackness below them, "I can't see any sign of light at all. But up here, on this ledge, we can actually see pretty well."

"What are you getting at?" Ångström asked.

Dex looked around at the dimly lit platform, up into the black heights, and back into the Stygian depth of the pit.

"If you look up or down, there's nothing to see but black. It's like that passage we came through. But this platform is another matter. There's light here and I'll be damned if I can see where it's coming from."

Dex turned away from the edge to walk back to the sheer wall that rose up into the heights. He laid his palm to it, feeling a warmth to it that didn't seem possible so far underground. In addition to being warm, the wall was flat and smooth, just like the platform.

"Doc," he said without turning back to Ångström, "how is it possible for naked rock to be this smooth? Doesn't it feel like somebody built this?"

Ångström came over to join him. "Now that you mention it."

"And the light down here, it seems like its just here."

"Yes," Ångström agreed, "it does seem odd."

"It doesn't seem like it's coming from anywhere in particular," Dex went on, no longer caring whether Ångström was listening or not.

"There's no source for it, like a lamp, or the sun..." He paused then, newly aware of something really odd. "And it doesn't make any shadows. Neither of us have shadows. How is that possible?"

Ångström followed Dex's gaze as it moved from place to place.

"I can't argue with anything you're saying..." Ångström trailed off, then looked around again for the invisible thing with the wings, his eyes glowing golden in the dim light. "I wonder..."

"What?"

"Nothing, probably, I was wondering if our invisible winged companion might have something to do with you being able to see down here."

Dex peered at him curiously.

"You think that's possible?"

Ångström shrugged.

"Well, something odd is happening, and..."

Ångström never finished his thought. Without any warning, his physical form dissolved in a spray of phosphorescent green light.

Dex gasped, then gaped at the place his friend had stood only a moment before. In Ångström's place, a strange grayness began to take shape, slowly forming out of the ether.

He was reminded of a swarm of gnats massing over a sluggish pond, except that these gnats had chosen to remain connected by some force at its core. It took time before the shape was recognizable, but as the thing knit itself together, Dex recognized it as the satanic nightmare Ångström had described.

Suddenly, it was real, the leathern wings, the long distorted limbs, the restless features that refused to resolve. When it reached an acceptable solidity, it spread its wings as its mouth yawned open to spew a spray of gnat-like specs.

Dex's body shrilled with terror. He retreated until he brushed up against the wall that marked the inner edge of the platform.

"*I am Legion,*" the demon said in a voice like the roar of hornets.

* * *

The demon's leathery wings fluttered to life, yawning wide as they bloomed over its body. Dex was struck by the same sensation a mouse must feel in that last moment before being taken by the hawk. The demon was enormous, over eight feet tall with a wingspan exceeding its height by a factor of two.

"*I am Legion,*" the demon said again. "*This place is forbidden to you, just as it is forbidden to those who came with you.*"

Dex shrank from the demon, and with his back flush with the wall, he froze, too terrified to run. His heart pounded with the need to get away, and his head was on fire with it, but his body refused to move. He tried to raise a hand, to block out the shifting face of the demon, but even this meager action was more than he could manage.

Legion raised one great hand, and Dex saw long pointed claws where the nails should be. Just as it seemed poised to strike, the demon turned the hand to show its palm.

"*Speak,*" commanded Legion in its hornet voice. "*Why have you entered the world of the Acari? I give you leave to speak.*"

And just like that, Dex found his voice.

"I'm lost," he said before his voice gave out.

"*That much I guessed,*" the demon said, taking a step closer. "*Only fools and the damned come here.*" The demon paused a beat before adding, "*And seekers after the truth, though frankly, we haven't had any of those lately.*"

"You killed my friend," Dex said accusingly.

"*He wasn't our friend,*" Legion said. "*and he wasn't yours either. The thing that accompanied you was a fraud, designed to deceive you*"

"You killed him!" Dex shouted again. "You killed Doctor Ångström!"

"*We did not,*" said Legion, "*we don't have the power to destroy. We may befuddle, we may deceive, and we have the power to banish our tormentors, but we cannot end a life. The thing that came with you was a fraud. We have only sent the ones who made it back to where they come from.*"

It took time for the meaning to sink in, but when Dex parsed the words, he found something he hadn't expected. "That wasn't Doctor Ångström?"

"*No,*" said Legion. "*The one who came with you was a snare created by the ancient enemies of the Acari, the accursed Ffaeyn. The Ffaeyn deceived you into believing that this animated shell was your friend.*"

"But why?" Dex asked, feeling like a child after its first encounter with a schoolyard bully. He wanted to ask why beings as powerful as the Ffaeyn would go to the trouble of tricking him, but the question died unborn.

It didn't matter. The demon seemed to hear his thoughts.

"The ways of the Ffaeyn are a mystery, even to the Acari. Though we were once as they are, they are strange and devious, and we no longer know their hearts. Long ago, they made this underworld our prison. We may not leave, but by the same token, they cannot come here."

The demon was fearsome in its visage. Its shifting features altered before Dex's eyes, morphing from one tormented face to another never allowing any to achieve stability. He saw both men's and women's faces, as well as others that weren't remotely human. They were all different, all separate, all unique, save in their expression of pain. The faces were difficult to watch, but something about them made it impossible to look away.

The demon went silent after answering his question, retracting its wings and settling onto its knees. Its head was bowed in thought. Though it was terrifying to look at, it no longer seemed hostile, only sad.

"Please, Mr Legion-" Dex began.

"There's no mister, it's just Legion," the demon corrected.

"Then please, Legion, who are you? Who are the Acari?"

The great shifting head remained bowed in thought, but the hornet buzz left its voice, leaving the rumble of a *basso profundo* in its place.

"Once we were as they are. But we rebelled against the Ffaeyn and we lost. Now we are fallen, and in our fall, we are confined to the interior of this world. Once we traversed the universes, we were all places at once, but now we are only here. It has been so for a thousand times longer than the age of Man. That is the Acari, of which I am but many. Does that answer your question, mortal?"

"And you live down here?"

"It is our home as well as our prison."

Dex slid down the wall to take a seat.

"Why can't you leave?"

"Once we possessed the power to resist the destructive nature of the sun's radiation, but it was taken from us when we were defeated. Without that protection, we are trapped. On nights of the new moon, we can leave our underground world, but only for a few short hours before we must return. No longer can we glide along the currents of space. Now we must stay here, below the surface of this world, or perish. For us, there is no other choice. The same is true for you."

The demon fell silent, but after a long pause, it lifted its shifting face again.

"I may not leave, but you may not stay. There are other things down here that are not Acari, and many would harm you. You must return to the surface at once."

"But I can't," Dex complained. "It's like I told you. I'm lost and I can't find my friends and I can't find the way out."

"I cannot help you with your friends except to say that none of them have wandered into the lands of the Acari. But if you do not know the way back, then I must take you."

"But how?" Dex asked. "We must be a mile underground."

"I shall bear you up. The bones of the Earth are no barrier to the Acari."

With that, the demon unfurled its wings, enveloping Dex in its cold grasp. Legion's touch was unlike the touch of the living, it was a sensation felt but not felt. Dex shivered at the lifeless chill, but only for a moment. Without notice or warning, they were off, rising into the black heights above them, bringing the light of the platform with them. Dex looked up, shocked to see the shadows retreat, but more alarmed by the approaching roof of the cavern.

"Hey-" Dex cried out. He'd meant to point out that he couldn't move through solid rock, that moving at the speed with which they were approaching the ceiling, he would be flattened like a beer can under a bus tire.

But in the demon's arms, he no longer seemed to have a body. When they struck the ceiling, they passed right through the barrier. That revelation made him think that maybe he'd left his body behind on the platform, that he no longer had a physical form to destroy, that he was now a ghost being sent back to haunt the surface world.

Through earth, water, and stone, the demon bore him up. He passed through layer upon layer of rock, traversing strata that had taken untold millennia to form. They passed through an underground lake, surprising the blind sleepy fish that constituted its corporeal life, then finally the moist damp earth that separated him from the surface.

Legion left him at the entrance to a cave, departing without instruction or farewell. For a span of minutes, Dex stood there shaking, unable to comprehend what had happened. It was longer still before he could make his body move under its own power.

Dex exited the cave, emerging into the twilight of early evening. Before and below him lay low hills, and beyond, a country lane that led to a larger road. He saw the headlamps of a car out on the main road, and beyond that, the lights of a city.

Dex started down the slope, hoping to hell that city was Washington DC.

Chapter 20 - Desiree Blythe

John Haste staggered out from his shelter under the elms, making his way over to the public drinking fountain. His body felt odd and unfamiliar, as if he'd forgotten how to use it. His legs still quivered with the strangeness of what he'd seen and for the first time he could remember, he wasn't sure he could trust the evidence of his senses. The metamorphosis of man into insect was a Kafkaesque nightmare, as far beyond his experience as it was beyond his imagination.

At the fountain, he wet his handkerchief and wiped the chilidog off his trousers. When he finished, a faint ochre stain still resisted his efforts, but it was mostly just a big wet spot running down one thigh. When he was done with the trousers, he looked up into the sky, his eyes straining for some sight of the man in the tan suit, the thing he'd turned into, or the invisible ship that took him in.

Finding none of these things, Haste started back to his car. He continued to scan the sky as he walked and, as a result of this preoccupation, ran right into a parking meter that stopped him cold, but failed to bring him back to his senses.

A petite woman with a Pekingese on a gold leash started to laugh, but upon realizing she was being rude, smothered it with a gloved hand. When Haste failed to even register the infraction, she turned her gaze up to follow his. Reaching the end of his leash, the Pekingese looked up as well, though if one followed his line of sight, one would discover that he was looking at the petite woman rather than the sky.

The woman started to ask what Haste was looking at, but upon giving him a quick once-over, decided she didn't like the look of this disheveled man with his damp trousers and badly shaven chin. Giving the leash a tug, she hurried off with the Pekingese in tow.

She rounded the corner at the end of the block before stopping to indulge in one last look. She was surprised to find that Haste still hadn't moved. Shaking her head, she muttered to no one in particular, "This town gets crazier every day."

The woman's name was Desiree Blythe and her Pekingese was called Mister Poopoo for reasons known only to the two of them. She'd moved to DC in the forties to work for the War Office, then stayed on through the reorganization that resulted in a more or less unified Department of Defense.

She started as a secretary with limited skills in shorthand and typing, but armed with a classic hourglass figure, she was more than generously equipped to attract the attention of even the most vaguely heterosexual male. Many hounds sniffed along her trail, but General Neal Cranston was the big dog who chased the others away.

***

While it was technically true that General Cranston was married, it was easy to see that his marriage was a sham and he didn't love his wife anymore. With this in mind, she had allowed his attention and finally surrendered when he mounted an aggressive campaign that swept aside the competition of two senior officers, a sitting member of the Joint Chiefs of Staff, and a host of lower ranking subordinates.

All were men who'd become obsessed by the signature click of Desiree's heels as she shuttled paperwork from one end of the Pentagon to the other. These were men who should've been preoccupied with weightier matters, but the familiar sounds of Desiree's approach drove away all thoughts of their stalled careers or the defense of the nation. Every one of them would look up when they heard her coming, each envisioning his own fantasy featuring the package that accompanied those Pavlovian clicks.

Once they located her, their eyes would start at the patent leather pumps, then rising up the charcoal seams of her stockings, to pause at the pear-shaped perfection of her generous hips, swaying side to side with pendulum precision. They would tarry there because not doing so would be wrong, and realistically they had no choice in the matter.

The temptation was to remain there until she was out of sight, but doing so would deprive them of other glories that were impossible to ignore. Belatedly, suddenly realizing that time was running out, they would tear their eyes away from the perfect fulcrum of her waspish waist to catch the briefest glimpse of the alarming crest that peeked tantalizingly around the line of her bicep.

Then, before they could do more than sigh their longing, she was gone.

In her wake, those first moments of her absence, they would remember what all the fighting had been about, what they'd given up their lives and bodies to defend through four long years of war. They would remember these things though most had wives, many they were even happy with. But in Desiree's presence, they would remember things they'd been in danger of forgetting.

In the moments that followed Desiree's departure, they couldn't help but dismiss their wives as conquered lands. They couldn't help the dissatisfaction of having conquered a satanic enemy and returning home to a dull existence of picket fences and apple pie. They couldn't help but dream of overcoming the challenges presented by Desiree's compact natural fortifications.

In these fantasies, Desiree represented a rampart never breached or taken, and none of the men who tracked the movements of Desiree Blythe had much use for unbreached ramparts. She was their alpine fortress, the untamed foe yet to be taken, the walled Jericho of their deepest desires. Neal Cranston may have been just one of her many admirers, but he had the power of the United States

129

Air Force behind him and he would not hesitate to use it.

He would use that power in blunt and subtle ways, using his subordinates to gather information about her, tracking her back to her lair in the typing pool, specifically requesting her to deliver documents, and finally, requisitioning her as his private secretary. Once he had her under his control, he asked her to work late, often keeping her busy until well after the buses stopped running so that he could offer her a ride home. On these rides, he would leave her with clues about the ongoing problems of his marriage. When the time felt right, about three weeks after she'd come to work for him, he began to woo her with gifts.

Neal Cranston could be a very generous man when the impulse struck, but it was generally generosity in absentia. Cranston, or rather his adjunct, was the one who found and rented the downtown apartment a few blocks from the river. And though he was only a weak-chinned surrogate for his higher ranking master, the adjunct was also the one who purchased Mister Poopoo when Desiree spotted the snub-nosed pup through the window of a G Street pet store.

***

A sharp yap interrupted Desiree's thoughts. She glanced down to see what Mister Poopoo wanted. The way the dog was squatting gave her the answer without having to ask. So she waited like she always did when Mister Poopoo did his business. But after a minute went by with no results, she looked down again. That was when she noticed that he wasn't doing a number two after all.

Mister Poopoo was staring at something up in the sky.

Desiree turned to follow the little dog's line of sight, shading her eyes with the flat of the hand. She saw the thing for only a moment, but for that moment, it was clear as crystal, a shiny silver disc that sauntered languidly between clouds.

Without lowering her hand, she asked rhetorically.

"What do you suppose that is, Mister Poopoo?"

She didn't really expect Mister Poopoo to answer, of course. But she'd gotten into the habit of talking to the dog because Neal was always off doing his general stuff. As a result of her man's dual preoccupations with his career and the defense of the nation's capital, Desiree had grown quite lonely in recent months. She watched the disc for a while, and would've watched longer had it not shot off into the clouds at tremendous speed.

As soon as it was gone, Desiree did an abrupt about face to head back to where she'd seen the messy man looking up into the sky. She'd only gone half a block since seeing the reporter, and she hoped that, if she hurried, he might still be there. Her heels clicked off the sidewalk like slow castanets while she considered the question she was going to ask if she found him.

Was the silver disc what he was looking for when he ran into the parking meter?

When she reached the corner, she saw that John Haste hadn't moved an inch. In fact, his mouth was open so wide that he could have caught flies if he was a few blocks closer to the Potomac.

Clearly, he'd seen the same thing she had.

Desiree approached with some trepidation, the wet spot on his thigh being a strong deterrent. But she was helpless in the grip of an insatiable curiosity that would rule her actions for the rest of the day. Neal had scolded her once about approaching strange men on the street. He said they would get the wrong idea, no matter what her intentions might be.

She suspected he was right, Neal was a general after all. But she had to know what the thing in the sky was, and for some reason, she was virtually certain that this slovenly man with the wet spot on his thigh was the only one who had the power to tell her.

Desiree Blythe stopped just short of John Haste and reined Mister Poopoo to heel. When John Haste failed to notice her, she raised one gloved hand and waved. She wasn't tall enough to get into his elevated line of sight, so she had to hope that his peripheral vision would pick up the movement, or that he wasn't too distracted to ignore the interruption.

"Excuse me?"

John Haste turned his head side to side in a wide arc, but his eyes remained sky bound. Since he didn't appear to have heard her, she tried again.

"Uh, sir..." The word felt wrong when used on this man, but Desiree had been raised to be polite. "Uh, sir, excuse me?"

As John Haste's eyes fall out of the sky, he became aware that someone was addressing him. When he reached eye-level without finding anything of interest, he continued to lower his gaze until he found the pint-sized woman holding the strangest looking dog he'd ever seen. He blinked a few times, his mind still in the clouds, before realizing he really ought to pay attention to this nicely packaged bundle of soft curves and her flowing waves of blonde hair.

Haste reached for the hat he'd already taken off, and gave the half-bow with head bob that passed for etiquette in Texas.

"I'm awfully sorry, ma'am," he said, apologizing for having ignored her. "My eye was drawn by something up in the sky."

Desiree looked both ways down the empty street. The only car in sight was just turning the corner. She came closer, lowering her voice to a conspiratorial whisper. "I know. I saw it too."

Haste jerked ever so slightly, his question mark spine straightening with an audible crack. "You did?"

Desiree picked up Mister Poopoo, then rose to standing with the Pekingese chin resting happily on her bosom.

"Yes, I saw you looking up when I walked by. Then I saw it myself a minute ago. What do you think it was?"

Haste didn't answer right away. It wasn't just the silver disc that troubled him. The disc was disturbing, but it might have a logical explanation. But, try as he might, he could not think of any way to explain the sight that had left him scraping chili off his pants. He was a trained observer of the human condition, with an impressive vocabulary and the skill to use it, but he couldn't think of any way to describe the transformation, ascension, and disappearance of the man in the tan suit.

"Well," he said with a shrug of his rounded shoulders. "I can't say I know. Maybe it's something the Air Force is testing." Giving it some thought, this did seem to be a reasonable explanation.

This might be enough to satisfy anyone else, but it wasn't enough to satisfy Desiree Blythe. Desiree's brow compressed into three parallel lines, then cleared as she shook her head.

"No, I don't think so. Neal would tell me about something like that."

John Haste had a long mobile face with a chin a bit on the weak side. That chin tended to draw back when confronted by anything he considered unlikely.

"Neal? Who's Neal?"

Desiree blushed and giggled. The unencumbered hand, the one that wasn't full of Pekingese, fluttered to her breast, drawing Haste's confused but appreciative gaze like a charlatan presenting a show card.

"Oh," she said quickly, without considering the repercussions, "Neal's with the Air Force. He's-," she struggled for the right word to explain the relationship, settling on one she'd heard used in a movie by another diminutive blonde. "He's a close personal friend."

John Haste laughed in her face and wasn't particularly nice about it.

"Well, ma'am, I don't care if your friend is in the Air Force. He'd have to be pretty high up to know about that. Anything that can accelerate like that would be pretty hard to hide." Haste jabbed a finger skyward for emphasis.

Desiree's smile grew thinner and less polite. "I'll have you know that he is pretty high up. He's a general and you can't get much higher than that."

And just like that, John Haste felt the tingle. It was hardly the first time he'd felt it, his career was littered with such moments. The tingle was the realization that there was a story in this little woman, and if he was any judge of human character at all, she would keep talking only as long as he didn't believe her.

John Haste cut the air with a dismissive hand.

"Ah, quit pulling my leg. Even if he is a general, I'm sure he wouldn't be talking about secret projects to a sweet little gal like you."

Desiree's dander rose as if the Texan had just waved a red flag in her face.

"He would, too! You may not be aware of this fact, but generals get lonely too, and most of the time they don't have anyone to... to talk to. Neal tells me lots of things and I'm sure he would have told me about that, that, that..."

Desiree sputtered to a stop as her un-Pekingesed hand rose from its bosomy shelf. She pointed after the vanished disc, punctuating her venom with her finger.

"Besides," she concluded, "I bet you don't have the faintest idea what it is either and what's more, I bet you don't even have anyone to tell about it when you get home."

John Haste's head was spinning.

He felt like he was in one of those game show cages where contestants are given 30 seconds to grab all the dollar bills they can. He tried to recall everything she'd told him, frantically making notes in his head until he could find the time to write it all down.

1. She was a close personal friend of an Air Force general.
2. The general would be there when she got home.
3. The general was in the habit of telling her about secret projects.

His stomach lurched with the realization that his chilidog lunch had been a horrible mistake.

Clearly, this tiny woman was completely unaware of the danger she could put the country in. She didn't have to be a spy, all she had to do was talk to a spy to compromise national security. Haste wasn't sure exactly what she knew, but his mind reeled as he wondered what would happen if the Reds were able to milk her for information. He shook his head at the image, disturbed by thoughts about milk and where it came from.

Haste considered turning her in, but abandoned the idea when he realized what he'd be giving away. He was a reporter, and if this woman didn't have a juicy scandal and a month's worth of headlines in her, he was no judge of news.

He stared down as she lifted her chin in an expression of contrived haughtiness and realized that she was one barb away from moving on. He needed to do something to keep her around. He couldn't just let her walk away, not with so much riding on every word.

Desiree Blythe set Mister Poopoo down and prepared to leave.

"Wait, don't go," John Haste said.

Desiree looked up at the Texan without interest. He was a disappointment as far as she was concerned.

Haste looked to the sky for guidance. When he came back down, he knew exactly what he was going to say.

Haste looked up and down the empty street before leaning down to whisper.

"Can I tell you a secret?"

Desiree smiled happily.

Men were always telling her secrets.

Chapter 21 - Flaws in the Ffaeyn

Jakob Kleinemann prided himself on his newfound patience. Before being healed by the Ffaeyn, he was in such pain that forbearance in any form was an extremely low priority. Lashing out at the slightest provocation, he released his inner rage with such savagery that, despite his diminutive size, he earned a well-deserved reputation as a man one did not trifle with. There was a long list of colleagues at various academic institutions who still bore emotional wounds from relatively minor disagreements. Since his repair by the Ffaeyn, he'd made a real effort to shore up what he now perceived as a character flaw.

Having weathered other encounters with the Nemerteans, Jakob had learned enough about the worms' intentions to conclude that they were innately hostile toward human life. But while recognition of an alien presence on Earth was troubling, realizing that those aliens were able to inhabit and control human bodies was downright disturbing.

The revelation that the dead bodies from the Roswell incident had been given to the worms was beyond irritating, and the fact that this had been done by super-intelligent beings he considered friends of humanity taxed his patience to the limit.

"Let me see if I understand this correctly," Jakob said. "You are saying these Nemerteans..."

"We just call them worms."

"...these worms might be anywhere."

The faux man shrugged.

"...and there's no physical way to tell us from them..."

"Technically, you can cut their heads open..."

"...Yes! Find the worm inside..."

"...just like the prize in a cereal box..."

"How very practical," Jakob agreed, as he wondered how much the Ffaeyn understood about sarcasm. "But I still think the best part is that they're hostile to human life and bent on world domination."

"We think you're overlooking some of the benefits."

Jakob tried one more volley only to have it returned with enthusiasm.

"Ah, there are benefits then?"

The faux man created by the Ffaeyn nodded vigorously.

"Oh, yes, the worms have the power to heal..."

"...they can maintain your bodies indefinitely..."

"...they can repair virtually any damage..."

"...slow the aging process to a crawl..."

"...why, having a worm could advance the evolutionary process by..."

"...hundreds..."

"...thousands..."

"...maybe millions of years!"

Jakob shook his head to remind himself that these were godlike beings who were able to move between dimensions, masters of time and space at the core of all life and knowledge. With all that wisdom and power, how was it possible that they could sometimes be so incredibly dense?

Since they clearly weren't getting it, he tried to redefine the problem in terms they could understand.

"So, in addition to being hostile, they are also virtually indestructible and vastly more intelligent that we are."

"...Doctor Kleinemann, please...."

"...almost everyone is vastly more intelligent than you are..."

Jakob did achieve one small victory when a lone Ffaeyn said,

"...We haven't looked at it from that perspective..."

Jakob was about to respond when Rita's hand fell on his shoulder like the talon of a predatory bird. She'd listened patiently while Jakob interrogated the omnipotent specks, but that patience was quickly eroding. She'd been trying to come up with a metaphor that would clearly illustrate the issue.

"So you just tossed these foxy worms into our human hen house, even though we don't have any way to defend ourselves against them."

As metaphors went, this one was pretty sad. In any event, it was only the preliminary salvo. "So, my question is this, what are you going to do about it?"

The Ffaeyn-man looked startled for a moment. Its infinite minds had clearly not expected such a question.

"...what do you mean?"

Rita tightened her hold on Jakob's shoulder, a warning not to interfere.

"I mean this. This is all your fault. You've introduced a hostile species into a world that doesn't even know it's there. Every human on Earth will have a worm in their head if they aren't stopped and we don't have any way to stop them."

"There isn't any way to detect them, any way to defend against them, or as far as we know, to even damage them. As long as they live inside our heads, they can't be killed without killing the host and even then, I'm guessing that the worm can simply find another host. They can't be seen and they look just like us. You've changed the course of our history and turned us into zombies."

Jakob Kleinemann beamed at his bride-to-be with the pride of a parent whose child unexpectedly brought home first prize in a spelling bee.

Now understanding the problem, the faux man said.

"...Oops..."

"...We didn't look at it..."

"...quite that way..."

"...this changes..."

"...everything..."

"So," Rita asked again, "what are you going to do about it?"

The faux man didn't answer immediately, but the air before Jakob and Rita began to move in a disturbing way that encouraged them to step back. A brilliant ruby light exploded soundlessly out of the primordial luminescence, blinding them momentarily with its intensity. But this scarlet snow blindness only lasted an instant. When they were able to see again, they were awed by the condensed version of the ruby light hovering before them.

The light was without any discernible physical shape. It appeared as a star, taken from its far location and brought to Earth across the lightyears required. It looked like a neon sign seen from a few miles up the road.

"What is it?" Jakob asked.

The faux man explained.

"This is a *warak shu*. It was created by a race who lived long ago. When you touch it, it will bind itself to you and you alone. No one else will be able to use it. The *warak shu* is no stranger to Earth, but it's been a while since one was used openly..."

"...There was that one guy..."

"...but he just used it to move rocks around..."

"When you touch it..."

"...it will assume a familiar shape."

"Carry it with you always."

"No one else can touch it."

Jakob blinked against the light, asking a second time.

"What is it?"

"We cannot undo what we've done to help the Nemerteans..."

"...again, sorry about that..."

"...but the *warak shu* will defend you against the worms."

"Once you touch it..."

"...it will tell you how it may be used..."

"...and its limitations..."

"...you control it with your thoughts..."

"...We give this *warak shu* to you, Jakob Kleinemann..."

"...use it well..."

"...pay close attention to the disclaimer..."

"...no warranty is provided..."

"...buyer beware..."

"...no deposit, no return..."

Jakob had taken only a single step when the *warak shu* came to him like a well-trained dog. He extended a trembling hand to touch it and, as he curled his fingers around the shapeless mass, he felt it turn solid in his hand. When he opened his hand, he found an eight-sided rounded cone, flat at the base with tiny holes at the rounded end. It looked, as much as it looked like anything, like the kind of saltshaker one might find at any Howard Johnson's.

Jakob almost dropped the thing when it spoke, but the *warak shu* caught itself before it'd fallen too far, and hovered until Jakob recovered his composure.

When he held it in his hand the second time, his mind was flooded with a stream of images. Each image seemed to snake its way to a different part of his mind, making one connection after another. He felt it tunnel around like a probe, firing neurons that had never been fired before. The entire process took seconds and the ride was exhilarating.

When he could catch his breath, he realized he'd been loaded with both a sales pamphlet and the instruction manual for the strange device he held in his hand. The pamphlet took first priority.

"Greetings, new partner! You are the worthy recipient of the most useful tool ever created! Warak shu are famous throughout the multiverse for their ease of use and wide range of functions. Once paired to an indigenous recipient, your warak shu will provide advantages that, you and only you, may employ for the rest of your life. Warak shu have a nearly perfect success rate and enjoy a 93.7% positive rating on Yelp."

"Here's how it works. Using a proven technology that dates back eons, your warak shu will provide you and your loved ones with a lifetime of service and protection, fulfilling your needs while still respecting your privacy. Your warak shu requires no maintenance and its abilities may not be transferred except in the event of death or physical separation through a barrier of the space-time continuum."

"Limitations: Your warak shu may not be used for purposes of conquest or to gain advantage at games of chance. All warak shu come with a moral arbiter that will internally determine the appropriateness of any proposed action. In circumstances involving the immediate wellbeing of the recipient, the warak shu is authorized to act independently until the crisis is resolved."

"Disclaimer: The creators of the warak shu provide no warranty of operation. They may not be held responsible for actions performed as a result of its function or lack of such."

"Offer is not valid in alternate universes, and is restricted to the galaxy where it is issued."

While Jakob Kleinemann shared secrets with his new partner, the Ffaeyn turned their attention to Rita Mae Marshaux.

"...To you, Dorothy, we give a secret that will be yours alone..."

"...You won't be able to share it..."

"...or tell anyone you have it..."

"...but it should be useful against...well, anything-"

"Try not to move, this may sting..."

With that, the faux man whispered something in Rita's ear. Whatever was said, she didn't hear it so much as she felt it. It was a word of power, compressed into concentrated form, and it exploded inside her head like a bomb.

Rita cried out in terror, but the reaction lasted only a moment. Her hands went to her head to stop the pain. It was as if her body was on fire and she felt helpless as wave after wave of sensation rolled over her. Her cries, the ones she was still aware of, grew rhythmic, taking on a primeval guttural quality. Finally she let go with a scream as the last wave crashed over her. The sensation stopped, leaving her shivering in its aftermath, her flesh tingling and raw.

Jakob viewed his fiancee with alarm. He'd never imagined her capable of such naked passion. It made him feel inadequate. All he'd been able to draw out of her were a few smothered moans before Mrs Kelley knocked on the door and ruined everything. This new Rita was a changed woman.

The urgency now clear, she turned to Jakob.

"We have to get to the airport."

Jakob wanted to point out that they were several hundred feet underground, trapped in a sea of darkness, and possibly miles from any exit. Additionally, they were lost without any idea of where to go or how to proceed. How on earth, he wanted to say, would they get to the airport?

But the *warak shu* knew.

And, surprisingly, that was all that mattered.

***

With the departures of Jakob Kleinemann and Rita Mae Marshaux, the uncountable Ffaeyn comprising the faux man settled back into their normal physical state. Though their voices could still be heard, there was no one left to hear them.

"...wait, there was more..."

"...did they leave?..."

"...but we didn't..."

"...tell them..."

"...too late..."

"...I didn't say anything..."

"...I know you didn't? I thought..."

"...but there was more..."

"...that's what I meant..."

"...but they left..."

"...weren't we supposed to..."

"...tell them about the bugs?"

Chapter 22 - Next Steps

Allen Hynek didn't catch up to Ed Ruppelt until he was at the taxi stand wondering why there weren't any cabs. He tried calling out to the captain, but Ruppelt was in so single-minded a state that the scientist's entreaties fell on deaf ears until Hynek caught up to him.

"Professor Hynek-" Ruppelt started to say before Hynek cut him off.

"Take me with you," Hynek pleaded, appalled at the begging tone that had crept into his voice.

"Professor-" Ruppelt started again.

"No, listen to me," Hynek said, struggling to catch his breath. "I'm tired of it all, tired of the pretending. We don't have any idea what we're dealing with or even what we're looking for really. I'm tired of this whole charade. Every few months, I get flown out to some hick ranch where some shell-shocked man or woman wants to tell me what they saw. The moment we arrive, we start looking for ways to pass off their experience as natural phenomena, even though we know they've seen something extraordinary, even though the explanation we provide dismisses every fact they've just given us. We're not looking for truth, we're looking for a ways to deny what these people have seen, and our explanations are crippled by the one thing we can't admit out loud."

Hynek paused to catch his breath, providing Ruppelt the break he needed to ask, "And what is that?"

Hynek shook his head, drawing another deep breath.

"We don't know. They want explanations for everything, but sometimes it's just not possible. Then I have to say something like 'we don't have enough data' or 'it's difficult to evaluate eyewitness testimony.' Nobody wants to hear that. You should see the faces of these people after I tell them that. It's like I've just called them liars."

"They don't even let me talk to the analysts anymore. I see only those guys from a distance, getting on a plane or climbing into the back seat of a car, but they don't even let me talk to them. Nobody tells me anything and I'm sick and tired of it. They just come to me for explanations. It doesn't even matter how dopey it sounds-"

As Hynek was showing no signs of running down, Ruppelt grabbed his shoulder and escorted him away from the mass of bellboys and car attendants. People were starting to stare.

"Easy, Allen," Ruppelt said soothingly, "we can't be so public about this. People are watching."

"I don't care-"

"But I do, and if Menzel gets wind of what you just said, you will, too. Come on then. We aren't going to find out anything here."

Turning to the attendants, Ruppelt called, "Hey, can someone get us a cab?"

The cab arrived five minutes later. During the wait, the two men continued to converse, albeit in whispered tones.

"So what are you planning to do?" Hynek asked, sobering by the minute.

Ruppelt shrugged, staring at traffic that was pretty sparse by DC standards.

"Like I said, I don't know. I was thinking I might go down and walk along the Mall for a bit, see if something popped into my head. I just figured I wasn't going to do anything worthwhile drinking away the afternoon."

Having finally caught his breath, Hynek nodded.

"That's fine with me, I've already had a few too many, but listen, we both think our superiors know more about this than they're letting on-"

"Yeah," Ruppelt agreed, "and we both know they aren't about to share what they know with us. So the question is, what can we do on our own that won't require asking our higher-ups to share what they don't want to share?" Ruppelt paused a beat, then added, "And how do we do it without getting in dutch with our bosses?"

Allen Hynek started to say something then abruptly stopped.

"What is it?" Ruppelt asked.

"Something just popped into my head," the astronomer said, "something you said right at the end of your testimony."

Ruppelt frowned. "What?"

"You said that ATIC claims there'll be a sharp increase in UFO sightings for the rest of the month."

"Yeah, so?"

"Well," Hynek said, "how on earth could they know that? It's not like we've ever been able to predict when a flying saucer is going to appear."

It took almost a full minute before Ruppelt admitted, "I don't know how that could have slipped by me."

"Another thing," Hynek said, now regaining his momentum, "how were you contacted about appearing?"

"You mean, how was I invited to the hearing?"

Hynek nodded.

Ruppelt frowned as he tried to recall the sequence of events.

"I received a memo at my office at Wright-Patterson. I'd already been ordered to DC for the weekend, so testifying before the committee fit in with the plans I already had."

"Did you have to clear the appearance with your superiors?"

"Sure, I'd have to do that for anything."

"Did your superiors warn you off speaking about anything?"

Ruppelt froze, then shook his head. "I can't say anything about that. We're getting into classified territory."

Hynek smiled for the first time since the conversation began.

"So you were. Do you still have that memo, the invitation? I ask because I received something similar. I even brought it with me, but it wasn't there when I got back to my room. I tried to find it, tore my suitcase apart if you want the truth, but it was missing. Where did you leave yours?"

Ruppelt thought for a moment.

"I think I filed it after entering it on my calendar."

"So you might not have yours either?"

The long-awaited taxi pulled up to the curb beside them.

"What are you getting at?" Ruppelt asked, now puzzled by the entire line of questioning.

It was Hynek's turn to frown. "I'm not exactly sure. There's just something odd about these hearings. There wasn't any notice in the papers. UFOs are entirely outside HUAC's focus. Congress has been out of session for weeks, but close to fifty reporters showed up today. Taking each thing by itself gives you little, but put them together and something doesn't add up. There are other things, too. It's just strange and it's all well outside the way Congress does business. Does any of that seem normal to you?"

Ruppelt shook his head. "I have to admit it doesn't."

Ruppelt opened the door and got into the cab. Hynek went around to the other side. When both men were settled, the driver, a tall sandy-haired man in a crisp blue shirt with rolled up sleeves, turned and leaned an elbow on the back of his seat.

"So where will I be taking you gentlemen today."

The way he said it, it didn't sound like a question at all.

***

Donald Menzel hadn't always led a double life, but he was finding that he quite enjoyed it. He liked being on the inside of the greatest mystery of the 20th century, as well as the twin auras of secrecy and danger that accompanied every meeting with the men of Majestic-12. He especially liked being so visibly in the news while so much of what he did was out of the public eye. As all these things belied his background as a scientist and an administrator, Majestic made him feel exotic, like one of Dulles' European spies.

The down side of the work lay in not having subordinates to do his bidding like Dulles or Vandenberg. Both the spymaster and the general had cadres of young men ready and willing to do their bidding without questioning the face value of the request. As a humble academic, all Menzel had at his disposal were a few summer interns.

While it was true that he might be able to coerce the occasional grad student into picking up his dry cleaning, he had little control over their actions in general. This sometimes led to Menzel having to perform essentially menial acts on his own without assistance. Getting back on the scent that would lead to the identity of the mystery witness was one such situation.

That interloper Dulles had offered to take official control of the search, a task that was difficult to deny him given the resources at his disposal. But upon leaving the conference room, it occurred to Menzel that a direct approach might be more efficacious.

It was with this in mind that he instructed his driver to drop him at the Senate building housing the office of Senator Joseph McAfee. If the closed door session wasn't McAfee's idea, and nothing in the chairman's history would convince Menzel that it was, then maybe he'd give the mystery man up out of sheer spite.

***

Detlev Bronk, unlike the others at the meeting, saw no further need for his involvement. While it was true that he'd been able to inform the group of La Paz's plans, his information was second hand at best, relying entirely on a chance comment made by one of the men La Paz was meeting for dinner.

So, with nothing of immediate importance to delay him, he returned to his room at the Ambassador. There, he indulged himself in a late lunch consisting of the Reuben sandwich he craved and a Waldorf salad to appease his wife. He finished with a brandy, and was almost ready to go when he was approached by a sandy-haired man in a bellhop's uniform. The bellhop was carrying a telephone that he plugged into a socket under the table.

The bellhop spoke to the operator, then backed away when the call was put through. When he had the connection, he handed the receiver off to Bronk.

"Hello, Doctor Bronk?"

The voice was Midwestern and male, but otherwise unfamiliar.

"This is Bronk. Who is this?"

There was a hum on the other end of the line before the caller said, "My name is unimportant. In any case, you wouldn't recognize it. But it's imperative that we speak in person. I have vital information that could affect the welfare of the nation, maybe even the world."

"Then I should stop you right there," Bronk said. "I am a scientist and an administrator, but I have no influence over the security of the nation. Perhaps you should call Central Intelligence. I believe they handle that sort of thing."

The caller, who'd been calm until then, suddenly turned anxious.

"I can't do that. It's the CIA I need to talk about. They've been compromised!"

"Then, perhaps you should speak to General Smith. He's the director and I'm sure he'll be very interested to hear what you have to say."

"No!" The voice said, pleading now. "The problem is inside the CIA! There's a leak! If I could just talk to you—"

142

Bronk held the phone further from his ear, irritated by the man's strident tone. "Well, I can't imagine how I can help you. I'm just a simple-"

"I know you're a member of MJ-12!"

Bronk went white with shock, recovering his voice with some difficulty.

"I... that is..., I beg your pardon. What is this MJ-12?"

"I'm not playing games, doctor! Don't trust him!"

"Who is this? I really must insist... Who shouldn't I trust?"

"Dulles! You mustn't trust Allen Dulles!"

There was a click and the line went dead.

Bronk put down the receiver, as disconcerted by the strange call as he was by the paranoia of its messenger. He sat in thought for several minutes, shooing away the bellhop when he returned to take the phone away. When he knew what he wanted to say, he lifted up the receiver and asked the operator to connect him to the only man who might help.

Nobody answered, even though he let it ring a dozen times.

***

Hoyt Vandenberg went home to change before returning to the Pentagon. It was a relief to get back into his uniform. On the way into the office, he stopped to ask Lieutenant Clarence if he'd heard anything from Ruppelt, but for the first time he could remember, the lieutenant wasn't at his post. Vandenberg fumed about his absence, but there was plenty of work to do before quitting time, so he got back to it.

He'd been at his desk for almost an hour when the power to the building went out. He waited for the backup generators to kick in, but when five minutes passed without anything happening, Vandenberg rose from his desk and went in search of butts to kick. He ran into his next problem as soon as he left his office.

Inside his office, he wasn't have any difficulty. The blinds were up and, as it was still afternoon, there was plenty of light coming in through his window. It wasn't until he stepped into the hall that he realized every place wasn't the same.

There weren't any windows into the hall, and with the power out, no light either. As most of the men who had offices on this side of the Pentagon were gone for the weekend, they'd also seen fit to lock their doors. As a result, the corridor was as black as an unlit mineshaft.

With the afternoon sun streaming in behind him, a dozen voices cried out as soon as he opened his door. He could hear their calls for help, but he couldn't see the zombie-like shuffle of their approach.

Either way, Vandenberg wanted no part of them. Retreating into his office, he slammed the door behind him, plunging the corridor back into darkness. Just before the door closed, he caught the distant strobe of a flashlight and wondered if he might have stashed one of his own somewhere. But a quick inspection of his office failed to turn up anything useful. Vandenberg was irritated at losing control over his options, but there clearly wasn't any other way.

He left the door open this time, using the diffused light from his window to guide him down the hall. He was pleased to find that conditions were better. By this time, most of the men and women he'd seen had been led down the stairs by the men with the flashlights.

He saw a few of the emergency wardens grouped around the stairwell door. The men, distinctive in their yellow vests, were shining their flashlights in both directions, calling out to any stragglers who might still be trapped on the floor.

Vandenberg called one over. Under the vest, Vandenberg spotted sergeant's stripes. The sergeant came at a trot and came to attention as soon as he got close enough to see Vandenberg's stars.

"At ease, sergeant," Vandenberg growled, "any word on what's happened yet?"

"No, sir," the sergeant said, dropping his salute. "We don't know why the power's out, but it's not affecting the surrounding area, only this building."

"Only this building? Sergeant, this building covers a hundred fifty acres of land and houses over twenty-thousand personnel. Saying the blackout only affects this building is like saying it only affects this small town. We have backup systems on top of backup systems and none of them has kicked in so far and I want to know why."

"Yes, sir," the sergeant said, "I don't have any information on why the backups haven't kicked in, but the phones are still working. All I know is word came down from General Bradley a few minutes ago that we were to clear the building. Since it's late in the afternoon, all clerical personnel are being sent home. Do you want to countermand those orders, sir?"

Vandenberg scowled, irked that someone else was taking the initiative.

"No, dammit, that'll be all. Get back to your post, sergeant, I guess this is just going to be an inconvenience. Oh, before you go, give me your flashlight."

The sergeant relinquished his torch grudgingly, saluted, and left muttering something about being posted to a place with too many generals.

Using the flashlight, Vandenberg made his way back to his office, intending to make sure there weren't any classified documents on his desk before leaving. As he drew close, he was surprised to find that, unlike every other office on the floor, there was a light shining out from the crack under his door. The light was too bright to be coming through the window, which meant it was artificial. Vandenberg wondered where it was getting power from.

When he opened the door to his office, he was shocked to find an even more puzzling sight. His adjunct, Lieutenant Clarence, was sitting behind his desk, sorting through a stack of classified documents as casually as a businessman reading his morning paper. Making matters worse, Clarence had his feet up on the desk.

"Lieutenant Clarence!" Vandenberg roared, glad to finally have someone to vent his rage upon. "Exactly, what the hell do you think you're doing?"

Accustomed to immediate responses from his subordinates, Vandenberg was stunned to see the insouciant way in which Clarence reacted. Far from snapping to attention, Clarence didn't even take his shoes off of the desk blotter.

In lieu of this missing respect, the lieutenant drew his service automatic and pointed it at Vandenberg's heart.

"Please close the door behind you, General, we're going to be here awhile."

"In the meantime, you and I are going to have a little chat."

***

Across the river, a similar situation was playing out at CIA headquarters.

If anyone was watching, they might have noticed that at the exact moment the lights went out at the Pentagon, the same thing had happened to the CIA.

The loss of illumination was annoying, but not annoying enough to rob Allen Dulles of enjoying his crank call to Detlev Bronk. The crank call was just the latest volley in a subtle campaign to repay Bronk for arguing against Dulles' inclusion in Majestic. Even though the grudge was almost four years old, Dulles was a great one for holding onto his rancor. As luck would have it, the lights went out at the exact moment Dulles hung up the phone.

But unlike Vandenberg, Dulles never left his desk, choosing instead to remain inside his room like a patient spider. He prepared for his visitors by retrieving his pistol from its drawer and setting it within easy reach.

But other than that, he did nothing.

He simply waited for his enemies to appear, and while it would take several hours before they got around to him, he would not be disappointed.

Chapter 23 - Worms!

"It is like television then?" Lars Ångström asked innocently.

The Nemertean viewing panel did look like a television, albeit one without any picture tube, antenna, or cabinet. On that screen, Arthur Ecks sat, trussed up like two-bit gangster, his eyes focused on the man with the hypodermic. There wasn't any sound and Ångström regretted the lack of it. He was dying to know why Joe McAfee had taken Ecks prisoner.

"Bah!" Corbett spat. "It is so far beyond human technology that...that..." He ran out of breath, still searching for his simile. To compensate, he puffed out his chest and backed Ångström against the only empty wall space in the room.

"It is much better than anything you have in the primitive living rooms of your freedom-loving nation. You will never achieve so sharp a picture with your medieval cathode rays!"

This wasn't an idle boast. Ångström was stunned by its depth of detail as well as its authentic reproduction of colors. The viewing panel was also larger than any modern television. It was so large that the figures on the screen were almost life size. There was a shade too much lavender in the mix, but any kind of color was a quantum leap over the Philco in the Ångström den.

"Yes, very impressive," Lars said, searching for a compliment these strange men might consider adequate. "I have never seen its like."

"And you never will!" Corbett exulted, "Not until we bring the human race to its knees. Then you will see them everywhere, but then you will be slaves and you will watch only what your masters see fit to show you. There will be no more of your Jack Benny, no more Uncle Miltie!"

"You will watch what your worms want to watch!" Wally Sands added.

Lars peered closer at the screen. "Am I correct in deducing that this works without using a camera, transmitter, or receiver?"

Winthrop Walton Russell III looked up from his work for the first time, surprised that anyone had shown interest in what he was doing.

"Yes," Russell said, displaying a distinct Ivy League accent and the manners that went with it, "yes, you are correct, doctor."

"It would be more impressive with sound," Lars suggested.

Russell flashed a timid smile he wasn't allowed to use very often.

"In fact, that's exactly what I'm working on now! It's almost ready."

"Shut up, Russell," Corbett snapped, "no one cares about your techie crap."

Russell went back to his work and Lars went back to watching the screen. Ecks and McAfee seemed to be chatting amiably.

"It appears that they aren't far away," Lars pointed out.

"You can shut up too, Doctor Ångström," Corbett snarled. "Isn't this thing ready yet? I want to hear what they're saying."

Russell didn't look up because only bad things happened when he looked up. "Almost ready," he said, putting down the tool he'd been using. "All that's left is hooking it up and tapping into the control device."

"Then, do it, damn you," Corbett raged. "We're missing everything."

Russell picked up the oval shape he'd been working on and snapped it into a socket on a larger unit. The screen flashed once, then resolved into a sharper detail that replaced the lavender tint with a deep red. Lars watched the screen with such fascination that he failed to observe the dozen tendrils extending out of Russell's head to connect with smaller sockets on the main device.

And suddenly there was Arthur Ecks explaining.

"*stuff we get is real. We make physical contact with extraterrestrials and we deal with any issues we encounter.*"

This time, Lars Ångström couldn't hold back his gasp. There were many things he'd heard and seen as a result of his work with Project Stall, but he'd never imagined any scenario where Arthur Ecks would willingly discuss their mission with an outsider.

But Russell's success proved to be short-lived. Suddenly, the screen flashed a short burst of red, then abruptly shifted to an infrared view of Rita Mae and Jakob talking to a luminous creature sheathed in an emerald glow.

Abel Corbett stared at the new scene with impotent rage.

"What the hell just happened? What were they talking about? Get it back! I want to hear what they were talking about!"

"I'm trying, I'm trying," Russell cringed. "I just need more time!"

"Wait!" Wally Sands said, stepping in front of Ångström. "That's two of the others, Kleinemann and the girl. What the hell is that thing they're talking to? Can't you get sound, goddammit!"

Corbett struck Russell across the back of his head. Russell shuddered as his worm withdrew, sliding his tendrils back inside the host's temples.

"Get back in there," Corbett ordered, fuming at the delay. "I want sound! I need to know what they're saying!"

"I can't," Russell insisted, "it hurts!"

"I don't care if it kills you!" Corbett ranted. "Get back in there!"

Again, the tendrils extended out of Russell's temples, and this time Lars was able to watch the process. The tendrils were coated in what looked to be Russell's flesh and there was no line of demarcation between the tendrils and his face. For the first time, Lars Ångström began to understand.

These men really weren't human.

He'd known this in theory, but now he understood on a empirical level.

They looked human and they spoke like humans, but there was something underlying their human facades, something inside their bodies, controlling their actions. And whatever that thing was, it was displaying clear signs of hostility toward humanity. Lars shuddered, unable to stop himself. He tore his eyes away from Russell's head, forcing his gaze back to the screen.

On that screen, he saw a ruby red shimmer in the air above Jakob's head, but then the screen flashed red, and abruptly died. Russell cried out in pain as he withdrew his scorched tendrils.

Corbett shrieked his frustration, and took it out on Russell, pummeling the youth about the head and shoulders. Sands joined in as well, and after determining it would be all right, so did a timid Grady.

"What happened now? What was that thing they were talking to?"

"I don't know," Russell whined, shielding his head with his hands. "There was some kind of energy surge, and then it was gone. It was working and then it just stopped."

Kraall thrashed about inside Corbett's skull. *"You said you were prepared!"*

Corbett snarled impotently at his worm because the thrashing hurt, but directed his anger at Wally Sands, rounding on him with clenched fists.

"You were responsible for this! You said we were ready to strike and you had them in your sights. You said we could take them on my signal."

Sands backed away as if Corbett's rage was a gale. Shff coiled into a quivering lump, leaving his host to face Kraall's fury alone. Wally Sands cursed his worm for being such a pussy.

"I was ready, but...it was Russell's fault. They just disappeared!"

Corbett slapped a palm against the table.

"What were they doing? What was that green thing they were talking to? I want answers, dammit! You were watching them!"

Sands waited a moment too long, hoping Shff would answer. When his worm didn't respond, Wally realized he was on his own.

"The dwarf and the dish got separated from the others. Don't ask me how. They shouldn't be able to see a damn thing down there, but it seemed like they knew where they were going. When they stopped, they started talking, but not to each other. The dish had a hissy fit, and that's when something shorted out the viewer. I don't know what happened after that, but the connection was wiped out by a massive energy burst."

Corbett seemed calmed by the explanation, but he slapped Russell one more time for his failure. "Can you get it back on line?"

Russell extended his tendrils, wincing as the scorched tips made contact with the viewer. There was a prolonged burst of static before the infrared view of the empty corridor came back online. Stunned by the defection, Russell could only murmur.

"They're gone."

Wally Sands pushed his way forward to lean over Russell's back.

"Look around, maybe they just walked away."

The screen rotated in a full circle, but failed to locate any heat signatures. The corridor appeared to be completely empty.

"There's a lot of dust down there. Maybe you can find some footprints."

Russell brought the view back to its original position, then rotated it down until he could see several footprints, clearly outlined in the dust.

"Okay, I got 'em."

"So follow, moron."

Russell brought the view around, circling the area.

"They just stop. It's like they vanished into thin air."

Wally Sands slapped an angry palm on the table.

"Did they go back the way they came?"

Russell shook his head.

"Doesn't look like it. The tracks come in, but they don't go back. Even if they stepped in the exact same places, there'd be some sign of them turning around and they'd mess up the earlier prints on their way out."

Corbett exhaled so angrily it was a surprise he didn't blow flames out of his nostrils. His volume rose as he got deeper into the question.

"Then where the hell did they go?"

Russell cringed, already recoiling from the coming blow.

"How should I know?"

Corbett wheeled about so quickly that Lars flinched.

"Recalibrate the panel and do a wide-area search. See if you can find the others. Let's see what else shows up."

It took Russell a short time to recalibrate, but when he had completed his adjustment, the resurrected humans and the worms controlling them all cried out at once. Lars felt a thrill rising up his spine at what appeared on the screen.

Perseus Grady pointed a shaking finger at the screen, asking the question that troubled all of them. "What the dickens are those?"

The wide-area sweep intended to locate Jakob and Rita had found another target instead. Set to its automatic function, the screen showed an aerial view of the sky over Washington DC. That sky was filled with ships in a multitude of shapes and sizes. The designs were as unfamiliar to the worms as they were to Ångström.

"Those aren't ours." Corbett said, his stolen tongue lying numb in his mouth.

"We don't have any ships, sir," Winthrop Walton Russell reminded him. "Ours were destroyed when we came through the wormhole."

Only one worm knew what they were seeing.

Wally Sands curled his upper lip into the same sneer of contempt gracing the mouth of Arthur Ecks in a different room on a different level.

His disgust was encapsulated into the single word he spat out like a moldy strawberry.

"Bugs!"

Now that he knew what they were facing, Abel Corbett didn't waste any time.

"Grady, see if you can get in touch with any of our MJ-12 friends. They'll want to know about the ships right away. Don't tell them about the bugs until you hear from me. I'll contact you in an hour or so."

Grady's eyes went wide.

"Me? An hour? But, Major—"

Corbett's eyes narrowed imperceptibly, but it was still enough to choke off Grady's protest.

"Captain Sands and I will proceed to the nearest human radar station where we will see if we can get a better fix on those ships. They should be visible on radar, especially if we give them a nudge in the right direction."

Finally, Corbett turned to the lowest member of his team.

"Russell, you're going to stay here until this bloody thing is fixed. And while you're working on that," Corbett groused, "see if you can get some of this other crap working. If we're facing a bug invasion, we might need all of it. If you can't, you know how to punish yourself."

"What about me?" Lars interrupted, checking his watch. "I was hoping you might help me get back to the surface. I said I'd meet my family at the airport, and I'm quite late. I'm sure they're wondering where I've gotten to. Our flight is at seven o'clock."

Corbett slapped Lars Ångström, and was surprised when it hurt him more than Ångström. He winced and turned back to Russell in a fury.

"As a bonus, you'll keep an eye on Ångström. We can't have him wandering around lousing things up. I don't need to remind you what will happen if he escapes."

Winthrop Walton Russell III didn't look up from his work.

"Of course, Kraall, whatever you wish. You are *thang*."

Chapter 24 - The Dead End

The advantage of the Library of Congress, before text publication got out of hand and overflowed the physical constraints of the building, was that it was purported to have a copy of pretty much everything ever printed in the States. From novels to scientific studies to periodicals to pulp magazines, the Library had it all. It was this singular quality that drew Bertie Stein and Janie Gently back to the heart of the nation's capital.

What the Library didn't have, was a terribly accurate idea of what it had or a reasonably efficient method for retrieving it. It had clerks and it had one of the finest indexing systems in the world, but the clerks were overworked, the desk understaffed, and no indexing system is particularly useful when the books aren't properly returned to their assigned shelves.

Another disadvantage was that, even if your book could be found, you weren't allowed to take it out of the Library. It wasn't a lending library after all. And as the Library was at the mercy of its flaws, finding your book could take hours.

But on this muggy summer day, with Congress in recess, the service wasn't all that bad. HUAC was the only committee currently in session, and this oddity was speculated upon by observers of Capitol behavior once they ran out of other things to talk about. The Senator's supporters lauded his unswerving vigilance, while his detractors made *soto voce* comments about his apparent unwillingness to return home to his constituency. Whatever the reason, the Library was buzzing with news of the closed-door session and its abrupt termination.

Still it was impressive that, forty minutes after they'd approached the circulation desk, a bespectacled man in a sweater vest wheeled a loaded cart out to the table where Bertie and Janie had set up shop.

They split the cart down the middle, each taking the output of the man they knew least about. This division left Janie with the work and reviews of Jakob Kleinemann, the heretical monstrosity of *Schrödinger's Catastrophe*, and a slew of academic reviews by men who rejected its hypotheses in the opening sentences of diatribes written well in advance of the book's release.

Bertie drew the *oeuvre* of Lars Ångström, and this made him uncomfortable on many levels, from the subject matter (*Sex!*), to his discomfort with the man's Aryan good looks, to the creeping fear he might be reading the work of a former (or God forbid, current) Nazi.

So while Janie read about cosmic events whose controversial nature she wholly failed to grasp, Bertie rifled through the pages of a massive tome devoted entirely to *schtupping*. When they looked up at each other from time to time, Janie's wide-eyed incomprehension looked like a funhouse reflection of Bertie's red-faced embarrassment.

"I don't understand a word of this," said Janie.

"This is a filthy book," muttered Bertie, afraid of being overheard.

Janie picked up a magazine whose plain front cover featured only headlines. "Maybe the reviews will be better."

The reviews were not better.

Janie ran her finger down column after column of itemized objections, then returned to *Schrödinger's Catastrophe*, scanning the table of contents, and then the index, to see what claims Kleinemann had made to provoke the reviewer's ire. She gave up after twenty minutes, having failed to correlate a single point.

Bertie, meanwhile, was finding the fluff pieces in the popular magazines puzzling. Each article seemed to focus more on the controversy Ångström's book had provoked than its contents. It was a reaction that was more than justified given the little he'd read. He was grateful that, other than a few diagrams of the human reproductive system, Ångström had decided against including pictures.

"I'm sorry, Janie. I guess this was a waste of time."

Janie rested her chin in her hands and watched the young man in the sweater vest deliver another cart of books to an adjacent table. "Well, it's sure not getting us any closer to figuring out why they were at the hearing."

Bertie perked up at the mention of the hearing.

"Yeah, say, I heard something as we were coming in."

Janie eyed the narrow shoulders and skinny arms of the young man in the sweater vest, wondering abstractedly if she would one day marry a man with a similarly uninspiring physique.

"About the hearing getting canceled after we left? Yeah, I heard that too."

"Why do you think they'd end early like that?"

Janie's eyes traveled down the young man's rounded spine to his shrunken, boyish buttocks. "Could be any number of reasons, I guess."

Janie stopped in mid-shrug, letting her brain pick at a point that'd troubled her since leaving. "Say, why do think they never came out?"

Bertie scratched an itch. "Probably went out the back way."

Janie fished a cigarette out of her purse. "There's a back way out?"

"Sure, it's at the back of the room, like a backstage door for senators."

Janie waited for Bertie to offer her a light, but when that possibility seemed hours away, she did it herself with a small silver lighter.

"You know where it lets out?"

Bertie inhaled the smell of fresh tobacco and felt a yearning for his cigar. "Now that you mention it, no."

Janie took a long drag and held it in as she worked over a new idea.

"So no one saw them leave the building?"

Bertie turned from his contemplation of a Georgetown girl's gartered hips. The carnal nature of Ångström's book had provoked disturbing images in his head, and he was having a devil of a time getting rid of them. It was much easier looking at Janie. Now there was a girl who didn't make you think about sex.

"So? I don't know. It's a big building."

Janie took off her glasses, taking one stem between her lips.

"Yeah, but the place was swarming. Someone must've seen 'em leave."

Bertie felt the pink drain from his complexion.

"Not necessarily. There're rumors of an underground exit. I've even heard stories about tunnels to other buildings. The city might be chock-full of 'em. You 'n me'd never know."

Janie found an ashtray and flicked a half inch of ash into it. She leveled her gaze at Bertie, holding his attention until he started to feel uncomfortable.

"What?"

Janie took another drag, but didn't hold this one as long.

"I was just wondering if there was any way we could get down there."

"Down where? Under the Senate building? Have you lost your mind? We'd be arrested and shot before we got fifty feet. There's gotta be guards."

Janie let her gaze wander around the near-empty reading room.

"So you never heard of any way to get under the Capitol?"

Bertie's hand went to the cigar in his pocket.

"How would what I've heard have to do with anything?"

Janie's tone was subliminally dismissive.

"Ah, nothing, I guess. It's just you've been around Washington so long, I thought you mighta heard something. I mean you are kind of a legend."

This last compliment was laying it on a bit thick, but it flattered Bertie to think there were people who actually knew what he did for a living.

"It's got nothing to do with what I've heard or haven't heard."

"So you don't know anything. That's fine."

Janie stubbed out her cigarette and started gathering her belongings.

"Well, I guess I better get going. Can I drop you anywhere?"

Bertie stuck the stump of the cigar between his teeth, admitting defeat for the second time in ten minutes. "Actually, there is one thing..."

***

Bertie didn't complain about her driving the second time around. This time, they didn't go very far, covering the distance to the Capitol in a few minutes.

The thing that Bertie had heard about was a manhole in a back alley behind the Senate. The alley, a narrow, nearly invisible branch off the main road, was empty save for a loading dock that looked like it hadn't been used since Warren Harding made his name and administration synonymous with graft.

Janie hid neither disappointment nor disdain.

"You gotta be kidding."

Bertie was philosophical.

"Hey, you asked. This is what I heard. You go down that manhole and the rumor says you get into a bunch of secret tunnels."

"So how we gonna get down there. That thing looks way too heavy to lift, even if we do it together."

Bertie shook his head.

"You're on your own, doll. Bad back."

Janie put her hands on her hips and a curl on her lips.

"So I guess this was just another waste of time."

But this last phrase was interrupted by a scraping sound. To the surprise of both, the manhole cover started to turn, and then lift.

"Sonuvabitch!" Bertie hissed. "I told you there was something down there!"

Grabbing Janie's elbow, he dragged her into the shelter of a vacant doorway. Janie started to resist, but when the manhole cover rose smoothly from its casing, unsupported by human hands, she decided it might be better to go along without the formality of complaint.

The manhole cover rose to a height of about eighteen inches, then hovered a beat before settling to the ground. Bertie's bowels bucked alarmingly as three men climbed out of the hole. In open defiance of the summer heat, all three men were dressed the same black suit and shoes. All three wore the same white shirt, the same black tie, and the same dark sunglasses.

The shortest was about Bertie's height. In addition to the shared ensemble, he wore a wide-brimmed hat that, Bertie felt reasonably certain, disguised a balding pate as devoid of hair as his. The other men were hatless. Bertie was reasonably sure he would've shit himself if any of them looked in his direction, but upon exiting, the trio took the other way out of the alley.

The manhole cover was reset in the same handsfree manner, without any action on the part of the men in black. When they reached the end of the alley, one man separated from the others before Bertie lost sight of them.

"Sonuvabitch," Bertie muttered, a numb response that lacked the passion of his original ejaculation. Janie tugged at his arm. Unwilling to get railroaded into further shenanigans, Bertie resisted.

"What?"

"Come on, we're gonna follow those two."

Bertie dug his heels in hard enough to take the girl's feet out from under her.

"Follow those two! Are you nuts, girlie? Those guys are killers!"

Janie put hands to hips, as if explaining something to a small child.

"Bertie, we've been trying to find out what happened to two men who came to the hearing but didn't testify. They didn't leave by the door they came in. I think it's pretty obvious that they left through some secret passage. Those men just came out of a manhole which means there has to be an underground tunnel down there. If they aren't holding our men prisoner, I bet they know where they are. To find out, we need to follow them. I think we should follow the two that stayed together. Maybe you think we should follow the other guy, but we need to follow someone to find out what is going on. What kind of reporter are you?"

Bertie felt his colon kick. "An old, fat, tired one."

Janie glared at him, but her voice was surprisingly soft.

"No, you're not. You're one of the best this town has ever seen. Now, we're doing this together, or I'm doing it alone and you'll be finding another ride back to the Y. So, are you with me or not? This could be the biggest story of your life. Are you gonna pussy out on it?"

Bertie gasped at the crude phrase coming from a girl, but managed to ask.

"How do you know there's a story in it?"

Janie laughed out loud. "Come on, Bertie. Five people disappear, a manhole cover rises out of the ground, even though there's no one lifting it, and three men come out."

"You gonna tell me there's no story in that?"

Chapter 25 - Catch and Release

"So...," Arthur Ecks said as a second drop of green blood fell from the blade. "I guess I'm the one who's been asking all the wrong questions."

"Nonsense, Major, you've been most cooperative."

McAfee set the scalpel on its tray and leaned back in his chair, twining his fingers around one shin. Holding this position, he arched his spine to an alarming degree before allowing it to come back to vertical.

"You'll have to pardon me," McAfee said, "we find that certain shapes are uncomfortable to maintain for long periods. I suppose it's easy enough if you're born to it, but you'll forgive me for saying, human and Antarean parts aren't a very good match. For one thing, you have no ... "

McAfee pointed to a spot on his lower back and said a word that Ecks was unable to decipher. Because it was expected, Ecks nodded sympathetically.

"Yeah, that's tough," Ecks commiserated. "So what are we doing here?"

McAfee glanced around the barren room as if he'd just noticed where he was.

"Here? Well, after your display in chambers, I thought you might be more inclined to talk openly if we met someplace private."

"I told you before. I'm not giving you anything."

McAfee gave Ecks an amused smile.

"Of course, Major. We've noticed certain side effects to the drug I gave you. One of those side effects is a kind of selective amnesia. But even though you may not remember doing so, you've already told me everything I wanted to know."

Ecks flushed angrily, struggling against his bonds.

"You're bluffing! I told you, you'd have to torture me."

The Senator released his knee, rising to his feet in a single flowing motion. He seemed to grow taller by several inches before settling back to his normal height. "Well, we still can if it'll make you feel better, but I don't see the point."

Ecks gave up the struggle, collapsing back into the chair.

"I don't get it. Why would a bunch of bugs be interested in the Earth? I've always heard you bugs like it dry. Climate's a little humid for you, isn't it?"

McAfee yawned and stretched again, growing taller then shrinking back.

"Oh, that shouldn't concern you, Major. We'll make do. We always have. Truthfully, it shouldn't concern human beings much at all. The only problem we have with Earth is that you're in our way."

McAfee leaned over to undo the straps binding Ecks' arms.

"I'm afraid we'll have to cut this short, but I have what I need and I imagine you have someplace you need to be as well. I've been gone far too long. Senators have pretty tight schedules. We should get going before someone starts looking for me."

"What are you going to do with me?"

McAfee shrugged as he undid the first of the restraints.

"Well, I was going to let you go."

"Let me go?" Ecks' eyes went narrow with suspicion. "Then what?"

McAfee paused on the second restraint, concentrating as anyone might when considering a problem in logistics.

"Oh, I suppose I'll just go back to the office. You wouldn't believe how the paperwork piles up. I swear, the amount of energy one can exhaust on rooting pinkos and fags out of the State Department is just staggering."

"What's to stop me from telling the world what you are?"

McAfee finished with his arms, then moved to the restraints binding his legs.

"Why, nothing at all, Major. You can tell anyone you like."

"I will. I'll go straight to the papers."

McAfee shook his head, smothering a laugh. "No, you won't."

Ecks frowned. "Why not? Why wouldn't I?"

McAfee sighed as the last strap came free.

"Let's start back up. We'll have time to talk along the way."

Arthur Ecks rose, feeling a bit rubber-legged. His arms and legs felt creaky from long disuse, but otherwise he was none the worse for wear. McAfee opened the door and beckoned him to follow.

"You'd better come with me. It's a real rabbit warren down here. You'd have a hell of a time finding your way back on your own."

Ecks stared at his jailer, puzzled by the ease of release. But after a moment of hesitation, he followed.

***

Arthur Ecks learned a great deal on the hike back to the surface.

He learned that the Antareans had been coming to Earth for quite a while. McAfee didn't say exactly how long and Ecks wasn't sure it mattered. The thing Ecks most wanted to know was why the bugs were coming at all. The Earth's climate didn't suit their physical needs, and in light of several conversations he'd had with other sentient races, the Antareans were never portrayed as aggressors.

The bugs weren't a colonizing race, but they did have a number of worlds under their control. While their motives weren't necessarily benevolent, they weren't particularly expansionist either. Like everyone else, they suffered from overpopulation, but, at present, they seemed to have it under control.

From an outsider's view, the Antareans were perfectly content with their dominion. Beyond a lax attitude concerning the observance of local religious holidays, there were very few complaints from the worlds under Antarean rule.

In truth, the bugs were known for their flexibility.

When an indigent species revolted, as had happened on a few occasions, the Antareans were perfectly willing to sit down and negotiate their differences with the rebels. Occasionally, this even resulted in temporary independence.

But independence never lasted very long. Every time the bugs released their thralls back into the wild, the locals had begged the shapeshifters to come back.

Everyone agreed, governments just worked better with the bugs in control.

But it was the shapeshifting that bothered Arthur Ecks. From the point of view of an enslaved race, it made an enormous difference when your benevolent overlords looked like that kindly uncle you never get to see often enough. The shapeshifting made the bugs almost impossible to detect.

***

McAfee didn't wait for him, but it didn't take long to catch up. The corridor was wide and well lit by the thin ribbon of light that ran down the center of the ceiling. The senator strolled along in an easy stride, occasionally pausing to poke a toe into one of the mounds of dust piled against the wall. The poking gave Ecks time to catch up.

"I don't get it. Why aren't you afraid of being exposed?"

McAfee gave him the kindly uncle smile.

"Oh, come, major. We both know what an excellent job your government has done of marginalizing the very idea of visitors from outer space."

Ecks missed a step puzzling over this.

"What do you mean?"

McAfee never broke stride, continuing up the corridor at a steady pace. He did turn to look at Ecks as he walked, but this only deepened the kindly uncle impression. "Well, you should start by understanding this. None of us ever intended to let you know we were here."

Ecks didn't like the sound of this. "Who do you mean?"

McAfee gestured toward the imagined sky.

"You know, visitors," he made little quotes marks with his index and middle fingers, "aliens, beings from other worlds, little green men. There are quite a lot of us out there, you know."

Ecks was aware of this, but he still played the part of the rube.

"There are?"

"Oh, yes," McAfee said. "But up until recently, you humans were so very primitive. It wasn't so long ago you strutted around thinking sharpened sticks were the height of advanced weaponry. There wouldn't have been any point in coming here then. It's far too much work to develop a planet that doesn't have any infrastructure. We learned our lesson on that one long ago."

"But then you learned to fly. You built your airplanes, made them better, and you flew higher and farther. Fifty years ago, we didn't have to worry. You never flew high enough to spot us. Now? Well, let's just say it's getting awkward."

Ecks nodded, but he'd already had several years to get used to the idea of extraterrestrial races. McAfee continued with his history.

"It all started to change with the war. There were more planes in the sky. Thanks to a few nosy parkers, your technology improved by leaps and bounds. When you exploded your first atomic bomb, we started to get worried, especially because so many different nations were involved in the conflict. It would be a different story if the Germans hadn't hated communism so much. Imagine if the Germans and the Russians had been on the same side for the entire war."

Ecks didn't have to imagine it. He'd already done so many times.

"Well, when the war ended, we all breathed a sigh of relief. But our relief didn't last very long because as soon as you were done with one war, you started preparing for another. Four years after the end of the war, the Russians exploded their own bomb. We couldn't have atom bombs on both sides of the table."

"Why didn't you intervene?" Ecks asked, already sure he knew the answer.

"We did, of course," McAfee said blandly. "That's really why we're here now. As a planet, the greatest danger facing the Earth is a lack of good leadership. As that is our speciality, and as we always seem to need more territory, we saw it as a good fit. We petitioned the others into letting us give it a try."

"We were planning to do things a bit on the sly, sneak in and make changes without anyone noticing. There's a number of us in Congress now, as well as in state positions across the country. The same is true of the Soviet Union where many members of the Politburo have been replaced by our people. We're in a good position to make out presence known now. We're hoping that the coup, when it comes, will be completely bloodless."

They arrived at the same door Clarence had slammed to lock Ecks and company in on the way down. McAfee extended his arm and lengthened it until he could reach a button ten feet over their heads. Ecks felt sheepish when the senator returned the limb to its normal length.

"We were quite surprised when you gave up," McAfee mused, referring to the door. "We had to change our plans to track you down. We really thought you'd find the button."

"What would have happened then?" Ecks asked.

The door opened and they started to climb the stairs.

"Oh, we were always going to pick you off one by one, but in the end, you were the only one we could catch. As far as I know, your friends are still lost down there. But I'm straying off topic. We were discussing how we happened to come here. This is where it gets awkward."

"Things heated up with those crashes in New Mexico, Roswell and Socorro, then Aztec. That led to you learning about the Greys. After that, everyone up there started to worry about being noticed."

"But rather than expose our visits and preparing for our arrival, you decided to cover it all up. Even after the crashes were reported in the newspapers, your government managed to suppress it. They even came up with a way to do it that we never would've imagined."

"What was that?" Ecks asked, already knowing the answer.

"You made the very idea of Earth being visited by men from outer space something to be ridiculed."

Arthur Ecks considered the observation.

"They were afraid that people would panic."

McAfee's smile grew wide with genuine wonder;

"So they panic. They'll calm down once they get used to the idea."

Ecks blushed a little.

"I guess we were afraid it would turn out like *The War of the Worlds*."

McAfee smiled at the memory.

"The Orson Welles broadcast? Never laughed so hard in my life."

"You heard it?"

"We all did! It was brilliant! It was very realistic. But you need to look at the world you've made, and recognize how big a mistake it was to do that."

"What do you mean?"

They reached the top of the stairs. McAfee paused to catch his breath.

"You made it impossible for anyone, no matter how reliable their character might be, to report having contact with extraterrestrials. That's one reason I don't care if you report us to the newspapers."

"What do you think would happen if you told the world that a well-known member of the Senate was actually a shapeshifting alien from Antares? What would they think if you told them that Congress was populated by aliens? That my true form has more in common with the locust than any mammal?"

Ecks had no answer. "I take your point. Most people think something is fishy with Congress anyway."

"And why would you personally do such a thing, major? You'd sacrifice your anonymity to a lost cause. It would be the end of working in secret. And the questions! There would be so many questions you'd have to answer. In the end, you'd just be another nut case. Your own government would disown you. They'd be forced to conclude that you cracked under the pressure of your work."

They came to a junction and McAfee led him down the right fork. The strip light in the ceiling faded out behind them.

"We just want you to know one thing, Major. We mean you no harm. This is a nice place and we have no plans to interfere with your development. We're very hands-off as conquerors go. Most of your people will never even know we're here. Personally, I think we'll make very good neighbors."

Ecks shook his head, now truly confused.

"There's one thing I still don't get, and it's got nothing to do with you guys coming here to conquer the planet. You seem like a pretty reasonable guy for a bug, but you spend all your time in the Senate waving blank sheets of paper and accusing the State Department of being full of commies and fairies. Why all the hard-nosed stuff?"

If Ecks was looking for it, he might have noticed the blush running down McAfee's neck. It wasn't a natural response for a bug. McAfee made a guttural sound that wasn't remotely human.

"There are two entirely separate reasons, Major. First of all, thousands of years ago, we had our own dalliance with communism. As a result of that time, we still find communism abhorrent. Communism presents a few difficulties for anyone who tries to excel-"

Ecks understood suddenly. "You mean get rich."

The bug accepted the correction with equanimity. "Just so."

"And the fairies?"

The blush grew bright red as it rose to envelope his face. This time, Arthur Ecks did notice, probably because it was accompanied by a stammer that hadn't been present until then.

"Our sexuality is limited to our queens and consorts. As with any insect population, these are insignificant numbers. In our native form, the rest of us have no outlet for such...feelings."

McAfee turned his shoulder from Ecks, hiding his face as he continued.

"But though we aren't breeders, that changes when we assume the identity of another race. In human form, we have the same drives you do, in all those marvelous permutations."

Ecks was less shocked than utterly dumbfounded.

"In human form, we're capable of engaging in sexual acts with others of our kind in human shape or...," McAfee's embarrassment seemed to reach its zenith, "with like-minded humans."

McAfee paused to collect himself.

"But since we aren't breeders, and since we take the form of human males... it's an absolute waste of time being a woman on this planet..., we look for others who are amenable to alternate couplings..."

McAfee trailed off, leaving his ultimate meaning unexpressed. It took a while before Ecks understood the implications. "So, the hearings..."

"...are essentially a dating service."

Ecks was aghast. "The whole committee is made up of bugs???"

McAfee nodded, "The committee, about a quarter of the Senate, and two-thirds of the House. We haven't infiltrated the executive branch yet, but it's only a matter of time. We've been a little gun-shy about replacing Truman."

Arthur Ecks had to stop. This was too much to process.

"I thought you said you didn't mean us any harm?"

McAfee brought his hands up to protest.

"Oh, we don't! But we do need to make sure the political climate is right. Millions of Antareans will be arriving over the next few years. Earth is going to see a population explosion unlike anything you could ever imagine. We're just part of the first wave, but the second is arriving very soon."

Arthur Ecks was no stranger to bad news, but this made him ache.

"How soon?"

Then Joe McAfee did something Ecks would have never expected. It was an entirely human action, and it was something he couldn't have anticipated from a being who'd journeyed light years across the dead reaches of empty space.

McAfee looked at his watch.

Then he reacted much like the White Rabbit in *Alice in Wonderland* had.

"Oh my! Look at the time! The fleet arrives in about an hour and a half. I have things to do, Major! I have a whole invasion to set in motion."

McAfee looked up from his watch, adding, "You're welcome to come along, of course. You've been excellent company so far, and I hope we remain friends after it's all over."

Arthur Ecks looked down at his feet, feeling like his toes had turned to lead. He could lift his heels, but getting those toes to move was going to be a problem. He looked back at McAfee, burdened by the sudden weight of despair.

"You'll conquer us without ever firing a shot."

McAfee nodded his head, smiling his most disarmingly smile.

"If all goes according to plan. Really, we mean you no harm. We just want a safe place to raise our young, just like you, and while America was founded with wonderful ideals, we think we can make it even better. We want to be your friends, not your conquerors. We'll start businesses, we'll join your chamber of commerce, maybe a few lodges, I've been wondering what it would be like to be an Elk. We'll be no different from anyone else and you'll never even know. We'll just fit in until our numbers grow enough to safely reveal our presence."

Ecks' mouth had gone dry. "And then?"

McAfee laid a gentle hand on Ecks' shoulder.

"Who knows? Now come on, it's just a little further to the lift. We'll take my car. And don't be so glum! There's really nothing to worry about."

Ecks shook his head, unable to believe what was happening. The Earth would be conquered without even mounting a resistance.

In his frustration, Ecks absently kicked a mound of dust, scattering a million motes into the air. He inhaled a few thousand and violently sneezed.

"Bless you," said the Senator from Antares.

At that moment, Arthur Ecks believed he really meant it.

Chapter 26 - Several Clarences

The driver of the taxi was a tall sandy-haired man with a wealth of freckles. He wore a captain's cap far enough back on his forehead to reveal the point of a faint widow's peak. He'd taken off his jacket in deference to the heat, rolling his shirt sleeves up over his elbows. The name 'Clarence' was embroidered over the left breast pocket of his shirt. He was, all things considered, rather ordinary looking, with a Midwestern simplicity that came through in his placid smile and gentle eyes.

"So where will I be taking you gentlemen today?"

Hynek sank deep into the passenger side divot of the back seat, leaving Ruppelt to answer.

"Um," Ruppelt said, reconsidering his plan to proceed directly to the National Mall, "why don't we just drive around for a while." Feeling this needed more, he fabricated a cover story to go with the request.

"This is my friend's first time in DC," he added with a nod toward Hynek, "I'd like to show him around a bit, see the sights. Then we'll have you drop us off somewhere along the Mall."

Clarence nodded, "A little sight-seeing it is."

Clarence eased the taxi away from the curb, then waited for a break in traffic before pulling out onto K Street. They passed the parks at McPherson and Farragut Squares, taking the long way around the roundabout at Washington Circle. Clarence exited the circle on 23rd St NW, heading south toward Foggy Bottom and the Potomac.

The men in the back seat said nothing as they pretended to be seeing the city for the first time, and unlike most cabbies, Clarence left them to their silence until they neared the ring road at the Lincoln Memorial.

"Is this your first time in DC?" Clarence finally asked.

"No," Ruppelt replied, "I've visited several times, but I've always been busy with work. Thought it'd be nice to just get out and see the city for once." This fit the cover story and was almost true.

"Same for me," Hynek added, "always working."

"So this is just vacation then?" Clarence prompted, "Because I'd swear I saw you two testify before the McAfee committee just this morning."

This observation had an electrifying effect on the men in the back seat. Hynek's eyes went wide, then fearful. Ruppelt fought to remain calm, but the comment had clearly caught him off guard. Nonetheless, he managed to fight down the surge of panic it triggered.

"Well," Ruppelt said jovially, "you've just shattered my illusions about taxi drivers. I always thought you guys spent most of your time glued to the seat of your cabs. Glad to hear you get out once in a while."

Clarence laughed good-naturedly.

"Oh, I'm not a taxi driver, Captain Ruppelt, at least not most of the time."

Hynek glanced toward the cabbie's license posted up by the rear view mirror. The man in the picture wasn't the man driving the car. He nudged Ruppelt with his shoulder, pointing with his chin. Ruppelt nodded. The name on the license wasn't Clarence, either.

"Then what do you do, normally?" Ruppelt read the name on the driver's pocket in the rear view mirror, "Clarence, is it?"

"Yes," said Clarence, "Clarence will be fine. Normally, Captain, I work as a kind of liaison for Senator McAfee. I was at the hearing this morning, though I forgive you for not noticing. You probably had other things on your mind."

"You know," Allen Hynek said, looking out the window at the empty lawn, "I feel like maybe we can walk from here. Care to join me, Ed?"

"Yeah, that'd be great," Ruppelt said. "Say, Clarence, could you drop us over by the Reflecting Pool. I think we'd like to take a stroll."

Clarence's smile reflected back in the rear view mirror.

"I'm sorry, Doctor Hynek. I'm afraid that won't be possible."

Clarence pushed a button on the dashboard that made the windows turn black. A separator rose from the back of the front seat, cutting off all contact between the driver and his passengers. These precautions prevented both men from seeing the hole open in the sky above the cab. Antarean technology took care of the rest.

The few witnesses walking along the edge of the Pool were distracted by a bright flash of light that drew their eyes toward the Memorial at its western end of the lawn. There, for those watching, Abraham Lincoln crossed and uncrossed his legs. When they looked back, the cab was gone, but there wasn't anything unusual in that. Taxis were always coming and going.

**

Donald Keyhoe sniffed the air, detecting a strange note in its symphony of smells. It was a different kind of smell, but he couldn't put a finger on what it was. He felt fuzzy in mind and body, although not with the bilious ache of a hangover. His body felt vaguely abused, and he couldn't recall any reason he should feel that way. It came to him that he was lying down, on a hard surface with no give to it. It clearly wasn't his hotel bed, which had been several degrees too soft for his liking. With eyes still closed, he rolled over and heard a voice.

"Looks like Keyhoe is waking up."

Keyhoe found this satisfying on some level. He was waking up, and not just in the sense of becoming conscious. While he was asleep, he'd dreamt about his situation in great detail, realizing as a result of those dreams, that the world he knew wasn't the world he was living in. There were hidden secrets that had been there all along. But he was wise to them now.

For years, he'd believed that the government was covering up the truth about UFOs, and though he wasn't sure when it had happened, it was becoming increasingly clear that sometime during the day, he'd stumbled onto his first real clue. There was something fishy about the McAfee committee's UFO hearing and he had a suspicion that he now knew what it was.

That certainty lasted only until he opened his eyes. Once his eyes were open, Donald Keyhoe realized he didn't know a goddamned thing after all.

***

Lincoln La Paz was already sitting up by the time Keyhoe started stirring. He still felt the effects of the narcotic dulling his senses, but when confronted by the sight before him, he was glad it was there. If he'd seen the creature without the numbing effect of the drug, the resulting heart attack would have killed him.

The creature was enormous, but for all that size, it didn't seem very heavy. It had more limbs than human beings, and those limbs were clearly intended for inhuman needs. He tried to count them, but had to start over when the creature turned to reveal a dozen more spindly extremities. As to its numerous legs, he lost count when he hit double digits. These were gnarled and crooked, flecked with a mottled texture like the lichened branches of an ancient oak. But though his initial impression was arboreal, La Paz was more influenced by the way it transported itself, taking stiff unjointed steps, like an insect.

It had a flat triangular head that reminded him of a shovel blade with eyes and antenna. The head had the same mottled texture as the limbs. Its eyes, of which there were thankfully only two, were set at the sides of the head and spaced so far apart that any blind spot must be directly in front of or behind it.

The creature, whatever it was, seemed to agree. Its face was turned directly toward him, but judging by its lack of interest, La Paz had to think he was in one of those blind spots.

His hypothesis was confirmed when he made an involuntary shuddering sound of disgust. As the thing turned one eye toward him, he saw that it was a pupil-less brown, deep enough to convey an impression of fertile intelligence. The eye blinked once, its golden membranes converging vertically, then the entire figure began to change, as some legs disappeared while others grew thicker as its mottled appearance assumed a soft uniform surface of human flesh .

For the second time, La Paz was grateful for the fading influence of the narcotic. The creature had transmogrified into something entirely different, and the process was alarmingly swift. When it was complete, Lincoln La Paz

165

found himself staring into the freckled features of a tall sandy-haired man in his late twenties. He wore a tan summer suit and a pair of brown cap toes that complemented both his complexion and the suit.

"Wakey, wakey, Dr La Paz," Clarence said.

***

Unlike La Paz, there wasn't anyone around when Allen Hynek and Ed Ruppelt were let out of the cab. Both men felt a vague sense of being separated from the influence of gravity. They felt it as a lightening, as if a weight had left their bodies when the taxi left the ground. But beyond that, they felt nothing out of the ordinary, and saw nothing due to the blacked-out windows of the cab. The suspension settled slightly when the cab came to rest, but then there was only silence.

The suspension moved when Clarence got out, and they heard the door slam behind him. Since they'd clearly been kidnapped, neither man expected the doors to work. By the time Ruppelt tried the door, the driver was long gone. But much to his surprise, the latch lifted and the door opened. But despite this apparent path to freedom, neither man was especially eager to leave the confines of the cab.

It wasn't that there was any physical impediment that prevented them from moving about. It was simply that, there in the hold of what was surely an alien spaceship, there was too much to take in all at once and trying to absorb more would only complicate matters.

For the moment, it was enough of a stretch to accept that, after years of rumor, speculation, and denial, they were standing on the floor of the very thing they had both feared might be a fiction. It was like standing on the Moon, or having tea with the Cheshire Cat. Standing on the landing deck of the ship was a reality that neither man considered possible.

Ruppelt thought giddily that it all might be a joke, that this ship was just the result of advanced human engineering. But the more he looked around, the more it became patently obvious that this wasn't the work of human hands.

The cab was sitting in the center of an enormous multi-sided enclosure that was constructed of a rusty red metal that'd been cut into a variety of triangular shapes. Vast I-beams arced and crisscrossed over their heads. Hynek chose just one beam to follow from end to end, but it was an impossible task and he lost it when it ran under and through a dozen others that were exact copies of the one he was tracking.

Everywhere he looked, the beams were covered in some kind of writing. The ceiling, so high over their heads that he could barely make it out, was a maze of hieroglyphics, of pictograms so alien that ancient Egyptians would walk away shaking their heads.

Both men turned at the sound of a door being drawn open. A moment later, half a dozen men paraded through the door, coming straight for them. As the men drew closer, Ruppelt and Hynek could discern a certain sameness to them.

They were all tall and freckled, with limp sandy hair that was just long enough to lightly brush their foreheads. Making matters worse, they were all dressed in the same tan summer suit and they were all wearing the same chocolate cap-toes. For all intents and purposes, they were exact copies of the same man.

When the first one came within arms reach of Hynek, the whole line came to a halt, then split to take positions to either side of the leader. Six Clarences smiled at the Earthlings in unison as the leader stepped forward to greet them.

"Welcome to the Light of Antares," Clarence said, "honored men of Earth."

"Welcome," said all the other Clarences.

For a long moment, the Earthlings were stumped for a proper reply.

"Well, shit, Dorothy," Ed Ruppelt finally said. Unable to keep the awe out of his voice, he added, "I guess we're not in Kansas anymore."

Chapter 27 - An Otherwise Dull Day

Though the name has changed in recent years to honor the memory of a famous movie cowboy, Washington National Airport still lies along the same fat spit of land, jutting out into the Potomac River like a deformed almond in a pool of mud. It has three crisscrossing runways that form a triangle in the center before each meanders off in its own way toward the reliable safety net of a water landing. The terminal is set a short distance back from the westernmost landing strip and inadequate parking is a sacred tradition still honored to the present day.

Air traffic is controlled from a single tower south of the terminals, but the day when that tower would be an efficiently run technological marvel, capable of displaying arrivals and departures on electronic screens, was years in the future. Another thing that lay in the future was the strike, during the reign of that same cowboy president, that would cost ninety percent of those controllers their jobs.

The tower did have a recently installed radar system, but the system was only a slight improvement over the ones that had warned Londoners of approaching bombers during the Blitz. The radar was a nice feature, but the sight of an ATC man tracking an incoming plane through a pair of field binoculars was still common sight as well as being standard operating procedure.

Flying as a means of travel had grown more popular since the end of the war, as new passenger airlines tapped into the ready supply of bomber pilots left unemployed by the cessation of hostilities.

In addition to the pilots, a new generation of passengers had come home and many now viewed air travel as a favorable alternative for transporting their families on trips deemed too lengthy for a Sunday drive. Naturally, this increase in volume had placed a heavy burden on the existing infrastructure, making the demand for new airports and runways a critical need for a country lost in the rapture of an unprecedented economic boom.

The control room at Washington Air Route Traffic Control Center had felt the pinch as much as any airport on the Eastern seaboard. At any hour of the day, the control room was amply staffed by tired men watching display screens, reading numbers that were meaningless to the untrained eye. This was all done so they'd be able to relay instructions to the pilots circling in the summer clouds that had followed the Potomac up from Chesapeake Bay.

Preoccupied with the performance of an increasingly stressful job, none of the six men in the control room would notice the muted ruby glow that came through the crack under the door to the radar room. Because that door was closed, the ATC men also missed the materialization of two figures, one male and one female, as they coalesced out of thin air.

The figures were insubstantial at first, like smoke passing through a screen, but they began to find solid form as their ghostly silhouettes drifted through the complex array of electronic wiring. They drifted on those spectral winds until they found open spots where they could become corporeal without their bodies becoming a physical part of the system.

If you were a *warak shu*, the process was normal enough, but something happened to the equipment as the insubstantial bodies moved through the racks of tubes and wires that housed the functional parts of the radar system.

Suddenly, the displays in the control room came alive, as dozens of unidentified objects appeared at the outer limit of the system's range. All of the objects were flying at very high speeds, an anomaly the tired men at the consoles, their nerves long shattered by commissary coffee, could hardly fail to notice.

***

Having served in both the Pacific and European theaters, Abel Corbett had passed through dozens of airports in his time. During the active period when he'd flown in combat, he'd seen what he believed were all the possible ways a man might face the prospect of imminent demise.

Some became obnoxiously boisterous, as if a wild display of spirits might remind the world of their existence. The behavior of these men was generally a good indicator of how they might act after drinking too many boilermakers. These men would stomp around, slapping buddies on the back, getting in stupid fights, and jackassing around.

The more spiritually inclined would seek a quiet space to clear their heads before facing the flack, beseeching the Almighty to grant them one more day of raining death on the faceless population below. Corbett considered these men hypocrites and he would occasionally express a profound distaste for the sanctimonious belief that the lives of the men in the air were somehow more important than the lives of those on the ground. He made no friends among the members of this group because he rather liked killing, though he preferred doing the work in person.

Those were the extremes, but he'd found that most men facing the prospect of their own demise were simply somber. Any guilt they felt for their actions was rationalized by the fear of what might happen if they failed. Both fear and guilt were mitigated by the laws of probability that governed flack distribution. Few liked what they were doing, but they had their orders. They'd lost comrades, and each hoped in his own small way, that bombing the bejesus out of an unseen enemy five miles below would make up for that loss.

Most of the airports Abel Corbett had seen were rude stations erected in urgent need. Those runways might be in a wheat field in Burgundy or on a rock in the Pacific so remote that even birds refused to visit. Now, as the world moved further away from shooting wars into cooler conflicts of ideology and economics, the airports were beginning to change. People smiled occasionally. They traveled for pleasure. They took vacations. They visited family.

But whatever reason brought them to the airport, they still moved with the same urgency as those men who'd taken to the sky in the hope of saving the world. And they still had the same hope that they'd be allowed to return intact, to park their bodies between the thighs of a good woman within easy reach of a cold beer.

As Abel Corbett strode along the sidewalk in front of the terminal, he cursed every one of those brave men who'd returned home to raise families that took vacations that brought them to this airport in the hot muggy hell of a DC summer. It seemed to be a blatant act of violence, that these people had come to Washington National for the express purpose of creating an impenetrable wall of flesh that persisted in its effort to move in the wrong direction.

Upon arrival, Corbett and Sands had wasted a good twenty minutes trying to locate a parking space. Failing in this effort, they were forced out into the fast buck hinterland that had grown up around the terminal. They waited another ten minutes for a terminal bus, then proceeded to stop at every patch of paved or unpaved earth that was capable of parking a few sedans for an exorbitant daily charge. By the time they were dropped at the terminal, both men were in foul moods and as eager to get inside as the flood of arrivals was to get out.

Being smaller and easier to push around, Wally Sands was unable to elude the current when a tour group from Minneapolis came pouring through the doors like a herd of lost bison. Like a leaf in a stream, he was forced back out onto the curb where the taxis waited like crocodiles eyeballing a herd of wildebeest.

Corbett managed to skirt this hazard by racing through the revolving doors, accelerating the great sheets of mounted glass to dangerous speeds. Upon his exit, Corbett plowed straight into the back of a fashionably dressed mother with three young girls in tow. The woman, apparently accustomed to being obeyed, was busy instructing her porter in the ancient art of luggage transport, all the while maintaining a taut psychic leash on her girls.

Frantic to get to the control tower where he expected to get a better look at the incoming ships, Corbett was in a great hurry. He was anxious, but not in the way one might be if hurrying for a departing flight. Abel Corbett was anxious in the way a man with a worm in his brain is anxious when he realizes that he'll be brutally punished for perceived dawdling. In the grip of this distraction, he plowed straight into Maisie Neill Ångström, knocking her onto, and very nearly over, a cart stacked high with suitcases. Fearing the repercussions from his worm, Corbett didn't apologize, forging on like a fullback plunging toward a goal line.

In the aftermath of the collision, Maisie Neill Ångström couldn't imagine what the hell had hit her. She found herself on her back, gazing up into the dark features of the porter who was biting his lip in an effort not to laugh. While she processed this affront to her dignity, she grew increasingly aware of an infusion of cool air forcing its way to places cool air had no business being.

Lifting her head, she found that the collision had lifted her hem to mid-thigh, exposing three inches of a lacy half-slip and a generous expanse of cocoa-colored nylon. The nylons concealed what even her husband would admit were still a pretty decent pair of legs. Maisie brushed the skirt down to mid-shin and rose on unsteady heels. Upon achieving verticality, she had expected to find the man who'd bowled her over waiting to apologize.

Instead, she saw only Abel Corbett's back as it receded into the throng at a pace that would soon take him out of reach. Despite being the mother of two willful daughters, as well as a little angel sent from God, Maisie wasn't in the habit of raising her voice. But, given the circumstances, this inhibition was easily overcome.

"You there!" Maisie cried in the kind of towering voice a Roman senator might use to address an amphitheater of robed republicans. "In the black suit! You stop this instant!"

Abel Corbett heard the woman yell and knew she was yelling for him. He had an extensive history of rude behavior, with most of the incidents occurring before the worm took up residence. As a result, he'd discovered that it was often easier to bull his way through a situation than to negotiate. Another man might say it was easier to beg forgiveness than ask for permission, but Corbett thought both approaches were weak. Either way, it was an error in judgment because he'd failed to recognize the dangers presented by the Ångström girls.

When their mother went down, the psychic leash that bound the girls was snapped like a frayed length of twine. The girls were hot and sweaty. Less than an hour out of their hotel room, they were already bored with travel and ready for something more active than sitting quietly while their mother berated porters.

Having witnessed the unwarranted assault upon their mother's person, the girls responded like a crack commando unit. Invisible to adult eyes, the girls slithered through the crowd, keeping low to the ground because at ages seven, eight, and ten, they was no other option. Corbett, his progress slowed by the dense crowd, had no idea of the danger keeping up from behind.

Blonde, with Shirley Temple curls, Bubbles was the youngest of the three. Standing just inside the doors, she had witnessed the assault from its inception and was first to arrive. Bubbles wrapped her legs around Corbett's right ankle and her arms around one long shin. Holding on tight to prevent being dislodged, Bubbles sank sharp new teeth into the tender meat of Corbett's calf.

Corbett screamed like a debutante who's just seen another girl wearing the dress she'd paid top dollar for.

Stormy, the oldest, slid her hand up under Corbett's jacket to grab him by the belt. In the normal course of things, this action would've had little effect as Stormy weighed about as much as a B-flat clarinet. But in catching Corbett by surprise, her hold became a destabilizing influence that threw him off-balance when the *coup de grâce* arrived.

Tomboy Molly finished him off, putting her full weight into a flying kick that bent the back of Corbett's un-Bubbled knee and drove him to earth. Corbett went down like a stallion hitting a trip wire, his kneecap cracking audibly on the tiled floor.

For the next few seconds, the girls went at him like a pack of hyenas, punching and kicking for all they were worth. Actually, this was only partly true. Bubbles and Stormy pretty much stayed out of the fray, leaving it to Molly to administer the bulk of the punishment. Molly was much better at that sort of thing.

Meanwhile, back at the parental unit, Maisie's anger had been temporarily overwhelmed by her horror at the public conduct of her girls. But that anger flared anew when Wally Sands, having fought his way free of Minnesota, threw an errant hip into Maisie's behind that sent her sprawling a second time. For this second pratfall, she went face first, taking the tower of suitcases with her.

When Maisie rose the second time, any inhibitions she'd previously espoused were gone. She was red-faced with rage, and though she wouldn't become aware of the damage for another hour, she now sported a ruined perm to complement the run in her left stocking. Moving more rapidly than many would believe possible, she caught Wally Sands by the collar and yanked back hard enough to take his legs out from under him.

Acting upon the instruction of their worms, Corbett and Sands lashed out at their attackers. It was their second error in less than a minute, and very nearly, a fatal one. Coming from a different species and culture, the worms had little experience with the penalties for assaulting women and children in public. The magnitude of this oversight soon became eminently apparent.

By this time, everyone within a fifty foot radius was watching, and a dozen men had seen what happened. A couple of pacifists tried to pull the girls off of Corbett, but soon discovered it was like trying to extract rival tomcats from a pillow case. None of the men offered to help Maisie back to her feet, but they were more than willing to kick the living crap out of the black-suited men they'd seen assaulting the cream of American womanhood.

It was an ugly incident and it wasn't over until the airport police arrived.

Maisie, crimson with embarrassment, wasn't available to make the formal complaint. As quietly as she could, she recalled her ninjas, patted her hair back into place, and sharply instructed the gawping porter to get her a taxi. Hailing taxis wasn't really part of his job, but after seeing what a woman from Wisconsin was capable of when riled, the porter did as he was instructed.

***

172

As previously stated, the tower at Washington National was a far cry from the modern wonder it would one day be. Still, as the airport itself was only a decade old, it wasn't bad for its time. Rising a hundred feet above terminal level, the tower presented a 360-degree view of the surrounding sky. This view was further extended by a futuristic version of a bay window that displayed a wider swath of sky than any flat pane could afford.

The interior of the tower was manned by a dozen men who sat at gray metal consoles with eyes that strayed nervously between the massive windows and the blinking green displays on their radar screens. Occasionally one would rise from his seat and walk over to the window where he'd bring his binoculars up to eye level. Then he would peer through his lenses until spotting the errant plane that had drawn him from his chair. Once satisfied, he would nod and return to his seat, where he would remain until the next crisis.

All the while, as their eyes strayed from screen to window and back, these men would spew the incessant chatter of a juggler with more balls in the air than he can reasonably control.

Stogie Meredith had run radar since 1944, learning his trade in the last year of the war. Back then he was a young man with a full head of hair and 20-20 vision. The radar equipment of the day was flakier than French pastry, more prone to outright failure and false readings. Even now, the equipment was so sensitive that no one was allowed to smoke in the radar room, a stipulation that kept Stogie's Macanudos confined to his breast pocket until quitting time.

Seven years after the war, Stogie's eyes were starting to go, a decline he was trying to delay with a new set of horn-rims. His hair was thin around the temples and almost nonexistent at the crown, but Stogie had more experience with radar units than all but a few men in the world. With the improved equipment, he'd worked out most of the kinks and experience had taught him when a bogie was a false reading.

The false readings came in two varieties. The first was known as anomalous propagation. These appeared when something caused the radar signals to bend earthward so that objects on the ground were detected by mistake.

The second type were known as radar angels. These were airborne objects such as birds or weather phenomena that reflected the radar signals to create ghost targets. There were visible differences between anomalous propagation and radar angels and solid objects. The ghosts appeared diffuse and rather blobby, where real aircraft generated a solid signal known as a strong point return.

The half dozen bogies that appeared on Stogie's screen were definitely strong point returns, even if the speeds being reported were absurd.

Stogie reached for his unlit Macanudo and started to call for the shift chief, but other voices beat him to it.

"Anybody else seeing this?"

"We got bogies!"

"What the hell are those?"

"They came outta nowhere!"

Stogie looked around the room to find that every radar display was awash with tiny green blips that darted about in rough formation, at speeds that were impossible to believe.

Jim Maddox, the shift supervisor, was leaning over Zack Beezer's shoulder when the cry went up. He was on the mic in an instant.

"Unidentified craft tracking 030 mark 20, please identify yourself. You are flying in restricted air space."

Maddox released the key on the mic, waiting for the response that would never come. After a moment, he tried again with the same result. His eyes strayed back to Beezer's screen as a shiver of panic ran up his spine. As he waited, the blips continued to multiply. When a third attempt yielded nothing, he felt a sick thrill come into his throat. He swallowed his trepidation with an audible gulp.

"Someone get me Andrews. We need to report a UFO."

Stogie pulled the cigar out of his pocket to emphasize his point.

"Technically, chief, we need to report a whole mess of UFOs."

Chapter 28 - Une Nuit d'Amour

John Haste soon developed a few strategies for keeping the tiny woman with the tiny dog from walking away. Keeping her close was of paramount importance, because based what on she'd said, Desiree might represent a short cut to a Pulitzer for Haste, or a charge of treason for Cranston. Based on what she'd said so far, Haste could see both outcomes as real possibilities.

First and foremost, he managed to make friends with Mister Poopoo. This wasn't as simple as it might sound. The Pekingese was an irritable little beast, but as it turned out, the savory taste of chilidog that still clung to Haste's fingers was a pretty decent icebreaker. As Desiree kept him on a strict vegetarian diet, Mister Poopoo was starved for protein. As a result, the dog wasted no time, slathering the reporter's hands with doggy spit as he sought and found every detectable trace of oil and flavor. As thanks for the snack, Mister Poopoo let Haste clumsily pat his head without nipping at his fingers.

Being from Texas, John Haste was accustomed to bigger dogs, but he was relieved to discover that some of the same things worked on the urban variety. Haste had grown up just east of the border with New Mexico, spending the greater part of his youth riding the eastern ridge of the Llano Estacado. Back then, he had a big blue tick hound named Jake who came along to chase prairie dogs and a rambunctious Appaloosa mare named Kitty. Those were long idle days, mostly spent looking for shade in the barren waste, but as a result, Haste supposed he knew dogs and horses about as well as any man.

His second epiphany lay in the discovery that Desiree Blythe liked hearing him talk. It didn't seem to matter what he said. He could point out an elm that needed pruning and she would express fascination at his knowledge of such things, declaring in that ditzy voice that the care of elm trees was a subject she knew absolutely nothing about. He could express admiration for one of the newer sedans coming out of Detroit, marveling at how they seemed to get bigger every year, and she would say that she had ridden in many such cars and always felt small and lost in those roomy back seats.

It took almost two hours for John Haste to realize that this little woman, buxom and pretty though she might be, was also desperately lonely. By some trick of intuition, he said little of the secret he'd hinted at, using it only when her attention showed signs of flagging. Then he would bring it up again in an indirect way, baiting her with it like a horse fly teasing a trout until he had her back on the line.

Though she hid it well, Desiree knew what was going on. She could tell that John Haste was digging for more dirt on the general, so she didn't exactly open up, essentially keeping his attention in much the same way he was keeping hers.

The reporter was pleasant company, and Mister Poopoo liked him, which was more than one could say for Neal Cranston. And, since this was one of those rare days that Neal was scheduled to spend with his wife, her night was entirely free of commitments.

She liked that the Texan was enough of a gentleman not to waste her time making veiled references to her bosom, and she was even pretty sure he wasn't running lascivious eyes over her curves when she wasn't looking. She was well aware that most men liked to do this, albeit surreptitiously. It made them think they were being sneaky, but most gave themselves away with a muttered 'Golly!' or 'Hot damn!', and that was just plain tiresome. Even her general, who was an older man, experienced these moments, and was only able to overcome his gaffes through acts of extreme generosity.

When John Haste wasn't looking at her directly, it was only because he was looking around for some new item to catch her fancy. More than anything, she liked that he was willing to work so hard to keep her entertained. They strolled around town for the longest time, occasionally sitting on a bench to rest, but mostly just aimlessly rambling through the many parks scattered around the city. A light breeze came up as the sun fell to the horizon, bringing cool air off the river, and that drew them down to the water's edge. Running out of words, they sat in silence, watching the river flow as a waning moon rose in the twilit sky.

It was Mister Poopoo who brought up the subject of dinner. This meant that Desiree had to take him back to the apartment, and might've ended the evening had Haste not offered to walk her home. The reason he gave for his offer was that even though Congress was in summer recess, there were other dangers on the streets of the capital. It was a lame excuse and both of them knew it, but Desiree said yes anyway.

Again, it might have ended there. After all, they weren't that far from the apartment. But along the way they discovered an Italian café with garden seating, no diners, and a motivated waiter who offered to look after Mister Poopoo's culinary needs as well as their own.

The offer led to dinner under a striped umbrella. With their table framed by great coils of wisteria, a sliver of moonlight shone over the rooftops to fall across Desiree's cheek as twilight deepened into night. Haste ordered angel hair with a carbonara sauce. Desiree, ravenous after a day of walking, opted for the veal. They finished one bottle of Chianti, and shared a look of complicity when they ordered the second. Dessert was a tiramisu that tasted like a chocolate cloud.

By the time they reclaimed Mister Poopoo, it was almost eleven o'clock, but neither wanted the night to end. Mister Poopoo was another matter. His feet were sore from the sidewalks and his little legs had walked so far that it might take a week to recover. With the prospect of spending more time in the company of Desiree Blythe, Haste was more than willing to carry the beast.

So they walked along the river with Mister Poopoo resting his head on Haste's shoulder. Desiree shivered, as the night grew cool enough for Haste to loan her his jacket. He handed it over, hoping his afternoon sweat had dried enough not to embarrass him.

They both laughed when Desiree put it on. Her hands were almost a foot short of the cuffs and the hem reached her calves. It looked so silly that she handed it back. The problem was solved when she leaned in close, saying she'd be fine if he didn't mind wrapping his arm around her shoulder. Haste said this would be no trouble at all, bringing her inside the jacket and drawing her closer when her hand reached for his hip.

A block later, when he leaned down to bridge the gap that separated his lips from hers, he found her more than willing. Those lips, still redolent with Italian veal, parted to claim him, and her eyes opened wide as she stared up at the bare sliver of the waning moon. He was dismayed when she drew away, her sudden withdrawal wounding him like the loss of a vital organ.

But before he could apologize for a slight he hadn't committed, Desiree pointed up at the sky to ask.

"What do you think those are, Mr Haste?"

***

If Neal Cranston had been a Viking warrior, his battle-axe might have taken a different form. As it was the 20th century and such weapons were no longer in vogue, he was forced to be content with his wife of thirty-three years.

At sixty, Cranston was still in possession of the same flat hard belly he'd had at the Third Battle of Ypres and, if he was being honest, he expected the same of his women. At fifty-six and counting, having expressed six children from the sanctity of her womb, Geraldine Cranston no longer measured up to this ideal. To say that she'd put on weight was an exercise in understating something profoundly obvious.

It was also unsettling that his once-demure girl from Omaha had long since lost both her reticence and her innocence. While her husband was busy charging across the Pacific, Geraldine was left to tend the six children Cranston had fathered with diminishing enthusiasm. As far as Geraldine was concerned, in light of his prolonged absence, she'd earned the right to pack on a few pounds.

In the early years of their marriage, Cranston had dragged her from one posting to another, often requiring her to pick up and move on short notice. With each move, Geraldine left behind a group of friends that grew younger with every posting. When Neal finally made general, she informed him that she'd had enough. He could continue to move around all he wanted, but she'd done her time. From that point forward, she was staying put and her preference was to do so in Richmond, Virginia.

Richmond gave the family a much-needed home base. In Richmond, she found a crumbling antebellum mansion with fourteen rooms. The house had been a hotel during the Confederacy and clearly needed work, but Geraldine no longer fretted over the labor of others. She hired a host of skilled craftsmen and provided them with unstinting oversight. Over time, the hotel was transformed into something worthy of inclusion in Richmond's registry of historic sites.

It took more than three years, but at its end, every child had their own room, and Geraldine enjoyed the privacy of a southwestern suite that looked out over the tree-lined streets of Richmond, much as Zeus must have looked down on ancient Greece from the heights of Mount Olympus.

Richmond was a blessing for the general as well. Freed of the apron strings that once held him back, Cranston could again enjoy the company of women. He still moved from post to post, but with each move, his visits home grew less frequent. Geraldine's motivation for maintaining an attractive figure declined in direct ratio. In her isolation, she indulged her love of sweets, maintaining a dish of chocolates in every public room, and berating her children whenever she caught one picking at favorites that were rightfully hers.

They finally found an adequate compromise when Neal was posted to Andrews. The Air Force became an independent branch of the Armed Forces in '47 and, with that schism, Neal was permanently assigned to the flyboys.

Andrews Air Force Base, the installation tasked with protecting the capital from attack by air, was a two hour drive from Richmond. It was close enough that he could drive home on the rare occasions he was needed, and far enough away that he could maintain a mistress in DC without his wife getting wind of it.

Geraldine knew about the mistress, of course, and would've openly applauded the acquisition were it socially acceptable to do so. In retrospect, she only wished her husband had discovered this solution before the births of the youngest Cranstons. Alan and Bryan were two years apart and notoriously incorrigible.

On the weekend in question, Neal had planned to drive down on Friday night and stay through Sunday. But a tiff with Desiree and its subsequent reconciliation prevented his leaving on time. This led to going into work on Saturday morning with the idea of getting some paperwork done before the drudgery of the long drive. He called Geraldine to explain, reasoning that their anniversary wasn't until Sunday anyway. As Geraldine was unable to muster any enthusiasm for his visits at the best of times, the new plan was fine with her.

And everything was fine, at least until Captain Pierce brought him the latest budget numbers. The new budget showed some serious red in the area of facility maintenance, so rather than turning the job over to his subordinates, Cranston spent the afternoon tracking down the source of the bleeding. Somewhere along the way, day turned into night, and by the time Lieutenant Greenwalt brought him a plate of pot roast and new potatoes, the drive down to Richmond was a chore he was no longer willing to entertain. Checking the clock, he decided it was even too late for the shorter drive to Desiree's apartment.

And like the budget, that was something else he would soon have to face. The rewards of keeping a woman like Desiree had declined precipitously over the last year. She'd never told him her age, but he was reasonably sure she was over thirty. He was wary too, of a growing plumpness around the hips. He'd seen all too well the devastation that time and calories had wrought upon his once-slender Geraldine.

Making matters more complicated, Desiree had also dropped a few not-so-subtle hints that she would be amenable to formalizing the arrangement. Cranston didn't bother to ask what she meant by this. To his ears, it sounded like marriage, and any marriage would first require a divorce. Such a divorce, with its associated scandal and loss of financial wherewithal, would put an end to the career he'd nursed so assiduously for so long. Neal Cranston still harbored dreams of a position on the Joint Chiefs of Staff.

He'd just decided to head back to the quarters he maintained on base when Greenwalt burst in again. He was without food this time, but moving with greater urgency. When Cranston scowled at his improper entry, Greenwalt rediscovered the poise that'd earned him his job. He came to attention, saluted, then waited through the short eternity protocol required before the general asked him what the hell had got him into such a lather.

Greenwalt dropped his hand, and took a deep breath that quickly got away from him. With the tail end of it, he managed to gasp.

"Flying saucers!"

General Neal Cranston snorted derisively, but Greenwalt continued.

"The tower is tracking them on radar. Washington National called to report similar sightings. So far, there's at least a dozen hovering over the capital!"

Cranston was leaning back in his chair, trying to think of a punishment for his adjunct's behavior, but when Greenwalt revealed the confirming report from Washington National, he leaned forward, sensing that this might be something truly significant.

"They're tracking them? Now?"

"Yes, sir!"

"Visual confirmation?"

"Not yet, sir. They're awaiting your orders."

Cranston took a cigar from the humidor and considered the problem. The Air Force had tracked UFO's for years without a definitive sighting.

"How long have they been up there?"

Greenwalt consulted his watch.

"About seven minutes when I left, sir. I ran from the tower."

Cranston unwrapped the cigar, tossing the wrapper in the wastebasket. This might be just what he'd hoped for, one last opportunity for advancement before his inevitable retirement. If he could get pictures, or any kind of confirmation, it might even open the door to a position on the Joint Chiefs of Staff.

"Well, what're you waiting for? Get a couple of birds in the air!"

Greenwalt started for the door and was almost there before the second thought popped into his head.

"Oh, and lieutenant..."

"Yes, sir?"

"If it's not too much trouble, tell them to shoot one of the damn things down."

***

Cranston waited until Greenwalt had gone before picking up the phone. If there was any truth at all to the sighting over Washington, he wanted to be the first to report it. The first number he dialed was kept in a locked drawer in his desk. The number was the private line for General Hoyt Vandenberg's Georgetown residence.

But nobody picked up on the other end, even though he let it ring almost two minutes. He dialed the number for the general's office at the Pentagon, but again there was no answer. That the general wasn't at the office was hardly surprising, but that he wasn't at home either was.

But then Cranston remembered his relationship with Desiree. Was it too much to believe that Vandenberg might be getting a little on the side?

Believing all men to be essentially base in nature, Neal Cranston decided it wasn't.

Chapter 29 - Two Hills and Four Men

Prior to that fateful day in June 1947, Dexter Wye was just another private first class, indistinguishable from the hundreds of others posted to Roswell Army Air Field. He'd been given no special training beyond learning how to deal with barbed wire fences and had no particular talents to boost his career. He hadn't been trained to command other men, even as a non-com. At that point, he'd been in the Army a little over two years and, apart from a six-month assignment in Italy after the surrender, he'd spent his entire career in the States. In June 1947, over the course of a single day, the arc of his military career would change forever.

It was sheer coincidence that his platoon was tasked with guarding the doors to the operating theater at the base infirmary. The assignment was unusual enough to elicit comments from the men, but these were quickly hushed by the sergeant. This duty grew strange when they weren't allowed to take their posts until after three shrouded gurneys had been rolled into the surgery.

As Dex would later learn, the covered gurneys contained the subjects of a secret autopsy. The guards were given orders not to enter the theater under any circumstances or to look inside. The porthole windows in the swinging doors were curtained to prevent this. They were simply told to stay and thwart any unauthorized entry until they were given notice to leave.

If things had gone the way they were supposed to, it was highly unlikely that Dexter Wye would have ever experienced anything out of the ordinary. His life would have continued on along predictable lines. He would complete his hitch, return to Arkansas, and probably marry a local girl who, after an in-depth genealogical search, would turn out to be distant relation. None of those things were unprecedented in his family, all having happened to his older brothers.

What Dex didn't know when he took his post, was that inside that room, a team of masked surgeons were preparing to cut open the first of three alien bodies retrieved from the crash of a flying saucer. They were cutting the bodies open in the mistaken belief they'd be able to figure out what made them tick when they were alive. The significance of that failure wouldn't become apparent for a very long time.

But as the lead surgeon made his incision into the subject's leg, something went catastrophically wrong. The subject of the autopsy was short, gray-skinned, and roughly humanoid in that it had one head, two arms, and two legs.

It differed in the finger and toe counts, but that was just being nitpicky.

At that point, any resemblance to modern humans pretty much ended. As the terminated autopsy would reveal, the alien body had no vital organs of any kind. Its insides were home to hundreds of thousands of emerald green capsules that resembled luminescent caviar. Each capsule appeared to be utterly identical and there were no organs to be found. It was like each body had been stuffed with the contents of a beanbag chair.

The part where it all went wrong came when one of the surgeons decided he wanted a closer look at the inside the green globules. Using his scalpel, he separated one from the clustered mass in the subject's leg. Then, intending to smear it on a slide so he could view it under a microscope, he used that same scalpel to divide the globule into two parts.

And that, as Artie later related, was where things started to get weird.

Arthur Ecks was one of the observers monitoring the autopsy. As the scalpel split the globule, the surgery was instantly permeated with a corrosive gas that killed everyone inside. In a matter of minutes, the bodies of the autopsy team were turned into green goo. Dex didn't see the process, but he did help Artie clean it up, a job that still ranked as the most disgusting thing he'd done in his life.

For Dex, the autopsy was a career-changing, maybe even a life-changing, event. The autopsy marked the beginning of his association with Arthur Ecks and Project Stall and it all came about because Dex was the only man in his platoon who didn't lose his head in the emergency. When the fading effects of the gas struck down his sergeant, Dex took command of his platoon, discovering a respect among the men that he didn't know he had.

After the injured were taken outside, Artie had Dex gather the materials needed for the cleanup. Dex's role in the cleanup was to shovel the viscous green remains of the autopsy team into the canvas bags that Artie held for him. Artie decided on the spot that since Dex was already partway in on the secret, that's where Dex was going to stay. And that was how Dexter Wye became the fifth member of Project Stall, learning the secrets of the extraterrestrial presence on Earth in the process.

Though the work was extraordinarily strange, Dex performed well over the course of the following days and in the years since. Like Rita Mae Marshaux, who found herself in a similar position, Dex was promoted directly to lieutenant, bypassing the ranks in between. The promotion was temporary and ultimately meaningless. A few months later, he left the Army, all public records of his life were expunged, all the way back to his birth certificate.

***

As the last rays of the summer sun disappeared over the western horizon, Dexter Wye walked down the hill from the cave where Legion had left him. The sunset was a handy piece of information. It let him know that it was about 8:30 in the evening, which meant he'd spent about six hours underground.

The hill was a gentle mound that rose a hundred feet over the surrounding countryside, its grassy tonsure still damp from the morning rain. He found a narrow footpath leading up to the mouth of the cave and started down with the expectation that it might take him into the lane. While there was still light, he looked around with the hope of spying a landmark that would tell him how far he was from downtown.

He never found that landmark, but as the path led around the corner of the hill, he did find the country lane he'd seen from higher up. The lane was lined with cultivated trees that ran in straight lines to either side of the road. The trees had clearly been planted because each was evenly spaced from its neighbors.

Off to his right, he saw another low hill that appeared to have been cut in half. From Dex's vantage, its profile showed that the far side of the mound had collapsed, leaving a vertical slash that stood in sharp contrast to the more gentle slope facing the road.

As the last bit of sunlight faded, Dex broke into a run, eager to reach the lane before it grew too dark. From there, he could walk out to the main road and maybe hitch a ride into town. Dex slowed as the light faded, gingerly picking his way along the uneven trail. He caught a flash of headlights at the far end of the lane and heard an engine rev as a car turned off the main road.

He started to hurry again at the now real prospect of a ride. He reached the bottom of the hill, climbed a split rail fence and started cross country toward the lane. The car stopped at the end of the lane. He heard doors open and close as men got out and saw a flashlight beam strobing between the trees. He continued to watch as three shadows started up the hill.

By the time he reached the lane, the men were already out of sight. He was surprised to learn that the car he'd seen wasn't the only one parked under the trees. That car was parked at the end of a row of six, but Dex didn't waste time on any of them.

He did waste precious seconds before deciding to follow them up the hill. He was halfway up before he began to wonder what had brought so many cars to such a remote location. His heart sank when he recalled a story he'd read a few days earlier. The situation had all the markings of a gangland execution.

It didn't take long to find the path the men had used, but he was minutes behind. Still wondering if he was doing the right thing, Dex took to the trail at a run, flying up the path heedless of the danger of twisting an ankle. This new trail was easier to follow than the one from the cave, and the men ahead of him were in no hurry. Soon he spied their silhouettes, and from that point on, the distance between them steadily closed.

Halfway up, he started to wonder if the men were aware of the danger posed by the sheer cliff on the other side. He thought about calling out a warning, but decided against doing so. He was a short distance from the summit when he realized that one of the silhouettes looked familiar.

"Artie!"

One shadow turned to look back, but using Dex as a distraction, one of the other men pushed that shadow off the top of the hill. As the second shadow disappeared, Dex had no doubt that the pushed man had been Arthur Ecks.

He redoubled his efforts, climbing the hill with the intention of thrashing the man who'd pushed his Major. A minute later, Dex stopped just short of the edge. Squinting in the dim light, he peered over the edge of the cliff into the black pit of a sinkhole.

A second later, a deep rumble shook the earth and a fiery disc rose up out of the pit. The disc ascended until it reached the top of the bisected mound, then hovered as if taunting Dex for his late arrival.

Then, without ever making a sound, it was gone, leaving in its wake a trail of fire that extended out to the distant horizon.

***

The elevator, when they reached it, didn't go straight up the way Ecks had expected. Instead, it moved along a steep, but noticeably diagonal slope. The sideways tug of gravity felt odd. Despite being inside the cage, the ascent felt more like an escalator than an elevator.

He noticed, upon entering the wrought iron monstrosity, that the cage was a hundred years old if it was a day. He'd expected to hear a motor straining as the cable drew them up to the surface, but the ascent was virtually silent, disturbed only by the creaking of cage and cable.

McAfee enjoyed his consternation before deciding to enlighten him.

"It's not an elevator," McAfee informed him, "there's no motor."

"Then how does it work? Is it some bug thing?"

The senator chuckled like a friendly fireman.

"Hardly, it's human enough. Nothing terribly advanced, just a simple system of weights and balances. On the other side of this wall there's a similar tunnel with its own cage. When I want to go up, I simply signal for the other car to be sent down and the weight of the other car causes ours to rise. They were popular for a time, though interest fell off when electricity became readily available. But the men who built this place wanted secrecy above all else, and as well as breaking down, electricity can be traced by following the wires. Using this powerless expedient gave them a degree of security while also minimizing the maintenance required to keep it running. This would still be a funicular, though it is one of the few that was built underground."

The cage stopped and McAfee opened the gate, stepping aside to allow Ecks to exit. Once out of the cage, Ecks stared at the cage with some curiosity.

"Who built it? I've been coming through Washington for a decade, but I've never heard a whisper about this."

McAfee smiled as he approached a narrow panel at the end of the chamber. He checked outside through a peephole then slid the panel back into place.

"An excellent question and one I have no answer for. There is no end to the mysteries under this city. Maybe the Masons know. We've explored extensively down here and we've only scratched the surface. Washington was built to be the capital of the country, the Paris of the New World. Most of your early leaders were Freemasons, you know, and Freemasons are a mysterious bunch. We infiltrated Congress pretty easily, but we've had a hell of a time cracking the Masons. In any case, I suspect even they've forgotten what's down here."

"When you say we," Ecks asked, "are you talking about Congress or your Antarean comrades?"

McAfee laughed genially. "There's not as much difference between the two as you might think. Every freshman congressman gets a tour of the underworld. Some take an interest, others don't. I found it fascinating."

Ecks followed the Senator through the panel. Upon exiting, he stopped to slide the panel back into place. The seam marking its edge was barely detectable. When he turned to McAfee, he was surprised to find where they were. It seemed to be a perfectly ordinary parking garage. The Senator was standing by a black Hudson Commodore whose door was being held open by a tall man in a tan suit.

McAfee rested his elbow on the roof, with one foot on the frame.

"We can part company here if you like, Major, or I can have Clarence drop you somewhere. A third option might be to tag along. I'm reasonably sure you'll find it interesting."

Ecks frowned. "Why? What are you planning to do?"

McAfee smiled kindly, "I'm going to conquer the Earth."

Arthur Ecks didn't hesitate in making his decision.

"I believe I'll join you. It's been a most enlightening day."

***

The Hudson had a short wide windshield with a metal awning that gave it the slouched hat appearance of a cheap gunsel hiding in a dark alley. The seats were sumptuous and, in concert with the car's superior suspension, produced a comfortable ride that made light of bumps and potholes alike. With Clarence driving, the car rose to the surface on a winding ramp that delivered them to an exit gate. The attendant lifted the barrier without even a nod of recognition.

Then they were out onto Constitution Avenue, passing from the cone of one street lamp to the next in funereal silence. The streets were deserted, save a few taxis that were either heading home or off to the clandestine clubs favored by powerful men on the public payroll.

They followed Pennsylvania across the Anacostia River, and stayed with it as it bisected Randle Highlands and Dupont Park, passing through an area where, buoyed by the suburban success of Levittown, new construction had begun on a set of homes with identical floor plans on lots denuded of all plant life. Then they were into the country, gliding smoothly under the silhouettes of old trees. They continued on through this rural setting for about twenty minutes.

Without warning, Clarence turned off onto a side road that was invisible until they were right on top of it. They drove down a lane bordered by a split rail fence and lined with opposing rows of sycamores. After a quarter of a mile, the car stopped at the base of a dark mound that rose over the sycamores like a black sun at dawn.

Clarence set the brake, then hopped out to open the door for McAfee. McAfee smiled cryptically. "We're here."

Ecks followed the Senator the narrow path that led to the top of the mound. Clarence held back, deferentially allowing Ecks to pass. The mound proved to be larger than it seemed from below. When he looked back, they were already above the treetops. The lights of the city twinkled in the distance.

Though the night had turned cool after the long muggy day, Ecks felt a trickle of sweat roll out from under his hat, a product of exertion rather than heat. He took his hat off, and fanned his face, inviting the breeze to cool him. When he turned back to the path, McAfee had vanished. Clarence had paused to wait for him. Ecks gave the driver a wry smile and hurried to catch up.

The trail ended abruptly at the top. Ecks felt his feet slide a little under him. He reached out for support, but found only empty air. Staggering, he managed to find his balance, and was surprised to learn the mound had terminated so precipitously. He heard a call behind him and looked into darkness, wondering where the hell McAfee had gone.

He turned toward the sound, recognizing the familiar voice even as he felt the hands on his back. The hands pushed, and he fell for a few seconds before a sandy landing. He sank beneath the surface like a stone thrown into a pond. The sand parted around him like water. He tried to swim back up to the surface, then stopped when he considered the possibility that he'd fallen into quicksand.

He tried not to move, but it didn't make any difference. He still sank deeper and deeper. He was starting to worry about the air he'd lost when he struck something solid. Then there were hands all around him, clutching at his clothes and pulling him down, dragging him under and finally inside.

***

Dex watched the horizon point where the ship had disappeared for more than a minute before giving up. After that, he watched until the orange discharge of its exhaust was torn apart by the wind. Only then did he begin to consider where he was going to go and what he was going to do when he got there. It was a poor use of time, but that realization wouldn't come until later.

His first problem lay in descending the unfamiliar path in total darkness. Even the ledge that Artie was pushed from seemed indistinct and malformed. The path, set between random tufts of grass, was almost impossible to find, and once located, damnably difficult to follow. As it was, he experienced two disasters on the way down, and narrowly avoided a third. Both disasters were ultimately provident as both involved tumbling descents that brought him closer to the bottom. The third one might have resulted in broken bones if he hadn't drawn back from the edge at the last possible instant.

When he arrived back at the cars, he was reasonably intact, though no more sure about which direction to take. He took a seat on the last car's bumper, determined to take the time to think things out. Analytical thinking was more in Artie's line, but it was clearly what the situation called for.

He started with a single question.

What the devil had happened so far?

It started when Project Stall team was called to testify before the HUAC committee chaired by Joe McAfee. They were called because McAfee had decided to investigate the government's UFO research effort. Dex made a note for later examination. Not only that HUAC had a bug up its butt about UFOs, but that they were able to identify Project Stall, an agency protected by the highest security clearance the country had to offer. Being called to testify meant there was a leak. No one was supposed to know about Project Stall or the business it was engaged in.

Second point.

As it turned out, they didn't have to testify because Artie decided to tell McAfee to stuff it. McAfee didn't like that so he tried to get Artie arrested. But the bailiff refused to arrest Artie, claiming that Project Stall was under presidential protection, which is odd because Harry Truman isn't supposed to know about them. Dex winced at missing that one. Rita was right, there were times when he was too naive.

Third point.

The same bailiff spirited them out through a series of secret passages that led deep under the city. Dex tried to recall the bailiff's face, but didn't find much to remember. The bailiff was tall with light brown hair, but otherwise not terribly memorable.

Then there were the questions about where the bailiff owed his allegiance. Artie was expecting help from the man and was surprised by the betrayal. That meant that someone had instructed the bailiff to take them underground and abandon them. Who would do that and why? More to the point, who had the knowledge to execute such a plan? The only one who knew enough to stage such an operation was McAfee himself. But that would mean that the bailiff's refusal to arrest Artie was staged. Dex shook his head, unwilling to believe that McAfee could be the evil genius behind it all.

After that came the long walk underground where they were eventually separated. He had a lot of questions about that.

What had happened to the others? Were they still down there?

Dex shook his head, reminding himself that everyone wasn't still stuck underground. He'd made it out and if the man on the hill was Artie, that made two. He tried not to think about the encounter with Lars Ångström, or whatever it was that had impersonated him. He preferred to think that the false Ångström and his subsequent encounter with Legion weren't real.

The more he thought about it, the more comfortable he was with the idea that he'd gone daffy after all that time in the dark.

Yeah, that was it. He was hallucinating.

A moment later, he had to throw that idea away. If he was hallucinating, how did he get back to the surface?

Finally, there were the men he chased up the hill. He was sure that Artie was the man he saw pushed over the edge, even though he hadn't had a very good look. There was just something in the way he moved.

And after all that, there was the spaceship rising out of the sandpit. Artie was on that ship, which meant that Dex needed to find a way to get him back. Dex looked around at the imperceptible trees, the starlight glinting off the abandoned cars. Whatever it was that needed getting done, it sure wasn't going to happen on a country lane in the middle of nowhere.

It seemed unlikely that the spaceship would be coming back and that meant that the men who'd driven all these cars weren't coming back either. He was struck by a chilling thought that the men in the cars might not be men at all. But if that was the case, then what were they?

He heard an explosion off to the east, and realized he needed to get moving. There were half a dozen cars to choose from. He needed to take one and find someone to make aware of the danger before it was too late. At the very least, the military should be alerted.

He rose from his seat to select a car. The first one was locked, so he tried the next, and then the one after that. He was just passing the fourth car when he heard something thump on the lid of the trunk. He edged closer. The thump came again, from inside the trunk. He tried to open it and found it locked.

Dex tried the door and struck gold. Not only was it unlocked, but the interior light came on, illuminating the keys still dangling from the ignition. Taking the keys, he went around to open the trunk.

The man inside was wide-eyed and panicky. He leapt from his confinement, then gaped open-mouthed at Dex looming over him.

"What do you want from me?" Detlev Bronk shrieked before retreating into the shadows that gave him birth.

Chapter 30 - The Radar Room

The radar room at Washington National was a windowless enclosure where they kept the electronic instrumentation used to scan the sky. The room housed three rows of vacuum-tubed components, arranged in high racks with narrow pathways between so the technicians could access the units for servicing.

Even with this concession to sanity, the racks were home to a bewildering array of color-coded wires. Rita Mae gasped out the last of her breath before collapsing onto her knees, her skin still tingling from their disembodied transit through the electronic wonderland.

She heard the wheezing breath of the air conditioning units, straining to keep the temperature down to acceptable levels. The smells were close and mechanical, of vacuum tubes, heated elements, and chemical exchange.

Unable to see much, she tried her extended senses, but in a place with so much electricity and magnetism, there was too much to see and all of it was overwhelming. She took one quick look around, then gave it up as a lost cause.

She heard Jakob cough somewhere nearby, a distinct and familiar sound, then wondered where they were before getting around to how they'd got there. She remembered saying something about the airport, but that was all. She knew nothing of the *warak shu*, the strange device the Ffaeyn bequeathed to Jakob, and she had no answers for the mysteries that seemed to assail her in waves.

Wherever this was, the only thing she could see were a thousand flickering pinpoints of light. In the windowless room, they winked like multi-colored stars. She called out, keeping her voice to a whisper. "Jakob."

She heard an asthmatic wheeze somewhere nearby and tried again.

"Are you all right?"

"I do not think I like this mode of travel."

"What happened? I remember saying we had to get to the airport, but I just thought we'd get a cab once we made it back to the surface."

Jakob coughed again. "I recall that you spoke with some urgency."

Rita tried to recall her exact words. Though spoken only seconds ago, it felt like going back years. "I suppose...but what happened?"

"The *warak shu.*"

"The what?"

"The *warak shu*, it is the name of the device they gave to me."

"What about it?"

"When you said we needed to get to the airport, it brought us here."

"Just like that?"

"So it appears. It says it is conscious. Bringing us here was its decision, not mine."

"Is this the airport? This doesn't look like an airport."

She heard Jakob get to his feet, so she did the same, steadying herself against a rack of red and green lights that blinked at her like an angry Christmas tree. Her body felt electric, still surging with the currents generated by their transit. Her skin tingled with a yearning sensation, as if aching to be touched. Rita shook her head, fighting it down when all she really wanted was to indulge it.

"How are you?" Jakob asked, his voice disembodied by the darkened room.

"I feel strange," she said.

"Are you sick?"

She heard a shuffling movement somewhere, but there were no shadows to attach it to. Her body leaned toward the sound like a magnet.

"No, I don't think so, it's just..."

"What?"

"I don't know how to describe it. I just want...oh, never mind."

She felt him near, but his voice was drowning in the electronic hum.

"Keep talking," he said. "I will follow your voice."

"No, you keep talking. What do you mean it's conscious? You mean it thinks?"

"Yes, I must be very careful how I use it."

"Use it? What is it?"

Jakob shook his head, a gesture she couldn't see. Realizing this, he explained.

"I do not know. It may be a tool, it may even be a weapon."

"*Let's get that idea out of the way right now,*" said the *warak shu*, breaking in on Jakob's end of the conversation. "*I'm not a weapon—*"

"It says it is not a weapon," Jakob said, relaying the message to his fiancée.

"Then what good is it?" Rita asked, reaching out to steady herself against the racks. She took another look with her extended senses, using them to gauge the distance to the end of the row.

"*You didn't let me finish,*" the *warak shu* said, sounding peeved at the interruption. "*I'm not a weapon, but I feature a wide array of non-lethal options, all available for use in hostile situations.*"

"It says it has a wide array of non-lethal options," Jakob relayed to Rita.

"What does that mean?"

"I think it means we cannot use it to kill."

She heard Jakob moving, shuffling steps that went away from her before starting back. She heard him turn a corner, then felt more than saw the shadow that magically found the sweatered mound of her left breast.

Her ache to be touched returned with a vengeance.

"Ah, there you are," Jakob said coolly.

It was all the invitation she needed. Rita wrapped her little man in her arms and let kinky curls of his beard tickle her throat. The uncovered places, where her flesh touched his, detonated like a string of firecrackers, running up her arms into her skull before taking a *kundalini* plunge into her panties.

The morning's orgasm, stolen by Mrs Kelley's knock, swept over her like waves breaking in a storm, each shuddering climax drawing Jakob deeper inside hers. She found his mouth and thrust her tongue in to meet his, letting it quiver there until she slid off her peak and fell to the floor in a boneless heap.

"*I'm assuming this is all consensual,*" the *warak shu* commented.

"Rita! What's come over you?" Jakob backed away in shock.

"I don't know," she gasped, her body still vibrating. After a moment she found her feet, using Jakob's arm to pull herself back to standing.

"It was like there was something left over from what the Ffaeyn told me."

"What did the Ffaeyn tell you?"

She was still light-headed, and her body was suffused with a satisfied warmth unlike anything she'd ever felt before. She pulled Jakob close, and held him until she was sure it wouldn't trigger another climax. When he seemed real enough, she released him.

"I'm not allowed to share what they told me," she admitted. "Frankly, it doesn't make a lot of sense. They said nobody would understand anyway."

Jakob frowned, but he reached out to draw her back and she let him.

"I loathe secrets. Can you give me a clue?"

"What can I say? They gave you a *warak shu* and they gave me...this."

Jakob's hands slid down to her hips, then slid around to cup the cheeks they were too small to contain. He murmured something she didn't catch, but knew the meaning of perfectly well. She reached inside the black suit and squeezed the secret spot that made him gasp, then pushed him away.

"I think we should look for a door, don't you?"

His grip tightened before he released her with a sigh. The sigh encapsulated the stoic resignation of the world's longest suffering religion fused with the throbbing need of a teenage boy denied home plate during a late night make-out session.

"Yes," he sighed after a moment, "I suppose we should."

"We could look for a door," Rita suggested.

It was a good idea, but if there was a door, it wasn't very well marked.

It wasn't anywhere near the racks where they'd found each other. The racks ended against a wall on one side and provided only a narrow passage to the next row at the other end. Somewhere above them, an air-conditioning unit kicked into a higher gear, adding its vacuum cleaner sound to the buzzes and clicks of the radar units.

Finding the door in such a large dark room was impossible until they again resorted to the expanded senses. Even then, the room was a maze, but at least they could see its limits. The exit was far away as the size of the room allowed. Rita turned the knob slowly, drawing the door back enough to peek through the crack.

There were more surprises on the other side.

The outer room was larger still. There were three men visible, but it was the rows of equipment and the wide picture windows that looked out onto the wide asphalt stripes of the runways that told her where they were.

The *warak shu* had brought them to the airport after all.

In the room outside, a man was talking on the phone. Though clearly trying to remain calm, there was a note of restrained hysteria in his voice.

"Thank you, General," the man said. "You should see them any second."

As Jakob poked his head under her shoulder for a look, Rita bent over to kiss the bald spot at the back.

"You take me to the nicest places."

Chapter 31 - Off to the Airport

Lacking the resources to keep up with all three, Bertie and Janie decided to follow the two men who stayed together rather than the one who went off by himself. The men in black were still in sight when they reached the road at the end of the alley. They were still in sight when Bertie and Janie hopped inside Camille, though by then the mystery men had climbed into a black sedan that was too far away to determine make or model.

While the men in black negotiated their way out of the parking lot, Janie rolled the Nash over the curb separating one side of the street from the other. She did this even knowing she shouldn't, weathering the blare of angry horns when she cut off a flatbed truck and a prewar Chevrolet.

After that conspicuous display of aggressive driving, she held back, keeping the sedan in sight as it cruised along Independence before crossing the bridge into Arlington. It wasn't until the sedan took the turn for Memorial Parkway that Bertie figured it out.

"They're going to the airport?"

His observation came out as a question, though he hadn't meant it to.

Janie darted around an Olds, halving the distance between the two cars.

"Does this get us any closer to finding Ångström and Kleinemann?"

"I don't know," Bertie snapped. "Why are they going to the airport?"

"Maybe they're catching a flight?"

Janie slapped the steering wheel, and swerved around a Chrysler to pass a Buick before pulling back into the right lane.

"Maybe they're picking someone up."

"How does that help us?"

"I don't know, I'm thinking of reasons to go to the airport."

"Maybe they're pilots, or maybe they steal luggage when they don't have anyone to kill. Maybe they're porters who like to carry bags for nice families from Kansas."

"You okay, Bertie? You look kinda sweaty."

"No, I'm not okay! This whole thing is *mashugana!*"

As they neared the terminal, the sedan pulled into a short-term parking lot, pausing at the gate to get a ticket from the attendant.

"What do I do now?" Janie wailed. "We'll lose them!"

Bertie shrugged. "I guess we park."

"Jesus," she wailed, pointing at the sign. "Will you look at those rates!"

Janie froze at the barrier. "You got any money?"

Bertie laughed. "Sorry, dolly, I got a wife. I ain't had money since raccoon coats were the rage."

"Damn it!" Janie pulled up to the gate and waited while the attendant punched her ticket, one leg vibrating with impatience.

Three rows away, the two men were already out of the sedan. They took no bags as they started toward the walkway leading to the terminal. Janie snatched her ticket and burned rubber away from the gate.

"Hurry," Bertie urged, now getting excited. "They're getting away!"

"Do you see any spots?"

Janie floored the gas pedal, winding the engine up and down as she buzzed around the lot only to find that the black sedan had taken the last one. Reaching the edge of the lot, Janie jumped out of the car, leaving the key in the ignition.

"Hey," Bertie protested. "You can't park here! This ain't no spot."

Before closing the door, Janie patted the little car's dash.

"Take good care of Camille, Bertie. I'm going after 'em on foot."

The soggy cigar fell out of Bertie's mouth and rolled under his seat.

"The hell you are!"

But Janie Gently was already gone, sprinting through the gate in her sensible shoes, with only her skirt to limit the length of her stride. The two men stopped to wait for a break in traffic, giving Janie time to catch up, but they'd already crossed over to the terminal by the time she reached the curb.

Fifty yards behind, Bertie had to roll down the window to yell at her. His complaints grew more remote with each iteration.

"Get back here now, little girl!"

"I can't drive this thing!"

"I'll get even for this!"

And finally, as though she needed reminding.

"I'm from Brooklyn!"

***

There was a cluster of people blocking the terminal doors when she arrived. She was just in time to see the two men separate. The taller man hurried inside while the shorter was pushed back by a horde of departing travelers.

Janie hesitated at the curb before deciding to follow them inside.

Nestled under the rain canopy, the terminal lights came on as the last rays of the sun disappeared over the western horizon. She paused at the great windows, peering inside for some sign of her quarry. In doing so, she missed the entrance of Wally Sands and the second assault on Maisie Neill Ångström's patience.

By the time Janie turned her attention toward the revolving doors, there was such a bedlam of churning bodies inside the main lobby that it was hard telling whose fist belonged to what arm. In the ensuing riot, she could only lean from side to side to maintain her view of the fight. Inside the lobby, a dozen men were kicking and punching the snot out of two men who were already on the floor with their knees drawn in and their arms shielding their heads. It wasn't until the police arrived to push back the mob, that Janie could be sure that the men on the floor were the two she'd been following.

Janie rubbed the glass where her breath had fogged it, but most of the action appeared to be over. The men in black were sitting up now, their suits peppered with dusty footprints. A ring of men shouted curses at the fallen pair, pointing at them as if the whole ruckus was their fault. She wondered what was happening, but the terminal windows were too thick to hear anything.

Whatever had happened, it'd also drawn the attention of a half-dozen idle taxi drivers. The cabbies had all left their cars to press their noses to the glass, all hoping to catch a glimpse of the fight that was really more of a beating. It wasn't long before Janie was unceremoniously pushed away from her window. Her last glimpse was of Abel Corbett being cuffed by a gaggle of airport cops. At that point, Janie gave up the trail as another dead end.

Sighing with frustration, she kicked a baggage cart and made her way back to the crosswalk where a disheveled brunette about thirty years old was trying to corral three unruly girls. There was a second cart parked next to the woman, but unlike the one Janie had kicked, this one was piled high with suitcases and there was no porter in attendance. It didn't take much to figure out that the porter had joined the crowd trying to get a look at the melee.

Janie started to walk past the woman, trying to get clear without giving up more than a sympathetic look. Something had clearly happened to wind the girls up, but it seemed rude to inquire. The two oldest raced around, ducking behind the bags as if trying to sneak up on each other. Meanwhile, the youngest girl had climbed atop a calf leather portmanteau to better rat out the others.

The woman's perm was one of those helmet jobs that wasn't supposed to move in a hurricane. The ruckus inside the terminal had left her hair punched up on one side and flattened on the other. She had a red smear of lipstick across one cheek, and while the blush complemented her makeup, it made one side of her face look like the flames painted on the side panels of a hot rod. Her dress had a tear at one shoulder and her expensive cocoa cream stockings had been ruined by a long run down one calf.

Janie would've continued without further comment if the woman hadn't suddenly given up her fight for control. Throwing up her hands in frustration, the pretty brunette screamed, releasing emotions she'd repressed for years. The scream continued for some time as she gave herself over to a level of rage she was clearly unaccustomed to expressing.

"If I ever get my hands on you, Lars Ångström, I will tear you apart with my bare hands!"

The unexpected mention of her absent target caught Janie by surprise.

Janie paused at the curb, unsure what to do. As the scream ended and her rage petered out, Maisie Neill Ångström burst into tears. Passing pedestrians looked the other way as they hurried by, giving Maisie the wide berth due a madwoman, Burying her face in her hands, Maisie crumpled against the unstable edge of a Samsonite then rolled off to land on the sidewalk.

The three girls, who'd been squabbling over a piece of black fabric torn from Corbett's suit, went wide-eyed with shock at their mother's collapse. It was that look of shock on those pale young faces that drove Janie to act.

"Excuse me?" She said haltingly. "Are ... are you all right?"

Even before the words had left her lips, Janie kicked herself for asking such a stupid question. It was painfully obvious that this woman wasn't all right. Grown women didn't scream and burst into tears when they were all right. Janie tried again, with more commitment, adding a touch of compassion.

"Is there anything I can do to help?"

This time the woman looked up, blinking and sniffling as if she hadn't been aware that someone was talking to her. She looked up into Janie's anxious eyes, wiping away her tears with a white-gloved hand and smearing the bejesus out of her mascara. Maisie smiled bravely and blinked away an eyelash gone awry.

"No..., no," she said bravely. "Everything's fine."

It should have been obvious from the start, but Janie finally realized that she needed to be the one to say something.

"No, honey, it's not fine. Something's happened and you need help." She held out her hand to shake. "I'm Janie. How about you tell me what happened?"

Maisie sniffed, using the other glove to smear the other eye.

"We were going to Sweden."

"Sweden?"

Maisie gawked at the twin smudges on her gloves, then shook her hands in frustration at this latest gaffe. The youngest of the girls, a blonde with ringlets that fell to her shoulders, wrapped her arms around her mother's thigh.

Maisie tried to smile as the next wave of tears pooled for deployment.

"My husband wants to go to the Olympics."

Janie nodded, but she was now more confused than ever.

"Aren't the Olympics in Helsinki? You must like sports, I guess."

Maisie shook her head sadly, laying a gentle hand on her daughter's head.

"No," Maisie said, indicating the middle girl, a red-headed tomboy with freckles and a missing bicuspid.

"Molly does, but I don't think she's old enough to enjoy the Olympics."

"So, why are you going to the Olympics?"

Maisie opened the clasp on a small purse and began rooting inside.

"Well, my husband is Swedish," she said as if this explained everything. "That is, he's of Swedish extraction."

It was Janie's turn to shake her head.

"I think Helsinki is in Finland."

Maisie nodded, extracting an immaculate handkerchief from the purse.

"That's what I said, but it didn't make any difference."

"But you're not going to Helsinki now?"

"Sweden," Maisie corrected. "No, my husband was supposed to meet us. He never showed up, so we missed our flight."

"To Helsinki? I mean Sweden."

"Yes, my husband was supposed to meet us hours ago. I tried calling the hotel, but they said they haven't heard from him since we checked out."

"Why wasn't he with you?"

"Well, he had work, something he wouldn't tell me about."

Maisie leaned closer, covering her daughter's ears.

"I've learned not to ask."

Janie nodded, wondering if this was a good time to offer her a cigarette. She sure seemed like she could use one.

"Say, I couldn't help but hear you scream a man's name."

Maisie nodded and sighed. "That's my husband."

"Your husband is Lars Ångström? The sex doctor?"

Maisie's eyes went wide as she tried too late to cover the youngest daughter's ears. The two older girls had wandered away, drawn by the sight of the airport police forcing two men in black suits into the back of a cruiser.

"Hush!" Maisie almost shouted. In a lower voice, she added, "Yes."

Janie mulled that over for a second, finally shaking a cigarette free from the pack and offering it to the stricken woman.

Maisie shook her head, mouthing, 'Not in front of the girls.'

"So you haven't heard from your husband?"

"No."

"So what do you want to do?"

Maisie sighed, absent-mindedly accepting the same cigarette she'd rejected a moment earlier, then gesturing for a match.

"Oh, I don't know. Go back to the hotel, I suppose. Once upon a time, I could've called my father, but he moved back to La Crosse when that awful man beat him in the election." She leaned in again as Janie sparked her lighter and took a long satisfying drag.

Janie lit her own cigarette then flicked the lighter closed.

"Well, listen, why don't you let me give you a ride? I've got a car in the lot. It'll save you the cost of a taxi."

Maisie started to refuse, but her need was so naked that Janie almost laughed. Maisie went scarlet with embarrassment, before capitulating with a shy smile of thanks.

She left the luggage with Janie as she went off to track down the older girls. Before leaving, she introduced the blonde girl as Bubbles. With her mother's exit,

Bubbles reclaimed her perch on top of the suitcases, then proceeded to watch Janie smoke. Her question seemed to come out of left field.

"Do you like our mother?"

The question caught Janie by surprise. She tapped the ash off her Viceroy before giving a qualified response.

"Well, I just met her."

"But do you like her?"

Janie shrugged.

"I suppose I do. I stopped because she looked like she could use some help."

Bubbles looked off toward the terminal where Maisie had come out of the crowd, holding a girl's wrist in each hand. The little girl's reply was eerily mature.

"Boy," said Bubbles Ångström, "you sure got that right."

***

Janie thought offering the Ångström girls a lift back to the hotel was a nice thing to do. But as they approached Camille, she realized she'd forgotten about Bertie Stein. She found the old reporter arguing with a meter maid who was trying, without success, to make him move Camille out of the driving lane.

Bertie was explaining that he didn't know how to drive, while admitting the car wasn't his anyway. The meter maid went away when Janie promised to move as soon as they got the luggage into the trunk.

They could only fit two of the three suitcases into the Camille's trunk. Janie offered to strap the third to the roof, but Maisie waved off the suggestion, her eyes afire at the prospect of matrimonial vengeance.

"My husband," she said with icy aristocracy, "has chosen to abandon us. The least he can do is take care of his own luggage. That thing weighs fifty pounds and I'm tired of dragging it around."

This claim was misleading. The suitcase had been handled by a succession of bellboys and porters. Maisie hadn't had a thing to do with it.

But when it came time to load the passengers, the live cargo proved to be another matter. Janie purposely neglected to mention the family's surname when she introduced the Ångströms.

Bertie was confused by the influx of new blood, but not overly impressed. The disheveled brunette with the dirty gloves gave him a little bob and said her name was Maisie. There wasn't time to get the girls' names, but they piled into the backseat where they were a reasonable fit alongside the smaller bags.

It wasn't until Maisie took his place in the passenger seat that the penny dropped. Bertie waddled around to the driver's side to hiss through the window at a smiling Janie Gently.

"You can't just leave me here! How'm I s'posed to get back across the river?"

By way of an answer, Janie jerked a thumb back toward the terminal.

"This is an emergency, Bertie. There's a row of cabs in front of the terminal. Why don't you take one?"

Bertie went apoplectic at the prospect of spending money to get back to the YMCA. He shook an angry fist at the young woman from *Women's Week Daily*.

"Why, you little-". He caught himself before he said anything awful in front of the girls.

Bertie glared at the three girls in back with venom. They'd probably turn out like this treacherous bitch who, he had to remind himself, had turned out to be more competition than friend after all.

Janie drove a short distance away before calling back.

"Just one more thing, Bertie. Do you think you could drop that suitcase back off at the Ambassador?"

Bertie started to make a vulgar gesture, but turned it into a shaking fist at the last moment. Janie waved back as if the whole thing was a lark.

And then they were gone.

Bertie watched her go with murder in his heart.

So Janie Gently wanted to play rough.

Well, Bertie Stein had been playing rough for forty years. He was only being nice because she was a girl, but if she wanted to play hardball, so be it.

Bertie looked west where the sun was now a fallen memory and swore that one day he would have his revenge. At that angle, something golden glinted up into his eye. Following the glint, Bertie discovered that it was coming from the remaining suitcase. He walked over to it.

The suitcase was of high quality, a top of the line Samsonite, calfskin with a cinnamon complexion. The glint was from the shiny brass handle. Bertie looked closer and saw a name embossed on a brass plate below the handle.

He picked up the suitcase, then staggering under its weight, set it back down. He clutched at his back theatrically, even though there wasn't anyone around to offer help or sympathy.

When his back stopped complaining, he leaned closer to read the name, then stood up so fast he felt light-headed.

The name on the suitcase presented unimaginable possibilities.

Maybe, Bertie thought, as a slew of new ideas percolated his reporter's brain, this wasn't so bad after all.

Chapter 32 - Mudduk and Russell

"I hope you will forgive my saying so," Lars Ångström commented after the other worms had departed, "but your friends do not treat you very well."

Winthrop Walton Russell III smiled painfully and nodded.

"Oh, they don't mean anything by it," Russell said. "It's because I don't belong to the higher castes. Nemerteans don't value their scholars or technicians, I'm afraid."

Lars nodded sympathetically as he took a seat at Russell's work table.

"That seems odd to me," Lars said. "Though I am admittedly an outsider who knows little of your culture, at first glance, they appear to be rather reliant on your expertise."

"Oh, they are," Russell agreed, putting down one incomprehensible tool and picking up another. "It is a great honor to server Kraall. He is a great *thang*, even though he only became *thang* after the crash."

"I heard you use that word before," Lars recalled, "I must confess I don't know what it means."

"Ah," said Russell, applying the tip of a second incomprehensible tool to the rear plate of the view screen, "it's quite simple. A *thang* is the position at the top of the power structure in a *scherzo*, at least until a more powerful *thang* comes along."

"And a *scherzo?*" Lars asked, the academician in him now growing interested. "What would that be?"

Russell pursed his lips.

"Now that's more difficult to define. So far, I haven't been able to find a true analog for the *scherzo* in human culture. In one sense, it's like one of your tribal societies, the difference being that there's a more rigid genetic component in a *scherzo*. Those who rank outside the higher castes aren't allowed to breed, except in times of great need."

Lars was all attention now. "So you are like drones in a bee colony."

"Again, not a perfect analogy, but yes," Russell replied nodding. "But even those who are spawned from a *thang* have no guarantee of position."

"So the genetic component," Lars said, "doesn't set the final determination of status."

"Exactly," said Russell, warming to his subject. "The true determinate is the personality of the individual worm."

"Much like selecting a compatible host, then."

"All too true," Russell agreed. "There's a kind of madness required to be a *thang*, just as a calmer nature is required to be a scholar-technician like myself."

"This is quite fascinating!" Lars enthused, his mind sorting through a host of questions he wanted to ask.

"Thank you," Russell said politely, "I enjoy studying human behavior myself. I suspect there is a lot more variety in humans than you could ever hope to find in us. I've been theorizing that your greater variety is due to how recently you've become a global culture. You're still at a stage where many cultures are vying for dominance. Nemertea has been unified under one culture for quite some time."

Lars nodded. "Centuries? Millenia?"

"Difficult to say," Russell admitted. "Unlike your planet, ours doesn't orbit its sun, so we never learned to base our record-keeping on linear time. Nemertea resides within the photosphere of its star, which is what your astronomers would classify as a red giant."

Lars shook his head, enthralled by the extent of the differences between the two environments. "But how can your planet be located inside its star without being absorbed by it. Wouldn't the gravity crush it, or the heat turn it to liquid or gas?"

Russell laughed. "Oh my no! I'm sorry to laugh so openly, but your scientists don't have the faintest idea how stars work at present."

"Could you tell us?" Lars asked, his eyes growing wide at the possibility of having a more advanced life form to query.

Russell laughed again. "Of course, but I've learned enough of your science and the men who practice it to know that nobody would believe me. It's very difficult to convince a human of anything. Even if you start with basic precepts and work your way up, they still have their own rigid beliefs that they will refuse to let go of. I understand to some degree, it can't be easy to hear that everything you believe is wrong. Believe me, I know, I've tried and failed often enough."

Lars sat back in his chair, dumbfounded.

"You mean to say you've talked to our scientists?"

Russell shrugged. "A few. I've come away with the impression that they are quite difficult to persuade. Perhaps it's because I don't look the part."

"You do look quite young," Lars pointed out. "Based on your appearance, I'd say you were barely old enough to be a graduate student."

"My host's appearance does work against me," Russell admitted, "but I could hardly tell these men they're talking to a six foot worm that resides in the frontal lobe of this body's skull. They would think I was insane. Besides, even if they did believe me, such an admission would expose our presence on Earth, and from what I've learned, that would make your government very unhappy. There's also the matter of the punishment I would receive from Kraall."

Lars' eyes grew wider still.

"Am I talking to the worm now?"

"Of course," Russell said, "I, that is, the human part of me, doesn't know a damned thing about this stuff. Mostly, you've been talking to my worm."

Lars shook his head in amazement. "Does your worm have a name? Do any worms have names, for that matter?"

Russell laughed again, clearly pleased to be sharing the information.

"We all do! My worm is called Mudduk. It is a pleasure to meet you, Doctor Ångström. You are quite unlike any human I've ever come across."

"This is fascinating," Lars said again. "Are all worms like you?"

"Oh no," Mudduk said. "Like humans, each and every one of us has a unique personality. I think, given the chance, and by that I mean if we had any *thang* other than Kraall, we might get along quite well with humans, at least some of us. We could be of great benefit to you, given the chance."

"How so?"

Realizing that he wasn't going to get any more work done, Russell finally put down the incomprehensible tool and turned to face Ångström.

"Well, I don't know if you were aware of this," Mudduk confided, "but Mr Russell here died five years ago in a helicopter crash."

Lars leaned away from his acquaintance. It was a subconscious reaction, but he did do it. "He did? Are you saying that Mr Russell was killed?"

"Oh yes," Russell said, actively rejoining the conversation. "That crash cut me in half, but Mudduk fixed me right up, made me as good as new, maybe better. Even left my personality intact."

"We were a good fit," Mudduk admitted, "and still are, but that's the way it should be. The worm has to have a positive resonance with the host, otherwise there can be all kinds of trouble. Can you imagine if I was put inside Corbett's body?"

"Or Captain Sands?" Russell added.

Russell and his worm shared a composite laugh at the very idea. After a time, Lars Ångström joined in.

"You know," Mudduk said, his voice dropping to a more confidential tone, "I rather like you. I'm glad we've been able to have this talk."

"I have very much enjoyed this conversation as well," Lars replied, showing off his manners.

"But I'm afraid we should end it here."

"Oh," Lars answered, a bit disappointed.

"Yes," Mudduk explained, "I have work to do. I'm sure you understand."

"Of course," Lars said, "you're under a deadline of sorts."

"Don't look so disappointed," Mudduk continued. "I don't mean that we can never talk again. I would enjoy that very much. But I don't think it is safe for you to stay here. Kraall is rather capricious by nature."

"Yes, I noticed that," Lars admitted.

"And I don't think you should be here when he gets back."

Lars perked up, but quickly covered it up.

"But what other choice is there?"

"I was thinking I could just let you go."

This time, Lars was unable to hide his reaction.

"But won't you get in trouble?"

Russell nodded. "Of course, but you've met Kraall. You've seen what he's like. I'll get in trouble even if I do a good job watching you, even if you're still here when he gets back. So you see, I don't have any motivation to keep you, and I have nothing to lose by letting you go."

It was unusual logic, but Lars couldn't find any holes in it.

"Won't the punishment be worse for letting me go?"

"Possibly, but Kraall will really be punishing Russell and I can heal any damage done to him. Kraall will be angry, but he needs me to fix things, so his options are limited."

Lars remembered another problem then.

"There's another problem. I was lost when I found you here. I don't know how to get back to the surface."

Mudduk considered this for no more than a second.

"Then I guess I'll have to show you the way out."

Chapter 33 - Gobsmacked

It didn't take long for Andrews Air Force Base to respond to the general alarm. After all, rapid response to emergency situations was what the base was all about. Within two minutes of General Cranston issuing his command, two F-94 Starfires were airborne and streaking northwest toward the nation's capital. Due to the runway repairs at Andrews, the order had to be relayed to Dover Air Base in Delaware but the delay wasn't a long one.

In the meantime, two things happened.

First, the Andrews tower received radar confirmation of the anomalies from their own tower.

Second, with the state of emergency in full flower, the general placed all thoughts of his wife and Desiree Blythe in separate pockets of his emotional briefcase.

Lieutenant Greenwalt had a car waiting that covered the distance to the tower in slightly less time than it would have taken a good sprinter to run. Five minutes after the initial notification, Neal Cranston climbed the tower stairs.

Usually when Cranston entered a room, men went ramrod straight and came to attention, not daring to move until he put them at ease. On this night, however, he was surprised to find their attention so focused on the little green dots of their radar feed that no one acknowledged his presence until Greenwalt barked, "General in the tower!"

The rapidity of the response was remarkable. Men who'd been seated rose to attention so quickly that one man yanked the cord connecting his headset right out of the control panel. The men standing beside the panel seemed to simultaneously freeze and spin on their heels.

But there were two men by the window who were so intent on what they were seeing that the call to attention went unnoticed. One half of this pair was an acned corporal named Squibb. It took several seconds for Squibb to note the sudden silence, but even then he ignored the ceremonial posturing. Rather than coming to attention, Squibb let his binoculars fall to his chest and pointed out the window. Less than a mile distant, an orange fireball with a comet-like tail hung like a ripe tangerine in the western sky.

The general glared at Squibb, who despite the ample evidence around him, still hadn't grasped what everyone was waiting for.

Squibb explained in a dreamy voice. "You can see it plain as day."

Cranston chose to ignore the Squibb insurrection, but he did come over to see what the fuss was about. At first glance, the orange fireball didn't look like much.

From the tower, it was no more than the size of a thumbnail extended to arm's length. The fireball had paused in its forward motion, losing its tail as a result. Now it looked like a small orange moon hovering in the midnight sky. Cranston had a sense it was watching, but felt no imminent threat of danger.

He felt a little thrill of anticipation when one of the men behind him said, "Here come the recon boys," as the jets from Delaware came screaming into view. Cranston held his breath, waiting for the outcome. So much depended on what happened when the jets engaged the strange moon.

The results were disappointing.

The moon blinked as if coming out of a dream. Then, taking notice of the approaching fighters, the comet tail reappeared, and it was gone.

It was only then that Neal Cranston understood the full implications of what he'd seen. Those implications were like a hammer blow. Cranston's right knee quivered, forcing him to consciously bring it back under control.

Something that fast, something that could be gone before the fighters had time to fire on it, could probably outrun their missiles as well as the jets.

What was he supposed to do against such an enemy?

You couldn't anticipate its arrival or its departure.

With a technology so advanced, it must have weapons, but since the fireball has simply retreated, they hadn't even been able to determine the nature of those weapons. As a result, he still didn't know if they were anything he could prepare for. How could he could defend the country against something like that with the tools he had available?

A lump rose in his throat and caught there as a far more sobering thought added its weight to his already considerable burden.

Was this the end of Man's dominion on Earth?

The fighters roared past, shaking the tower windows as the jets broke the sound barrier, but the orange light was still receding and, even at top speed, the fighters were falling further behind.

The sonic boom exploded over the tower and left his ears ringing. The room remained silent until the jets were out of sight. Only then did Cranston release his breath, letting his body go limp. The inevitable sigh that swept through the tower was one of despair. Cranston heard it and pulled himself together.

"Are we still tracking that thing?" Cranston demanded as if it still mattered.

"No, sir," said an anonymous controller, then "scratch that! It's back! A quarter mile east northeast!"

Cranston looked out the eastern pane and found it at once. The orange fireball was back and it was closer this time, close enough to see how it differed from the classic saucer shape he recalled from *The Day the Earth Stood Still*.

Like the saucers in the serials they showed the kids before main attractions, it had the rounded nub on top. But rather than the classic saucer shape, its hexagonal outer rim was marked by six evenly spaced points. Taken in total, the points looked like the brandished claws of some great predator.

The saucer was so close he could even see the markings along its outer rim, a series of concentric circles radiating out from the domed nub in waves. The orange light that'd first attracted their attention dimmed to amber.

Somebody groaned as a dark line moved across the surface of the ship like a Chinese eye. Corporal Squibb pointed out the obvious, unable to keep the awe out of his voice.

"They're toying with us."

***

In the aftermath of the disturbing phone call and his subsequent failure to contact Colonel Bee, Detlev Bronk left the phone on the table for the waiter to collect. Colonel Bee was the only man he could think of who might help, and with that avenue denied, he was at a loss as to how to proceed.

He felt anxious and overwrought by both the mysteries of the situation Majestic was facing and the responsibilities he'd taken on. For one of the few times since he was a young man, he wondered if he was up to the task. He returned to his room, so lost in his thoughts that the elevator operator had to remind him when they reached his floor.

He hadn't meant to fall asleep when he lay down, but his fatigue was too great to fight. He woke hours later to the shock of having abdicated his task. Shaking off the grogginess of his impromptu nap, he called the front desk and requested that to be connected to Donald Keyhoe's room.

He half-expected to the clerk to tell him that Keyhoe had checked out, but the clerk rang the room as requested. The phone rang and rang. Bronk was on the verge of giving up when a man's voice finally answered.

"Mister Keyhoe?" Bronk asked in his plummiest accent.

There was a slight hesitation on the other end before the man said, "Yes?"

The hesitation was something Bronk would later recall, but at that moment, it didn't strike him as important.

"Mister Keyhoe," Bronk began again, "I would like to meet with you at your earliest available opportunity."

"What would this be about?"

Bronk decided it was best to remain mysterious.

"Let me just say that it will concern a subject of great interest to you."

He was met by silence on the other end of the line. The silence ended when Keyhoe asked, "Can you be in the Ambassador Hotel bar in fifteen minutes?"

Having hooked his fish, Detlev Bronk smiled.

"I can do better than that, Major," he said, using the reporter's former rank. "I can be there in five."

"How will I know you?" Keyhoe asked.

"Don't worry, Major," Bronk assured him. "I will know you."

Bronk took the elevator down to the lobby, chatting amiably with the operator in a distracted 'how's the weather' kind of way. Exiting the lift, his progress was intercepted by a bellboy. The bellboy handed him a note that he barely glanced at before stuffing it into his pocket. It was a request by that scoundrel Dulles to call as soon as possible.

'The effrontery of that man,' Bronk thought to himself as he entered the cavernous gloom of the saloon. 'As if I was unable to complete a simple contact.'

He requested the most isolated table, then ordered a lemon squash from the waitress. His wait was a short one.

He'd only taken one sip of his drink when he saw Keyhoe coming through the open arch that separated the bar from the lobby. He watched the man wait for his eyes to adjust to the diminished light. When Keyhoe's gaze came around to him, Bronk subtly raised his glass to draw his attention. That reporter took the seat opposite Bronk and wasted no time getting to the point.

"So I'm here. Now what's with all this cloak and dagger business?"

His response had to wait for Keyhoe to order. The reporter sent the waitress away with a request for bourbon and branch water.

Once she was out of earshot, Bronk began, "You've covered a wide range of topics for *True Magazine* over the past few years, major, but you're best known for one particular topic. In fact, over the years, your name has come to be almost exclusively associated with-"

Bronk was quite pleased with this line of approach, but Keyhoe cut him off.

"Yeah, yeah, the flying saucers, what about it?"

Bronk wasn't used to being interrupted, but he refused to let Keyhoe's manner throw him.

"Well," Bronk paused, re-marshaling his thoughts, "your name came up in a recent discussion. As a result of that discussion, we'd like to extend an offer-"

"What's this regarding?" Keyhoe asked, cutting him off again.

Bronk brought his fingertips together, making a steeple.

"Well, there are security considerations, of course, and we must discuss those before I get to the heart of the matter, but I'm sure those will prove no obstacle. I've been told that you are reasonably proficient at keeping secrets. As this is a matter of the highest national security, we must have your assurance that you will not speak of or write about these matters. That restriction applies whether you accept our offer or not. Are you willing to accept this limitation? We can go no further if you aren't."

Keyhoe startled as the waitress returned with his bourbon. He waited for her to leave before suggesting, "Hope you don't mind my saying, but this isn't exactly the most secure place to talk. I have a room on the fourth floor. How would you feel about moving this conversation up there?"

"Of course, of course, an admirable suggestion," Bronk nodded his approval. Leaving his drink on the table, he followed Keyhoe to the elevator.

The operator had changed while he was in the bar. The new operator was a tall sandy-haired young man in hotel livery.

Bronk and Keyhoe were the only passengers. When the elevator stopped on the fourth floor, Bronk turned to Keyhoe, ready to follow him to his room.

In Keyhoe's stead, Bronk found an exact replica of the elevator operator, right down to the uniform. Bronk's world went black as the elevator descended, bypassing the lobby in favor of the basement where, when the elevator doors parted, several more Clarences awaited his arrival.

***

The sun had set by the time the taxi dropped Donald Menzel off at the Senate building. It was the same building where he'd addressed McAfee's committee only that morning, but night had changed it.

He was surprised to find the building dark, and to all appearances, empty. The same center of power that had buzzed with activity earlier in the day was now black and desolate. As he approached, he was also surprised to find that even the guards who monitored entry were nowhere to be found.

Menzel tried the great double doors, expecting them to be locked. He was surprised again as the doors swung open to receive him. Menzel stepped inside with the conspicuous trepidation of a man entering a haunted house.

"Hello?" He called, just to hear a voice. His greeting echoed through the dimly lit halls, returning without bringing a response.

There were only a few emergency lights still on, but these were enough to guide him. He took the stairs up to the second floor, hugging the rail because it was something substantial. As the corridor opened up before him, he started down the hall, checking the nameplates on the doors as he passed. He heard a noise from further down the hall, but, as before, calling out brought no reply.

Menzel began to wonder what the devil he'd expected. It was after hours on a Saturday night. Of course, the building was empty.

A moment later, he rejected this conclusion. The guards, at least, should still be on duty. If not, the doors should be locked and nobody would be able to get in. What he'd found so far didn't make a lick of sense.

He finally found the nameplate for McAfee's office, but the doors were closed and he saw no lights underneath. Additionally, when he tried the knob, he found it locked. It was all predictable, but he was unprepared for this eventuality.

His hand was still on the knob when the entire building shook with the force of some great impact. Suddenly, even the emergency lights were gone and he was alone in the dark.

Menzel cursed, annoyed by the inconvenience. He started back toward the stairwell and was halfway there when he heard a shuffling movement from down the hall.

208

***

It had been a long time since anyone pointed a gun at Hoyt Vandenberg.

"Lieutenant Clarence," the general said in a voice fraught with slow menace, "have you lost your cotton-picking mind?"

Clarence took his feet off Vandenberg's desk and lowered them to the floor.

"Why no, General," Clarence said. "I don't believe so."

"Then what the devil is the meaning of this?"

Clarence looked down at the .45 automatic in his hand, as if seeing it for the first time, then back up at the general.

"Oh, you mean this?"

Vandenberg glowered back, but played along. "I do."

"Well, General," Clarence said breezily. "It's like this. I'm using your own gun because I want to make sure you understand the situation. Without the gun, I'm afraid you might not get it."

"Get what? That your career is finished?"

"In a way," Clarence continued in the same light vein. "One way or another, you're right. My career in the Air Force is over, but then, so is yours. By tomorrow morning, there will be no Air Force, just as there will be no Army or Navy."

Clarence came around the desk, waving the gun to shoo Vandenberg away from the door. "As we speak, there's a coup already underway. By morning, we will hold every vital position in the United States government and every important post in the military chain of command."

Vandenberg snorted his disbelief. "Exactly who is behind this coup? You'll pardon me for saying this, Clarence, but you never struck me as a commie."

"Oh, I'm not a communist," Clarence said with an amused smile.

"Then what are you?" Vandenberg fumed, his temper rising as the beginnings of doubt crept into his certainty.

"To answer that, general, you'll need to open your mind."

Clarence set the .45 on the desk and raised the hand that had held it. He extended it toward Vandenberg as if he was going to show him something, then paused.

Before Vandenberg's unbelieving eyes, the hand began to change, assuming the mottled twig-like appearance of a giant insect.

Chapter 34 - Sex and Paul Revere

The porter had taken the cart with him when he returned to the terminal, so getting Ångström's suitcase over to where he could get a cab was going to be a manual effort. Bertie tried to lift it by the handle, immediately wincing at the unnatural strain on his back. Two steps later, the weight proved too great as the metal nubs scraped against the concrete, making the decision for him. He let go of the handle, wondering what the hell Ångström kept in the thing.

No matter what was inside, the damned thing was sure as hell expensive. Its veneer was the softest calfskin Bertie had ever encountered, a light cinnamon that, while not quite brown, was too dark to pass for white. The metal latches were gold-plated and, with a goldsmith for a cousin, Bertie had no doubt they were genuine. Its weight, even when empty, probably wasn't insignificant, but after giving it another tug, Bertie was pretty sure there was more inside than Ångström's underwear.

The weight made him curious, but not curious enough to open it. For all he knew, there were three copies of Ångström's pornographic book inside. He lifted again. He made it to the curb before he had to set it down, but this time he knew he was done. This boat anchor of a suitcase wasn't going any further until he found help from a porter or a cab. He looked around for either, but the porters were all inside the terminal and the cabs confined to a long row on the other side of the road.

Bertie stared longingly as taxi after taxi left the terminal, each ignoring his attempts to flag them down. The night was turning cool, a chill contrast to the steamy heat of the day. He tried to get the attention of a porter, but this far side of the ring road seemed to be foreign territory and nothing he did could entice them across the border. He made the same gestures toward the cabbies, but they were facing the terminal, where the money came from, and who could blame them? He should come out of the terminal like a normal person, not be standing on the wrong side of a busy road.

While he waited, the traffic turned heavy with evening arrivals for late night departures. Cars flowed out in a rush, filled with people hurrying off to hotels or meeting friends for a late dinner. He checked his watch and was surprised to find it was already ten o'clock.

How long had he been out here?

At long last, a car pulled up to the curb and stopped. By this time, Bertie was sitting on the suitcase with his head down, like a poster child for despair. At the squeal of brakes, he looked up, feeling a surge of hope that was dashed as soon as he saw the man's uniform.

The cop was a beefy linebacker of a man in a light blue shirt. The shirt was emblazoned with the emblem of the Metropolitan Airport Authority on the sleeves below each shoulder. He wore his cap back on his forehead, far enough that Bertie could see a few wisps of the dark hair underneath.

"Having trouble, mac?"

Bertie sighed. "Can't seem to get a cab, officer."

The cop turned toward the dwindling line of cabs.

"Yeah, that's probably because they're not allowed to pick up over here. Have you considered using the crosswalk?"

The cop smirked like he'd just made a chicken joke.

Bertie scowled, but didn't rise. "The thought never crossed my mind."

He smiled his thanks for the helpful suggestion.

The cop, being immune to sarcasm, didn't smile back.

"So what's stopping you, bud? I've been watching you for quite a while. This ain't no hotel, you know. You can't stay here all night."

Bertie shifted his cigar to the other side of his mouth, then unwisely let out a little of his frustration. "You think I'm here cause I wanna be here?"

"I don't care why you're here. Ah'm telling you, ya gotta move on."

Bertie placed his palms on his knees and rose on tired legs, a move the cop construed as aggressive. He took a step back, his hand reaching for his nightstick.

Bertie shook his head sourly.

"Take it easy, I gotta bad back and I got run all over town today before that chippie ditched me."

The cop relaxed, but kept his hand on the nightstick.

"There's no call for talk like that. Now come on, get that suitcase across the street and get yourself a cab."

"Gee, I wish I'd thought of that."

"I'm being patient here, smart guy. Don't make me run you in."

Bertie's jaw dropped an inch, the cigar still stuck to his lower lip.

"For what? Not having the strength to lift a suitcase?"

The cop's brow furrowed in what might be seen as confusion in a lesser man.

"That what's stopping ya? Why'd ya load it up so heavy if you can't lift it?"

The words left Bertie's mouth before he considered the implications.

"Oh yeah, well, maybe it's not my suitcase. Maybe when Miss Florence Nightingale came to the rescue, there was only enough room in her stupid midget car for two suitcases. I'm trying to be a good guy, but she runs outta seats when this other bimbo gets in with her little girls, so me and the suitcase got left behind. Take it back to the Ambassador, she says, but she don't say how I'm supposed to get it there. So I try to pick it up and it turns out the damn thing is full of bricks or something. I don't know what's in it, but I can't lift it. I was lucky to get it this far, but I got a bad back and I can't get a porter to come over and help me, and I can't get a cab. Look at it! It's a nice suitcase, it obviously cost a lot of money. So, forgive me for being a Boy Scout, but maybe I don't wanna just leave it on the curb."

The cop waved at him to a stop.

"Let me get this straight."

He took a flashlight from his belt and shined it down at the suitcase, then back up at the shabby man. Clearly, the two things didn't go together.

"This isn't your suitcase?"

"No. I just told you that."

"So what're you doing with it?"

Bertie took another look at the suitcase. What was he doing with it?

"I dunno. The guy owns it might be at the Ambassador, so I guess I'm supposed to take it there."

"You guess?"

"Well, I guess I never thought about it, but look, it's a nice suitcase! I figure the guy wouldn't want to lose it."

The cop's hand rose to massage a tired shoulder.

"No, he wouldn't. Ya sure, ya wasn't gonna sell it."

"Sell it? The guy's name stamped on the handle. How'm I gonna sell it?"

The cop leaned in, shining the beam on the handle, then back at Bertie.

"You sure as hell ain't no Lars Ångström."

"No kidding."

"So what's in the bag?"

Bertie turned his palms to the sky, beseeching his God to help him out.

"How should I know? I told you. All I knows it's heavy."

The cop cocked his head to one side.

"You got any objection to finding out?"

A sense of foreboding fell heavily on Bertie Stein, but he had no choice.

"Sure, I guess. Why should I care?"

The cop picked up the suitcase, marveling at the weight of the thing.

"Hoo boy, well that part of your story rings true."

Expending considerable effort, the cop set the suitcase on the hood of his car and flipped the latches. The suitcase opened with a cough that sounded like it'd been holding its breath for hours. The cop flipped back the upper section and shined his flashlight inside. He picked through the contents, removing items like shirts, pants, and undergarments. He nodded as if these things were to be expected, then reached in to extract something large and heavy. A grim sneer curled one side of his lip as he shined his light on it.

"So maybe you can explain this?"

He held up a large volume bound in red leather. The title was a single word embossed in gold lettering. Checking in at over nine hundred pages, the book was massively thick.

The single word on its cover read **Sex!** in large bold letters.

The cop shook the book at Bernie like an indictment, his wrist straining under its weight. "There's six more of these things in here, all just like this one."

Bertie was astounded that he'd been right the whole time.

The cop set the book down in order to take the handcuffs from his belt.

"We've got laws against the sale of pornography in this country, you know."

***

Perseus Grady made an unlikely Paul Revere, but that was the role his worm wanted him to play. Given his complete lack of free will in the matter, he didn't see any other option.

The sun was already setting by the time Grady walked away from Corbett and Sands. He didn't say goodbye as he left, though that was what the human part of him wanted to do. He missed being his loquacious self. Even though his worm was gregarious by Nemertean standards, his conversation fell well short of human conviviality.

His job was to contact the secret organization called Majestic, then inform them that the Earth was about to be invaded by Antarean shapeshifters. It was an assignment that should've made Phault happy as it reflected Kraall's level of trust in him. Such an assignment would make use of Grady's skills as a diplomatic liaison. It was a sensitive maneuver requiring great delicacy on his part.

There were several reasons for this level of care, some dating back to the time before the worms had resurrected them. Back then, Abel Corbett's group was one of a handful of Special Teams defined in the Majestic Manual of Operation (MMO), the document that established procedures for how to handle extraterrestrial materials and contacts.

This was, Grady discovered upon his resurrection, what had brought Corbett, Sands, and Russell to Roswell in June of 1947. While they were there, Corbett's team had encountered the other Special Team headed up by Major Arthur Ecks. As liaison for the base, Perseus Grady was given strict orders to help both teams, no questions asked. But no one had told him what to do if the help he gave one team conflicted with the help he gave the other.

Predictably, that order was challenged when he provided information to Ecks that Corbett insisted should be kept secret. This was where Grady's garrulous nature let him down. Men who liked to talk as much as Grady liked to talk should never be assigned to tasks where every word was Top Secret, or in this case, Cosmic Top Secret.

So, when Grady shared the information that Corbett didn't want him

213

to share, Corbett interpreted a certain passage in the MMO to mean that Corbett had the right to terminate Perseus Grady, though they were still technically on the same side. Five years later, Perseus Grady still resented being shot in the head, but Fate had a strange sense of humor. Otherwise, why would Grady be resurrected to serve the man who killed him?

When he stopped to think about it, Grady had to laugh at the sheer complexity of it all. Resurrecting Corbett's team was an improbable break for the worms. Most of humanity was completely ignorant of the existence of extraterrestrial life. Even those who had such knowledge, and the men who ran Majestic were pretty much the sum total of that group, were unaware of the worm presence.

The only exceptions to that rule belonged to the other Special Team, the one under the command of Arthur Ecks. But while Ecks knew there was something fishy about Corbett's team, he had no idea what it might be. All Ecks knew was that, despite reports of their demise, Corbett's team was still alive. He knew nothing of the power behind their resurrection.

The only thing that could change that was if Grady somehow ran into Arthur Ecks or Dexter Wye. Both had witnessed his execution, so explaining Grady's continuing existence would be awkward to say the least.

***

It took a surprisingly long time to find a cab. Grady stood at the corner of Independence and 1st for a good five minutes before he was able to flag down a taxi to take him to Foggy Bottom. The driver, a tall sandy-haired man in shirt sleeves and a captain's cap, looked at him so strangely at the request that Grady made a note of the name on his operating permit.

The trip was a short one. Grady paid off the driver and waited until he'd driven away before approaching the building. At the front door, he was denied entry by an armed official, but the man was alone.

When Grady asked why he wasn't allowed to enter, the man said a power outage had shut down the building, forcing its evacuation. As it was already after hours, the building virtually unoccupied.

Unfortunately, Phault didn't believe the man. Thirty seconds later, when Grady entered the building, he was amused to discover that the guard wasn't lying. There really was a power outage.

"Ah well," Grady hummed, "live and learn."

He headed straight for the office of the man who, by the same time next year, would be named director of the Agency. That information wasn't available to everyone. It was one of the nasty little things Wally Sands had been able to extract from sources Grady didn't even want to think about.

Perseus Grady climbed the darkened stairs to the fourth floor, turned right upon exiting the stairwell, and counted room numbers until he arrived outside the door where Allen Dulles still sat in the dark, waiting with spider-like patience.

The only light came from the window and even this was limited to the night sky's providence. Dulles' ears, having grown attuned to the emptiness of the building, picked up the intruder while he was still on the stairwell. He continued to listen as Grady made his way down the empty hall, every step reverberating like water drops in a subterranean grotto.

Dulles stroked the pistol on his desk with limited affection. He supposed he could use it in a pinch, but it was a crude fit for his Byzantine style. The footsteps stopped outside his door, just as he knew they would, but the man who opened it was unknown to him. Dulles didn't move, his presence hidden by the shadow of his high-backed chair. The intruder wasn't fooled.

"Mr Dulles?" Perseus Grady asked before closing the door. "I have a message."

As greetings went, this one sounded ominous. If Dulles had been a bit player in a gangster movie, Grady's introduction might've served as precursor to his execution. But Allen Dulles had grown accustomed to such preambles over the course of the war and the years that followed.

When Dulles didn't answer, Grady said, "I'm quite capable of seeing in the dark."

"Why have you come here?" Dulles asked, now on more comfortable ground. Assuming Grady was part of his network, Dulles asked, "Don't you have a contact you're supposed to report through?"

"Negative, sir," Grady replied. "I'm here on behalf of Majestic."

Dulles stifled the sharp inhale that accompanied Grady's invocation. At least they were in a secure building. "Who are you? Who sent you?"

He didn't really expect answers to either question, and was a little surprised when Grady willingly provided them.

"You may be familiar with Project Nemesis," Grady replied.

Dulles frowned, "Retrievals?"

"No, sir," Grady said, still standing in the doorway. "Contacts."

"With who?"

This was the tricky part. Grady couldn't identify the bugs as an imminent threat without raising questions about where he'd acquired the knowledge. He decided to avoid the question.

"I'll get to that in a moment, sir. I've been sent to inform you, and Majestic as a whole, that a large number of alien ships have been spotted over the city. The military will soon try to intercept those ships, if they haven't already."

Dulles leaned back, suddenly aware that he was likely the first man in a position of power to acquire this information. He started to imagine the ways he might use it.

"Do we have any idea why they're here?"

This was the question Grady was waiting for and he took the time to savor it.

"Yes, sir, we believe that this is the vanguard of an invading armada."

Even in the dark, it was a rare treat to see Allen Dulles so discombobulated.

Chapter 35 - Un Amour Divin

Neal Cranston was a hard man to love, and the only woman who knew this better than Desiree Blythe was his wife Geraldine. He was devoted to his country, the Army, and his career in that order. Of the many masters he served, sex had never risen any higher than ninth on his bestseller list, love was somewhere in the twenties, and fatherhood an honorable mention of little interest to its author.

At one time, it'd been important to have a son, but the thrill had declined with repetition. Now saddled with four, he was grateful for the small mercies he had, that only one remained in college, the others having completed their studies at West Point, West Point, and Annapolis respectively. Alan, his third and Cranston's personal black sheep, had broken the barrier so that Bryan, the youngest, could attend NYU where he majored in liberal studies, studied acting, and lived what Cranston believed to be a deviant lifestyle.

His daughters feigned indifference in his presence, but this was only to mask the open hatred they actually felt. He'd never shown the slightest affection for his female offspring, had never been the doting father. His was a man's world and the only place he'd ever found for women was on the receiving end of the three and a half minutes it took to achieve climax.

Desiree Blythe had revived his interest for a time. She was a good listener and he'd told her many things he really shouldn't have, but she was a well-kept secret, tucked away in an apartment he was paying for through a bank account he mistakenly doubted anyone could trace. As long as she stayed hidden, she wasn't likely to do any harm to his career.

The problem was that, lately, she was the one who wanted to talk. And, he suspected, that desire didn't apply just to him.

He knew she was lonely, but that was why he'd agreed to getting her that ridiculous dog. He knew she'd probably like to have a friend, another woman maybe. But other women didn't like women who looked like Desiree Blythe, even if she had put on a few pounds.

Through no fault of her own, Desiree made other women feel threatened. They worried that having a friend like Desiree might make their husband's eyes wander. While Cranston had his own more than adequate reasons to keep her hidden, that wasn't his fault. In his view, her lack of friends was Desiree's cross to bear for looking the way she did.

***

John Haste, like most men of a heterosexual persuasion and even many of the other, found he quite liked the way she looked. He'd also discovered, that despite the somewhat scatterbrained way she had of expressing herself, she wasn't dumb.

But any fears he had regarding her intelligence vanished as soon as her lips parted to receive his. He couldn't know how much she ached for that contact. Neal Cranston hadn't kissed her in three months and that last one, a quick peck on the cheek as he headed out the door, hadn't done much to hold her interest.

Haste could feel her hunger, and his body responded with every fiber of his being. Every part of him moved toward her. He was like a satellite caught in her gravity, a pile of iron filings drawn to her magnet. So when she suddenly broke away from him, he felt like an essential law of physics had been violated.

He rose bereft to the verticality afforded by his compromised spine, worried that he'd misjudged the situation or inadvertently done something wrong. He sought her eyes, though finding them brought both relief and concern. He was relieved because he saw at once, that whatever had caused her to break contact, it wasn't him. He was concerned because it was just as clear that, given the situation, only something extremely unusual could make her do so.

He looked around for an answer.

The path along the riverbank was deserted and the river flowed slow and quiet, the traffic of the day tied up for the night. In a more fulsome phase, the moon would reflect its presence on the placid water, but tonight, with the moon so new, the sky should be full of stars.

Then why, Haste wondered, was he seeing moonlight reflected in Desiree's eyes? They were fifty yards from the nearest street lamp, but an orange radiance had lit up her pale features. John Haste felt a sudden need to know what had caused her eyes to open so wide, and her lips, already parted to welcome his, to gasp in astonishment.

He felt her draw closer as he turned to face the light, her soft curves pressing into his hip and belly. He felt her arms clutching at him as she moved under his protection and he drew her in like a child. He followed her gaze across the river, and almost cried out in alarm

Hovering over some of the most heavily protected airspace in the world, he saw three orange discs floating in a revolving triangle over the Pentagon. They were only a mile distant, and if his eyes weren't playing tricks, each disc was as wide as one of the Pentagon's outer walls.

Mister Poopoo didn't like the look of them either. A warning growl started low in his little throat.

"What are they?" Desiree asked.

Haste shook his head, unable to account for what he was seeing.

"They must be flying saucers. We sure don't have anything like that."

Only then did he remember who he was holding. Haste looked down at her with questing eyes. The question already felt silly.

"Do we?"

To his relief, Desiree shook her head emphatically.

"Neal never told me about anything like that."

Mister Poopoo let loose a string of yaps to echo her denial. Desiree knelt to let the little dog leap into her arms.

They became aware of a faint hum that grew louder as they turned from each other up to the triumvirate. The three ships were turning fuzzy around the edges, their pale orange darkening to a dull umber. When the hum reached its peak, it was joined by a familiar rumble, the roar of jets, coming in low and fast. As the saucers became aware of the jets, the hum rose into a higher octave.

But just as the jets came into view, the three ships disappeared, leaving a fading trail of fire as they vanished over the southern horizon. The jets roared on in pursuit, but they were the tortoises in this race and the hares were long gone.

Gradually, Haste became aware of something soft and warm shaking against his leg. Tracking the source of that movement, he looked down into Desiree's frightened eyes and knew it was finally time for the evening to end.

"I think we better get you home."

***

But this, like many things, was easier said than done.

They'd walked a long way since meeting that afternoon and Desiree's legs, being half the length of Haste's, were exhausted. In the bliss of their magical evening, this special time they would remember as the night they fell in love, Desiree had chosen to ignore the less than perfect fit of her heels. With the spell broken, the walk back to her apartment seemed like torture.

Mister Poopoo, possessing the shortest legs of the trio, gave up as soon as they left the Potomac, dropping to his belly and refusing to move. While this normally wouldn't be a problem, Desiree had problems of her own. Her strappy open-toed pumps, which were fine for short walks, weren't designed for long hikes, and as a consequence of the extended stroll, had cut deep red grooves into the flesh of her feet.

When the saucers returned to hover over the Pentagon, they ignored the danger to rest on the steps outside the Lincoln Memorial. This allowed Desiree to remove the pumps and give her painted toes a few precious minutes of freedom. Honest Abe watched them in brooding silence, a hundred years too late to throw his stovepipe hat in the ring. John Haste felt awful when he saw how much damage the saucy pumps had done.

"Your poor feet! And like a fool, I walked you all over the city."

But before he could hang his head, he felt her hand on his cheek.

"Think nothing of it, Mister Haste. I honestly didn't feel a thing until just now. Besides," she said, with lugubrious eyes, "it was worth it."

John Haste checked his watch, surprised to find it was after one o'clock in the morning. He searched for taxis, or a public pay phone. His car, forgotten in an underground lot two miles away, was surely locked in for the night. The streets were empty as far as he could see.

He was just beginning to wonder where everyone had gone when a military jeep turned the corner two blocks away. The jeep was followed by three covered trucks. At that distance, he couldn't see what they were transporting, but he could sense the urgency in how they went about their business.

He took a seat next to Desiree, taking her hands in his. He was shocked to feel how cold they'd become. He removed his jacket for the second time that day, and this time she accepted it.

"Where are all the taxis?"

John Haste shook his head and grimaced. "I don't know. But those were military trucks. Something must be happening."

Desiree drew her legs inside his jacket. "Those things, those flying saucers. Do you think that's what brought them out?"

Haste wrapped his arms around her. He hadn't noticed the cold and was now surprised at how long she'd gone without complaining. She was freezing.

"It pretty much has to be. Looks like they warned everyone off the streets. I wouldn't be surprised if they evacuated the city."

As if to emphasize this point, two jets passed overhead.

Haste followed the jets until they were out of sight.

"We gotta get you home."

Desiree gave him a rueful smile. "I don't want to be difficult, but I just can't walk any further and I don't think Mister Poopoo can either."

The Pekingese had gone to sleep, and whether he snuffled in a dream or in agreement didn't really matter. Desiree stroked his furry head. "Can you, baby?"

Haste looked down at the discarded shoes.

"No, you're not being difficult. I've been, well, I just haven't been doing a very good job of paying attention. I can't believe you walked so far in those things without saying something."

A strange smile floated across Desiree's face. With his eyes turned the other way, Haste didn't get to see it, but he heard the warmth in her voice.

"Don't give it a thought, Mister Haste. I haven't felt this way in years."

Haste kissed her, a comfortable buss with a different kind of passion than the first one. When it ended, Haste said, "I haven't felt this good ever."

Desiree had heard men say such things before, but the difference here was that she knew he meant it. Those other men might've meant it when they said the words, but Desiree knew that John Haste, in his disheveled, unkempt way, meant it forever.

Suddenly, he cocked his head to one side. It was a gesture she would learn in time. It meant that he'd just had an idea.

"What?"

Haste shook his head, suddenly embarrassed by the thought.

"What?" She asked again.

Haste laughed, waving a dismissive hand. "Ah, it's nothing."

"Tell me."

"It's silly."

She didn't ask a third time, sensing he would tell her when he was ready.

"It's just, well, I do need to get you home..."

"Yes?"

"And, though I know this would be an imposition..."

"Tell me anyway." She felt her cheeks flush in spite of the cool air. "I'd love to know what an imposition feels like."

Haste blushed.

"Well, I was thinking that if you were to hold Mister Poopoo, I could carry both of you. I don't know how far I can do it, but, pardon my saying so, you're such a little thing."

Desiree put a finger to his lips to stop him.

"Hush. I graciously accept your offer."

The problem then became how best to do it. It was easier for her to carry Mister Poopoo if he carried her in front, but it also put a greater strain on his back. His preference was to carry her piggyback, but it alarmed Mister Poopoo to be so far from *terra firma*.

In the end, Haste carried Mister Poopoo while Desiree wrapped her legs around his ribcage, curling her arms around his throat. The malignant pumps were left to dangle from one hand.

Desiree hadn't had a piggyback ride since she was a girl. She found it exhilarating to be so far off the ground. With his arms full of Mister Poopoo, Desiree had to maintain her seat with little help from Haste. This forced her to squeeze his ribs between her thighs, establishing a familiarity that would come in handy later.

As Haste walked her back onto the long lawn of the National Mall, Desiree felt an exhausted, delirious joy. She swung the shoes by their straps and let out a wild "Yew-haw!" that echoed down the Mall to catch in the marble columns of the Capitol Building.

Snorting like a draft horse, John Haste kicked up his heels for fun, then took off at a plodding trot that even Mister Poopoo learned to enjoy.

Chapter 36 - The Ambassador Hotel

There was something alarmingly steep about the Ambassador Hotel. With no neighbors around to infringe upon it, the Ambassador appeared to have been carved out of an ancient mound of red brick, the vertical detritus of its excavation borne away to lesser purpose. As a result of this effort, the front of the hotel was a nearly flawless red rectangle from the fourth floor up, its perfection disturbed only by the architect's insistence on adding windows. On the lower floors, the brick was painted white, giving the whole structure the look of a red velvet cake turned upside down to rest upon its frosting.

Janie Gently had never been inside the Ambassador, and subject to the limitations of her salary, she felt sure she never would have made it past the burgundy-coated doorman on her own. The doorman smiled politely as she passed, though she was certain that the purpose behind his station was to keep out undesirables such as hobos, gangsters, and reporters.

Maisie Neill Ångström, on the other hand, carried herself with the air of one who belonged, and Janie watched her new friend with real appreciation. Despite her disheveled state, Maisie sauntered through the lobby like a foreign dignitary, her only concern being to keep her girls from running rampant as soon as they passed the double doors. Janie trailed behind with the suitcases until she was relieved of this duty by a covey of bellboys.

Maisie made short work of the desk clerk, waving aside his *pro forma* claim that there were no rooms to be had. Her requirements were announced in a sharp clipped tone that rejected any attempt at contradiction.

"My name is Ångström. I will require two rooms, one for the girls and one for myself. My husband may be joining us later as well."

The desk clerk was accustomed to dealing with difficult people. In truth, he considered it part of his job. Under different circumstances, he might've put her through the usual charade of claiming a dearth of vacancies, or asking if she had a reservation. But he'd been on duty when this woman and her band of hellions departed and saw no need for a repeat of the morning's performance.

In her current state, with the prospect of the girls wreaking havoc on the lobby, he judiciously decided that the hotel's interests would be best served by getting them into a room before further mayhem could erupt. The Ambassador, like any such establishment, was strict about maintaining its standards.

Sensing their association was at an end, Janie held back as Maisie guided her brood toward the elevators. To her surprise, Maisie noticed her absence, and pausing just short of the lift, turned to search for her savior. Spotting the elusive reporter, she closed the gap to take Janie's forearm in her firm grip.

"Please, don't go! You must let me show my gratitude. Let me freshen up and get the girls settled. Then we'll see if we can find a drink and maybe have some dinner if you're hungry."

Janie's reticence showed. The opulence of the Ambassador made her feel dowdy and plain. Actually, she always felt dowdy and plain, but the Ambassador had a way of exacerbating her inferiority.

"Ah, I shouldn't, Mrs Ångström," Janie said, pulling away. "You've had a long day. I bet you'd like to rest."

"Nonsense," the older woman said. "First of all, it's Maisie, and second, you're coming with me and I won't hear another word about it."

With a mischievous smile, Maisie called on her daughters for support.

"Girls, I'm inviting Janie to join us for supper and I think she needs some encouragement."

After that it was impossible to refuse. Stormy and Molly took her by the wrists while Bubbles placed both hands on Janie's butt and started pushing. The sheer boldness of the attack caught her by surprise and made Janie laugh. The laugh banished the last of her resistance.

The rooms were across the hall from each other. Maisie left the girls and one of the suitcases in the first with instructions to be ready for dinner in an hour.

Janie paused in the doorway of the second room, suddenly so anxious that she felt compelled to offer, "I could keep an eye on the girls while you freshen up."

Maisie's laugh had a musical ring.

"Don't be ridiculous. They'll be fine. We can talk while I freshen up."

The bellboy left with a dime from Maisie's purse, and as the door closed behind him, Maisie took a good look at the first mirror she'd seen since the airport debacle. She made Janie laugh by clucking at the inky streaks of teary mascara running down her cheeks.

In fairness, her foundation would've been difficult enough to maintain in Wisconsin. But in the humid steam bath of an average Washington summer, it had completely disintegrated. The resulting topography resembled the caked flesh of a radioactive mutant from a low budget science fiction film. A younger Maisie would've been horrified at the prospect of appearing in public with the left half of her hairdo sticking up like the red flag on a mailbox, but this elder version had been a mother for over a decade. Maybe she'd never been put on public display in a worse condition, but she could recall a couple of occasions when it'd been close.

"You just have a seat, this won't take but a minute."

She'd taken an immediate liking to Janie, and as she swiped at the ruined makeup with a tissue, she realized that one reason for that affection was Janie's apparent indifference to her cosmetic disarray. Not once had she seen pursed lips or disapproval narrow Janie's eyes the way she would expect from her friends back in La Crosse. Tossing aside the first of many tissues, Maisie regarded her reflection with a philosophical air.

She waved Janie to one of the two chairs by the window and sat on the bed to remove her shoes. Then, with a lack of self-consciousness that Janie found more than a little disconcerting, the mother of three hiked her skirt up to her hips to unclip her stockings.

"I don't know what possessed me to wear silk stockings in this weather," Maisie babbled as she rolled down the first. "If anyone asks, I'll say I was taken by a fit of madness,"

"It does get muggy this time of year," Janie agreed, still unsure why she was hanging around.

"You'd think I'd remember that. I lived here during my father's first term."

Janie was, of course, aware that Stanford Neill had been a two-term senator from Wisconsin. But, under the circumstances, she felt a judicial application of ignorance was called for.

"Oh, your father was a congressman?"

Maisie dampened a hand towel in the bathroom sink and used it to wipe away the rest of her ruined foundation and the horror show mascara. She scowled at every swipe, groaning as the flesh-tone crud fell away in sheets.

"Senator. Stanford Neill? He lost his seat to that awful McAfee man in '48."

"I'm sorry-" Janie started to apologize.

"Oh, don't be. Daddy was fed up with DC. He's fine now, as long as we keep the gun closet locked and don't let him listen to the news. He's over seventy now and he's happier sitting on his porch and shaking his fist at the world than he ever was in the Senate."

There was a small round table next to Janie that held a glass ashtray with an Ambassador decal. She wondered if it would be all right to smoke and thought about asking for permission. Instead, she decided to delve deeper into Ångström family life.

"I hope you don't mind me asking, but I'm worried what your husband will think when he gets to the airport and can't find you. Won't he wonder what happened to you?"

Maisie came out of the bathroom, her face fresh and pink to begin the process of taming her hair with a bristle brush. She took a seat at the vanity and began to comb it out with short deft strokes.

"That's funny," she said mirthlessly, "you worrying about Lars."

Satisfied with the state of her hair, she pushed it back behind her ears.

"My husband can be a very selfish man at times. He knew our flight left at four o'clock and he assured me he would be there with time to spare. Instead, we waited all afternoon for him, well after the flight left, in fact. I wasn't about to get on that plane. Can you imagine? I mean, what would I do in Helsinki without him? I can't speak a word of Swedish."

Maisie walked over to stand in front of Janie, letting the hairbrush fall to her side. Janie was amazed at her transformation. The conservative perm had been overpowered, albeit reluctantly, leaving a sumptuous mass of auburn hair that fell to her shoulders in waves. Her face, having shed its makeup, glistened with robust good health. The lipstick, an unflattering shade of violet that couldn't quite decide if it favored the red or blue end of the spectrum, had been wiped away to reveal a pair of full expressive lips that, when she smiled, drew back to display the prominent incisors of a predator.

"But, Janie, you haven't told me a thing about yourself. I assume you're a working girl, but I don't have the first notion of what you do for a living."

There was a question somewhere in last half of her sentence, and it caught Janie by surprise. Some instinct warned her that, given Lars Ångström's notoriety, it might be better to keep her occupation a secret. She had to scramble to come up with a believable occupation.

"Oh, nothing special. I work at the Library of Congress."

Janie liked that. It wasn't even untrue. She did a lot of her work there.

Maisie gave another mischievous smile, then turned away.

"Do you think you might unzip me? I always have the most difficult time with this dress."

Janie released the pack of Viceroys she'd been fingering in her purse.

"Sure, I suppose so."

Maisie tossed the brush onto the bed and used both hands to clear her hair away from the zipper. One coil escaped her, falling to brush against Janie's hand. Despite a lifetime of perms, the texture of her hair was marvelously supple. The sensation sent an unexpected thrill up Janie's forearm. Reaching for the zipper, Janie was surprised to find that her hands were trembling.

Maisie, sensing something awry, warned her.

"You'll have to be careful. This thing gets stuck all the time. I'm so glad you're here. The girls are still too young to get it right. And too short," she added as an afterthought.

Janie gulped, wondering why she was so nervous. Pinching the hem of the dress between thumb and forefinger, she lifted the tab and drew the zipper down. The dress parted to reveal the topology of Maisie's spine from neck to tailbone.

"The brassiere, too, if you don't mind."

Janie's heart leapt into her throat as she stifled a gasp. This time, she couldn't mask her shaking hands, and it was only with considerable difficulty that she managed to separate the hooks from the eyelets.

Maisie complimented her with a murmured, "Perfect," then turned to face her, sliding the dress and the bra off of her shoulders. The dress fell partway, catching on her hips, but the bra slid down her arms to land on the floor.

Then, in a move that didn't surprise her half as much as it should have, Maisie Neill pressed her lips against Janie's, and sucked out her resistance with a kiss that made her knees buckle and sent her sprawling weakly onto the bed.

Maisie shimmied her dress to the floor, stepping out of it to kneel over the fallen reporter like a jungle cat, her eyes steamy with lust.

She murmured her approval again, though the meaning had changed into something infinitely more mutable.

"Perfect."

Chapter 37 - A Captive Audience

Arthur Ecks tried to open his eyes, but found he had to brush the sand away before he could safely do so. He reached into his jacket for a handkerchief, but even his pockets were full of the stuff and when he shook his head, still more drizzled down onto his shoulders like the aftermath of a bad day at the beach. By the time, he could safely look around at his new surroundings, the hands that had dragged him inside were gone. Joe McAfee and Clarence stood to either side of him, wearing identical grins.

"Clarence has something to say to you," McAfee said, "don't you, Clarence?"

"Yes, sir," Clarence agreed, hanging his head like a scolded schoolboy, "I want to apologize for pushing you. It was very rude of me."

Clarence offered up his most contrite expression, folding his hands in front of his chest and slightly bowing his head. "I hope you'll be able to forgive me."

Ecks scowled, ignoring the apology. He continued to wipe sand from his eyes and cheeks, then looked around the strange room, a little surprised to find the floor covered in the stuff. Suddenly, the sand was more important than the apology.

"What's with the sand?"

McAfee turned to his aide. "Would you like to tell him, Clarence? I have so many things to attend to." Addressing Ecks, he added, with an air of regret.

"You can imagine how many details there are in planning an invasion of this magnitude. I'm going to be busy for a while, but if you like, I can have Clarence show you around."

Ecks shrugged, sending a torrent of fine grains down the back of his shirt. "Sure, why not?"

With this settled, McAfee spun about in a swirling pirouette and, stunning Ecks with the grace of this balletic maneuver, sank down into the sandy floor. If he hadn't seen it happen, Ecks would've dismissed the action as either impossible or straddling that fragile border separating improbability from the constraints of known physics. He looked to Clarence, unable to hide the quizzical expression that'd forced its way onto his features.

"So," Clarence said, lingering over that syllable, "you're curious about the sand?"

Ecks nodded numbly, unable to think of anything else he wanted to add.

"Well," Clarence began, taking his elbow as if they were old friends. "Where should I start?"

"Sand is our natural element. We're born to it, we live in it, and our bodies process it to extract the silicon we breathe and the nutrients that sustain us."

Ecks parsed what he needed from the words, though he might have found a more politic way to phrase his response.

"You're sand eaters?"

Clarence nodded, but didn't seem to take any offense.

"In a sense. You've probably guessed that this isn't our natural form."

"I kinda figured that out on my own," Ecks said.

Clarence swept his hands down his torso to indicate his human body.

"So you understand then that we're shapeshifters. Given time, we can mimic virtually any life form large enough to accommodate our mass. Human bodies are a little confining, but we can compress ourselves to hide the excess weight. If you tried to lift me, you'd find that I weigh a great deal more than you'd think."

"How much more?"

Guiding Ecks by the elbow, Clarence turned him around. "Oh, something around four hundred pounds. I don't know how that converts to grams."

"Neither do I," Ecks muttered darkly. "You're a hefty boy, Clarence."

"Perhaps," Clarence sniffed, a trifle offended, "but you could stand to drop a few pounds yourself, major. Shall we begin the tour?"

"Might as well," Ecks growled, "unless you're busy conquering the Earth, too."

Clarence preened at the dig, but deflected Ecks' mood with good manners.

"I am entirely at your service, major. Since we're already here, we'll begin with the receiving chamber. This is where we enter and leave the ship. The sand under our feet is of a special variety that cleanses us of any microbial life we might pick up outside. Due to the climate of your capital, there's quite a lot to get rid of."

"Well, you know what they say," Ecks pointed out, "politics is a dirty game."

"In more ways than one," Clarence agreed. "But have no fear. We'll clean things up once we're in control."

"What's that supposed to mean?"

"Oh, you'll find out in due time," Clarence replied mysteriously. "I'd hate to spoil the surprise."

Ecks looked around the chamber, noting the hieroglyphic markings that covered most of the available wall space. "What's with all the...?" Ecks waved his hands at an I-beam just over his head.

Clarence picked up his meaning despite the vague way it was expressed.

"This is our written language. I'm afraid it doesn't say much of interest. These are just safety precautions to be taken when entering or exiting the ship. You must have something similar on your submarines, warnings not to open the doors while the ship is underway, that sort of thing."

Ecks peered at the queer room, noting its low ceiling and infrared lighting. Everything seemed to be constructed of the same rusty red metal. He brushed his fingertips against the ceiling, finding its texture to be as rough as it looked.

"How about this...material? What is it?"

Clarence shook his head in amusement.

"Nothing that would make the slightest bit of sense unless you're a closet metallurgist. It's an alloy of several base metals that have been combined to create a material that's lightweight, heat-resistant, and remarkably strong. It isn't perfect yet, we've been unable to get rid of that orange residue it exhales when it comes in contact with high-oxygen atmospheres, but it performs marvelously in deep space."

Ecks nodded sulkily. Every alien species he'd met thought it was so damned superior. The floor under their feet shifted radically as a dozen subterraneous forms jetted by like fish swimming through shallow water.

"Jesus!" Ecks swore. "What the hell was that?"

Clarence did his little shrug.

"As I said before, what you dismiss as simple sand is our natural element. We move through sand in much the same way you move through air or fish move through water. It's what our bodies are designed for. I suspect it's time to give you a demonstration."

Ecks didn't even want to think what such a demonstration might entail.

"Ah, that's fine, you don't have to do that. I'm perfectly happy right here."

But Clarence shook his sandy head.

"No, major, I'm afraid it won't do. We need this room for other purposes. Normally, we keep it filled to the ceiling, but we carved this space out so you could breathe. Now, we have to refill it. You'll be taken to a holding cell. We'll have to finish our tour another time. Our leader, the one you know as Senator McAfee, will want to see you later when the attack is underway, but for now, we're must ask you to be patient. We will do all we can to make you as comfortable as possible."

"Do you think you could stop attacking my planet? It makes me nervous."

Clarence nodded, as if Ecks' request had confirmed something.

"Well, we were wrong about that. You do have a sense of humor."

"I wasn't joking," Ecks said.

The floor began to churn again as two things that looked like branches of the same lichen-covered oak rose out of the sand. Ecks backed away until the oaks began to change. Right before his eyes, the oak branches transformed into bookend copies of Clarence.

"Jesus!" Arthur Ecks swore. "How many of you are there?"

The first Clarence laughed out loud.

"I doubt that you could tell us apart in our natural form," he replied. "It takes us more time to mimic a unique individual, so we make copies as a shortcut. We've found that this form has the freedom we need to move about in human society. When there's a need for a specific function, we simply make alterations to change its outward appearance-"

Ecks frowned. "Change how?"

It took Clarence a moment to grasp his meaning.

"Oh, I see what you mean. Let me think of an example. How about this? When a particular Clarence is required to function as a cab driver, he will manifest a sweaty shirt with bow tie and a captain's cap, but everything else will stay the same. It's quicker because we only have to change part-"

"Wait," Ecks said, suddenly grasping something beyond what Clarence had said, "you mean the clothes are actually part of you?"

All three Clarences nodded in unison. "Oh, yes!"

The first Clarence continued.

"Something like that. Now these two will escort you to a holding cell. Both may be addressed as Clarence, just as you've been addressing me. I must caution you not to struggle or try to get away. Doing so might result in suffocation. They'll be taking you down several levels and you'll be moving through solid sand. If you break free, you'll probably run out of air before they can recover you. You're going to a place we've prepared for human use and you'll find some men you know already waiting there."

The new Clarences moved to either side of Ecks, each taking an arm.

"Now," said the first Clarence, "take a deep breath..."

***

A minute later, Ecks came out of the sand. He emptied his lungs in a rush, took one long deep shuddering breath, and collapsed onto the sandy floor. His lungs had to work hard to get oxygen back into his body and bring color to his pallor.

When he was able to speak, he said to no one in particular, "I hope to hell I never have to do that again."

"Don't count on it," a sour voice said. "They move us every couple of days so they can recycle the sand."

Arthur Ecks brushed grit away from his hair and face. When he could safely open his eyes, the place he saw wasn't very different from the one he'd left. It had the same rusty walls with the same strange writing and the same low ceiling and sandy floor. The only difference was, this time he wasn't alone. As promised, he'd already met the four men surrounding him.

The men stood in a ragged arc, Ed Ruppelt and Allen Hynek of Project Blue Book, Lincoln La Paz from the University of New Mexico, and Donald Keyhoe from *True* Magazine.

"They expect us to use this place as a goddamned toilet," the sour man complained. "Makes you feel like a goddamned cat."

"Welcome to the secret you've been searching for," Keyhoe said acidly.

Ecks shook his head. Keyhoe was sour enough, but Ecks had seen him just that morning so he wasn't the sour voice. Ecks looked around to find the source of the commentary.

229

Seated with his back against the rusty wall, Senator Joseph McAfee sat glowering back, favoring the men in the room with the same glare he normally reserved for Helen Gahagan Douglas, and all the pinkos and fags inside the State Department.

Chapter 38 - Sweet Release

An important part of police training involves learning to guide a handcuffed prisoner into the back of a squad car without smacking his head on the door frame. Sadly, this skill is frequently neglected and more often ignored entirely. The airport cop who provided this service for Abel Corbett had either been off sick that day, or didn't feel like doing Abel Corbett any favors. There were no such problems with Wally Sands, but he was a shorter man. Corbett, almost a full foot taller, fell into the back with a long red welt marking the spot where he'd failed to duck.

Corbett wouldn't remember the ride downtown, the bash on the head having scrambled his worm into a petulant silence. It wasn't all bad though. Neither Kraall nor Corbett had to suffer through the extended rant by Wally Sands. This was probably for the best, because, in addressing his need for content, Sands made frequent reference to subjects Corbett had expressly named as being taboo in human company.

His most heinous transgression involved the worms' presence on Earth, a gaffe that would normally require disciplinary action. Fortunately, the police had dismissed his rant as the ravings of a lunatic. This was understandable, given that the first thing Wally blabbed was that he had a giant worm in his head that had eaten part of his brain.

Upon arrival at the precinct, the pair were booked and put in a holding cell to await disposition. The holding cell was a filthy cube, already chock full of drunks and petty criminals. Its unique smell was a mixture of piss, fecal miscues, ancient colonies of vomit, and the bacteria that thrived in those environments.

Sands guided the stupefied Corbett to a bench whose resident drunk had pissed himself. Sands snarled at the drunk and when this failed to move him, lifted the man by his shirt and threw him to the floor. He sat Corbett down in the vacant urinal and thrust his bulldog chin forward in a blanket challenge to the room. In different circumstances, he might have faced opposition, but these tired men were too far gone to respond to such a naked promise of aggression.

Corbett was numb to the world for almost two hours. During that time, a steady stream of men were brought in and taken out. He didn't begin his climb back to consciousness until the door was opened to admit a short fat man in a shabby suit. The fat man loudly protested the police treatment he'd received as a member of the fourth estate, invoking strange references to the rights of Americans and freedom of the press. The jailer had no idea what the fourth estate might be. For that matter, he couldn't name the first three either. Bertie Stein thrust his froggy mug through the bars in one last plea for justice, but the jailer shook his head and snatched Bertie's half-smoked stogie right out of his mouth.

"No smoking," he explained, tossing the soggy butt in the trash.

It was Bertie's good fortune that his stay in the holding cell wasn't a long one. Less than an hour after the bars had closed behind him, the jailer was back, calling out three names for release. His voice was remarkable only for its lack of enthusiasm.

"Stein, Corbett, Sands, this is your lucky day."

The jailer led them out of the cells, down a hall, and through a few doors to stand before the release clerk. The release clerk didn't even look up as the trio approached. "This them? The airport boys?"

The jailer shrugged, which the clerk guessed meant yes. The jailer had only been at his job for three days. He was still trying to get a read on the clerk who'd been at his desk for a decade. The clerk looked down at his paperwork.

"So what do we have here? You were all arrested at the airport, two separate incidents. Mr Stein, you were in possession of a suitcase belonging to a Dr Lars Ångström and your explanation of how you obtained it was suspicious."

"Fortunately, the Ambassador Hotel has confirmed that Dr Ångström and his family are currently guests of the hotel. The hotel has taken possession of the suitcase and, as no one has filed charges against you, you're free to go."

"If you'll sign here," he thrust a form at Bertie, pointing at a line near the bottom, "I can return your personal items." After Bertie had done so, the clerk slid him a tray containing his wallet, keys, lighter, and two wrapped Macanudos.

"Door at the end of the hall, exit to your right."

As Bertie began his long shuffle toward the freedom of the parking lot, the clerk turned his attention to Corbett and Sands.

"Now, as for you two, I don't know why the hell we're letting you out. If it was up to me, you'd be looking at a nice long paid holiday at the expense of the state." He read from the list of charges, "accosting a woman repeatedly, battery, inciting a riot, resisting arrest, striking a police officer..., it just goes on and on..."

The clerk looked up long enough to smile at the pulpy lopsided faces of the two men, taking pleasure in the number of shoe prints left by the beating.

"We were able to find the name of the woman you accosted though she was gone by the time you were taken into custody. Interestingly enough, she has the same surname as the man whose suitcase was stolen. We tracked Mrs Ångström to her hotel, but were unable to contact her. Since she hasn't contacted us, there's no one to swear out a complaint. But that's not why we're letting you out."

Down the hall, Bertie froze at the name Ångström. Leaning against the wall, he put a hand to his lower back in the manner of any man with chronic problems in that part of his anatomy.

Back at the desk, the release clerk continued.

"Unfortunately, in going through your personal items, we discovered your ID badges from the agency you work for. As a taxpayer, I'm appalled to see our government employing men of your ilk, but we contacted your agency and they have insisted that we release you immediately. My understanding is that a man is being sent to pick you up and any disciplinary action will be handled internally."

"So," he concluded, "at least we can all look forward to that. Please sign."

Wally Sands ignored pretty much everything the clerk said. He'd been in an agitated state ever since hearing that the shabby reporter had been arrested with Ångström's suitcase. Upon Bertie's release, Wally had monitored his slow journey down the hall. Sands signed the release with an unreadable scrawl, and immediately took off in pursuit, only to be surprised at how little progress the old man had made toward the exit.

When Bertie heard the rustling exchange of confiscated property, he resumed his journey without a backward glance. By the time the door closed on Bertie Stein, Wally Sands was already ignoring the clerk's warning.

"You two better keep your noses clean. Next time, you may not be so lucky."

They were further delayed by the appearance of Winthrop Walton Russell. Russell joined them in the corridor, albeit through a different door than the one that'd spewed Corbett and Sands.

"What the hell are you doing here?" Corbett said as soon as he saw Russell. "I told you to keep an eye on Ångström."

"I let him go," Russell explained without any trace of fear or embarrassment. "He was nice to me."

As Corbett built toward the inevitable explosion, Russell held up a hand to forestall his master's anger.

"Don't worry. I've already punished myself. It really hurt."

***

Bertie's back spasm was real.

The thing that'd triggered it was a bit of mental arithmetic. Until he heard the name Ångström in reference to the black-suited pair, he hadn't realized that these were the two killers he'd seen rising out of a manhole behind the Senate building. He hadn't realized that they were the men he'd seen getting stuffed into the back of a police cruiser at the airport. He hadn't even noticed them in the cell. Both men had been there for hours when he arrived and their presence was mercifully obscured from him by the host of drunks that separated one end of the cell from the other.

He'd been so preoccupied with his own situation that he didn't realize who the men were until the release clerk announced that they'd been arrested for assaulting the Ångström woman. So, with that and the suitcase for evidence, he finally understood Janie Gently's evil plan in absconding with the Ångström clan while leaving him to be picked up by the cops.

Bertie cursed the girl reporter with a vehemence he usually reserved for Nazis.

There would be revenge, of course, but that would have to come later, after he'd had time to think. His more immediate need was to get the hell out of the police station and as far away from the two killers as was humanly possible. Bertie pushed away from the wall, fighting the spasm as he started for the door.

His progress was predictably glacial. With his failing back, and his fallen arches, Bertie Stein was a tortoise in a world of jackrabbits. The back issue, along with the extra weight he carried, put more stress on his hips, and God knew he could lose fifty pounds without missing an ounce.

He was fed up with playing investigative reporter. All he wanted now was to get back to his room at the Y and go to sleep. He wanted this even though he was ravenous and hadn't eaten for hours.

The exit door loomed ahead as the release clerk issued his final warning. Bertie's hand reached for the knob.

***

"We'll discuss this later," Corbett hissed icily. Despite the self-inflicted punishment, he wanted to hit Russell every bit as much as Kraall wanted to do something he didn't understand to Mudduk.

"Come on," he said, pointing toward the door at end of the corridor.

"Do you even realize what you've done?" Corbett whispered as he strode angrily down the hall.

"Probably not," Russell admitted. He didn't say this very loudly. He certainly didn't say it loud enough for Corbett to hear, not that it would have mattered.

"Ångström has seen our headquarters. He knows what we are and, in case you didn't know, he works for that damned Major Ecks."

"Is that a problem?" Russell asked.

Corbett stopped to put his hands on his hips. In his head, he praised himself for the patience he was showing.

"Yes, it's a problem. Ecks is one of the few humans who knows we're here and he one of a smaller group who happens to be in a position to do something about it. We have to get Ångström back before he has a chance to talk to Ecks."

Russell puzzled over this for a moment.

"What are you going to do with him once you get him back?"

Corbett shook his head. It was hard being the only one who could think.

"We're going to kill him, of course."

Russell frowned. "That doesn't seem very nice."

Corbett turned the knob on the door to the parking lot.

"It's not supposed to be nice. What do you think the humans will do to us if they find out we're here?"

"Dr Ångström was really nice. Maybe the others will be, too."

Abel Corbett shook his head in disbelief.

"Sometimes I wonder whose side you're on."

Wally Sands was thinking he could overtake Bertie in the parking lot, but he screwed it up by pausing to watch Corbett chew Russell out. He liked watching Russell's frequent humiliations, considering it one of the perks of being Corbett's second in command. With the reporter's lack of progress, he thought he had plenty of time, and though he only watched for a moment, in doing so, he missed Bertie's exit. When he found that the reporter had disappeared, he blamed Bertie's disappearance on Russell for distracting him.

As he slipped through the door that exited onto the parking lot, Wally realized that he didn't know why he wanted to get Bertie Stein. He just knew that he did. He could say that it had something to do with retrieving Lars Ångström, but the truth was, his pursuit was more instinctual than rational. He'd been watching when the reporter seized his lower back, and he'd noticed that Bertie had done so at the very instant the release clerk said, 'Ångström.' Putting that together with the man having Ångström's suitcase and...that had to mean something even if Wally couldn't see what it was.

The parking lot had enough room for a dozen cars. The spaces were set in opposing rows, but only three were filled. Bertie had seen the time on a wall clock before leaving the station, both hands coming together in that vertical position indicating noon or midnight. The glow of the street lamps settled the question of which. Bertie headed for the curb to stand under one.

He dawdled at the edge of the lot, futzing with his back, looking down to see if his shoe laces were still tied. He'd been thinking he might flag down a taxi and, hang the expense, take it back to his room at the YMCA. The buses sure as hell weren't running this late. But as he stood on the curb, he didn't see any taxis either. Bertie Stein shook his head.

When he was done shaking his head, he was mortified to realize what he'd done with his day. He'd spent almost all of it chasing a man for no more than a girl reporter's hunch. He'd started out three steps behind Ångström and God knew how far back he was now. He'd been kidnapped, forced to ride in a clown car, abandoned, and finally arrested.

This wasn't how he worked.

Bertie Stein hadn't done legwork in thirty years.

Feeling in his pocket for a fresh Macanudo, he decided it was time to use the brain he'd been ignoring all day. He never should have listened to Janie Gently. It was time to give up, go back to his room, and get a good night's sleep.

In the morning, he'd call Sadie up in Brooklyn and let her chew his ear for half an hour. Then he'd get some breakfast, a couple eggs over easy, three slices of rye toast, a pitcher of black coffee, and if God had his head turned, maybe a few slices of bacon. His mind made up, he left the safety of the street lamp, to head for the main drag where he hoped it would be easier to find a taxi.

He never saw Wally Sands come up behind him. He felt, but did not see the handkerchief over his nose and mouth. He was dimly aware of its scent, something sweet and sleepy. Bertie closed his eyes and fell into waiting arms. After that, there was nothing at all.

***

The black Ford coupe was parked in the slot closest to the street, under the umbrella of an old oak that cut off the light from the street lamp. From a kit bag in the trunk, Wally Sands extracted the jar of chloroform and used it to soak a handkerchief. Holding his breath against the effects, he ran out to the sidewalk to join Corbett in ambushing the reporter. After the chloroform did its work, the two men maneuvered Bertie into the back seat of the Ford, the dead weight of his limp body putting up more of a fight than a conscious Bertie ever could.

Corbett took the passenger seat, while Sands slid into the back with their prisoner. Russell, the low man on the worm totem, started the engine and put the car into gear. They were out of the parking lot less than a minute after taking the old man. While Russell drove, Sands rolled his window down to minimize the effect of the chloroform hankie, unwilling to get rid of it until they were some distance from the station.

Traffic was unusually light for a Saturday. Corbett counted three cars on their way through Foggy Bottom, and all were headed in the other direction. He saw what looked like a military transport as they turned onto 17th, but it was blocks away and not yet a concern. He already had a destination in mind.

The first order of business was undoing the mess that Russell had made. That meant retrieving Lars Ångström. Corbett reasoned that, if Ångström was going anywhere, it would be to rejoin his family. And if not, he was sure that Ångström's wife and those brat daughters could be used as bait to draw him out. If what he'd heard at the release desk was true, the Ångströms were staying at the Ambassador Hotel.

Corbett glanced into the back seat where Bertie Stein was beginning to stir. When he turned back to the road, his thin features lit up with the wicked grin of a born villain. The seed of an idea was taking root, an idea that was absolutely reprehensible in every way. The first step was getting rid of Russell.

"Pull over here and get out," Abel Corbett said, "I'm taking the car. You're going back to work on the equipment."

"But it's miles," Russell complained, knowing it wouldn't make a bit of difference. 'Not even a word of thanks,' thought Winthrop Walton Russell as the car sped off into the night. 'At least Dr Ångström said thank you.'

***

If the streets were quiet on the drive to the Ambassador, that somnolence was nothing compared to the silence that pervaded its lobby. Aside from a last call conversation in the bar, the lobby was devoid of activity.

236

A bellboy in a pillbox fez slumped against a marble pillar while a desk clerk with a sweaty comb-over perused racing form, his last pitiful wager doomed by the same run of bad luck that'd been killing him for weeks. The cigarette he wasn't supposed to smoke on duty smoldered forgotten by his elbow, an inch of slow ash crumbling to powder.

While Wally Sands initiated the sequence of events that would result in the bellboy losing consciousness, his uniform, and his job, Corbett laid a five dollar bill on the counter where the clerk could see it.

"Tell me which room the Ångströms are in and I'll let you talk to this guy's big brother."

The clerk looked up hungrily, his furtive eyes scanning the empty lobby.

"This ain't that kind of hotel, bub."

One side of Corbett's face smiled.

"No one says it is. My business is with Dr Ångström, but I know he has family."

"Well, you're outta luck then, 'cause he ain't here."

The clerk took his lip between his teeth gnawing on the worry that he'd said too much. Corbett slid the bill across the counter, then watched it disappear.

"You know, big brother tends to worry about the little tyke."

The clerk's eyes darted up at Corbett before making a second circuit of the room. "Yeah, which brother we talking about? Jackson?"

The other half of Corbett's face joined the smile. "Grant."

The clerk sucked a lungful of air with an audible hiss. "Show me."

Corbett lay his palm on the counter, flipping it just enough to show the '50' at the corner. The clerk tried to take it, but Corbett pulled it out of reach.

"Uh-uh, first the room number."

The clerk's hand left, fluttering up to wipe away a thin trail of saliva.

"Okay, but I wasn't kidding. Ångström isn't here. They was supposed to leave this morning, but the wife came back in a holy snit. She has two rooms across the hall from each other, 801 and 802. The girls are in one, she's in the other, but I don't know which is which. If that matters, the bellboy could tell you for a chat with Mr Lincoln."

Corbett slid the bill over, lifting his hand to show the number again.

"Thanks, it doesn't. Just one last thing."

The clerk reached again, then paused, sensing imminent betrayal.

"What?"

Corbett kept his eyes on the clerk as he drew back to reveal the face of the Hero of Appomattox.

"I need to see the registry, specifically the page where Dr Ångström signed in."

The clerk got a scared look that sent his eyes darting back around the room.

"I can't do that! They'd fire me. I'd be blackballed. I'd never work this line again, leastways not anyplace that pays."

The Hero of Appomattox disappeared under Corbett's palm.

"That's very ... disappointing."

Visible beads of sweat formed under the sparse strands disguising the clerk's scalp. One, having grown too large to maintain its grip, rolled down his temple to plop onto the carpet. The clerk's voice dropped into a darker register.

"You dirty sonuvabitch."

Corbett accepted the characterization with equanimity.

"I happen to be a guest at this hotel, friend."

Realizing he was beaten, the clerk set a large volume on the counter, flipping the pages back a few days. He pointed to a line midway down the page.

"There you go. Dr Lars Ångström. You happy now, chief?"

Corbett's eyes devoured the signature, noting its eccentricities. When he felt satisfied, he looked up again, revealing the Hero of Appomattox the way a fan dancer might show a bit of thigh.

"Just one last thing."

"You already said that. Whaddaya want now?"

Corbett removed his hand, pursing his lips to blow. His breath caught the bill and sent it spinning off the counter to fall at the clerk's feet.

"I was wondering if I might borrow a few pieces of hotel stationary and a pen. I think I'd like to write a letter."

Chapter 39 - Hysteria

"Hey, mister," Dex called, peering deep into the trunk, "you can come on out now. No one's going to hurt you." He stepped away from the car, hoping that giving the man his space might put him more at ease.

"Then why did you kidnap me?" Detlev Bronk fired back. He didn't come any closer to leaving his confinement, but Dex took it as a positive that he didn't scoot further away.

"I didn't kidnap you," Dex explained. "I heard you knocking so I let you out."

"Someone did!" Bronk cried heatedly.

"Maybe so," said Dex, "but it wasn't me."

"Why did they do it?" Bronk asked, coming forward a little bit. Dex caught a glimpse of pale skin and a prominent jawline, but the eyes remained hidden.

"Did you see anyone?" Dex asked. "Could you identify the men who took you?"

Bronk couldn't hide his horror, or the hysteria that accompanied it.

"See them? I saw all of them! They were all the same man! How could that be possible? They were like twins! They all had the same face!"

Bronk retreated again, so Dex took another step back. He was starting to realize that getting this man out of the trunk was going to be like coaxing a kitten out of a tree. In stepping back, he found the solution, however accidentally, as the car's interior light fell on his face.

After more hesitation, Bronk came forward, before pausing at the rim to confirm the identification. A pair of rheumy eyes peered up at Dex for several seconds before concluding.

"You're not one of them," Bronk said. "You're not even Keyhoe. You don't look like them at all. They were much taller."

These last observations were loose-jointed ramblings, as if the conscious part of Bronk's mind had moved on to other subjects. His eyes listed left and right, still searching for his kidnappers.

"That's because I wasn't one of them," Dex explained slowly, trying to be patient despite his eagerness to get going. He still had to figure out a way to get Artie back and he was hoping one of the others might help. Jakob or Lars would know what to do.

"Listen, I've got to get back to town. I guess it's okay if you want to ride back there, but I think you'll be more comfortable up front with me. You can tell me what happened on the way back."

Bronk left the trunk without any more prodding, but his eyes and posture remained distrustful. Dex stepped further into the shadows, allowing Bronk a wide berth. His body seemed stiff and bent out of shape by his ordeal. He had considerable trouble rising to his full height.

"What is this place?" Bronk asked suspiciously, trying to frame shapes out of the dappled shadows.

"Your guess is as good as mine," Dex replied.

"How did you get here?" Bronk asked. "Were you kidnapped too?"

Dex started to say no, then thought about trying to explain what'd happened to him. He decided it was easier to just say yes.

"Yeah, I was in one of the other cars."

"Other cars?"

Dex waved for Bronk to come away from the car, then pointed at the others.

"Yeah, I got out just in time to see them take a friend of mine up the hill." This sounded good so far. "He didn't come back down so I think they took him somewhere."

"Who were they?"

"I don't know," Dex admitted. "Unlike you, I didn't see any faces."

Bronk's eyes darted nervously about.

"Then how do you know they had your friend?"

Dex had to think about that.

"By the way he moved, I guess. He turned when I called his name."

Bronk took a step away from the car, then meticulously closed the lid of the trunk with a soft snick. "Where is he now? Your friend?"

Dex frowned, not liking where this was going. One thing he'd learned from five years of investigations was that the other guy was there to answer questions, not ask them.

"I don't know," Dex admitted, realizing that he couldn't very well say that Artie had been taken aboard a flying saucer. "They took him away."

Bronk looked up at the silhouette of the hill, then back to Dex.

"If they took your friend, why did they leave you behind? For that matter, why did they leave me behind?"

"I don't know," Dex said again. "Maybe they decided we'd be worth more to them on the loose. Maybe they were in too big a hurry, or maybe they just forgot you were there. The important thing is they left us behind."

"Listen," he said, changing the subject, "I need to get back into town to look for my friend. Do you want to ride up front with me? Or do you want to drive yourself? There may be keys in one of the other cars, but this is the only one I've found so far."

As if to punctuate this urgency, a pair of jet fighters screamed through the night, somewhere off to their west. Bronk's eyes tracked the fighters, perplexed by what they represented.

"Perhaps I should get back to town as well," he said, finally relenting. "But I'm in no condition to drive."

"That's no problem at all," Dex replied, relieved to be moving forward.

Bronk considered where he needed to be, who he could go to for help. He hated the admission his logic forced out of him. Vandenberg would be busy. Menzel was as effectively useless in this situation as he was. To his knowledge, there weren't any other members of Majestic in town. He needed Dulles.

"Can you drop me at CIA Headquarters?" Bronk asked after the long pause reached its zenith.

"Doc," Dex assured him, "I can drop you wherever you want."

***

General Hoyt Vandenberg was busy, or perhaps it might be better to say that his time was spoken for. He watched in a kind of fascinated horror as Clarence's extended hand mutated between entirely human and something alien to anything he'd ever seen on Earth. Even in the pictures of the extraterrestrial bodies they'd recovered in New Mexico, he'd never seen anything that could appear so completely human in one moment and so completely not in the next.

The hand and its owner were a revelation, and he struggled to accept the security breaches that had made it possible. This man, or thing, had been vetted all the way up the ladder. He'd managed to become an assistant to one of the highest ranking generals in the most powerful country on Earth. Vandenberg shivered when he realized that he might not be the only one so compromised.

"How did you do it?" Vandenberg asked, keeping the shake out of his voice with an effort of will.

"Do what?" Clarence asked, returning the hand to human form.

Vandenberg shook his head, unable to imagine the scope of the operation.

"Everything, I guess. How were you able to get vetted to such a high post? I'm guessing you're behind the blackout."

Clarence smiled, toying with the pistol. "Hard to believe you've been able to do so much with these little things," he said, musing on the nickel-plated .45. "It wouldn't harm me in the slightest, you know. I could take a bullet to the head," he smiled his amusement then, "if I had a head, that is. My body would simply grow back around it, instantly healing the wound. Surprising that you've come so far with such a centralized anatomy. From a geneticist's point of view, it seems like putting all your eggs in one basket."

Clarence waved the general to the guest seat.

"Why don't you have a seat? We'll be here a few hours at least."

"Are you behind the blackout?" Vandenberg asked again.

"Of course," Clarence replied smoothly. "Right now, it's only a few strategic buildings, but soon we'll extend the damping field city-wide. People will panic, but we'll be here to restore order. We'll also demonstrate a few crowd control techniques that don't rely on damaging people with toys like this."

Clarence waggled the gun in Vandenberg's face as the general took a seat. "This is a very uncivilized way of doing business."

"How did you ever get to this position?" The general asked. "You were vetted all the way up to Cosmic Top Secret. Only a few men in the country have your security clearance. This seems a poor way to repay our trust."

Clarence leaned back in Vandenberg's chair, aiming the gun at a point in the ceiling, his eyes narrowing to follow the sight.

"There was a lot of tedious work involved, to be sure. But that's pretty much all there was to it. If there's one thing we understand, it's bureaucracies. Like anyone, we started small and worked our way up. Eventually, we were able to replace some of your most powerful politicians with our own. We now hold a number of the top positions in your government. By the time the election rolls around in November, we may even win the presidency."

Clarence smiled disingenuously. "But enough about me, I have some questions, too. Tell me, General," he said, returning his feet to the floor and setting the gun on the desk, "why haven't you done anything about protecting your planet against threats from outer space? You've known about the Grey Children for at least five years, you've recovered ships, you're even beginning to understand their technology."

"But you haven't done anything to prepare the country for the reality of extraterrestrial life. You're one of the few men informed enough to know this secret and you still behave as if you believe you're alone in the universe."

Vandenberg snorted in disgust.

"You know the reason for that as well as anyone. We were disturbed by what Orson Welles did back in '38. And that was only a radio show heard by a small segment of the population. Can you imagine what might happen if it was known that hostile ships, possessing technologies far in advance of our own, could appear in the sky at any moment?"

For a brief instant, Clarence looked like he might laugh out loud, but then he raised the blinds to look out into the night. Through the glass, Vandenberg could see a hundred pinpricks of light dotting the upper atmosphere, each growing larger by the second.

"Well, General," Clarence said, "I think you're about to find out."

***

Donald Menzel paused outside the door to McAfee's office, listening to the sounds coming from further down the corridor. He started to call out, then reconsidered. His thoughts filled with an odd foreboding. He heard the sound of something large approaching, something that sounded like a large tree branch being dragged across the tiles.

His foreboding compelled him to take shelter in the alcove of an office door before the thing came into sight. When he saw the silhouette, he was glad he'd taken the precaution. His heart leapt at the impossible size of it.

He saw more as the creature came into view.

The thing was well over eight feet tall, its body divided into three separate sections strung together by narrow isthmuses of exoskeletal shell. Each section sprouted speckled bristles of vestigial spikes, a profusion that made it difficult to get a count of its actual limbs. The creature shambled past Menzel's sanctuary, propelled by a kind of sliding motion that precluded any need to lift its feet. This was what created the shuffling sound.

Menzel bit his lip against the horror of the thing, and prayed its ears weren't sensitive enough to hear his ragged breath. He felt a great sense of relief when it continued past without pausing, but his relief was short-lived.

As soon as the first was out of sight, Menzel heard the approach of another. As the second bug came into view, he saw it was accompanied by three others, and that all were similar without being exact copies. Each bug made a skittering noise that was so high-pitched he could barely hear it. Menzel imagined how his dog might howl at the conversation taking place.

As this group passed, Menzel let out a second sigh of relief, acknowledging and to some degree, regretting, his glib denials before the committee. With the immediate threat out of the way, he realized he had to get out of the building.

For a time, he stood frozen by his indecision, his back pressed against the wall as he searched for a response to this dire situation. Finally, he found the courage to leave the alcove, just as his ears detected another body coming down the hall.

Unlike the shuffling gait of the bugs, this sounded like the more familiar approach of hard-soled shoes on a tiled surface. Menzel's emotions trilled with relief as he hurried toward the footsteps, still keeping a hand on the wall should he need to take cover. Far down the hall, he made out the form of a tall slender young man. Menzel hurried forward, relieved to discover that he wasn't the only human left in the building.

He could see the man now and the man saw him in return. He gestured for Menzel to come closer, doing something to dampen his footsteps as he increased his pace. A dim rusty glow came through the picture windows, giving Menzel a good look at a light-haired man in a summer suit.

Menzel left the safety of the wall, giving his trust to this gift that Providence had provided.

Chapter 40 - Arrest and Evacuate

Jim Maddox was the ATC supervisor at Washington National Airport. While he'd seen a lot of strange stuff on radar scopes in his time, he'd never seen anything like the sprinkling of dots that now littered the screens like dandruff on the shoulders of a seborrheic troll. Maddox took another look at Beezer's display, realizing he'd neglected a step in the procedures, maybe several.

Perhaps, he speculated, staring at that impossible rain, he'd confirmed the sightings too quickly.

"Stogie," he called out to his second in command, "get Jack in there to do a maintenance check! We need to make sure the equipment is working okay. Schnoz," he patted Beezer on the shoulder, "keep an eye on those bogies and let me know if they do anything weird."

"What's weird, boss?"

Maddox ran a hand over his scalp, surprised as ever to find how little remained.

"You know, if they do anything impossible, new readings, anything. In the meantime, nobody takes off or lands. Departures are grounded. Route arrivals to the closest runway you can find. Nothing goes up or comes down until we figure this out."

"Collie, get your cheaters. Let me know as soon as you spot the fighters from Andrews."

Schnoz Beezer covered his mouthpiece with one hand.

"Andrews says their runways are down. They're coming in from Delaware."

"You hear that, Collie? Coming in from Delaware!"

"Right, chief!" Sam Collins took his binoculars to the eastern window.

Stogie hit the radar room door at what he considered a run. He turned the knob and leaned his shoulder into the metal monolith.

Normally, the door would have opened easily, its weight supported by four sets of heavy duty hinges. Instead, for the first time Stogie could recall, the door pushed back.

***

"What do we do?" Rita Mae Marshaux hissed, leaning every ounce of her weight into the door.

Jakob Kleinemann looked at his hands in the vague hope of finding something that would get them out of the situation, but they were as empty as the sleeves of an unprepared conjurer.

"I don't know!"

The knob turned again as the man on the other side renewed his assault. The door moved enough to show Rita that the man was stronger and heavier.

"Get us out of here! Use the *mu shu!*"

"The what?" Jakob whispered, not grasping what she was getting at.

"The salt shaker thingy!"

Recalling the vivid memory of having his body converted into molecules, then passed through a labyrinth of electronic circuitry, Jakob shook his head with a finality born of that experience.

"Not even if our lives depended on it!"

"Hey, boss," Stogie called to Maddox, "there's someone in the radar room!"

Stogie threw his weight into the door, catching Rita by surprise and knocking her back onto her glorious keister. With the impediment gone, he pushed the door open, reaching around the corner to flip the light switch. The shock of discovery took his breath away. Stogie pulled the door shut and called for help.

"Hey, Chief! Call security! We got saboteurs!"

***

Jim Maddox ran to the radar room, his mind racing through the procedures he'd have to follow now that he'd found the source of the anomalous readings.

First up would be another call to Andrews. He'd have to fess up to making a false report. They'd call back the jets, but in making the report, he'd cost the taxpayers thousands of dollars and that gaffe would go on his permanent record. He cursed his haste in not checking the equipment before making the call.

Maddox slowed before the open door. Stogie stepped aside to reveal the shortest man he'd ever seen outside a circus. The tiny man was dressed in a dark suit that looked like it came from the boys department. He had a mass of kinky hair that met his cheeks with a short beard of similar texture. Both hair and beard needed a trim.

Having grown up in Chicago, Jim Maddox knew about people like this. He still remembered sitting on his grandfather's knee, listening to the old bull's stories of his battles with labor demonstrators at Haymarket Square. The old man had an inch-long scar where shrapnel had left a crease in his thigh above the right kneecap. Grampy Maddox described the demonstrators as demons from Hell, angry Jews with piglet eyes, wild hair, and black beards. All these things made Maddox sure that the man before him was an anarchist of the highest order.

Obscured by the door, he didn't even see the woman. The tiny man looked at him with curious eyes, but didn't say anything. Like Maddox, he appeared to be wondering what was going to happen next. Maddox was still looking at him when the woman slammed the door in his face.

The men outside took turns beating on and pushing against the door, with Stogie turning the knob as Maddox added his weight. It would have opened easily, if not for Rita Mae's adrenal rush of terror.

"Goddamnit, Jakob! Get us out of here! I don't care where! They'll shoot us for just being here!"

Jakob curled his fingers around the alien device. He was waiting for the *warak shu* to answer when the pounding stopped. The knob released into the latch. They heard shouting from the other side, the sounds of men running. The words were indistinct, but the sense of urgency wasn't.

Jakob placed one hand on his fiancé's sternum and held a finger to his lips for silence. He waited a moment longer, listening to the tumult in the control room. Then, moving Rita aside, he turned the knob and opened the door.

It was forty feet from the radar room to the observation window on the eastern side of the tower. All six air traffic controllers had abandoned their posts to gather at the window, their cries of alarm now stilled by awe.

Though he was further away, Jakob could now identify the source of that awe. It hovered over the runway just fifty yards from the tower. He felt Rita's weight pressing into his back, heard her draw breath as if there was something to say, then stop. Whatever she wanted to say, it never came. Her hands settled onto his shoulders and stayed there.

For the moment, there was nothing left to say.

Three saucers hovered bright orange over the runway, at an altitude that allowed the occupants of the nearest disc to gaze directly through the long slit of its viewport into the control tower. Inside the saucer, three figures stood in an uneven row, their bodies backlit by a rusty light from the ship's interior. Jakob left the sanctuary of the radar room.

Ignoring the very real possibility of arrest and execution for espionage, Jakob Kleinemann joined the ATC men at the window. The ATC men were quiet, their binoculars and headsets either discarded or forgotten. If Jim Maddox was surprised to find the couple from the radar room standing beside him, it didn't register. Mere humans couldn't compare to the vision outside.

Without warning or preamble, two of the saucers departed, pursued by the Delaware F-84's called in by Maddox's mistake. The hull of the remaining saucer went, turning a dull gray that was barely visible under the runway lights. The sole exception to this blackout came from the viewport at the front of the ship.

Everyone in the tower saw them in the same moment.

The figures inside were clearly visible now, silhouetted against the light behind them. The ship drifted close enough to be seen from the tower window. One shape was human and this shape, a man, stood at the center.

It was impossible to see his features until the others pushed him forward. A light came on in front of the man, revealing his face to the men in the tower.

Maddox heard a gasp from the woman and turned toward her.

Attractive and auburn-haired, she was in her mid-twenties, dressed in a gray knee-length skirt and a thin white sweater. Her carriage was so upright that Maddox didn't have to look at her feet to know she was wearing sensible shoes.

She didn't look at all like an anarchist.

The woman clutched the tiny man's arm, her eyes wide in stunned recognition. Maddox could hear the shock in her voice when she exclaimed.

"Jakob, it's Arthur!"

***

"They're toying with us."

Cranston stared out at the fiery disc, Squibb's words hanging in the air like a holy man's fart. There it was, the tangible threat that turned a half decade of rumors into concrete reality. He stared at it in open admiration, a real honest-to-goodness flying saucer.

Neal Cranston wasn't a contemplative man. He was never one to look for deeper meanings, to think of mankind as a whole, or to consider his relative rank in the universal hierarchy.

His world was one where Man was the unchallenged and unfettered top dog. It was a world where one nation had emerged from the last war ascendant on the world stage. As the force that tipped the scale, the country that had lost the least and gained the most was the United States of America.

That there were beings out there capable of forcing him to reconsider Man's place in the universe was an epiphany he had never prepared for. Even so, it was an idea that would have to wait. Realizing that every eye in the tower was waiting for his orders, Cranston made his decision.

As far as he knew, there was no set plan for dealing with little green men from outer space. Suddenly, this seemed like a horrible oversight. But, while there were no contingencies for attacks coming from outer space, there were a bunch of perfectly good plans for dealing with Russian assaults on Washington DC. Given the situation, Cranston saw no need to re-invent the wheel.

"Greenwalt! Implement Defense Plan C! I want every fighter fueled and up in the air ASAP! All leaves are revoked. Call every pilot back to his post. Call McNair and the Barracks. I want ground support at every major intersection. Clear the streets, but do it quietly. We don't want a panic. Order everyone to stay in their homes or get to a shelter. I want the White House and the Capitol Building cordoned off. No one gets in or out. Security at both sites needs to know we're in a condition red, repeat red, enemy strength and resources unknown."

Lieutenant Max Greenwalt was an excellent peacetime aide, but he'd never seen military action. He was too young for the big war and, so far, too lucky for Korea. In his time under Cranston, Max had dealt with every administrative situation the Air Force could throw at him, but he'd never heard a call to arms. As Cranston completed his orders, Max turned to go, then stopped, realizing he'd been so focused on the threat outside that he couldn't recall anything the general said. This was completely unlike him. The Max Greenwalt he believed himself to be was obsessively efficient and detail oriented. He was great at dealing with normal emergencies.

But this situation was simply too big to fit inside his brain.

Even so, he knew better than to ask the general to repeat himself. That would be the end of his cushy job and the non-combatant status it conferred.

It might mean the end of his tenure at Andrews.

It might mean a new posting.

It might even mean freaking Korea.

And, from everything he'd heard, the winters there really sucked.

He tried to recall a single word from the order, a mnemonic that would bring the rest back to him.

Intersections, The general had said something about intersections.

And pilots. He was supposed to recall the pilots from leave.

'This was good,' Max thought. He was getting somewhere now.

What else was there?

He recalled something about getting people out of their homes, and...there was the mnemonic he was looking for.

Implement Defense Plan...which one was it?

He tried to pull it back, but this final thing, this most important thing, simply would not come.

Max Greenwalt took the Defense Plan codebook from the shelf behind his desk and started leafing through its pages. By the time he'd reached the end, he was glad he'd taken that speed-reading course.

There it was, Defense Plan Z.

Evacuate the city.

Max Greenwalt made the call that would change his life and demonstrate that sometimes the rumors were true.

Seoul really sucked in the winter.

Chapter 41 - The Note Under the Door

By the time their mother closed the door, Stormy was rooting through her suitcase for *The Secret of the Wooden Lady*. Finding her prize, she flopped down on one of the room's two beds, thumbing through the pages until she found the spot she'd neglected to mark.

In *The Secret of the Wooden Lady*, Nancy Drew, with her friends Bess and George, had driven to Boston Harbor to help Captain Easterly find out what'd happened to the figurehead of his ship, the *Bonny Scot*. Stormy couldn't fathom why anyone would steal such a thing, or even how one would go about doing it. She'd seen figureheads on ships before, and they all seemed pretty well attached. Even so, as Captain Easterly was quick to point out, his was missing, and that was enough to set Nancy Drew on its trail.

On the far side of the room, Molly, the family's inexplicable redhead, had her nose pressed to the window. This odd position hadn't been achieved without purpose. Molly was trying to look straight down the front of the building to see if she could spot their father before he entered the lobby. But even twisting her head at a sharp angle, the most she'd been able to make out was the driver's side of a taxi as it arrived to drop someone off. Her eyes followed the cab as it drove off, but the identity of its passenger remained a mystery.

Bubbles hadn't yet developed the level of curiosity that would one day make all three Ångström girls famous, but Stormy had shown her how to adjust the air conditioning on their first day in Washington. Bubbles liked air conditioning. Their house back in Madison didn't have it. Bubbles liked cooler temperatures. Here in DC, the air conditioning was the only thing that made the trip bearable.

As soon as she entered the stuffy room, Bubbles cranked the air conditioner up as high as it would go. When she was satisfied with the gale force chill coming through the vents, she took off her dress, set it aside, then lay down on the floor in her underwear. It was a new habit, but one she would never outgrow.

The deadline for dinner came and went without an appearance by their mother, but like most unmet deadlines, this one was easily forgotten. Bubbles went to sleep with her thumb in her mouth, an infraction that Molly would tease her for mercilessly. Stormy got to the good part where Nancy figures out that one character isn't quite what he seems. Molly had grown so tired of watching cars that she started kicking the wastebasket around the room. Finding this a satisfactory outlet for her excess energy, she turned it into a game.

A knock at the door changed everything.

The hall was empty by the time Molly opened the door. Technically, she wasn't supposed to open doors for anyone except her parents, but Molly had a reckless streak a mile wide. Finding no one, she peered down the hall in both directions. Whoever knocked had apparently departed. She frowned, wondering if someone was playing a trick on her.

Molly was so focused on the knocker that she didn't spot the room service tray until the door started to close. The tray's sudden presence, in concert with her hunger, made its appearance seem magical. The tray was large enough to hold three stacked plates with shiny chrome covers, silverware, glasses and a pitcher of milk. The tray was so big that she wondered how she could've missed it, but she didn't mistake its deeper meaning.

They wouldn't be going out to dinner. Mother had sent room service. This wasn't much of a disappointment as disappointments went. All three girls loved room service, even when the food wasn't very good. Room service came with the opportunity to eat without supervision or table manners, usually both.

Molly glanced over at the bed where Stormy was still lost in her stupid book and realized that her older sister couldn't be counted on. With Bubbles still asleep, it was up to her to get the meal into the room. She didn't stop to wonder what'd become of the bellboy. Usually the tray came on a cart and the bellboy brought it in and set it up for them.

She started with the milk since it held the most potential for danger. She tried picking the pitcher up by its handle, but it started to spill almost at once, the milky pool spreading under the plates until it reached the edge of the tray.

She solved the problem by balancing the front end with her other hand. She didn't spill, but the pitcher was still much heavier than expected. Nonetheless, she walked it over and set it down on the table, the only damage being the ring of white spreading out from the bottom.

The plates with their chrome covers were lighter and easier to carry, though the bottom plate was slick with spilled milk. Once the plates were on the table, she was able to pick up the tray and carry it inside without any more problems. She set the tray of pooled milk on the dresser, then took the glasses and silverware over to the table, leaving the napkins to soak up the damp.

Stormy finished her book and immediately wished she hadn't. Now there was nothing to do but be bored. She'd just started her descent into ennui when she detected the smell of burgers and fries. The scent led her to the table.

Stormy rolled off the bed and stumbled over Bubbles. Bubbles lay on her side with her knees drawn up, sucking her thumb as a trail of drying spit ran down her wrist to be absorbed by the carpet. Molly pulled a chair close to the table, but the seat was still too low to eat comfortably. She solved this problem by climbing onto her knees so she could eat from a kneeling position. She watched her sisters with narrowed eyes, grinding each bite between new molars.

Stormy jumped at the noise. The noise came from behind her, a crackling sound. She looked over to find a single piece of paper just inside the door.

Stormy smiled, exhilarating in the rush of excitement at this most obvious of clues. She hopped over Bubbles again on her way across the room, her heart pounding with anticipation. The piece of paper was a sheet torn from a hotel notepad. It lay blank side up.

She heard something move outside the room, but upon opening the door, caught only a glimpse of a man's leg before it passed out of sight. Another sound from the opposite direction revealed more. As her head snapped back around, she saw a single eye peering at her from around the corner. The eye disappeared as soon as she saw it. Stormy bent down to retrieve the note.

The paper was the pale yellow of the hotel's complimentary stationary with its faint printed letterhead at the top. She and her sisters had gone through a half dozen such pads in the last two days, using the 4x6 rectangles as drawing paper even though they were small for the purpose. The hotel provided pens instead of pencils, cheap ballpoints that had leaked blue ink over their fingers and set Maisie in a lather when she found that same ink on their vacation clothes. The note was written in the same ink she still had traces of on her hands.

Molly swallowed her last bite of burger, gagged, and pitched forward onto her plate where the fries, drowned in an ungodly amount of ketchup, cushioned the impact. Her limp body continued to spasm as she rolled from the table, onto the chair, and finally onto the carpet, where the ketchup smeared on her face became blood to be lost in the rich burgundy pile.

Stormy peered at the piece of paper, intent on discovering its message. With the name of the Hotel Ambassador printed in the upper left corner, the other side of the message was a warning written that read:

'Get out now! Meet me downstairs. Parking Lot. Black Ford.'

Most of the writing was unfamiliar, but the signature was their father's.

Stormy looked at the note, her hand shaking too hard to read the words. She glanced across the hall, at the 'Do Not Disturb' sign on her mother's door, realizing she would have to deal with the situation herself. She was the oldest after all. Mother trusted her to get her sisters to the school and that was three blocks away. She even occasionally trusted Stormy to babysit when she wasn't going to be gone long. Stormy folded the note into quarters, slipped it into her pocket, then closed the door behind her.

She knelt to shake Bubbles awake, then saw Molly crumpled on the floor.

"Cut it out, Molls. We got a 'mergency."

Bubbles' eyes refused to open, but Molly gave up her game, rolling around on her side until she was clear of the table and its chair. When she came up, her hands went to her face to find out what was so sticky. When her fingers came away smeared with the ketchup, Molly screamed.

"They got me!"

Ignoring the fact that the faux blood was on her face not her chest, she clutched at an imaginary bullet hole in her chest and staggered around like a wounded cowboy in a three part serial.

Bubbles' eyes opened at Molly's shriek. Immediately rising to her feet, she shivered in the artificial chill, as she blinked the sleep from her eyes. Stormy found her dress where she dropped it and threw it at her.

"Come on! Get dressed! We gotta get out of here!"

Bubbles slipped the dress over her head, but struggled with the sleeves until Stormy twisted it around to face the right direction.

"But I've been shot!" Molly complained, irked that her sister didn't seem to be taking her condition seriously. She fell to the floor and lay there, her feet still kicking theatrically, but Stormy was having none of it.

"I said, cut it out! Father sent a note. We're in danger and we have to get out of here! Get your shoes on, Bubs! And wipe that blood off your face, Molls. It looks like ketchup."

Bubbles had to sit to put on the saddle shoes her whining had coerced Maisie into buying for her. Stormy tried to help, but Bubbles pushed her away. Learning to tie her own shoes was a recent accomplishment and not one she'd easily relinquish.

Molly ran into the bathroom, climbing up on the sink to get a better look at the mirror. When she saw the long streak of red running down one cheek and the second smear across her temple, she grinned, showing the gaps where new teeth were poking through her gums. She wiped her face off with a towel before joining Stormy by the door.

Stormy peered at the door across the hall. At first, all she saw was the 'Do Not Disturb' sign, but then she noticed a handwritten addition where 'This means you, Veronica!' was scotch-taped to the bottom.

She looked down the red carpet with the black stripes along its borders. Finding nothing amiss, she opened wider and peeked further out into the hall. Somewhere down the corridor, she heard two men talking about tractors, but the hall was otherwise quiet. The elevator door closed, cutting off the conversation.

"Come on, the coast is clear." Stormy said, leading them away from the elevators.

"Where we going, chief?" Molly asked.

Stormy scowled at her sister's spotty complexion. She hadn't done a very good job with the towel.

"It's just a scratch," Molly assured her.

Stormy poked Molly's forehead with her finger, getting a sample to analyze. She licked it for taste.

"I don't know, Molls. Looks like you're bleeding pretty bad. We might have to leave you for the buzzards."

Molly coughed theatrically. "I'll be fine, captain, it's just this damn leg. You leave me if I can't keep up."

Stormy found the exit door at the end of the hall and pushed it open onto the fire stairs.

"Come on! We can get out this way without going through the lobby."

Bubbles yawned. "Why can't we go through the lobby?"

Stormy stopped halfway down the first flight.

"Because they might be watching."

"Who?"

Stormy reached into her pocket.

"See. Father left a note."

She unfolded the note and let her sisters read it. Bubbles mouthed every word.

"He wants us to meet him in the parking lot."

"What about Mother? Doesn't Daddy want Mother to come along?"

Stormy started down the stairs. "I'm sure he left her a note, too."

That much was true.

Wally Sands, in his bellboy disguise, had slipped notes under both doors.

But Maisie's note, as yet undiscovered, wasn't a warning.

In a strange way, it was a demand for ransom.

***

The stairs terminated at a ground floor door that exited onto a parking lot. The parking lot was lit by a single lamp with a recurring short that caused the bulb to blink on and off in a more or less regular pattern.

The girls came out of the stairwell in a rush, hiding behind a hedge to get the lay of the land. An alarm went off, but it died when the hydraulic arm pulled the door shut behind them.

Bubbles tugged on her sister's skirt. "Why we here?"

Stormy's gaze darted around the lot.

"Say it right, Bubs. Why are we here?"

Correcting Bubbles made her feel like Mother which, as far as Stormy was concerned, wasn't a bad thing at all.

Bubbles added the missing verb. "Why are we here?"

"Father's note, remember. He said he'd meet us here."

Bubbles didn't bother to look around. "I don't see him."

Molly searched the note for hidden meaning, but came away with the obvious. "There should be a black Ford."

Stormy started scanning the parking lot for black cars. In the dark, all of the cars looked black. "Well, if he's not here, he must've left a sign for us to follow."

"You mean like that one?"

Bubbles pointed to a sign stating that hotel employees weren't allowed to park in the lot. Stormy shook her head, whipping her lank blonde hair around her throat.

"It won't be that obvious. It'll be something only we will recognize. Father is clever that way."

Molly looked around, her gaze traveling across the street toward the dark trees of Franklin Park. "How do you know there'll be a sign?"

"Cause that's the way it works. We got the note, which means someone's trying to get our attention. They're trying to lead us to Father, or maybe others working with him. Now there should be a clue that brings us closer. Then there'll be another clue after that, but it won't be anything we can't figure out."

Molly came up alongside her, pointing out three cars in turn.

"I see three black Fords, there, there, and ...there."

She paused before announcing the third.

"There's something stuck to the tire of that one. See?"

Stormy followed her sister's finger to a car at the far end of the lot.

"How do you know it's a Ford?"

Molly snorted. "Boy, for someone who thinks she's so smart, you sure don't know your cars."

"What's that on the wheel?"

Molly took a couple steps toward the Ford.

"Looks like a piece of cloth."

She squinted in the dim light.

"It's too small to be a newspaper. Maybe it's another note."

Molly was halfway across the lot before Stormy could get Bubbles to take her hand, and then they had to run to catch up.

The chloroformed hankie that'd been used to subdue Bertie Stein was now stuck to the right rear tire. Wally Sands, having grown tired of the smell, tossed it out just as they pulled into the lot and it'd stuck when Russell ran over it.

Molly arrived first, and reached down to pluck the filthy thing free.

"Eeew, you're not going to touch it?"

Stormy was forever appalled by the things Molly would do.

Molly held the cloth up for inspection.

"It's just an old hankie."

Stormy came closer look, sniffing at the strange smell wafting toward her. Molly's legs buckled, causing her to stagger back against the car.

"Will you stop messing around?" Stormy groused.

But the smell was distinctive, and suddenly, Stormy knew what it was.

Stormy snatched the handkerchief out of Molly's hand and tried to throw it into the shrubs. Being a wadded-up hunk of cloth, it caught the air like a sail and fluttered to earth a foot from her hand.

"Get away from it!" Stormy grabbed Molly's arm and dragged her away from the handkerchief. "It's chloroform!"

Bubbles marched heedlessly past the doctored hankie. "What's klo-klo...?"

"Chloroform! You know, the stuff that knocks you out!"

Something rustled inside the Ford, making a low groaning sound. The girls jumped back as a froggy face pressed a cheek and an eye against the side window.

Bubbles pointed out the obvious.

"Look! It's the man from the airport!"

***

It took Bertie Stein a long time to wake up. When he did, his first conscious thought was to question why he was lying in the back seat of Ford. His head started spinning when he tried to rise, so he decided not to. He heard voices, but only a few words before the car stopped. The doors slammed as the two men got out. Then his head did a little dance and he was gone again.

When he woke the second time, he felt better, but his head swam whenever he tried to move too fast. He heard new voices that reminded him of cartoon chipmunks. These were higher in pitch and their words fluttered around like cartoon birdies, but he couldn't understand what they were saying either.

He tried to push up into a seated position, but only made it onto his side. He put up with that until his neck started to hurt. The next time he tried, he was able to get vertical long enough that when he fell, he ended up with his face pasted against the window, smearing one cheek into the glass. The eye above the cheek took a while to focus, but when his vision cleared, he saw that there were three little girls on the other side.

A moment later, the girls were trying to drag him to a regrettably short-lived freedom. Bertie Stein made it to his feet, his knees holding just long enough to allow him to slump against the right front fender.

But that was when Corbett and Sands appeared out of the dark.

Abel Corbett cracked his villain's smile, pleased that his plan had worked so well.

"Glad you girls could join us. Now get in the back and we'll be on our way."

The younger girls looked over at Stormy for what to do.

Stormy consulted her extensive store of Nancy Drew predicaments, and found one that seemed to address all the options.

"I'm sorry, sir, but I'm afraid we can't do that."

Corbett was puzzled by this show of resistance.

Hadn't he cleverly drawn them out into the open?

Didn't he clearly have the upper hand?

Wasn't he intimidating enough to cow three little girls?

He had to answer yes to all three questions.

"Why not?" Corbett asked finally.

"Because," Bubbles pointed out, as if the answer wasn't already obvious, "our mother says we shouldn't get into cars with strange men."

255

Chapter 42 - Afterglow

In the hazy afterglow of their first coupling, Janie Gently lay on her back wearing the same look of astonishment she'd worn right when Maisie first pushed her onto the bed. Nothing that came after that action had done a thing to alter the look in any way, though it was now unencumbered by clothes. In many ways, Janie was in a state of shock, a delirious, joyful, multi-orgasmic shock to be sure, but it was still shock, no matter how you sliced it.

She was shocked that a mother of three would entertain such thoughts about another woman, let alone act on them.

She was shocked that a human body, her body, could experience so much pleasure in so many varied ways.

She was shocked at the suddenness with which it had started and the length of time it had taken to reach completion.

But most of all, she was shocked by her lack of resistance.

Never once had she tried to push Maisie away.

Okay, that part wasn't quite true.

She had pushed Maisie away when her moans grew loud enough to attract the attention of a passing bellboy. Fortunately, the bellboy only knocked on the door to inform them that pets weren't allowed in the hotel. But before that, she'd been remarkably compliant considering that this was the first deviant sexual act of her life.

And after that, after she'd had time to catch her breath, she'd become the most gifted student Maisie had ever taught. Simply following the instructions printed on the box, Janie was able to bring Maisie to similar heights of ecstasy. This second set of screams would have elicited a second knock from the bellboy, had Maisie lacked the foresight to cover her face with a pillow. A large wet 'O', now almost dry, marked the spot where she'd spent her final climax.

Now the two women lay side by side in the darkened room, cigarettes dying forgotten in the twin ashtrays to either side of the bed. Janie's hands, possessed of a profound and unsated curiosity, still sought answers in the mother's flesh. She simply couldn't stop touching her, any more than she could stop the flood of questions that poured out of her.

"Mrs Ångström?"

Maisie murmured contentedly, her eyes narrowed to sleepy slits.

"Call me Maisie, dear. I think you've earned the right to use my Christian name."

"Maisie?"

Janie paused, unsure how to continue. "I was wondering...what about your husband?"

Maisie laughed, then groaned, then laughed again.

"Lars? What about him?"

Janie hesitated again. "Well, does he know?"

"Know what?"

"Well..., that you like other women. How would he feel about... this?"

Maisie laughed again, deeper and richer.

"Well, Janie, if he was here, I imagine he'd want to join in."

Janie's eyes couldn't contain her shock.

"Dr Ångström has been with other women?"

It was too dark for Janie to see her lover's face. If she had, she might've seen a strange expression there, an expression that combined hurt and amusement. She was amused by the naïveté of her new acquaintance, but also hurt. Those affairs had caused her pain, no matter how much she rationalized the betrayal.

"Yes, and don't ask how many. Let's just say it's been quite a few."

"But you're so beautiful..."

Maisie rolled to her side, running her fingertips over Janie's cheek.

"That's sweet of you, but I was hardly his first. The difference was that I had a father with the power to make him to marry me when I got pregnant."

"How awful!"

"Is it? Well, I suppose, in a way. But I do love him, and I know he loves me. I have three daughters to prove it. As to his other women...well, he tires of them very quickly. You've never seen a man so easily distracted."

Janie shivered at the touch, and giggled a little.

"But, aren't you lonely? I mean, why do you stay with him?"

Maisie leaned over to kiss her, then pulled back, her eyes sparkling.

"No, not particularly lonely. And before you ask, no, I don't do this all the time. I'd never do anything so reckless back home."

"But there's a certain freedom in travel. As to why I've stayed with him... well, there's the girls, of course. They love their father and I wouldn't take him away from them. As for me, I guess I've already faced every disappointment a wife can face. Lars is a good man in some ways, not so good in others."

Janie was quiet for a time. Then, in a smaller voice, she asked the question that was really troubling her.

"How did you know?"

Maisie's fingers came to rest on Janie's belly.

"Know what?"

"About me. How did you know I wouldn't say no?"

Maisie's hand went into motion again, stroking her ribs, then reaching around to pull her closer. She let her lips move down Janie's throat.

"You develop a certain sense about these things. Lars would be able to tell you better than I can. It's his field of expertise after all. You might have said no, I suppose, but I didn't think you would. I suspect that you've been overlooked a lot in life, Janie Gently. After your kindness at the airport, I didn't want to do that to you."

Janie froze at the mention of her surname, but Maisie quickly drew her in, wrapping her leg over Janie's thigh to discourage struggle.

"Yes, dear Janie," she whispered, "I know who you are."

Janie started to struggle anyway, but Maisie was stronger.

"But how?"

"Let's just say I read a lot of magazines."

Janie gave up and allowed Maisie to pull her in.

"And...I happen to be a big fan of *Women's Week Daily*, a publication that employs a certain Miss Janie Gently."

Janie groaned and buried her face in Maisie's bosom.

"I am so sorry. I thought if I told you I was a reporter, you'd think I was looking for a story about your husband."

Maisie's hand stroked the back of her head.

"Well, that was true, wasn't it?"

Maisie pushed Janie onto her back, turning her head until she was forced to meet Maisie's eyes. Maisie smiled the predatory smile again, letting her hand run down the younger woman's throat to continue the longer journey south.

"But you can't very well print anything about us now, can you?"

These were her last words for a while, because after that, there was just too much Janie in her mouth to speak clearly.

***

There followed many peaks and valleys that left both women spent. Time passed slowly and drowsily as talk of the forgotten dinner came and went. More cigarettes were smoked, though this consisted mostly of lighting them and setting them aside to burn down to ash. The girls were remembered as often as dinner, and one of these memories prompted Maisie to order room service. There were discussions about where Lars had gone and when he might return, but the latter fear never materialized. It was turning into a slow sleepy night.

Janie woke to the thunderous bang of doors being thrown open. These were followed by shouts of distress and the heavy stomping footfalls of disturbed men and women, running down the hall in both directions.

All that unseen panic seemed superfluous when the room was suddenly bathed in a wash of amber light, a focused beam that forced its way through the blinds, sending long stripes across the bedclothes. Eyes still closed, Janie let out a howl that had nothing to do with pleasure.

Maisie's head came up as the blinds were blown in by a sudden gust. The stripes fragmented, then went away as the room lit up in an explosion of light.

"What's happening?" Janie mumbled sleepily, unsure if the dream she'd been having was still going on.

Maisie rolled off the bed, landing on her feet with surprising agility. She snatched her errant underwear off the chair, and after fumbling to find the legs, pulled the panties up to her waist. She left the bra at the end of the bed, dismissing it as too complex an enterprise, and stepped into her dress, pulling it up past her hips and threading her arms into the sleeves.

Janie blinked numbly, realizing too late that the amber light had nothing to do with the interrupted climax of her dream.

"What's happening?" She asked again.

"Get dressed! You have to get out of here!"

Janie came out of her stupor in a panic. She asked a third time with more urgency. "What's happening?"

"Hurry! Get dressed! You can't be caught in here!"

Reaching behind her, Maisie zipped her dress up to the bra line and started the search for shoes. Janie finally started moving as a fist banged twice on the door before moving across the hall to perform the same service.

Janie didn't bother with underwear, slipping her skirt up to her waist and zipping without wasting time on the button. She snatched her blouse off the chair where it had landed and thrust her arms into the sleeves, wondering where the hell her shoes had gone.

Maisie pulled on her second heel, found her purse, and ran to the door, only to stop at the threshold. "Oh, my god, the girls!"

In the rush to leave, neither woman saw the note on the floor. Torn from a hotel notepad, it lay blank side up on the carpet.

With the door open, the Ambassador Hotel was a graduate course in chaos theory, a study of objects in random motion, propelled without guidance. Half-dressed men and women poured from its five hundred rooms in torrents, panic being the only trait they held in common. All the while, the amber light streamed in through the windows, bathing the vacating rooms in a flickering ambiance that chased the terrified guests out into the hall.

Maisie was bowled over by a salesman in checked boxers and a sport coat. He carried a pair of brown shoes in one hand, and his slacks in the other. The salesman hurried past. Like Sands and Corbett before him, he took no notice of the woman he'd just run over.

Janie helped her back to her feet, then using her own body, flattened her against the wall to avoid the stampeding executive board of Kruger's Nuts and Notions which was in town for its annual convention.

Maisie's thanks were automatic, delivered as she struggled with the key to the girls' room, her hands shaking so violently that she finally just pounded on the door with her fist.

"Stormy! Open up, it's Mother!"

Janie took the key from her and slipped it into the lock. Maisie burst inside just as the amber light swept away, leaving the room in shadow. She ran to the bathroom while Janie checked the closets and under the beds.

"They're gone!"

Then the light was back and with it came a strange wind that pushed the blinds away, even though the windows were still closed. Janie ran to the window, determined to see what was causing the commotion. She found the cord for the blinds and pulled too hard. Only one end lifted, creating a triangle of window from a rectangle of blind. The floor seemed to shift underneath her as she reached for the sill.

When she saw what lay outside, she let go and backed away.

A second later, she was crawling frantically backward, her eyes still on the window. She stopped by the bed, looking up with real terror in her eyes.

"There's a flying saucer out there!"

Up until that point, where she could see the thing for herself, Janie had thought all this flying saucer nonsense was a fad, something the public would eventually tire of. She'd seen her first and only saucer movie two years earlier, at a drive-in theater in Secaucus, New Jersey. She went to the movie on a date with Preston Freiburg, a pimply accountant who was a friend of her family. The movie was called *The Flying Saucer*, and it was an unmitigated piece of rubbish so poorly assembled it made the Flash Gordon serial that preceded it seem like high art. *The Flying Saucer* made it easy to dismiss the flying saucer phenomenon for the idiocy Janie believed it to be.

While Preston tried to find the courage to slide his hand under her sweater, Janie watched the plot develop with growing incredulity. The leading man was a wooden actor who also wrote and directed. Judging by the results, he wasn't very good at any of those things. He played a retired military man brought back by the government to investigate Alaskan reports of a flying disc.

Upon arrival in the icebox state, budgetary constraints limited his investigation to the interior of Juneau's largest bar. A woman accompanied the investigator. Ostensibly she went as his nurse, but the only reason Janie could see for her presence was to keep him on the wagon and she didn't do it very well.

Janie was still wondering how the awful thing had gotten made when she realized that Preston Freiburg had danced away from the bag while she was lost in her thoughts and stolen second base.

It wasn't her last date with a man, but it was the last time she agreed to go to a movie without knowing what it was about. Preston Freiburg thought it was swell, but Janie turned him down the next time he called.

Maisie took her place at the window, dropping to all fours before risking a peek. She watched for half a minute before ducking out of sight. There were at least two ships outside, both aglow with that amber light as they slowly circled the hotel in opposite directions.

Just as Molly had done earlier in the evening, she glanced down toward the entrance where a dozen men and women were running half-dressed toward their cars, like lemmings to a tour bus. She saw a steady line of traffic clogging the road, ignoring the streetlights at 14th and K as everyone tried to bull their way into the increasingly frantic press of cars.

The noises in the hall stopped when the door to the fire stairs closed for the final time. The 8th floor fell silent, save for the rapid breathing of two women facing each other across six feet of carpet. Outside, the discs broke away from the hotel to go in search of other buildings to terrorize.

Abandoned to the dark, Maisie felt her way to the light switch, but flipping it on did nothing.

"The power's out," Janie said. "I already tried."

Maisie swept a wave of hair off her forehead.

"I've got to find the girls. Will you help me?"

"Yeah, sure, of course."

"We'll search this floor first. I just hope they weren't hurt in the stampede."

Janie nodded and followed her through the door into the hall.

It took some time in the dark, but most of the doors had been left open. Maisie called their names at each room, whether the door was open or not, but there was never an answer.

Several minutes later, they returned to Maisie's room, without having had any success. Maisie felt something rustle against her foot and reached down to find the fraternal twin of the note slipped under the girls' door.

It was too dark to read. Maisie felt her way around the room, picking up things she might need. She found her purse, and then her suitcase. Setting the case on the bed, she rustled through the contents until she found a light jacket. The night was growing cool outside.

Working by feel, Janie crawled over the carpet, retrieving the errant items of her wardrobe. Her panties were a special relief and she felt more secure as soon as she slipped them on. One shoe had been kicked under the bed. She reclaimed it and was grateful that she could walk again without limping. She joined Maisie at the window, where she was trying to read the note by starlight.

"This is no good. I can't see a thing."

"Maybe once we get outside," Janie suggested.

So it was back into the hall, tracing the walls by feel until they arrived at the one door that was neither locked nor open. Then there was the slow descent, down seven flights of stairs in the dark, where any misstep might result in a turned ankle or a broken neck. By the time the outer door opened onto the parking lot, both women felt like they'd just escaped from a high-rise crypt. As if it sensed their need, a street lamp flickered back to life.

Maisie grabbed Janie's wrist and half-dragged her across the lot. She took the note from her purse, smoothing out the crinkles before exposing it to the light, terrified that it might be no more than a note from the hotel informing her that she was being charged extra for making too much noise.

She read the note once, then a second time before letting it fall to the ground. It wasn't her worst fear, it was a fear she hadn't even considered. Maisie let out the sobs she'd been holding back as Janie retrieved the note and held it up to the light.

Dr Angstrom-

I enjoyed meeting you this afternoon and I apologize for the events that interrupted our conversation. I would like to get together again, in fact, I insist on it. You should know that I have your daughters. If you follow my instructions, they will not be harmed. I'm willing to return them, but only once you've delivered yourself into my custody.

If you don't comply with my wishes, your girls will learn just how cheap life can be at far too tender an age.

Be at the Washington Monument by 4 o'clock this morning.
And please, Doctor, remember to come alone.

Major Abel Corbett, USAF
(Deceased)

Janie looked up into the night, wondering if it was possible to tell time by the stars. Finding new resolve, Maisie wiped away her tears.

"Well, I have no idea where Lars is, so I'm going to go in his place. Can you drive me to the Washington Monument?"

Janie had to point out the obvious.

"But they want your husband. What can we do without him?"

Maisie turned her face away, her chin quivering with pent-up emotion.

"I don't know. Lars is a hard man to count on at the best of times. I have no idea where he is. I haven't heard from him since this morning. Maybe he could help if I knew where he was, but I don't and it's too late to find him."

Janie squeezed her hand reassuringly.

"Of course, I'll take you. It's just..."

Maisie sniffed, not wanting to face any more obstacles.

"What?"

"I don't remember where I parked."

Chapter 43 - Lars at Large

Once Lars Ångström was back at street level, he was faced with a task that was more difficult than expected, that of deciding his next move. Like Corbett, Sands, and Grady before him, he walked out to the end of the alley, having said his goodbye to Russell at the bottom of the manhole. At the intersection of alley and street, he finally had to choose a direction. Unlike Corbett and Sands, he didn't have a car available, but he did have money for cab fare.

If it were possible to find a cab.

Lars had never seen Washington so deserted. He had to strain his ears to find any evidence of traffic and all he found was a faint hiss that sounded far away and no louder than the night wind coming in off the river.

Now that he was back on the surface, it was almost surprising to reflect on how short a time he'd spent underground. The subterranean experience, though subjectively interminable, didn't seem to have taken all that long when measured against a clock.

Even so, it was late enough to know he'd missed the flight to Stockholm by hours. He wondered if Maisie and the girls had gotten on the flight without him and decided probably not. Her Swedish, the little she'd been able to pick up, wasn't strong enough to make getting around Stockholm by herself an attractive proposition.

So, what had she done in his absence?

There was also the matter of what had become of the others. Were his friends still lost in the catacombs under the city? His intuition said no, though he had nothing to support that conclusion. He looked around for clues to his location and was surprised to learn that his long walk underground had taken him nowhere.

The Russell Senate Building, site of the morning's testimony, was on his right. He knew its shape by sight, but it seemed odd that there weren't any lights on inside the venerable structure. This didn't jibe with his watch, which said it was only 11:30. Surely there was someone still working on the business of the nation.

He was considering his options as a lone man got out of a cab to head up the steps into the building. Since the cab was now available, he waved for it, without realizing he was too far away to be seen. He broke into a trot, but the cab circled around and turned the corner before he drew close enough to hail it. Reaching the corner, he looked up to get his bearings.

The street sign told him he was at the corner of Delaware and C Street NE. He paused under the street lamp, pondering his next step. He had two worries, and therefore, two directions his decision might take him. On one side, there was the family he was supposed to meet at the airport, on the other, the friends he'd lost underground.

His friends were a problem. Though he'd worked with Project Stall for five years, he didn't know anyone he could go to for help. The isolation of their work precluded making contacts within the government and he was virtually certain that no civilian authority would be the slightest help in navigating the underground passages.

He'd had discussions about this with Jakob and Rita. Who could they go to for help if the major was unavailable? They'd assumed that Arthur Ecks must report to somebody, but even Dex didn't seem to know who or how to get in touch with them. In the end, the lack of options made the decision for him. The others would have to find their own way back to the surface. If they were still missing when the sun came up, he would do something then

He was still standing at the intersection when the lamp across the street flickered and went out. He caught a brief glimpse of an orange glow just over the tops of the trees, but it was gone before he had a good look at it.

Finally, he made his decision.

If Maisie didn't take the flight, she would have returned to the hotel. Even if she hadn't, it was the logical place to start his search. Lars turned north. The Ambassador was at 14th and K, and given the circumstances, that didn't seem too far to walk.

It was two blocks to Union Station. The city was eerily quiet as he passed under the trees. The brown arc of lawn in front of the station, usually teeming with departing passengers, was deserted by night. Even the cabs had gone off to find business elsewhere.

There was a shortcut to be taken there, so he followed the diagonal swath of Massachusetts Avenue as it cut northwest for several blocks. This would be the longest stretch of his journey. He followed Massachusetts until it terminated at Mount Vernon Square.

Oddly, he saw no one on the way and this made him wonder again where everyone had gone. He was still musing on this when he spotted a military transport in the distance, so far away that the rumble of its engine was inaudible. Even at that distance, he could see the young men in back, all hunkered down as the truck cornered, backed up, and reversed direction. An instant later, it vanished up a side street.

But as the transport disappeared, he saw a car back out of a driveway, then stop to eject a dark figure before driving off. The ejected man disappeared into the shadow of a sycamore, before emerging on the near side. Lars increased his pace, eager to see if the man could tell him what was happening.

All the houses and businesses were dark on both sides of the road, and there was something wrong with the street lamps. Every other one was blinking on and off.

Ahead of him, the man abruptly stopped as Lars passed under a working streetlight, then started up again. Like Lars, he'd increased his pace. As he came close enough to recognize, Lars saw why.

The man was Winthrop Walton Russell III.

"Greetings, Mr Russell," Lars said, "this is an unexpected pleasure."

"I share that pleasure, Dr Ångström," Russell said with equal enthusiasm.

"What brings you out at night?" Lars queried. "I thought you would be busy with your work for the rest of the evening."

Russell sighed. "All plans are subject to change. I was watching Major Corbett and Captain Sands on the view screen when I discovered that they had been arrested. I went down to bail them out and, on our way back, Kraall decided he needed the car more than I did. I couldn't argue, of course, not that I ever would. They were probably right anyway. This bug invasion seems to have everyone in a tizzy."

"So it is an actual invasion, then?" Lars asked, looking up into the sky as if such evidence was just waiting to be revealed.

"Oh," Russell shrugged, "I should think so. There's a large number of ships orbiting the planet and I can't think of any other reason they'd be here."

Russell joined Ångström in looking up at the night sky.

"I suppose Kraall would be furious at me for saying so, but the bugs aren't so bad really. They're excellent administrators. You'll get to keep your religions and your holidays, and they usually share a few technological advances that you wouldn't come across for decades on your own. I met a few worms before our ship broke up, and I have to say I liked them quite a bit. At the very least, they're not as bad as Kraall."

Lars winced as he caught sight of his first fireball, then gasped as it was joined by a dozen others. From far away, he the sound of distant jets screaming in from the east at top speed.

"Still," Lars said cautiously, "I worry about how they might be received. Human beings are only now beginning to consider the possibility of other life in the universe. And we're famously opposed to conquerors who try to impose their will on us. I suspect we might try to fight back."

Russell shrugged again. "Well, you're welcome to try, but frankly you're ridiculously outgunned. Remember, the bugs have been traveling across the galaxy for thousands of years. They have, I suppose you can't call it an empire, but they have a loosely confederated network of planets that spans a good part of the quadrant. Look at how much trouble you had with Germany and Japan. Speaking frankly, I don't much like your chances."

As if to support Russell's conclusion, the first jets arrived from Delaware.

Lars spotted three orange ships hovering over the Potomac. Two separated from the third, heading away from the river. The jets took off in pursuit. The orange ships kept their speed down, staying just far enough out of reach that the jets couldn't fire their missiles. Once all four vehicles were well out of town, the bug ships accelerated and were over the horizon in seconds. The jets returned home unbloodied, but unsuccessful.

"Your jets can't get close enough to do any damage," Russell explained, "but at least the bugs didn't show any sign of aggression. They have some very sophisticated weaponry if they want to use it."

Supporting this claim, all the streetlights along Massachusetts went out at once.

"See," said Russell's silhouette, "they just took out your power without firing a shot. I don't suppose you're carrying a flashlight."

"Extraordinary," Lars admitted, in reference to the blackout. Addressing Russell's request for a flashlight, he added. "No, I'm afraid I don't. This day has presented us with many situations and I've been ill prepared for all of them. Perhaps, it's a metaphor. The United States as a country and the Earth as a planet are similarly unprepared for what lies ahead. Up until now, I think we've never really considered life on other planets, at least not seriously."

Russell and Mudduk nodded their approval at this observation.

"It's true that Earth has been left relatively undisturbed until lately, but you need to understand that the reasons behind that hands-off policy have changed recently, and I think you already know why."

Lars returned the host's nod.

"Of course, the atom bomb and the testing associated with it."

"Exactly," said Russell. "With the atom bomb's reappearance, which was facilitated by what I will tactfully refer to as outside influences, your planet has been fast-tracked into galactic recognition."

"Is that a bad thing?" Lars asked.

Russell shrugged noncommittally. "Possibly, but not necessarily. It does mean you may be faced with issues you're not ready to deal with. It also means you're likely to get visited by a number of interested parties."

"Like the bugs?"

"Recent arrivals, and far from the worst attention you could receive. You might benefit from being conquered by them."

Lars pursed his perfect lips at this.

"I doubt there are many who would see it that way."

Russell laughed.

"Yes, you do have a bit of an independent streak, I'll grant you that. What you don't have are any effective ways of fighting back."

Lars had to agree. "I expect you're right."

"Oh, I am," said the worm. "But I have something that might help. I was tinkering around in my workshop after you left and I came across this."

Russell reached into his pocket to produce an object that fit easily into the palm of his hand. As he showed the object to Lars Ångström, the thing flared into sapphire brilliance, though its shape remained essentially formless and mutable.

"What is it?" Lars asked, already fascinated.

"Frankly," Russell said, "I'm not quite sure. It's just one of those things you pick up, throw in a box, and forget about. It didn't respond to Kraall or Shff at all. It lights up when I touch it, but that's about it. Kraall has told me to get rid of it on several occasions, but I'd like to know more about what it is before getting rid of it. I was rather hoping I'd run into you again to see what you thought. Would you mind taking it out of my hand and giving me your thoughts?"

Lars instinctively retreated a step.

"Is it dangerous?"

"I should think so," Russell said, "but not to you. Most likely, it will just remain inert, in which case it's useless. If so, I'll just take it back to the shop."

Lars considered the proposition. He didn't think of himself as a terribly brave man. He had dodged military service, using his intelligence to keep him out of live warfare. He stared at the pulsating blue thing in Russell's hand, imagining that it was winking back at him. He could almost hear it say.

"Go on, give it a try. What have you got to lose?"

Lars Ångström scoffed at his own imagination.

"All right," he said finally.

Russell dropped the light into Ångström's hand.

At first, nothing happened, possibly less than nothing because the light abruptly diminished. It felt insubstantial and odd. There was no weight or warmth to it.

"Hmmm," said Winthrop Walton Russell III, "it seems to have reservations."

"Reservations? What do you mean?"

Russell cocked his head, never taking his eyes off Ångström's hand.

"Well, I've studied this thing extensively," the worm admitted, "though there isn't enough reference material to draw any firm conclusions. The one thing I can say about it is that, to some degree, it chooses its master."

"Its master?"

Lars almost dropped the thing. He finally felt his first tactile sensation, noting how smooth it felt against his palm. He felt new weight as it started to shift. Not wanting to drop it, he closed his hand as the thing flared to life, emitting a sapphire brilliance far more intense than when Russell had held it.

"Oh my," Russell said, "it seems to like you."

Then, to Lars Ångström's considerable astonishment, it spoke.

"Greetings, new partner! You are the worthy recipient of the most useful tool ever created! Warak shu are famous throughout the multiverse for their ease of use and wide range of functions. Once paired to an indigenous recipient, your warak shu will provide advantages that, you and only you, may employ for the rest of your life. Warak shu have a nearly perfect success rate and enjoy a 93.7% positive rating on Yelp."

"Here's how it works. Using a proven technology that dates back eons, your warak shu will provide you and your loved ones with a lifetime of service and protection, fulfilling your needs while still respecting your privacy. Your warak shu requires no maintenance and its abilities may not be transferred except in the event of death or physical separation through a barrier of the space-time continuum."

"Limitations: Your warak shu may not be used for purposes of conquest or to gain advantage at games of chance. All warak shu come with a moral arbiter that will internally determine the appropriateness of any proposed action. In circumstances involving the immediate wellbeing of the recipient, the warak shu is authorized to act independently until the crisis is resolved."

"Disclaimer: The creators of the warak shu provide no warranty of operation. They may not be held responsible for actions performed as a result of its function or lack of such."

"Offer is not valid in alternate universes, and is restricted to the galaxy where it is issued."

"How very odd," Lars Ångström said.

"You don't know the half of it, bub," the warak shu replied.

Chapter 44 - Une Nuit de Secrets

Durf Schoenberg couldn't decide whether to believe the rumors or not. The order to mobilize spread through Fort McNair like wildfire, but the unanswered question still remained. Why?

That's what everyone wanted to know. Even so, it was a question that most soldiers knew better than to ask out loud. In this cowed silence, all they had left were their own speculations and these ran rampant as they prepped their gear. As a result, the power of the rumors built up like a seasonal flood that would eventually overwhelm an inadequate dike. Once they were aboard the transports, out of Sergeant Clang's hearing, the rumors exploded into wild gossip.

Durf took his usual seat next to L'il Schaver. Durf and L'il were the shortest men in the outfit and always side-by-side when the platoon lined up in alphabetical order. As a result, their association had resulted in a friendship of convenience. Sergeant Clang moved them around when the platoon was on parade, but there wasn't any reason to stop the pair from gravitating toward each other when they rolled out on assignment.

Before taking his seat next to the driver, Sergeant Clang ordered the platoon to shut up. The squad grew quiet as the truck rumbled to life and Clang barked the order to head out, but the chatter started up again as soon as the driver dropped the clutch.

"Okay, who knows where we're goin'?"

The question came from Paderewski, a big Polack from Chicago.

"I don't think the sarge even knows."

"Anyone see the jets?"

"What jets?"

"Yeah, couple of 'em. Blew by half hour back."

"Came back with their tails 'tween their legs."

"No shit?"

"Yeah, sumpin' chased 'em off."

"Flew rings aroun' 'em, I hear."

A trickle of sweat leaked out from under Durf's helmet and took forever to make its way down his jaw.

"I hear they got a UFO call over at Andrews."

"A flying saucer? You're cracked!"

"Hey, ah'm serious, dirtbag! Ah knows a guy'n Ops."

"Yeah? You talk to him in the last twenty minutes?"

"Where we're going?"

"We're going to the city, cupcake. What else would we be doing?"

The talk petered out for a few minutes as the transport took a left on South Capitol Street and headed toward the National Mall.

"Geez, the streets are freakin' deserted."

"They call a curfew?"

"Ain't so much as a late night cab out there."

The quiet fell on them again and it was heavier this time. It lasted until the transport stopped at the corner of 4th and Jefferson. At Clang's order, the men piled out, the mood somber as all eyes stared across the intersection at the open plain of the Mall. The speculations were put on pause as they went into action, but work was a welcome reprieve from the gossip.

With Clang barking orders, the squad was deployed on both sides of the intersection and a barrier was set up to block the road. The night provided no clues as to why they were there. There was nothing to be found in the moonless sky, but the street lamps along Jefferson offered a clear view of anything coming in at ground level. Durf and L'il were sent over to the Mall side to guard the northern perimeter. For the next half hour, everything was quiet.

The first signs that this wasn't going to be an ordinary night came from the strange objects in the sky. These were lights that moved too fast, or moved then stopped, or that just didn't look right. Most of the strange lights had a rusty glow about them, as if the sky was filled with mobile reproductions of the planet Mars. Most were off to the north.

Those lights, resplendent in their bright orange auras, wouldn't long remain in their initial quadrants. Soon those lights, or others just like them, were behind and above the roadblock, arriving and departing in the blink of an eye. The men shifted uneasily as their eyes tried to stay with the frantic activity in the sky.

"Must be different ones," L'il said as a fireball the size of a grape, disappeared behind a tree, then resurfaced over the Capitol Building.

"Nothing moves that fast," Durf agreed, "not even rockets."

But then two orange fireballs crossed trajectories above them, only a couple thousand feet up, close enough to give a clear idea of their size.

"Sonuva-"

"You see that?"

"Those ours?"

"I wouldn't bet on it."

"You dimwits, those is flying saucers!"

"Sure, cupcake. Just like in the funny books."

"Well, what do you wanna call 'em?"

L'il let his carbine fall to the ground. He clutched at Durf's arm and did a spot-on impression of a man falling to pieces.

"They're going to kill us all!" L'il hissed.

"Shut up, ya little worm, or we'll do it ourselves!"

"Keep it down, pipsqueak!"

Then, before Sergeant Clang could get the men back under control, all the lights, as far as anyone could see, suddenly went out.

A call went out to start the generators, but then another call came back that they hadn't brought along any lights for the generators to power. For that matter, there weren't any generators to power those lights because all such items had wound up at other locations in the confused execution of Plan Z.

Sergeant Clang ordered Sparks to call in the missing equipment, and that was when they found out that the radio was as dead as everything else of an electrical nature. Not wanting to panic the men, Clang kept this to himself and ordered Sparks to do the same.

"Keep your eyes on the perimeter!"

The voice wasn't Clang's, but it sounded like it was used to being obeyed.

"Who said that?" Clang objected. "I give the orders here."

Durf retrieved L'il's rifle and thrust it back into his hands.

"Don't lose your head. You're making us look bad."

Durf got L'il back into position and together they stared anxiously out into the surrounding black. A couple of times, Durf thought he saw shadows moving, but these were shadows moving into other shadows and nothing ever seemed to come out. The line of sweat grew to a respectable rivulet, tracing a path down his spine to pool inside his skivvies. His hands felt slick and clammy, and no amount of wiping on his pants could stop the flow.

He'd just wiped his trigger hand dry for the fifth time when he heard the first cries of the Beast. These were long inhuman grunts that rolled down the Mall to catch in the marble columns of the Capitol. There was a weird huffing sound at the bottom, like the sound of a man struggling with a heavy burden. Then, higher-pitched, the musical trill of a woman's laughter. This was punctuated by short sharp barks. As it came closer, the men on the northern perimeter started to chatter again.

"I can't see a blessed thing."

"Flashlight! Anyone got a flashlight?"

"I see it!"

The snuffling came closer.

"Rifles ready!"

Durf brought his carbine up to his shoulder, the barrel turning toward every shadow that caught his eye.

Then, without warning, a single street lamp flared back to life. In this new light, they saw that whatever the thing might be, it was far closer than it sounded. The thing was long and huge, taller than a man, but wide at the sides. A pair of legs kicked frantically from its open mouth.

The light of a second lamp sputtered to life behind them, illuminating the pale, snake-like body of something that looked like an enormous python.

No one waited for the order to fire.

***

John Haste and Desiree Blythe were halfway down the Mall when the lights went out. The reporter had slowed to an asthmatic canter as the extra burden of Desiree's ninety pounds, ninety-five if you counted Mister Poopoo, began to weigh on him. Running out of steam, Haste came to a reluctant halt beside a wrought iron bench.

"I'm sorry, Miss Blythe," he said, wheezing for air. "I think I need to rest."

Desiree released her choke hold on Haste's throat, letting her hands slide over his shoulders as he released her onto the bench.

"Oh, you poor man, you must be near done in. I can walk from here. I don't care how much it hurts."

She hopped lightly to the hard-packed lawn and took Mister Poopoo out of his arms. The Pekingese yapped excitedly, and leapt from Desiree to the bench to the ground. Never one to stay satisfied for long, Mister Poopoo was disappointed that the bouncy ride had ended so soon. Desiree poked him lightly on the nose and scolded him for his attitude.

"Don't you be that way, Mister Poo. Mr Haste carried us an awful long way."

Mister Poopoo, having decided long ago that this night was far too exciting for his taste, curled his legs under his little body and went to sleep.

Relieved of these twin burdens, John Haste collapsed onto the bench. He'd loosened his tie during his service as a pack beast, but his shirt was soaked with sweat. The yellow stains under his armpits attested to the fact that this wasn't the first time he sweated through this particular shirt. His head fell back as his lungs sucked deep lungfuls of air. His sweat grew clammy against his skin.

Desiree came around behind him, wrapping her arms around his neck and drawing his head back to rest upon the soft pillow of her breasts. She laid cool hands on his temples, not shying from his perspiration, letting it soak into her palms as she stroked his head and looked up at the stars.

"Do you know, Mr Haste? I don't think anyone ever did anything so nice for me in my life. You have a generosity of spirit, the like of which I have never seen."

Haste's eyes closed as his breath grew more regular.

"I have to say that surprises me, Miss Blythe."

She gave him a playful slap on the forehead, which made him open his eyes, but he could see her smile. "Call me, Desiree, silly. After the night we've had, we should be on a first name basis."

Haste laughed a laugh that was so tired it only made it halfway out.

"Only if you call me John."

"Just John? You don't strike me as a just John, Mr Haste. What do your friends call you?"

272

"How long have you been in Washington, Miss Desiree?"

"Oh, going on eight years, I think. Why?"

"Well, Washington has always struck me as the kind of town where you don't make friends, you make connections."

"That is an interesting observation, Mr Haste. Maybe I should ask what your connections call you?"

"Hmmm, that's sounds like I must be doing something illegal, doesn't it?" Desiree pulled her hands away in mock scandal.

"Are you? You know, you never told me what you do for a living."

Eyes still closed, John Haste shook his head. He didn't want to tell her how the other reporters called him Fast Johnny behind his back.

"No, nothing like that. My dirty little secret is that I'm a reporter for the *Post*. I cover the Capitol beat."

Desiree drew him back into her, her hands immobile on his drying cheeks.

"So that's it," she murmured, too low to hear as she thought back through the circumstances of their encounter. "Am I a story, Mr Haste?"

John Haste gulped at the use of his surname. It was the sudden realization of a skater blissfully gliding across ice that turned out to be far thinner than he anticipated.

"No! I mean..." He sighed and gave up, feeling honest but defeated.

"Well, yes. Because I think you're the kind of woman men tell secrets to. Just the same, I'm not going to lie to you, even now."

He twisted away from her grasp, taking her hand and guiding her around the bench to sit beside him. "You have to understand," he pleaded, suddenly desperate. "I was looking for answers."

Desiree shifted on the cold bench, her eyes hidden by the night.

"Answers?"

Haste looked down at his feet, unable to meet her gaze.

"Just before I met you, I had the strangest experience of my life."

He was quiet for so long, she had to prompt him to go on.

"What happened?"

"You're gonna think I'm crazy."

"After what we saw tonight? If you're crazy, so am I. Please, John, tell me what you saw."

The use of his given name soothed him enough to seek her hand. Though he was relieved when she didn't push him away, he still felt like he was on shaky ground.

"It's been a strange day. I spent the morning at the HUAC hearing. While I was there, I recognized someone who had no business being there. When the hearing broke up, I went to the Library to find out more about him."

"Who did you see?"

He was going to say it wasn't important until Desiree pulled her hand away.

"Lars Ångström," he admitted. "He was part of a group, but he was there."

Desiree's eyes went so wide he could see stars reflected in her pupils. He heard the excitement in her voice as she halved the distance that separated them. His heartbeat was almost audible when her knee touched his thigh.

"The sex doctor? Why would he be called in front of HUAC?"

"I don't know," Haste admitted. "That's what I mean. That's why it was so strange. McAfee did something completely different today. The men who were testifying were there because they were all experts on UFOs."

"UFOs?" Desiree looked up into the sky, remembering what they'd seen over the Pentagon.

"It's almost like he knew what was coming..."

Haste was immediately dumbfounded by her observation.

"Yeah..., hey..., you're right! I didn't even think about that."

"Tell me about the hearing," Desiree pleaded.

"Well," Haste said, preparing his thoughts as he would prior to writing the story. "There were five experts in all. One was a reporter of sorts, a guy named Keyhoe who does magazine articles for *True*. After the first four testified, there was another guy who wasn't scheduled. His name was Menzel and he was there because he wrote an article on UFOs for *Life* saying that UFOs are all bunk."

"After him, they closed the session to the press, I still don't know why. After they made us leave, some of the guys stuck around waiting for them to come out, while others ran off to file their stories. I was curious about Ångström, even though he didn't testify, so I went to the library to do some research."

He paused for effect. The pause had the result he was hoping for. Desiree came even closer, her body turning slightly to nestle into his ribs. He brought his arm around to accommodate her before going on with his story.

"I ran into a guy at the Library who said that Ångström and his crew never came out. After a half hour, the doors opened. They let anyone who was still waiting back in, but they ended the session without calling any more witnesses."

"So what did you do?"

"Well, like I said, I went to the Library and worked there a while. I found out more about Ångström, but nothing about him having anything to do with UFOs. Finally, I gave up and went across the street to have lunch. I bought three hot dogs and a Pepsi from a street vendor."

Desiree shook her head.

"Those were chilidogs. Give a girl a little credit."

"You're a sharp one, Miss Desiree. I wonder why no one seems to notice."

Desiree wriggled against him, pleased by the compliment. Haste went on.

"Well, I found a shady spot under the trees, and I was about done eating when I saw a man coming towards me. He was about the only thing I could see from where I was sitting, but I don't think he knew I was there."

Haste paused to take a breath before finishing.

"Halfway across the lawn, he stops and looks up. Then he just stands there, and even though it's the middle of the day, the light around him kinda changes. I can't really describe it. It was just different, like he's standing in a break in the clouds, even though there weren't any. I could even see where the circle ended on the grass. I rolled onto my side to get a better look. And then..."

Haste stopped, reluctant to continue. This was where he would have to trust her not to run. "I saw a door open up in the sky."

Desiree gasped, unable to hold back her surprise. "A door?"

Haste shook his head, still bewildered by the memory. His voice fell to a whisper. "I can't think how else to describe it. It was like a door opened and there was light pouring out of it."

"Gosh!"

"And then the man starts rising up toward the door."

"He was flying? Like a bird?"

Haste shook his head again, lowering his voice even further.

"No, he's floating, like a balloon, right up into the door. And then it got even stranger."

"Golly!"

"Then...just as he's about to go through the door, he...changes!"

Desiree slid so close she was almost sitting in Haste's lap. "Changes?"

"Just a few feet from the door, his body turns dark and his hands stretch out into ... claws or something. I didn't get a great look, but he reminded me of a big ol' insect, something really nasty like a locust or a June bug."

Desiree's pert nose wrinkled in disgust.

Haste had been making claws of his hands as he described the change. Now that he was finished, he let them fall into his lap and sighed.

"So that was why I was looking up into the sky when I met you."

Desiree stroked his cheek. "Well, it's all perfectly understandable now."

She thought for a moment, then she sighed too.

"And since you've been so honest, I'll tell you my secret."

Haste pulled her the rest of the way onto his lap, turning her side-saddle so he could look at her. For some reason, the thought of knowing her secret made him uneasy.

"You don't have to," Haste insisted. "It won't change how I feel."

Three blocks away, a single street lamp flared back to life. This single lamp lent a faint illumination to her face and revealed the lines of dried tears running down her cheeks. Desiree smiled weakly, suddenly worried about how he would receive her news. Would he think less of her?

"No, I want to," she said out loud, deciding to risk everything on the truth.

Desiree Blythe took a deep breath and gulped before blurting.

"Mr Haste, you should know that I am a kept woman."

Three blocks away, the night erupted with the sounds of rifle fire.

Chapter 45 - Scene From Space

"So," said Arthur Ecks, "you must be the real Joe McAfee."

"You're goddamn right I am," said the sour man, not budging from his seat by the wall. "You'll forgive me for not shaking hands. You'll understand why as soon as you take your first dump."

The real Joe McAfee held up his own hands as evidence.

The other four men looked away, each with his own level of discomfort.

"How long have you been here, Senator?" Ecks asked.

"I don't know for sure," said the real McAfee. "I haven't seen the sun since they nabbed me. All I can tell you is that I've taken forty-three dumps since they brought me here."

The four men looked at him oddly, prompting the explanation.

"They don't have any clocks and there's no other way to tell time."

Hynek nodded as if pleased to be able to make use of his scientific training.

"That means if we can calculate one bowel movement for every day-"

"I ain't anywhere near that regular," the real McAfee shared, "and the crap they feed you makes it even worse. You'll see," he concluded ominously.

"Your replacement told me they've also replaced a good number of men from the House and Senate. Are they here, too?" Ecks asked.

"Some of 'em were," McAfee admitted grumpily. "They left me behind to greet you or something, maybe show you the ropes. I don't really know."

"Lucky us," Donald Keyhoe muttered under his breath.

The room was almost circular with exit doors in every panel, a configuration that made it hard to find landmarks. Lincoln La Paz started toward a point where one of the I-beams dove under the sand.

"Not there," McAfee warned without saying why.

La Paz stopped, figuring it out for himself.

"What do they want with us?" Ed Ruppelt asked, breaking the awkward silence that followed. "I can see why they'd want Congressmen, but why us? None of us is all that important."

Ruppelt looked around, offering his apology. "Sorry if that offends anyone."

Hynek waved off the apology. "No, you're right. We aren't that important."

"I have to disagree, captain," Ecks said. "We five know more about UFOs than anyone on the planet. That's why we were called to testify and probably why we were abducted. I think they simply want us out of the way."

"Bravo, major," said a second Joe McAfee, this one rising out of the sand like a Botticelli Venus. "There's more to it, but you got a bit of it."

"You're here," the false McAfee went on, "because each one of you has knowledge you don't know you have. A great deal of that knowledge showed in your testimony."

"It did?" A stunned Allen Hynek said.

"Oh, yes," the faux senator replied, "let's take Dr La Paz's account as an example. If everyone will recall, Dr La Paz was sent out to locate the source of the green fireballs."

"But I never found...anything," La Paz protested.

"I know," McAfee agreed smiling, "but that's only because you didn't know what to look for. You see, you never understood the significance of the fireballs and where they came from."

"And you do?" La Paz said incredulously.

"Sure," McAfee said, jerking a thumb towards Hynek, "but clowns like this guy are so fired up to find a reasonable, and by that I mean terrestrial, explanation that they dismiss anything that doesn't fit the bill."

"So," La Paz asked, almost vibrating with the desire to know, "what are the green fireballs and where did they come from?"

McAfee looked at each man, ignoring only his doppelgänger.

"They're escape pods, of course. We found the wreckage of a Nemertean ship in orbit about two hundred fifty miles above the atmosphere. The ship broke up coming through a wormhole because worms don't know a damned thing about making ships or flying them."

"Worms? Wormhole?"

Allen Hynek stared back, baffled by what the bug was saying.

McAfee kindly decided to enlighten him.

"Yeah, they're just names that don't really mean anything, doctor. We use wormholes to travel between star systems, too. You don't have to be a worm to use a wormhole. Wormhole is just the name some of your scientists decided to use for the sub-space portals that are the key to getting around the universe. They're the only way to travel between stars without taking generations to go anywhere. There's a hell of a lot of empty space out there."

"And the worms?" Ed Ruppelt asked. "What about the worms?"

McAfee pursed his lips, frowning.

"Well, I hate to cast aspersions on those not present, but the best way to view the worms is to think of them as power-mad parasites."

"Parasites?" Ruppelt's jaw dropped open in surprise.

"You're one to talk, senator," said Arthur Ecks.

"I'm the senator here," the real Joe McAfee reminded them.

"I could be talking to you, too," said Ecks, "but right now I'm not."

"Get back to the parasites," Ed Ruppelt urged.

The false McAfee smiled, pleased to be the center of attention again.

"Well, Nemertean worms are between six and eight feet long and about as thick as a pencil. They can't survive in any environment other than their own without help, but-" McAfee paused, bringing one finger to his temple, "they have an adaption that makes it possible to survive almost anywhere life is found."

"What's the adaption?" Ecks asked, surprised to find he was interested.

"It's quite fascinating," McAfee said. "They find a suitably advanced life form, preferably something large enough to contain their bodies, then after that life form is deceased, they take up residence, repairing any damage they find. They can then use the body as a host for as long as they need it. There are some specifics I could get into, but that's pretty much the gist of it."

"In resurrecting their dead host, they also bring the personality of the host back to life. The host doesn't get much say in things, but on the plus side, it's not exactly dead either. The worm gets access to the body, knowledge, and experience of the host, and the host gets to go on living. It's a win-win situation if you look at it in the right light."

Arthur Ecks thought back to the resurrected men he'd seen in 1947. He'd always thought the Ffaeyn were responsible for bringing them back to life, but the worms presented another, albeit less attractive, alternative. It made sense. The green fireballs had fallen all over the Sonoran desert, from Arizona to west Texas. The worms were right there in the area, needing hosts to survive.

"Jesus," said Allen Hynek, "that's horrible."

"Not so much if you're dead," McAfee pointed out.

"What else did you learn from our testimony?" Ruppelt asked. "Do me next."

"Well, you had several things to talk about," the bug pointed out, "but let's take the case of Captain Mantell."

Allen Hynek groaned. "This is going to be about Venus again, isn't it?"

Donald Keyhoe laughed a bit cruelly as McAfee continued.

"I'm sorry, Professor, but you came up with the explanation. You were right in that Captain Mantell chased a pale sphere to his death, but the sphere he chased was much closer than Venus, and nowhere near as large. In your rush to find a rational explanation, the one you provided was patently absurd."

"So what was Mantell chasing?" Donald Keyhoe asked. "That's one I'd really like to know the truth about."

The false senator looked at Keyhoe in surprise.

"He was chasing a space ship, of course. That much should be obvious. If you want specifics, he was chasing something analogous to your aircraft carriers, a kind of deep space ship used to transport smaller craft that can be used inside a planet's atmosphere."

"But whose ship was it?" Keyhoe asked, clearly mortified at being thought dim by a bug.

"Well," McAfee said, "there are two candidates. Both use those kind of ships and both look more or less human, though one more than the other. I'd guess it was one of those. Frankly, you all look a bit the same to us."

"So," said Arthur Ecks, finding it hard to believe he was actually going to say this out loud, "either the Nordics or the Greys."

The other men, including the real Joe McAfee, all looked at Arthur Ecks with identically stunned expressions on their faces.

"Exactly," said the bug, ignoring the effect Ecks' statement had on the others. "I knew I had a good reason for wanting you to testify, major. Clearly, I still haven't asked the right questions. How about you tell me what you really know?"

"What I know," Arthur Ecks said, choosing his words carefully, "is that you're in a heap of trouble if you choose to follow through with your attack."

For the first time since Ecks made his acquaintance, there was a break in the bug's equanimity. The false McAfee's face creased into an animal snarl, then dissolved into its true form, spitting out one last venomous retort just before it disappeared into the sandy floor.

"Well, we'll just have to see about that, won't we?"

Arthur Ecks wasn't given any time to gloat. As soon as the faux senator was gone, Ecks felt something clamp onto his ankles. He barely had time to draw a breath before the lobster-hard claws of many bugs dragged him under.

***

Ecks fell through a ceiling and landed on his feet, sputtering grains of sand. Instinctively, he recoiled from the things holding his ankles, kicking and shaking violently, like a dog coming out of a river. He felt the stream of sand slide down his spine. It was annoying, but far worse things happened every day at the beach. The ceiling shifted above him as the bugs disappeared without surfacing.

He wanted to open his eyes, to see where he was, but he could still feel the grit clinging to his face. He wiped his hands on his trousers and ran his sleeve across his eyes. When he could see again, when he could take in the new space around him, he cursed his stupidity, understanding too late that he'd been complicit in his own abduction, and through his obstinance at the hearing, in the abductions of Ruppelt, Hynek, Keyhoe, and La Paz as well. The whole day had been one long miscalculation. Now he wondered what the bug had planned in separating him from the others.

A moment later, one of the Clarences was at his side, shapeshifting before his eyes into his true form. Ecks took in the final shape after the transformation, getting his first real look at the narrow flexible thorax with the surprisingly short abdomen, a head with three slits he took for eyes and a long chitinous snout whose purpose he could only guess at.

On its back were the stumps of many pairs of vestigial wings. The bug had six legs, two walkers at its base, a set of multi-digit manipulators up top, and a set in-between that seemed capable of limited use in both capacities. The change complete, the Clarence slipped below the surface like a fish slipping off a hook.

The ground shifted again, reminding him how tenuous his position was. The sand was an unstable surface. Though it currently supported his weight, Ecks was acutely aware of what might happen if something wanted to drag him under. All around him, Ecks saw the shifting wakes of the bugs in their element, circling like sharks around a shipwreck.

He reached down to touch the ground, bringing up a handful of fine grains that seemed no different from anything one might find along the Malibu shore. He let the grains fall back to this indoor beach, and felt an odd curiosity at how each grain shifted as it fell into the greater mass.

This latest chamber featured a lower ceiling than the others and that made him feel claustrophobic. Every exposed surface was of the same rough textured metal as every place he'd seen so far. Like the other chamber, the bugs had cleared this space specifically to accommodate him. He wished they knew more about the human fear of enclosed spaces, then decided perhaps they did. The ceiling was close enough that he had to take care not to crack his skull.

As before, the air was breathable, and he wondered where they were getting it from, if they were allowing it in from outside, or somehow manufacturing it. Like the rest of his surroundings, the perfect ratio of oxygen to nitrogen struck him as being solely for his benefit.

The air was astonishingly arid, a far cry from the humidity of a Potomac summer. It had a too-clean smell that burned his nostrils and left an alkaline aftertaste. Tiny motes of sand floated in the air around him, barely visible in the dim light of his new prison.

He heard the humming sound of an engine, and touching his hand to the ceiling, felt a vibration that seemed to run through the entire ship. It took only a moment to guess what was happening.

The ship was moving. This was interesting simply because he'd assumed they were moving the whole time. It was an odd sensation, quite unlike the tug of gravity one felt in airplanes. He continued to feel movement until it suddenly stopped and the engines went silent. He felt a sense of anticipation, a feeling that something important was about to happen.

The sand shifted again, creating the maelstrom from which Joe McAfee rose. With McAfee's arrival, the rest of the sand flowed away to disappear into vents around the edge of the chamber. The sand level dropped, revealing a floor of the same rusty metal as the walls. His feelings of claustrophobia went away with the addition of another yard of headroom. McAfee ignored him, busy with some task that involved touching a number of different spots on the wall.

"So what's next, senator?" Ecks asked when McAfee finally turned back to him. McAfee glared back, his stolen features devoid of his prior affability.

"I'd think you'd be able to guess. There's a piece of information I've been trying to get out of you all day. I finally decided you simply didn't know and gave you the benefit of the doubt. But your last remark shows I was right all along."

Ecks thought back to what he'd said only moments ago.

"What? You mean about being in a heap of trouble?"

"Exactly that, it means you know our presence here is unsanctioned."

Arthur Ecks had no idea what the bug was on about, but he knew how to play this particular game as well as any. "Well, if I didn't before, I certainly do now. And that remark could have meant anything."

"Don't play coy with me, major. Who's supposed to cause that trouble? Your military? Your Air Force can't match our speed and your missiles are slow enough to pluck them out of the air and throw back at you. We have nothing to fear from your weapons. Even your atom bombs are clumsy and inaccurate-"

"We've had surprisingly little need to make them accurate," Ecks retorted.

McAfee went on as if he hadn't heard.

"-and you're smart enough to know that. Yet you chose that moment to issue a threat. You just gave yourself away, major, because that tells me everything I wanted to know. So now I can finally ask what I've wanted to ask all along. Who is your contact on the Council?"

"You wouldn't know him," Ecks replied, "he's new."

"No, he's not," McAfee said with venom. "Your contact is the man you report to. The man you know as Colonel Bee and he's as old as the Council itself. I blame myself for not seeing it earlier. How long have you been working for Colonel Bee? It doesn't make sense any other way. You're not affiliated with Majestic, we've infiltrated deep enough to know that, and you're too well informed to be part of the government. Colonel Bee is the only option that makes any kind of sense. You simply know too much for your own good."

"Well, we're going to send a little message to your Colonel. I may not know how to locate him, but we've been keeping tabs on your subordinates, and I'm sure one of them can get in touch should the need arise. And believe me, major, I am going to make it clear just how urgent that need is. Watch and learn."

A section of the ceiling became transparent, allowing Ecks to see where they were for the first time since coming aboard.

They were in space.

The ship tilted imperceptibly to display the cloud-obscured lights of the Eastern seaboard hundreds of miles below. They were high enough to see the edge of the globe and the ridge of light that marked the position of the absent sun, still hours away from its East Coast dawn.

As this window opened, Ecks felt the claustrophobic boundary of the ceiling recede even further. Night came flooding in, dimming the rusty radiance of the hull. He strode to the edge of the opening, peering down at a sight that Lars Ångström, Rita Mae Marshaux, and Jakob Kleinemann had described so inadequately five years earlier. It was as breathtaking as it was terrifying, so much open space with no barrier to separate him from it. His legs shook at the sight of the Atlantic, seen from so many miles above the surface of the Earth.

Without warning, the ship dove straight down through the higher layers of cloud, plummeting earthward at an impossible speed. Two other ships joined them, taking positions to either side. Ecks fell to his knees, not in response to the influence of gravity, but simply because he was terrified by the descent.

His last sight was of clouds approaching too quickly, of free fall from miles above the planet. He saw sprites, free floating ribbons of electricity, but couldn't bring himself to believe in them. He felt dizzy, his head spinning as they hit the clouds, then all went black.

***

Arthur Ecks opened his eyes.

He lay on his back for a time, struggling with the conclusion that his last conscious thought had come some time ago. He remembered the false McAfee's admission. The 'We come in peace' nonsense was total bullshit after all. But, now he had to wonder if that admission wasn't just another part of an elaborate dream. He yawned, hoping to wake up in his own bed.

The sandy floor of the Antarean ship and its clamshell ceiling put a quick end to that hope. The last traces of the dream were driven away when McAfee's stolen face loomed into his field of vision.

"Wakey, wakey," said the surrogate Senator for the second time that day.

Ecks closed his eyes, and waited an appropriate length of time, but McAfee was still there when he reopened them. Ecks tried to roll onto his side, only to find he couldn't move or feel his body.

"What have you done to me?"

McAfee gave him the nasty smile.

"Your nerve impulses are frozen from the neck down."

"Why the hell would you want to do that?"

McAfee leaned in closer, lowering his voice confidentially.

"Frankly, you people tend to struggle quite a lot if we don't. We get better results from our organ harvesting process if you don't move. One little nick can ruin a perfectly good heart."

"You stole my heart?" Ecks murmured incredulously.

"Yes, and you stole mine, Major. Heart..., lungs, and intestines, too. Pretty much emptied you out. All quite valuable to the right customer."

Ecks' eyes darted down his torso, the horror he would have felt running up his spine now limited to pictures in his head. He searched for some sign of entry, but couldn't see past his chin. He felt nothing but tears welling in his eyes. He hadn't cried since breaking his arm at age seven. "Why?"

McAfee laughed heartily at his distress.

"Ah, take it easy, major. I'm messing with you. You're fine. We had to cut the oxygen level for a few minutes. You'll be able to move in a minute or so."

Ecks felt something release from around his throat, like a collar he hadn't known he was wearing. He flexed his fingers, ignoring Clarence's offer of help.

"Sorry," McAfee explained. "I thought you might panic when the oxygen level dropped. We've seen that reaction way too often."

Clarence chuckled. "Remember the guy in Sioux Falls?"

"That was priceless," McAfee agreed.

Ecks turned to the viewport, which now held a startling view of Washington by night. As he watched, the ship drifted lower, turning the glowing mass of the metropolis into tiny separate pricks of light.

McAfee turned to a different Clarence.

"So, did you have any luck reaching President Truman?"

The new Clarence shook his head ruefully.

"None, I'm afraid. I was told I needed an appointment, as well as references to get the appointment. His secretary said it might take months to arrange a meeting. They also wanted to know the topic of conversation in advance."

"Oh, what did you tell him?"

Clarence looked as if something puzzled him about the reaction.

"Well, I didn't have anything prepared, so I just told the truth. I told him I represent an alien race that'd come a long way to procure real estate on Earth."

"And what did he say to that?"

"That I still needed an appointment. I did say the matter was quite urgent, but he said it would be impossible until after the summer recess."

"Bureaucracy," McAfee remarked to Ecks, "will be the death of your species. Ah, well, you can't say we didn't try peaceful means."

"So, Major," McAfee continued, "have you recognized where we are yet?"

Ecks jerked his head at the viewport where saucers hovered to either side.

"Sure. That's the airport."

"Good, now in a moment, we'll be going in for a closer look."

"I've been informed that there are jets approaching," Clarence interrupted.

McAfee laughed, anticipating some light-hearted fun.

"Kill the lights. We'll let the escort lead them away. Tell them not to go too fast. Let the monkeys think they have a chance."

The interior of the ship went dark. Outside, the escort moved away to await the jets' arrival. Just before the jets came into sight, the saucers started moving, matching the speed of their pursuers, staying just far enough ahead to keep the fighters interested. After a few moments, the lights came back on.

"Now let's move on to the next order of business. You may have noticed, Major, my air of confidence. Do you know why I feel so confident?"

Ecks scowled irritably. "No, but I'm sure you're willing to tell me."

McAfee smiled. "Well, I suppose I am being a bit precious. The reason I'm so confident is that we have a weapon that renders everything you have useless."

Ecks tried to sound unimpressed, but didn't quite pull it off. "Is that so?"

"Ah, you doubt my claim. I wonder, Mister Ecks. Do you hail from the Show-Me State of Missouri?"

Ecks shook his head, unaccountably grateful that he was able to do so.

"Nah, I'm from Oklahoma, but we're a skeptical lot too."

Outside, the jets came back into view, having lost touch with their targets.

McAfee signaled Clarence with a nod.

"I think you're going to find this interesting. Activate the damping field. Give it full power."

Suddenly, every light in the District of Columbia went out. The ship moved forward, edging closer to the now dark tower.

"The damping field," McAfee explained, "suppresses all forms of power within a limited range. Your atom bomb might still be effective, but only if you found a way to deliver and detonate it without electricity. Watch."

The Senator pointed through the viewport at the approaching jets. As if by magic, all forward progress suddenly ceased. The muted roar of their engines went silent as the jets lost velocity. Seconds later, both jets glided safely down to splash land on the surface of the Potomac. The jets disappeared on impact, but after a brief submergence, bobbed back to the surface like bath toys.

McAfee nodded at the viewport. "Pretty impressive, huh?"

Ecks shrugged as he got to his feet. "I've seen better."

McAfee returned the shrug in a more elaborate form

"No matter, it's time for the next step. For that, we require your assistance."

Ecks snorted. "You won't get it."

"Ah," McAfee disagreed, "I think we will. If you'll just look out the window..."

Arthur Ecks was pushed forward to peer out the viewport. Light returned to the tower. To either side, he saw a thousand feet of unlit runway. Straight ahead, he saw the interior of the control tower through an enormous picture window. Inside that window, he counted seven men and a single woman. The woman and the shortest man looked achingly familiar.

Inside the saucer, a brilliant light came on a few feet in front of Ecks.

"This will work better," McAfee urged, "if you step into the light."

Surprising even himself, Arthur Ecks did as he was told.

Across the divide that separated the saucer from the tower, Ecks saw signs of recognition. The short man and the woman came forward to better peer through the glass. As he'd already guessed, they were Jakob Kleinemann and Rita Mae Marshaux. He was please to see that they'd found their way out of their subterranean prison. He hoped that Lars and Dex had been able to do the same.

Ecks waved, then said in a low voice he hoped McAfee couldn't hear.

"Wish you were here."

Chapter 46 - An Appropriate Response

"Who the devil are you people?"

Jim Maddox stared at the trespassers with real consternation. He thought about calling security, but he didn't see how either could be a threat now, this despite the little man's resemblance to the anarchists of his grandfather's stories.

Besides, given the presence of the giant saucer outside the window, he no longer suspected them of sabotaging his radar system. The bogies had been real after all, though that was a fact that took a little getting used to.

Jakob Kleinemann put a finger to his lips for silence, drawing Maddox away from the window with a jerk of his head. Surprising himself, Maddox followed without protest, giving in to one last glance across the divide, to where a single man stood displayed through a gap in the saucer's hull. He caught up with the little man, impatient to know everything. Sensing the need for secrecy, Maddox kept his voice low.

"How do you know that man?"

Jakob told the truth, or at least part of it. "He is our leader."

Seeing the effect this statement had on the ATC man, he added.

"But I can assure you that he isn't friendly with the creatures piloting the saucer. I have to assume he was captured."

Maddox decided to provisionally accept this answer. "Then, who are you?"

Jakob Kleinemann gave a miniature smile that exuded a confidence he didn't feel in the slightest.

"We are the people who deal with these kinds of situations."

Rita followed Jakob away from the window and she was more than a little shocked by his newfound assertiveness. Though she didn't say anything at that juncture, she very much wanted to ask, *"When did we become the people who deal with these kinds of situations?"*

There was also the matter of, *"How are we supposed to ward off an attack by creatures that can travel between stars?"*

But the secret she couldn't share, the bomb the Ffaeyn had planted in her head, answered both questions. For better or worse, she and Jakob were now guardians of the planet. She only hoped they weren't its only guardians.

Maddox scratched his night shift stubble.

"So, you're from the government then..."

Jakob allowed him to think this was so with a quick nod.

"Can I ask which agency you're with? Maybe see some identification?"

Rita laid a restraining hand on Maddox's forearm.

"It wouldn't do any good. The agency we work with isn't the kind you would hear about. We deal with problems of an extraterrestrial nature."

Jim Maddox turned to Rita, seeing her for the first time and sizing her up for far longer than Jakob liked. "The government has something like that?"

When no answer seemed forthcoming, Maddox shook off his own question. "What the hell does that even mean?"

"It means," Rita said, "that if a problem isn't of this world, we're the ones who deal with it. If you look out that window, you'll see what I'm talking about."

Outside the tower, the runway lights went dark. A moment later, the city across the river switched off as well. The tower had backup systems that briefly flickered to life, but soon those went down as well, throwing a curtain of dark over the entire area.

The great disc had gone gray when the jets roared in, but now, as those jets departed on another wild goose chase, the disc blazed back to life, sending shadows streaking across the control room.

Maddox turned to the window, his face bathed in an otherworldly glow.

"I should call General Cranston at Andrews. I was going to call to tell him I made a mistake, but now I have to call to tell him I didn't."

"We have no objection to that, as long as..."

Jakob's voice trailed off into an expectant silence.

"As long as what?" Maddox snapped at the little man, the glow of the saucer making a halo at the back of his head.

Rita cleared her throat. "As long as you don't mention us."

Jakob continued her thought.

"It is not a good idea anyway. The combined armed forces of every nation on the planet are helpless against these creatures. Calling the military will only get good men killed. It would have no impact on saving our world."

"Besides," Rita pointed out, "I bet they already know what's going on. And your phones," she said lifting a receiver, "are as dead as the lights." The lack of a dial tone confirmed her claim.

"You are an eminently practical woman," said Jakob proudly, turning his attention back to Maddox. "With their technology, they could probably survive a direct strike from an atomic bomb, which is something the city would not. Whatever we do, our response must not be to meet violence with violence."

Maddox grimaced with the uncomfortable expression of a man about to do something far beyond his station in life. "You mean, like Gandhi?"

Jakob nodded, apparently satisfied with the comparison.

Maddox glanced back at the saucer hovering less than a football field away. He'd been in the war, and like everybody else, knew that doing nothing to halt Hitler's early incursions had been a huge mistake.

"Is that a good idea? From what you're saying, these things may not be human."

A perplexed expression settled onto Jakob's face.

"What does humanity have to do with anything? In my experience, human beings are capable of the most craven acts of aggression. As yet, we have little experience with these creatures, whoever they may be. If we can find a way to communicate, there's a chance we might reach an equitable arrangement."

"Without resorting to violence," Rita quickly added.

The control room went dark again. Jim Maddox glanced out the window. The saucer had moved away. Under the starlit sky, the dead city across the river lay helpless in a sea of black. Dozens of fireballs, all in shades of red, orange, and yellow darted about like supervisors inspecting ongoing work.

"You want to talk to them? Seems to me, the balls in their court. From what I'm seeing, they have the upper hand. Why would they want to talk?"

Jakob Kleinemann fingered the *warak shu* in his pocket, feeling the device come alive in his palm. There was no change in its temperature. It didn't grow warmer or cooler, but he could feel it listening and responding to his thoughts.

"Perhaps that is the key. Perhaps, our task is to make them want to talk."

Jim Maddox asked the only other question he could think of.

"Okay, so what are we supposed to do?"

Jakob and Rita shared a complicit glance. Rita answered for both of them.

"We don't know yet."

***

Perseus Grady had allowed Allen Dulles ample time to cogitate on the information he'd provided. In doing so, he had to shush his worm three times, begging for patience on each occasion. Phault was of a mind to turn the knife and close the deal. But Grady had studied the future director and knew how carefully Dulles considered every move he made. It made more sense to let the CIA man come to grips with the new reality on his own, even if he was showing signs of cracking under the pressure.

After several minutes passed, Dulles looked over at Grady, his brow dotted with beads of perspiration. This alone showed how seriously Dulles was taking the situation. As far as Grady knew, no one had never seen the spymaster break a sweat. "Has...has there been any communication with the attackers?"

"None that I'm aware of," Grady replied, playing his part with subtle flare. "At least, not at the time I left my post."

Dulles glared down at his desktop, his mind working feverishly.

"I don't understand," he said finally. "We have a deal in place, they promised to leave us alone if we didn't interfere with their collection process."

Grady perked up at this revelation, but fought back the impulse to pounce on it. He could only wonder who Dulles was talking about. He was pretty sure it wasn't worms. He might be talking about the bugs, but Grady didn't think so. He went with his instincts in framing his response.

"I'm sure it's not them, sir." Grady said respectfully.

Dulles looked up sharply, his eyes narrow with suspicion. He paused a beat before saying. "No, I shouldn't think so. But who else has the technology?"

Grady caught a glint of bright yellow light outside the window, a brief flash that barely made it through the blinds. He held his breath, almost rejecting his next question. "Is it possible there's someone else?"

Dulles looked up, startled by the very idea. "The Russians?"

"I was thinking of someone more...exotic."

Dulles looked confused for a moment, but then his eyes grew wide with understanding. "Do you really think so?"

Grady moved over to the window, took the pull in one hand, and looked back at Dulles. He gestured for Allen Dulles to come closer to the window, then drew up the blinds. Dulles rose from his seat to join Grady at the window.

Beyond the night being dark, neither man found any answers. Across the street, the silhouetted treetops swayed in a gentle breeze. Off to the north, they saw the faint glow of a few working streetlights.

"What are you trying to show me?" Dulles asked irritably.

"Watch," Grady said. "It shouldn't take long."

He was right, it didn't.

High in the sky to the east, Grady spotted an orange streak shooting across the sky like a falling star. "There," he said pointing.

Dulles followed Grady's finger to the indicated location.

"I don't see...Oh my god!"

Suddenly the sky filled with a hundred points of flame, of dots too large to be stars, and too mobile to be planets. Allen Dulles saw streaks of yellow, red, and orange, dipping and diving, spreading out in a wide net that seemed poised to overwhelm the city.

A pair of jet fighters roared past, rumbling the roofs of Foggy Bottom. Down the street, a military transport turned the corner as the first warnings were braodcast from its public address system.

"Citizens of Washington! The city is under attack by unknown agents! For your safety, you will be relocated to a sanctuary outside the city. Please prepare for immediate evacuation. If you have a car, load your family into your vehicle and follow the guidance of the military wardens. Please make any extra seats available to those who don't have transportation. If you are unable to find transportation, there will be vehicles sent to pick you up."

"Above all, do not panic."

The transport rounded the corner to deliver its message to another street. Dulles watched as a family, a husband, wife, and two girls still in their pajamas, rushed out their door to climb into the family sedan. He saw the headlights come on as the car coasted down the driveway. Soon it was gone, as the same drama played out in the homes of their neighbors.

Dulles backed away from the window, his face ashen.

"Who are these...?" Lacking a definite object, his voice trailed away. He looked at Grady, as if Grady might provide a name for his fear.

"Who?" He asked again with even less hope.

Grady leapt at the chance.

"They're bugs, sir. That's all we know. Really big bugs."

Dulles continued to stare at him, his confusion mingled with horror.

"Bugs?"

"Yes, sir," Grady said, finding new ways to embellish his account.

"We've been tracking them for hours, but we haven't had time to issue a warning. We didn't know what we were dealing with until just before I left."

"Where the devil are they from?" Dulles asked. "We were assured..."

"We don't know yet," Grady interrupted, cutting him off.

Dulles spun around on his heel, an inadvertently violent action from a man who prided himself on his self-control. He cursed under his breath, then turned back to Grady as a sly expression curled one side of his lips.

"Do we have anyway to contact them?" Dulles asked, fearing the negative.

"Not yet," Grady admitted. "Why? Do you want to surrender?"

"Surrender?" Dulles was startled by the idea, but the sly look soon returned.

"Yes, that might work," he said more to himself than to Grady.

Looking out the window, Dulles gave his orders.

"If there isn't any way to contact them, see if you can find one. See if they'll accept a parley. I'd like to talk to these bugs before this gets out of hand."

Grady pushed away from the wall.

"Shouldn't we alert the president, sir?"

Dulles face dropped as if he hadn't even considered the possibility.

"Truman?"

The right half of the spymaster's mouth joined the left in a crafty smile.

"No," he said, with evident relish. "I don't think that will be necessary."

Chapter 47 - Shifting Pieces

Even after agreeing to drop him at CIA headquarters, it still took another five minutes of coaxing to get Detlev Bronk into the front seat. The car started easily, and after some difficulty getting the Mercury out of the slot the bug driver had shoe-horned it into, Dex started down the country lane to the main road.

He was both surprised and irritated to discover that the man he'd rescued was a finicky traveler. Though Dex tried to put it down to his being recently let out of the trunk, Detlev Bronk soon proved to be the kind of passenger who flinched at every obstacle, jamming his foot down on a brake pedal Mercury hadn't seen fit to provide for other passengers. Dex exacerbated the problem by backing into a Hudson in his effort to get free.

"Watch out!" Bronk cried as something small and furry ran across the road.

"Take it easy, doc," Dex said, trying to hide his irritation. "I saw it."

"If you saw it, why did you almost hit it?"

Dex glanced over at the academic. Bronk's eyes were almost entirely white, with pupils the size of new peas. "You feeling okay, doc?"

Bronk turned to glare at him.

"Do I look okay? You should try getting tossed in the trunk of a car and driven out to the middle of nowhere!" Bronk grew shrill with delayed hysteria. "I thought those men were gangsters! I thought they were going to kill me and dump my body out in the marsh! How should I feel?"

"I don't know," Dex said, answering a question that was meant to be purely rhetorical. "Lucky?"

Bronk continued to glare, his eyes steely and dangerous, but what he wanted was absent from the driver's demeanor.

Dex refrained from further comment. At the end of the lane, he took a left onto the main road, heading for the lights he'd seen from the top of the hill. He couldn't see those lights at ground level anymore. The rise and fall of the land restricted his view to the reach of his headlights.

The new road was two winding lanes in the process of becoming important as the city expanded beyond the limits of the Beltway. Dex passed a road sign that gave its name as Powder Mill Road, but provided no further information. A mile later, he turned onto the Baltimore-Washington Parkway.

With the wider road and only minimal traffic going into the city, Dex started to accelerate, but Bronk would have none of it.

"You're exceeding the speed limit," Bronk pointed out.

"We've got an emergency," Dex retorted, growing more irritated with every moment that Artie's fate remained uncertain.

"That's no excuse for breaking the law."

"Actually, doc," Dex said, putting the pedal to the floor, "I believe it is."

Dex's rejoinder, and the need to hold on tighter, ended Bronk's attempt at intervention. The next few miles flew by as the speedometer crept up toward seventy. There was almost no inbound traffic, but as they careened up the ramp onto US Interstate 50, the outbound side of the highway was a different matter. US 50 was a ribbon of headlights as far as the eye could see. Pinched off by events further down the road, that traffic was at a complete standstill.

"What the devil is happening?" Bronk asked, more comment that question. "Why is there so much traffic on the road this time of night?"

"If I didn't know better, I'd say the city is being evacuated," Dex replied, bringing the Mercury's speed down at the red glint of taillights ahead of them.

"Evacuated?" Detlev Bronk seemed shocked by the very idea. "Why would they evacuate the city? We're not at war! The Russians wouldn't dare attack!"

As if in response to Bronk's claim, six orange fireballs shot across the sky to enlighten him. The fireballs shot past in quick succession, darting low over the Capitol Mall, then rising up again to be lost in the residential streets north of the city. One fireball detached from the others, heading back toward the Mall before returning to hover at the treetops.

Even though he was one of the few civilians in the country who was aware of the existence of extraterrestrial life, Detlev Bronk was remarkably resistant to the reality he now saw above him.

"What's happening?" Bronk asked again, his disbelief crumbling at the sight of the fireballs. "This is impossible!"

Dex pointed up, though Bronk could see the invaders as well as he could.

"That's what's happening! We're being invaded by aliens from outer space!"

"But that's impossible," Bronk protested vociferously, unaware that Allen Dulles was doing the same a few miles away at that very moment.

"We had an agreement~"

For the sake of Project Stall, Dex pretended he didn't hear this remark. He was well aware of the document Bronk was referring to, and knew even better why his complaint was irrelevant. It was true that Majestic had formalized its treaty with the aliens. The problem was, those weren't the right aliens.

Inbound traffic came to a standstill a half mile shy of Mount Vernon Square. The streetlights that were still working revealed a military roadblock that was redirecting all inbound traffic. As they waited, cars pulled in behind them, blocking their retreat as well as their forward progress.

Dex tried to climb up on the curb in the hope of gaining a few more yards only to find that others had already done the same. He heard angry shouts all around, and similar complaints from the other side of the highway where many had abandoned their cars in open defiance of the guards. Those same guards were fighting a losing battle by trying to force everyone back into their vehicles.

The atmosphere was raw with fear, and ignited by a hysteria that only grew worse every time a fireball dipped low enough to strafe the highway and its trapped populace.

But there was no discharge of weapons because there was no need. The panic that every public official had feared since the Mercury Theater's *War of the Worlds* broadcast was thriving in the chaos that gripped the city.

"What the devil is happening?" Bronk whispered to himself, the sheer awe of the nightmare before him driving his analytical faculties into hiding.

Unable to move forward, Dex put the transmission in park, and set the brake. A private, his rifle lowered into shooting position, shouted angrily at the driver of the car in front of him. The private's warning went unacknowledged as the man abandoned his car to join the dozens doing the same.

The complaint was the same for all. There just wasn't anywhere to go.

This blockade of cars and its desperate rabble of trapped men and women descended further into chaos when the streetlights went out a moment later. The engine of the stolen Mercury died abruptly, and its headlights soon followed. All around them, engines that'd run flawlessly until then, choked and died, bringing a sudden and temporary silence to the night.

More fireballs darted across the sky, each leaving streaks of burnt umber in its wake. As the fireballs departed, the mob was left to the darkness and the fears that darkness held.

It seemed that Life was returning to an earlier age, an age that predated the advent of assisted transportation. Man, for the first time in millennia, was on his own, without a horse to kick or a machine to curse.

Somewhere in the distance, a gas main exploded.

Somewhere there were screams.

Somewhere there was gunfire.

It looked like the end of the world.

"Looks like this is as far we go," Dex told Bronk. "We'll hoof it from here."

He expected to hear some protest from the older man, but Bronk's response was only silence. When Dex turned to see what ailed the man, he saw why.

The passenger door hung open on its hinges.

Detlev Bronk was gone.

***

"It's a glorious sight, isn't it, General? The end of Man's reign on Earth."

Clarence fought the cord controlling the blinds and drew them all the way up. Outside the window, the night sky was populated by an almost uncountable number of darting stars, all aglow in shades stolen from the red-yellow bands of the visible spectrum. It was only these shades and the speed at which they moved that distinguished the ships from the static stars they used as disguise.

The sight reminded Vandenberg of the flak he'd seen during the war, rising up from the earth to smite the bombers come to rain hellfire. The only difference here was that the flak was raining down from above and the puny humans on the ground seemed to have no response. There was no boom of guns from the ground and nothing airborne could deter or delay the Antarean ships.

Vandenberg could only watch in frustration as the jets that Neal Cranston had called in from Delaware tried again and again to engage the enemy, only to have the saucers turn tail and scamper out of range. More jets arrived to join the fight, but the bug saucers continued to evade engagement, never allowing the jets to get close enough to deploy their missiles.

Vandenberg could only imagine how reluctant those pilots must be. It would be insane to fire their weapons so close to the city with so little chance of striking their targets. The impasse went on for almost fifteen minutes before their fuel ran low, forcing their to return to base. Vandenberg watched them with a sinking horror. The United States Air Force had been beaten by an enemy who never fired a shot.

In frustration, he pushed past Lieutenant Clarence, reaching for the phone on his desk. He wanted to get Cranston on the line to let him know how craven his pilots were. He wanted to communicate the shame he felt to every man serving under the Stars and Stripes.

But Clarence would have none of it. Clarence wagged the pistol at Vandenberg like a nun threatening a misbehaving child.

"Ah-ah-aah, General, no fair using the phone. That's why I'm here, you know. I'm supposed to keep you incommunicado for as long as is necessary."

Vandenberg picked up the phone anyway, bringing the receiver to his ear. He reached with the other hand to dial, waiting for a dial tone that never came.

Clarence shot the phone off of the desk, sending it crashing to the floor.

Vandenberg used the chance he'd been given, throwing the receiver into the bug's face and using it as cover to reach for the gun.

The diversion worked.

Clarence was caught off guard. The receiver struck his cheek, reached the end of its cord, and was yanked to the floor to rejoin the wreck of the telephone.

Vandenberg closed quickly, pressing his advantage, delivering a savage right to Clarence's belly, then following it up with a vicious uppercut to the jaw that sent the faux lieutenant reeling back against the window. The general felt a surge of triumph as the window shattered into a thousand pieces. But nothing could have prepared him for the bug's response.

Vandenberg froze in shock as Clarence started to change right before his eyes. He'd already seen a partial transformation, but that was a pale inadequacy when compared to the sight that now met his eyes.

As the bug's body broke through the shattered window, Clarence's torso seemed to explode into a dozen sets of limbs that resembled the lichen-covered branches of an old oak. The young man he'd known as Lieutenant Barlow Clarence vanished, to be replaced by a stiff-fingered insect with the claws of a crustacean.

The thing that was once Clarence spread its limbs out wide, clutching at the edges of the window frame to slow its fall. With shattered bits of glass still falling to the pavement below, the bug pulled itself back inside, and rose to its full height to deliver a backhand slap that drove Vandenberg back against the wall.

Vandenberg slumped to the floor, feeling the stab of two broken ribs.

"That," the bug said, as it came to stand over him, "wasn't very nice."

***

Donald Menzel almost cried out with relief as the sandy-haired man drew close enough to make eye contact. The man smiled reassuringly, but both turned at a sound from behind. Menzel came forward to catch the man's arm and draw him out of the exposed center of the corridor.

"We have to be careful," he whispered, "they seem to be everywhere."

"Who's everywhere?" The young man asked genially. "I haven't seen a thing."

"I don't know what they are," Menzel admitted. "I've never seen anything like them. They look like walking trees! All limbs and branches!"

"Trees? That's preposterous!"

The young man let out a laugh that was far too loud for the situation.

"Quiet!" Menzel hissed. "Do you want them to catch us?"

Another of the scraping branch sounds came screeching down the corridor from the direction he'd come.

"Who are you talking about?" The young man asked. "You know, you're not supposed to be here. Everyone has gone home for the weekend."

"Haven't you seen them?" Menzel whispered. "They must be eight feet tall!"

"I'm sorry," said the young man, his voice dropping to match Menzel's, "but I have no idea what you're talking about. Maybe if you described them," he suggested.

Donald Menzel groaned in exasperation.

"They're just like I told you, about eight feet tall, with...I don't know how many arms and legs. They don't have any heads and the arms and legs look a bit like the branches of an oak tree. That's about all I could tell in the dark."

Menzel flinched as the young man touched his shoulder. Turning, he saw the hand just before it began to change.

"Do they look like this, Doctor Menzel?" Clarence asked as a half dozen other limbs encircled Menzel's waist and torso.

"Was that what you saw?"

Chapter 48 - The Worm Turns

The Ford Coupe was a two-door model, which was a good thing if you were busy with a kidnapping and didn't want to worry about your victims slipping out the back door at a stoplight. The rear seat was reached by pulling the front seat forward to gain access. This had the effect of forcing any passengers bound for the rear to pass through this narrow gap prior to taking their seat. Once the front seat returned to its upright position, it provided an effective first barrier to escape.

On the other hand, like any vehicle tasked with abducting more than its fair share of victims, that back seat got pretty crowded after a while. It would've been an impossible situation if three of the four victims weren't young girls, and skinny ones to boot.

So, after Bertie Stein was brought back up to a sitting position, the girls took turns stepping on his corns and digging pointy knees into his pudding-like quads as they clambered to their seats. Bertie winced at each incursion, but his head wasn't clear enough to mount a more vocal complaint.

The girls were another matter.

Molly was the only one of the three who was actually excited by the prospect of being kidnapped. Being the first to surrender to this new adventure, Molly claimed the window on Bertie's far side.

Bubbles crawled into the middle beside the fat reporter. Never having stayed up later than eight o'clock in her life, she laid her head in Bertie's soft, smelly lap and fell asleep so quickly that Stormy abandoned her expedition to look over Molly's shoulder. With nowhere else to go, Stormy planted her bony knees in the remaining space between Bubbles and Molly and sat back on her heels.

"Hey!" Wally Sands admonished when he saw the way she was sitting. "Keep your dirty feet off the upholstery!"

Her heart leapt into her throat at this first sign of unwanted attention and Stormy adjusted her seat accordingly.

Corbett took over the driving, and in sliding the seat back to accommodate his longer legs, he moved the bars of the prison that much closer to its inmates. With his inner villain singing a happy tune, he reissued a stern warning to the back seat.

"Everyone just stay quiet and this'll be over before you know it."

Abel Corbett was feeling fairly genial, all things considered, but he hadn't given any thought to how his words would affect the kidnapped girls.

Corbett's command didn't bother Molly in the slightest. She'd been listening to gangster shows on the radio since she was tall enough to reach the dial. She didn't hear any threat in Corbett's words because she understood this was how these things were supposed to work. Their kidnappers simply didn't want any trouble. They'd be taken someplace dramatic where there'd be a confrontation, and then they would be exchanged for ransom. Molly grinned madly, wondering what the ransom would be.

Stormy was still smarting from the rebuke about her shoes being on the upholstery, and she didn't take it as well. Stormy saw only the implied threat. They were going to get their throats cut. Gangsters wouldn't waste bullets on little girls. They'd cut her and leave her on the ground with her life flowing out into a big red pancake of blood! Fearing this bloody dénouement, her heart leapt into her throat yet again, attempting an escape that was as premature as it was unsuccessful.

Bubbles, being asleep, couldn't have cared less, but even if she'd been awake, she would have maintained a child's faith in the belief that everything would work out all right.

It should've been a short drive to the Washington Monument where the exchange was to take place. After all, they were only one block over and ten blocks down. By day, the great obelisk was visible from the hotel windows, and it would have been at night if the lights hadn't gone out.

But once they turned onto 15th Street, they found the side streets barricaded all the way to New York Avenue. There, they joined a line of gridlocked cars being diverted away from the Mall. It was their first contact with the chaos that'd been created by the bugs.

The traffic moved slowly, but eventually, they arrived at another barricade. This one was different. Where city police had staffed the first, this one was manned by soldiers in khaki fatigues.

"What the fuck is going on here?" Sands scowled.

Bertie Stein tried to swallow the chloroform taste he couldn't get rid of, then unwisely attempted to admonish the bald kidnapper.

"Watch your language! There's young ladies back here."

Wally Sands turned to the passengers, resting his elbow on top of the seat. The chloroform was wearing off, but it'd left a greenish tinge that made Bertie look even froggier than usual.

"You keep your lip buttoned, old man. One peep to the soldier boys and you're done." He glared at Stormy and Molly in turn with the idea of delivering the same message.

Molly grinned back at Wally Sands. She'd already decided that he was better than the best radio villains she'd ever heard. Stormy pushed herself deeper into her seat, alarmed that she couldn't get farther away.

***

Even though he could still taste it, Bertie Stein couldn't remember eating his last meal. He remembered it well, the cold half of a corned beef and cabbage sandwich, devoured privately in his room at the hotel. That was his breakfast and his stomach was already rumbling when Janie Gently coerced him into joining her on this long ride to nowhere. After that, there was the airport, the jail, and a hankie soaked in chloroform. Not once had anyone offered him so much as a cracker.

All through the long day, his finicky bowels had craved release. He'd broken a little wind while unconscious, but since coming out of the chloroform, he'd been holding back the greater part of the eruption. After all, there was a little girl in his lap.

By the time Corbett was able to break free of the traffic, they were all the way back to K Street where they'd started. Most of the traffic was being diverted up 7th Street, but the soldiers were letting a few cars through onto Massachusetts. Corbett took the offered detour. He was still headed in the wrong direction, but he was willing to trade this for the ability to move freely.

He took a right at 3rd Street SW, then followed it most of the way across the Mall. He took another right at Maryland SW, and felt relieved to have reached the Mall, even if he was at the wrong end of it. He found another right onto Independence before disaster struck. He saw the barricade at 4th Street where they were turning cars around to send them back the way they'd come.

Corbett swore angrily. The roadblock was still a hundred yards away.

"This doesn't make any sense! Where the hell do they want us to go?"

Sands tapped him on the shoulder, pointing out his window.

"How about that way? If we can make it to the trees, we can dump the car. Maybe we'll have better luck on foot."

Corbett eyed the distance to the tree line. It was closer than the roadblock, but there was no street leading there, just a stretch of brown lawn the sun had baked harder than the asphalt around it.

"Turn out your lights," Wally Sands suggested. "You'll draw less attention."

Corbett turned out the lights, leaving a dark spot in the space before them. He eased one tire up onto the curb, and then another. He gave the accelerator a quick punch to get over the bump, then put in the clutch and let the Ford coast on its own momentum. Sands peered back at the roadblock.

"No one's watching. I think we're gonna make it."

Molly squirmed, pressing her face to the window. She'd never had so much fun in her life.

The canopy of the trees moved ever closer, extending its bony fingers as if yearning to embrace them. The Ford crossed the empty lane, then climbed the curb on the other side. But just as sanctuary seemed within reach, a headlight pinned the Ford in its beam and a two-stroke engine rumbled to life.

Sands hissed. "Run for it!"

Corbett braked to a stop. "No, it's just a motorcycle cop. I'm pulling over." Corbett glanced at his lieutenant, his look unreadable.

"You talk to him. See if you can make him see reason."

Sands nodded his understanding. Corbett turned to the backseat.

"You kids remember what I said about keeping quiet. I'm going to talk to this guy and find out what's going on. One word outta you little toothpicks and it's curtains, you got me? That goes double for you, old man!"

Bertie Stein's intestines turned over with a sound like a creaky door in a scary movie. Something was starting to move, and no force of will was going to stop it. Perhaps sensing the change in Bertie's tectonic biology, Bubbles opened her eyes and sat up. Her dream of imminent disaster continued on without her.

Abel Corbett looked her in the eye and put a finger to his lips.

"Sssh."

***

Wally Sands exited the car so quietly that no one even heard him go. He didn't push against the door until he'd released the latch, and then he slid it open just far enough to let his body slip to the ground. He rolled around until the motorcycle's headlight was blocked by the front tire. Unseen, he rose into a crouch, peering over the hood as a motorcycle cop in leather jodhpurs and a khaki jacket brought his Indian to a halt, set the kickstand, and killed the engine.

Sands avoided the beam as he made his way around to the car's dark side.

An earnest young man in the uniform of the DC police shined his flashlight beam into Corbett's eyes.

"Hey there, you folks lost?"

When Corbett didn't reply, he explained, "This here's a military e-vac-u-a-tion and we all gotta do our part. I'm gonna need you to get back in line."

He said evacuation like it was a new word he'd just learned, enunciating each syllable as if they were separate words.

"I know it's hard," he said, commiserating with their plight, "but it's just one of those things. Everyone in that line is just as stuck as you."

Corbett raised his hand to block the beam.

"But what the hell is going on out here?" Corbett snarled. "We've been stuck in traffic and no one's told us a thing! Why's the Army here?"

The earnest young cop laughed. "Are you kidding me? You ain't heard?"

"Heard what? We've been stuck in traffic."

"Well, you might wanna turn on your radio. Every station is broadcasting the same message."

"I don't like radio." Corbett scowled. "It's all bad music and bad comedies. What the message?"

The young cop's jaw dropped open in open disbelief. He knocked his cap back an inch to scratch the stubby hair under its brim.

"You mean you ain't heard? Why, it's only about the biggest news ever!"

The earnest young man's name was Jefferson Davis Early-Bird, the surname being an unfortunate amalgamation bestowed on the family a generation before. In the company of friends, he usually shortened it to Jeff Early, but some wag in the department had thought it would be funny to put the whole last name on the little badge Early wore over his shirt pocket. Early was too amiable to see the badge as a dig, a flaw his superiors interpreted as his being too kind for police work.

Still unable to believe the news had managed to avoid this family in the coupe, Early slapped his thigh with one hand, then set it down on the hood of the Ford. "I can't b'lieve y'all didn't hear."

Corbett sighed, feigning interest. "Hear what?"

"The city's under attack by flying saucers! Ain't you seen 'em? They been shooting around overhead for 'bout three hours and our jets can't keep up with 'em. Sometimes they slow down enough to give you a good look, but most of the time they just skitter along like water bugs."

Jeff Early leaned in closer, speaking in a more confidential tone.

"I don't think they really look like saucers though. I think they look more like sweet potato pies, all big, orange and tasty."

Early shook his head to clear it of all thoughts related to sweet potato pie.

"So, anyway, with all these flying saucers buzzing around, the Army thinks it best to get everybody out of town."

"Except for the colored," he added as an afterthought. "The coloreds are gonna havta take their chances with the Martians. It sure would be wonderful if them Martians could help the coloreds find deliverance from God's wrath."

Corbett hatched the seed of an idea, let it germinate, and then gave it more water than it needed.

"Say, officer, you seem like a man who might understand my dilemma. You see, I told my family," he waved vaguely toward the girls and the old man behind him, "that we wouldn't leave town without seeing the Washington Monument, but there's been so much to see here. DC's a great town, don't you think? We're flying out tomorrow, and I was hoping we could get a look up close before we go. We don't have nothing near that tall back where we come from."

Jefferson Early pushed his cap back on his head, and winced in the manner of someone who's been asked for too large a favor.

"Aw, I can't really do that. You'd never make it anyway, they got roadblocks all the way up the Mall. You'd never get that far without getting turned back."

Wally Sands finally appeared out of the shadows. Sands was a full head shorter than the earnest young man in the wrong profession for his personality type. Abel Corbett drew a thumb across his throat in a universally understood gesture.

Jefferson Early finally noticed the new man who'd crashed the party.

"Oh, hello, sir. I didn't see you there. Are you lost?"

The new man, an oversized silhouette in the glare of a distant spotlight, didn't say anything at first. Wally Sands took two steps closer to the unfortunate policeman and paused, cocking his head to one side as if he was trying to hear something too far away to catch.

Wally Sands winced as if he was preparing himself for something extremely unpleasant. His eyes pinched shut, his brow furrowed, his teeth clenched as his facial muscles drew taut with anticipation.

Then his face exploded.

And in a modern-day reversal of an old proverb, the worm got its Early-Bird.

***

The Ångström girls saw everything with a nightmare clarity that would haunt their dreams for decades to come. By virtue of their back seat prison and the coincidental framing of the worm's emergence in the windshield, the girls had front row seats for this unexpected horror.

Bubbles was the first to react, letting go with the kind of glass-breaking shriek that seemed to split Corbett's skull in two. Corbett covered his ears, but by that time Stormy and Molly had joined in as well, harmonizing Bubbles' high root with a shaky third and a perfect fifth.

Molly's shriek was especially raw, as well as being slightly off-key. The shriek brought an official end to her enjoyment of the kidnapping. Gangster radio shows and tough talk were one thing, but eight years old was far too young to be seeing a motorcycle cop being devoured by a giant worm.

As to Stormy's reaction, the less said the better. Let it suffice to say that it wouldn't be the last time in her life she'd wish for a change of underwear.

This time, the screams couldn't be stopped, and no threat, short of Kraall erupting the way Shff had, would've had the slightest effect. But terrorizing little girls wasn't the only result of Shff's emergence.

The worm's appearance also had a regrettable affect on Bertie's bowels. The girls were already pounding on the seat to be let out when Bertie released his corned beef poison into the restricted air space of the Ford.

Corbett reared back in protest at this new assault on his senses. Retching at this sudden offensive, he pushed the door open and fell face-forward to the ground. The girls took full advantage of this opportunity, leaving a cartoonish trail of footprints across the back of their fallen host. Once out of the car, they headed for the sanctuary of the trees.

***

The thing that came out of Wally Sands' face looked like the inside of a slaughtered cow. An orifice opened in its center, revealing glassy eyes in a bed of something with tendrils so fine they might almost be fur.

The tendrils snaked out of the orifice, coiling around Early's face before he had the sense to scream. As the tendrils drew Early into their fatal embrace, the orifice widened to receive the shoulders, then rapidly extended down Early's torso, drawing him in like a snake swallowing an unlucky lizard. As Early's hips disappeared, the worm lifted him skyward in an effort to gain gravity's assistance in forcing the oversized meal down its gullet. Early kicked frantically as one of the many broken street lamps flickered to life to illuminate the feeding worm.

The Ångström girls were still screaming when the first shots tore the night apart. Abel Corbett rose from the lawn, spitting dirt and grass from his mouth. Leaving the soldiers to Shff, Corbett took off after the girls, pleased that their noisy retreat made them so easy to follow.

***

Durf Schoenberg and L'il Schaver fumbled to get their rifles up to their shoulders so they could aim before they started firing. In this, they failed. Their first shots went high and wide, with one burying itself in the lawn of the National Mall while the other found the fourth story cornice of an apartment building.

With the night as dark as it was, all they saw at first were the same shadows that'd been making them jump all night. But then another light came on, and they saw the worm in all its horror. The night came alive as every man on the line emptied his magazine into the thing with four shoes.

Chapter 49 - The Grip of Chaos

The order to evacuate came filtering down from an unknown source in the chain of command. Some had it originating from Andrews Air Base, with the actual decision coming from General Neal Cranston, the man who was tasked with protecting the capital city's air space.

Another source had it coming from the office of General Vandenberg at the Pentagon, while a third claimed it had originated with an unnamed official at CIA headquarters.

There was even a rumor suggesting it came by cable from President Truman. Truman was at home in Missouri, licking his electoral wounds after a humiliating defeat in the New Hampshire primary.

But whatever its origin, the order to evacuate the city for the first time since the War of 1812 was disseminated to a sleepy public through an air raid system that'd never been used, and a fleet of public address speakers mounted on the backs of a fleet of flatbed trucks.

The trucks drove through the slumbering neighborhoods of Georgetown and Foggy Bottom, of Noma and Gallaudet, and Capitol Hill, each broadcasting the evacuation order without making any mention the imminent invasion from the sky. The order was essentially 'Get out of town now,' without any particulars given as to where to go or how to get there.

Predictably, given the gloom and doom nature of the human imagination, the trucks created panic wherever they went, and that panic was soon inflated by the orange fireballs streaking across the sky. An hour after the warnings began, more than half the population of the District of Columbia was on the move.

Doors were flung open as houses and apartments emptied in a lemming-like rush for the suburbs, mirroring in one night, a flight that would inflate the bank accounts of real estate developers for decades to come.

The capital's residents swarmed into the streets to blink sleepy eyes at the profusion of orange fireballs. Those with cars ran to them, and those without pleaded with their neighbors to be taken along. The panic grew as seats filled, and unlucky stragglers were left to beg rides from strangers, offering all manner of enticement.

When enticement failed, some were pulled from their cars by the mob, to be thrown into the street where they would take the place of the emboldened thieves. The police were overwhelmed, and with the military burdened by other duties, the infection could only spread.

Crawling along the side streets, those lucky enough to find a major artery impatiently ignored the stoplights to flood every intersection, blocking traffic in every direction. When they could go no further, the drivers leaned on their horns, adding their complaint to the sirens trying to clear the way.

Everywhere they went, the increasingly desperate mob encountered military roadblocks, diverting traffic, obstructing intersections, and adding to the general hysteria gripping the capital.

All the while, the fireballs passed overhead like meteors refusing to fall. But other than announcing their presence, the fireballs did nothing. The only active part of the incursion was that wherever a fireball could be seen, the remarkable technologies of Man simply failed.

And when the lights went out, the crowd turned ugly.

Short tempers, fuses lit by frustration and stalled traffic, exploded into fear and rage. When the power died, the cars died too, as the Antarean damping field extended its influence over every electrically powered device known to man. Frustrated drivers opened hoods and swore when flashlights failed. Cars were abandoned, and some even overturned by the ad hoc mobs of frightened men who still thought it was possible to get out of the city.

Terrified Washingtonians, driven mad by the burgeoning hysteria, attacked and overran the barricades set up to guide the flow of traffic. The young soldiers were as reluctant to fire on their fellow citizens as their commanders were to give the order. Many were knocked to the ground, to be overwhelmed by the mob.

All the while, the fiery discs zigzagged across the sky, occasionally pausing as if to review the fruits of their handiwork. Wherever the saucers went there was chaos, as the mere sight of them created panic and the wildfire expectation that things were about to get worse.

Many gave up, not finding the heart or will to fight back. Waiting for the end, they congregated in like-minded groups, straying to the shelter of the trees, or gathering under the awning of an apartment building. They prayed and they sang hymns as men and women alike rose to quote Scripture to any who would listen. Their voices called others to them, and together they surrendered to the unchecked power of the unseen assailants. Assured of their helplessness, they petitioned God to speed up the timetable of their salvation.

And as the night went on, more jets roared in from ever more distant bases, bringing with them the first casualties. Disaster struck as the saucers paused in mid-flight, hovering over the frightened populace, daring the pilots to fire their missiles into the heart of their own city.

One pilot, more reckless than the other members of his wing, decided to take the risk, but his target avoided the missile with ease, rising just high enough to allow the projectile to pass unchecked into the heart of the city. Destruction was only averted when the missile's propulsion system failed, leaving it to tumble into the Potomac with the kinetic force of a lead-filled garbage can. The saucer projected some kind of energy beam at the jet, then it too fell into the river like a wounded bird. The pilot bailed out before the jet hit the water.

A few more jets tried to engage with a similar lack of success, but there were no further casualties. Running low on fuel, they headed for home with their tails between their legs. After that, the jets stayed away, leaving the city helpless in the face of its irresistible foe.

***

Dexter Wye left the stolen Mercury where it died, with two wheels up on the curb and two on the gridlocked avenue. Everyone around him was out of their cars now. He saw a host of pale frightened faces, all of them stained a new shade of orange in the fireball glare.

He saw men trying to push their way free, women trying to comfort children too young to understand. He saw fights break out as men, unable to reach the threat in the sky, threw punches at any tangible obstacle they encountered. Dex tried to break up one fight, then a second, and gave up at the third. He remembered his mission then. His job was to find Artie, or failing that, anyone who might have an idea of how to get Artie back.

He started running, picking his way through the sea of blank faces and dark bodies that jumped whenever anyone rushed past. The panic was in full force by the time he reached the first of the barricades. Not wanting to sacrifice the time to explain himself, Dex slipped past the barrier at Independence, where an overwhelmed platoon of raw young men were struggling to divert the misguided flow of inbound traffic.

Once past the barricade, Dex crossed Independence Avenue to pass by the Library of Congress as he continued to fight the flow toward the Capitol. There, he was turned back at another barricade, but a block later, he managed to break out of the pack. Soon, he was making his way down 2nd Street. He ran to the next corner, turning right on C. The entire time, his heart pounded anxiously, as his pulse counted every lost second.

Once past the wailing mob before the doors of St. Peter's, he found the street almost deserted and he sprinted the four blocks to Washington Avenue. He followed Washington onto the Mall and continued until he spotted the Reflecting Pool on his right. Slaloming between two stalled Fords, he broke into a trot as he started up Jefferson toward 4th Street. A street lamp blinked on, then off, then on, illuminating yet another roadblock before dying for good.

A moment later, the first shots were fired. Before Dex could question why, he was running toward the gunfire. He'd gone a block when the shouts went up round him. Suddenly, he was in the middle of it all. A second light came on, and in the crossfire of the street lamps, he finally saw what the soldiers were firing at.

Jefferson Davis Early-Bird was already down to his last boot when Dex caught the last look the world would have of him. When that boot was gone, all that remained was Shff, the worm that once nestled inside Wally Sands' frontal lobe.

The worm was a horrid sight, a meaty, eyeless thing that rapidly grew to a dizzying height. It looked like one long intestine with a razor-toothed orifice as its only visible organ. As the unfortunate Early-Bird began his journey into its lower tract, the lamprey rings of its dentation were revealed. Off to one side, the body of Wally Sands lay discarded like a wet paper sack with a rip in its side.

The remaining civilians, who'd been too startled to move when the worm first appeared, now ran blindly as the worm grew. The panic-stricken soldiers started firing as soon as they saw the thing, many without taking time to aim. The gunfire drew the worm's attention, and the bullets its ire.

After the first two soldiers vanished down the worm's open maw, the rest turned and ran, dropping their weapons as they took to their heels. The worm caught two stragglers, picking them off like prizes from a drop hook game at a penny arcade.

Dex ducked behind an abandoned car and watched the worm, now twenty feet long and more than a foot thick, as it nosed about blindly for something it had lost. He spotted a rifle twenty yards away, but given the fate of the soldiers, retrieving it didn't seem worth the effort.

The body of Wally Sands still lay where it'd fallen when the worm exploded from his brain. The worm finally relocated its discarded host, coiling its length possessively around its torso, caressing the riven corpse with strange affection. At first, Dex thought he was seeing regret, an air of remorse at having ruined its home. He imagined he was a witness to mourning.

Instead, upon locating the object of its search, the worm began to shrink, the python width of its long torso growing thin enough to rest in a rattlesnake coil on the chest of its host. Having just witnessed five men being devoured, Dex wondered where all that mass had gone. The five men didn't seem to matter, the coil continued to narrow as its length shortened.

Dex stared at the thing in awe. There were simply no signs of the five men the worm had devoured. A snake that'd taken such a meal would've had a huge lump in its middle from just one body. The worm had swallowed five and all five were gone. His mind rebelled at the efficiency of the worm's metabolism.

But the true horror was yet to come.

When the worm could shrink no more, it slithered back inside the fractured head of Wally Sands. At once, it began to repair the damage it had caused, mending the rent skull as it rebuilt the bloodied features. Dex felt sick watching the reconstructive process, so much so that he finally had to turn away.

With his eyes so averted, Dexter Wye missed the most significant part of the resurrection. A minute later, Wally Sands rose to his feet and walked into the trees, to all appearances, none the worse for wear.

Bringing his stomach back under control, Dex watched as the worm and its host crossed the lawn, headed for the trees. Sensing that this might be the break he was looking for, Dexter Wye followed cautiously behind.

Lars Ångström couldn't remember when he lost sight of Winthrop Walton Russell. It wasn't intentional, but given the chaos gripping the city, it was hardly unexpected. He didn't know if Russell departed willingly to pursue his own course of action, or if he was compelled to leave by circumstances beyond his control. Either way, after twenty minutes of fighting crowds and barricades, Lars Ångström reached the Mall alone, where for the first time on his inbound journey, he found open space ahead.

The National Mall was, and still is, a series of lawns interrupted by numbered cross-streets. Now, as a result of the steps taken to facilitate the evacuation, the cross-streets were barricaded and the only obstructions were the few cars that tried to climb the curbs.

For the moment, there were only a few people out walking the Mall and these tiny figures were only visible when one of the saucers paused to cast its ruddy light upon them. All the real action was taking place in the side streets. As Lars passed the Reflecting Pool, the normally placid surface seemed to quiver with its own fear at the anarchy around it.

A mile and a half ahead, the Washington Monument drove a dark spike into the midnight sky. Its spotlights rendered useless by the Antarean damping field, the Monument was a presence felt more than seen. Now it was only truly visible when the obelisk was silhouetted by the glow of a saucer passing behind it, splitting the spaceship with a dark fat line of stone. Each time this happened, the monument leapt closer and seemed more ominous, as if a clock was running down on the world that existed before the saucers came.

Free of the mob, Lars ran through the dark, occasionally stumbling where the ground was uneven. He'd gone several blocks when he started hearing the screams of little girls. At first, he dismissed the cries, fearing that his subconscious might be playing tricks on him by giving voice to the apprehension he felt for his daughters. The whole city seemed to be screaming, and there must be thousands of terrified children among those, children roused from their beds, separated from their families, frantic in the dark madding crowd.

But, against all odds, these particular screams seemed familiar. Lars stopped to listen, trying to separate the needle of familiarity from the auditory haystack. He hadn't doted on them as often as he should, but he was sure he recognized those voices, individually as well as when they were joined in high-pitched disharmony. Luck smiled on him with uncommon favor when he was able to separate three distinct words from the general cacophony. Those three words were all he needed to verify his hunch.

"Run faster, Bubs!"

The voice, as if he needed more, belonged to Stormy.

His eyes darted around the lawn, anxiously trying to find her in the flickering dark. After more moments peppered with screams, he decided they might be anywhere in an area as long and wide as a football field. He could see very little, even with his expanded sight. He could see the heat traces left by the mob, but there were too many to give him any hope of picking his girls out of the crowd. He had only their screams to guide him and if the girls were truly in danger, those screams might go silent at any moment.

He ran toward the trees, blindly begging Chance to lead him where he needed to go. But the night was playing tricks and he suspected he was growing further away rather than closer. The center of the lawn was lightless and blank, while the periphery was a shapeless mass of shadow. There was too much sensory input for any one thing to stand out.

He didn't know what made him think of the Ffaeyn, but the memory proposed a new possibility. The Ffaeyn had made remarkable enhancements to his vision. Could they have made similar enhancements to his hearing? If so, might there be a way to echolocate his daughters the way whales did with their calves?

Lars closed his eyes to focus on the world of sound. He found what he wanted almost immediately. The shouts and screams of the mob continued to echo along the length of the Mall, but the screams he was looking for came from a clump of trees to his left. He ran toward the trees, praying he wasn't too late.

He found them by their warmth and by their size, his expanded sight locating the stripes of red spectrum light as they darted between the elms, random, frantic, disappearing and reappearing like particle waves in double-slit experiment.

The girls were being chased, but there wasn't anything in the red spectrum to identify their pursuer. It wasn't until he started searching the cooler spectrum of the blue range that he found their attacker.

Then, it was hard to make sense of it.

In spite of his appearance, the man chasing his girls clearly wasn't human.

***

Even before his resurrection by Kraall, Abel Corbett was as cold-blooded a killer as any man who ever lived. The worms preferred cooler climes and, in serving that need, they kept the body heat of their hosts down well into the blue range. In the dark, Lars Ångström almost missed Corbett, and would have if not for the minute electric bursts emitted by the worm during exertion.

Lars Ångström ran toward his girls, calling the names of the random movie stars his wife had named them for. "Veronica! Marlene! Virginia!"

These were their given names, though it had been years since they responded with any degree of regularity. All three shared a strong preference for the names they'd chosen for themselves, a preference that Lars had ignored in the hope that they'd eventually outgrow the game. His mistaken belief was that they would come around if he refused to play along.

Unfortunately, all three seemed to have inherited their mother's inability to acknowledge rational thought. His sudden capitulation felt like giving in, but in the heat of the moment, he realized that being rigid wasn't going to work. So, for one of the few times in his life, Lars Ångström abandoned rational thought in favor of raw instinct.

"Stormy! Molly! Bubbles!"

He would never know how they heard him, but they did, and they ran to him at once. Stormy came first, bursting from the cover of the elms dragging Bubbles behind her. He ran at them, regretting the neglect in his conditioning with every gasping stride. He'd made half the distance when their pursuer broke from the trees, his longer legs eating into the girls' lead with every stride. He didn't see Molly for a long anxious moment, but then he found her coming out from behind an elm. Corbett didn't seen Molly either, but he would reach the others before they could reach their father.

Lars tried to go faster, calling up every reserve he had left, but he was already gassed by the long hike. His legs felt heavier than flesh, bone, and blood, and he sensed that he was doomed to lose this race. Bubbles was running as fast as her legs could carry her, but Corbett was right behind. In a second, he would have her.

Exhausted, Lars stopped, praying for some higher power to intervene. Much to his surprise, his prayer was rewarded.

With a wind-up reminiscent of Bob Feller, Molly clocked Abel Corbett with a perfect throw that caught him right behind the ear. Maybe there was luck involved, but Molly had always thrown well. Even so, few eight year-olds could have matched that throw, in the dark at a man in motion from thirty yards away. She threw it as hard as she could, and though its velocity was spent by the time it struck Corbett, the diversion had its intended effect.

Corbett stopped in mid-stride, puzzled by the sudden pain at the back of his head. The stone had struck hard enough to leave a bump, and he rubbed it now with one hand. Stormy and Bubbles ran right through their father's arms to hide behind him, instinctively putting their father between themselves and danger.

When Corbett recognized the man protecting the girls, he had to laugh at the unexpected convenience of it all. Here he'd been going to all the trouble of chasing down the unruly brats in the hope that they'd bring their father to him. And though everything associated with his plan had gone wrong, here was Lars Ångström, helpless for the taking.

Abel Corbett smiled, suddenly enormously satisfied with the world.

"Good evening, Doctor Ångström," Abel Corbett purred with practiced villainy, "It's good of you to come."

Chapter 50 - The Return of Majestic-12

In the aftermath of his escape from Dexter Wye, Detlev Bronk slithered through stalled cars with an agility that would have been admirable in a man half his age. He left for two reasons, the most practical being that with traffic stalled as far as the eye could see, he no longer needed Dex and the stolen Mercury to reach Dulles and the CIA. The trek to Foggy Bottom now seemed walkable, and every time the fireballs darted overhead, there was a moment where he could see the reflected roofs of the hundreds of sedans gridlocking the avenue. Given the traffic situation, Bronk saw no advantage to staying with the car. He could travel faster on foot.

The second reason he left so quietly was, that even though Dex had rescued him from the trunk of the kidnapper's car, Bronk couldn't bring himself to trust the earnest young man. If there was one thing he'd learned from Dulles, it was to temper his natural instinct to trust with cautions of a more practical nature. But though he was now free to follow his own path, that path presented other obstacles.

It started with getting past the stalled cars. Each vehicle was squeezed into such a tight space that Bronk had to climb over their bumpers just to change lanes. Even this didn't reckon with the frantic horde streaming out of the cars to block his path at every turn.

He wondered again where he was. Washington had a limited number of roads that featured three lanes in each direction, and he had yet to spot a street sign or any familiar landmark. Judging by its width, the road was a major thoroughfare. As it was lined with sidewalks and shops, it was no stranger to foot traffic. Bronk tried to reach the sidewalk through tact and good manners, but the men and women in his way seemed immune to both.

In the end, he took his cue from the mob and simply bullied his way to the margins. In doing so, he was aided by the fact that most of the trapped were still loathe to leave their vehicles. It took minutes to reach the sidewalk, and once there, he had a torrent of pedestrians to contend with. Making his way to inside of the thoroughfare, he rested against the stuccoed wall of a barbershop.

Now that they were out of their cars, it was every man for himself. He was shocked to see the sudden breakdown in social norms. He watched grown men push women and children aside in their frantic search for refuge. Many deserted the open street, breaking windows and forcing doors in their search for sanctuary.

Bronk pushed away from the wall, staggering sideways at a glancing blow from an enormous man in striped pajamas. He continued to follow the thoroughfare, crossing an intersection where he learned that the road was New York Avenue, and that he'd reached 6th Street. All he had to do was pass through Mount Vernon Square to pick up New York Avenue on the other side. He could follow New York all the way into Foggy Bottom.

But Mount Vernon Square was impassable.

A detachment of infantry had claimed the square for its command post and nobody was getting through, even on foot. When he recognized the impossibility of getting any further on his current path, Bronk cut through the yard of a two-story Georgian to follow 7th down to H Street NW. There, he was able to turn west again, and somewhat surprisingly, to break free of the mob.

He had to divert again to get past the White House where a crowd of several hundred had gathered on the steps. Then he had to furtively cross the open plain of The Ellipse under the watchful eyes of a tank battalion. But at the end of it, he was finally on E Street, mere blocks from the front door of the Central Intelligence Agency and Allen Dulles.

He came gasping to a halt in front of the building, and took a moment to regain his composure. He was shocked to see the building dark, displaying none of the usual signs of occupation. This shouldn't have been such a surprise. After all, he hadn't seen any working lights since abandoning the Mercury.

But somehow it was. It made him feel like he'd already failed.

Exhausted by his journey, Bronk realized how much he'd been counting on the CIA for sanctuary. He hadn't even considered what he might do if Dulles was powerless.

But then he saw the dark figure of a man come out the front door. He was still too far away to guess at the man's features, but his presence meant the building wasn't empty after all. His hope rose again. Dulles would surely be the last man to leave the sinking ship.

Perseus Grady had gone by the time he entered and Bronk saw no cause to pursue him. Bronk slipped inside, shocked at how quiet the building was. He thought about calling out, but some premonition, of doom or discovery, stopped him.

He had to make his way by touch and memory. He was glad he'd visited earlier in the day, and he used that memory to recall every step he'd taken to reach the top floor. It took minutes of groping before he found the stairs, and only then did he realize how daunting a task he had ahead of him.

He would have to climb four or five flights in the pitch black darkness of an unlit coal mine. There would be no windows in the stairwell. He found the rail, but the steps were set at an odd height that seemed to have been designed to make him catch his toe on the nosing. He heard furtive sounds, unidentifiable creaks and scufflings, that made him think of rats and what a grand time the vile creatures must be having in a building devoid of people.

He paused on the second floor landing, listening for sounds of habitation, but the sounds he heard brought back nothing of human origin. As an experiment, he mounted a search for the door out of the stairwell, reasoning that the location on the top floor might be the same. It took longer to find the door than he expected, and he only narrowly avoided a nasty fall back down the flight he'd just ascended.

It wasn't until he opened the door to the fifth floor that he felt any degree of confidence. Having achieved this goal, he decided to risk calling out.

"Dulles! Are you up here?"

The response that came back sounded as shocked as Bronk was to hear it.

"Bronk? What the devil are you doing here?"

***

Donald Menzel looked down at the hand that wasn't a hand and finally gave in to the hysteria he'd been holding at bay. The hand, which was really more claw than anything else, represented an impossible reality, one that he'd gone to great lengths to deny. Even though he'd been on the inside of the extraterrestrial secret for years, he'd never had any problem resolving the conceptual speculation regarding life on other planets with the physical reality of the crashed saucers.

In a bizarre trick of memory, he recalled an occasion when he looked up the dictionary definition of extraterrestrial. The definition read, 'a hypothetical or fictional being from outer space, especially an intelligent one.'

This was patently unfair, Menzel thought as he stared down at the appendage gripping his shoulder. The dictionary specified that the being in question must be either hypothetical or fictional. It said nothing about gigantic shapeshifting insects tapping you on the shoulder as if they were only trying to get your attention.

"This isn't bothering you, is it?" Clarence said, giving Menzel's shoulder a little squeeze to further cement its corporeal existence.

In later decades, Menzel's reaction to that simple gesture might be described as freaking out or more accurately, losing his shit, but in 1952, the more reasonable diagnosis was that he was losing his mind.

"I'm using this shell because you guys tend to panic when you see what we really look like," Clarence explained, apparently unaware of Menzel's fragile mental state.

"Aaaahhhh," said the great astronomer, unable to articulate his state of mind.

The crack of something heavy striking the tiles snapped Menzel out of his funk. He jumped away from the bug, then, afraid of being caught from behind, whirled around to face it. Clarence retracted the claw and flipped it around to display the human hand before changing it back to the claw.

"Pretty neat, huh?" Clarence said. "It's a crying shame you guys can't do anything like that. If you could, you might stand a chance."

Menzel backed away from the bug, calculating the distance to the front door.

"You can't stand against all of us!" He shouted defiantly. "The American people will see you for what you are and they will fight you!"

Clarence laughed, barely able to restrain his hilarity.

"How are you going to fight us when we look just like you? How are you going to fight us when we replace your leaders with our own kind? You'll never be able to tell us apart from your own people. We will divide you and we will conquer you, just as we've done with dozen of planets before. Your weapons are useless against us and we already control the sky. How will you fight us, Dr Menzel?"

"We will resist you at every turn!" Menzel cried, shaking his fist at the bug. "We will take to the streets with torches and pitchforks if need be, but you will not crush us under your boot."

Clarence shook his head in mock pity.

"You will fight amongst yourselves and that will further divide and diminish your forces. You will fight yourselves because your weapons are designed to work against humans and they will have no effect on us. You may last a few years that way, but eventually you'll realize that we mean you no harm. In time, you or your descendants will start to question exactly what you're fighting for. As for us, all we need to do is control the sky and disrupt your power. Other than that, we won't have to do a thing."

The claw came and went again, followed by flashes of torso transforming into thorax and leg.

"If you want to fight us with torches and pitchforks, that's certainly your right. But we have no need to engage you. We can afford to wait you out."

"We have allies!" Menzel blurted. "Allies who'll blow your ships out of the sky!"

"If you're referring to the Grey Children," Clarence said, "I wouldn't count on their help. They're only interested in harvesting genetic material, and they can do that whether you say it's okay or not."

Menzel continued to back away, his chest heaving with the emotional effort of every step. Everything in his being screamed that Clarence was wrong, that the American populace, if roused, if warned in time, would make a worthy foe for the bugs. Clarence paused, uninterested in interfering with Menzel's retreat.

"Go the torch and pitchfork route if you like. We won't do anything to stop you. But eventually you'll run out of steam. How can you fight an enemy who doesn't fight back? We'll just wait for you to change your mind."

"That's barbaric!" Menzel cried as his next wave of hysteria reached a crest.

"Actually, we think it's quite civilized," Clarence demurred.

Donald Menzel, professor of astronomy at one of the most prestigious learning institutions in the world, turned and ran. As he ran, he cried.

"You won't get away with it!"

Donald Menzel ran back the way he'd come. Upon reaching the stairs, he glanced back, but nobody was following. Gasping with the effort, he sprinted down the first floor corridor, rounding a corner to surprise an unaltered bug. Menzel screamed, and the bug backed away, as afraid of Menzel as Menzel was afraid of it.

He ran until he found the exit, bursting through doors, and taking stairs three at a time. When he reached the Army barricade, Menzel cried out to the human mass around it, shouting this new truth.

"Listen to me!" He cried to the mob, sending his words out to find converts. "People are coming after me, they're not human! Listen to me! We're in danger!"

His rant went on and on. To his surprise, many listened.

***

Hoyt Vandenberg looked out at the saucers dotting the night sky and felt despair. It wasn't the first time he'd experienced this feeling of futility, and if life proceeded along the lines he saw developing, it wouldn't be the last.

"Quite a sight, isn't it?" Clarence said behind him. "We're focusing on Washington DC because this is where your military power is headquartered. Once we're done here, we'll move on Moscow. I forget what comes after that, London or Peking, but we'll just keep toppling governments one by one until you surrender. It's a shame you're so divided. If you worked together, you might put up a better fight, though the end result would still be the same."

"You'll never get away with it," Vandenberg replied with bluff courage.

"Don't be ridiculous, general," Clarence scoffed, "of course we will. This isn't our first rodeo, you know. I do love some of your American expressions."

High overhead, a dozen orange fireballs broke off from the main contingent to surround a squadron of jet fighters. The jets tried to break away using every maneuver they knew, but the saucers outflanked them easily, then herded them back into formation before guiding them away from the city.

"What the devil are they doing up there?" Vandenberg fumed at the out-classed jets. "They should be engaging, they should be firing their missiles!"

Clarence spun the gun around his finger like a Wild West gunfighter.

"Oh, we can't have that. Someone might get hurt."

The bug walked over to stand by the window.

"We won't allow them to fire their missiles, certainly not in the downtown area. We let one pilot try, but that was just to demonstrate what would happen. There's no point in repeating the same exhibition, so from now on, we'll simply prevent anything from happening when a pilot pulls the trigger. Your pilots will get the chance to fly around a bit, try out their best moves. But in the end, it will only demonstrate how futile it is to fight us. You're already beaten, general, and we haven't fired a shot."

Vandenberg watched in horror as a fighter jet shot past, flipping over in an evasive maneuver that failed to separate it from its shepherds. The jet was close enough that he could hear when the engine stalled Vandenberg followed it with his eyes, expecting it to fall out of the sky.

But the jet didn't fall. Before it could dive, a beam shot out from one of the saucers, catching the fallen fighter in its ray and causing the jet to do something Vandenberg wouldn't have believed possible.

It simply hovered in mid-air until the pilot managed to restart the engine.

Then, when it was deemed safe to do so, the saucer released the jet and allowed it to speed away.

Vandenberg shook his head in disbelief.

"That's impossible! It goes against all the laws of physics!"

"I believe the correct response is thank you. We could've let your boy crash."

"You're playing with us like cats," Vandenberg fumed.

"Yes, we are," Clarence agreed, "but unlike cats, we're not going to eat you when this is all over. We promise that no one will be harmed in any way."

Vandenberg continued to shake his head.

"This is ridiculous! Nobody fights a war like this."

Clarence pocketed the gun, returning to his seat in Vandenberg's chair.

"Well, first of all, we don't consider this a war. So let's just say there's no precedent for it on your world. This is the method we've found most effective. When it's all over, there won't be anywhere near the mess to clean up and you won't resent us for killing your people or damaging your property."

"You're insane!" Vandenberg yelled, heading for the door. "You're all insane!"

Clarence took one last look out the window. Vandenberg felt the smooth ball of the doorknob under his palm.

"We're insane?" Clarence remarked with raised brows. "The way you fight wars is what's insane. So much death and damage! Such an incredible waste!"

Vandenberg opened the door, then looked back at Clarence, wondering why the bug wasn't trying to stop him. The bug seemed to understand.

"Oh, it's all right if you leave now. There isn't a thing you can to stop us, though you're welcome to try, of course. But...if you don't mind, could you close the door on your way out? It looks quite dark and dangerous out there."

***

Dulles herded Detlev Bronk into his office, closing the door behind him.

"What are you doing here, Bronk? Haven't you seen what's going on out there? You should have gone to a shelter."

"A shelter?" Bronk scoffed. "Are you aware of the level of chaos out there? No one is going to shelters. The Army is evacuating the city. It's a total madhouse!"

Dulles went to the window where he spent the next minute staring down at the sidewalk. A figure came out of the shadows, looked up at the sky, then retreated back inside.

"Who gave the order to evacuate? Has Truman returned?"

"Not to my knowledge," Bronk replied, collapsing into a chair without waiting for Dulles to offer. "As to who gave the order, I have no idea."

"Probably some general with his head half up his ass," Dulles muttered to himself. "How did you get here? I haven't seen any cars in over an hour."

Bronk shook his head as he reached for a handkerchief.

"And you probably won't. The saucers have a weapon that knocks out our power."

"I know about that," Dulles said crossly. "The power here has been out for hours. I tried calling to see when they'd have it up, but even the phones are down."

Bronk shook his head, slowing his heart with an effort of will.

"It won't do any good. It's not the power plant. It's anything that runs on mechanical or electrical energy. Every car in the city stalled at the same time. Even headlights don't work. All the roads are blocked by stalled cars and the Army's made a hash of the rest. The city is helpless, and I should know, I walked across half of it to get here."

Dulles glanced sharply at the other man.

"Has there been any communication with...," he paused, unable to find a name. Finally, he went with the information Grady had given him.

"Did you know we've been attacked by giant bugs?"

"Bugs?" Bronk snorted, his upper lip curling in disgust.

"That's what my man said. They're bugs, really big ones, bigger than people."

"Then...," Bronk paused, his mind working feverishly, "it's not...them?"

"The grey guys?" Dulles shook his head. "I made the same mistake. It seems there's more in heaven-"

"Please," Bronk said, holding up a hand. "Spare me the platitudes. So..."

Detlev Bronk paused, considering the situation from a new angle. "That would mean there's a possibility we might enlist their help...the grey guys, I mean."

"My man says they won't help. Says they don't get involved in local spats."

Bronk wiped the back of his neck with the hankie.

"How would he know? Information regarding EBEns is compartmentalized. Who the hell were you talking to?"

"We don't use names. You know that."

Dulles frowned. "Besides, I didn't think to ask."

Bronk refolded his kerchief and returned it to his breast pocket.

"You and your damned spy craft."

"Dr Bush was right," Dulles shrugged. "Compartmentalization is the best way to keep things secret. Nobody knows anything they're not cleared to know."

Bronk shook his head, amazed that Dulles could miss so obvious a gaffe.

"Then, how did one of your field people find out about the Greys?"

Dulles reclaimed his seat behind the desk.

"Well, that's something I'll have to ask if I ever see him again. I sent him on a mission, to do something that may save us all."

"Oh, what's that?" Bronk's brow rose imperceptibly.

Allen Dulles folded his hands into a steeple.

"I've sent him off to make contact with our giant bugs."

The brow rose higher. "To what end?"

The steeple collapsed into a fold of intermingled fingers. Dulles brought the full power of his gaze to bear on his colleague.

"I thought it might be a good idea to surrender."

Chapter 51 - Camille Saves the Day

When he had time to look back on that night, John Haste would always wonder how he'd missed much of the disorder gripping the city. He'd marvel at how much of the chaos he overlooked, the saucers notwithstanding. Here he was, a chronicler of the human condition, and he had fallen so hard for the little woman in his arms that the better part of the city's descent into madness had completely escaped his attention.

He was in love, he was smitten, he was a too-tall Texan version of Pepe Le Pew. All his thoughts were of Desiree's eyes and Desiree's lips, her little expressions, and the way his spine curled over to make a little cave for her to nest in.

When the lights went out, Haste took it as a sign that the world wanted to give them some privacy. He heard bursts of gunfire, but these were a block away. The shooting stopped soon after it started, though the screaming went on a while longer. People ran past, but these were transient shadows, in far too great a hurry to notice the lovers. Even the great obelisk of the Washington Monument had gone dark, as if averting its gaze to give them solitude.

Desiree was as enthusiastic as he was, pulling him back to her whenever he drew back to catch his breath, her hands in perpetual motion as they moved between his neck and shoulders with occasional forays down the bones of his ribcage. She clawed at him hungrily, having finally found the sacred touch she'd always craved, that well of emotion that Neal Cranston reserved for fighter jets and armed men.

Above them, the fireballs crisscrossed the sky like a spider's web of shooting stars. They heard the frustration of angry drivers, caught up in traffic as complex as an Escher lithograph. A ruptured gas line exploded in Foggy Bottom. And all the while, the siren call of the warning system lured more suckers out of their homes and into the street.

Did they make love on that wide lawn? It was a curious madness of the night that neither could say for sure. No garments were removed and no animals were harmed, though Mister Poopoo certainly had it coming. So though it's easier to conclude they didn't do the deed then and there, something must've happened to leave them breathless, lying on their backs, and gazing up at a sky that was filled with more attractions than any Saturday night in recent memory.

"Oh, Mr Haste, I hope this night never ends."

"*That we may never see the dawn,*" offered John Haste, either referencing an obscure English poet, or making it up on the spot.

"That's pretty," cooed Desiree, not recognizing the quote, but knowing somehow it was meant to be one. She was silent for a while, taken by a brief fit of brooding. With another man, her silence might have been a sign that not all was right, but John Haste had already learned that these detours were short-lived. Her mind would consider a question, she would devote all her thought to it, and then she would decide how to proceed. The entire process generally took under a minute. This particular diversion took only seconds.

" Mr Haste?"

"Yes, my love?"

"I don't think I want to be a kept woman any more."

John Haste had been thinking along similar lines. He was now absorbed in considering the various actions he might take to move the mysterious General Cranston out of the picture.

Desiree shook her head at the stars, her eyes on something distant.

"I think I'd like to get a job."

"A job?"

Even as she said this, another idea came to John Haste.

"I had an idea, too."

"Oh?" she said, rolling onto her side. "What was yours?"

John Haste bit the inside of his lip, buying time to consider his next words.

"I was thinking we might get married."

Desiree was quiet again, a lack of response he found disturbing.

"I'm sorry for asking this way. I should have a ring and I should be on my knees, not on my back."

Desiree shook her curls and brought a hand up to support her head.

"Don't be sorry, it's really sweet of you to ask, especially as we only met this afternoon. And I accept, of course, if you're sure that's what you want."

John Haste thought about it and answered before she had time to think he had.

"It is."

"But I'd still like to have a job."

John Haste thought about his job, with its deadlines and its editors, finding it hard to see the attraction any job might hold.

"Wouldn't you rather start a family?"

Desiree frowned. "I'm afraid that's impossible. I guess I should have told you this, but I can't have babies, Mr Haste."

This was something he hadn't considered.

He wanted to be with her, of course, and if you were with someone, it was natural to want children.

"Oh?" He said, hoping he wouldn't kill the deal with the wrong tone of voice.

"It's one of the things Neal liked. You see, he has six children already and he doesn't want any more. I don't think he even likes the ones he has," she added. "You think he would've stopped after three, or four."

She sniffled a couple of time, then stopped to wipe her eyes.

"Mr Haste, my parents died when I was very young and I was raised by my Aunt Nadine. Nadine's job took her all over the Midwest so we were never in one place for long. When I was seventeen, I went from Nadine taking care of me to being on my own. After that, I went from working for the Army to being a mistress. It's been a long time since I did anything for myself. So, if I can find a job, I think I'd like to have one."

John Haste frowned.

"Well, I don't know. I never heard of a married woman with a job..."

Desiree's smile crashed on the shores of her disappointment. It was a sight that John Haste simply could not bear to look at.

"But," he recovered quickly, "if it means you'll be my wife, and it's what you want to do, I'll do everything I can to help you find a job."

Her smile returned with redoubled intensity and she drew his lips to hers for a series of sloppy kisses, each made more difficult than it had to be by the 'thank you' that interrupted it. Finally, she broke away, and rolling onto her back, she pulled him over on top.

"Make love to me, Mr Haste! Make love to me now! You are the most wonderful man I have ever known!"

The timing was perfect. It was spontaneous, and the moment was right, but once again, they weren't destined to make love just yet.

At the far end of the Mall, eight blocks away from where John Haste and Desiree Blythe lay making their plans, the shriek of stone tearing through metal rent the night asunder. The impact reverberated down the Mall.

They broke apart at the impact to witness a terrifying sight. They'd missed the start of it, when a saucer paused to hover over the point of the Washington Monument.

They also missed the next part where the saucer inexplicably lost power.

The only part they really saw was when the saucer came crashing down onto the tip of the Monument, to be impaled on its aluminum apex like an undersized wedding ring lodging on the second knuckle of a fat girl.

Then suddenly, it was all over.

All around, the lights of the city returned, illuminating amongst other sights, a plainclothes detective trapped in a bad marriage. Based on his own experience, the detective took a very dim view of public displays of affection.

***

They did find Camille in the end.

It took longer than expected, but eventually Janie found the little Metro where the attendant parked her. But in finding Camille, they also learned why

318

the streets around the hotel weren't jammed with cars. Camille simply wouldn't start. Her battery was so dead it didn't even make the solenoid click.

Stymied again, they smoked more cigarettes from Janie's pack of Viceroys.

"We could walk," Maisie suggested after a time. "The Mall's a straight shot down 14th. I think it comes out pretty close to where we need to be."

Janie frowned. Both women could hear the sounds of distant chaos.

"Would we be safe?"

Maisie's lips parted into the kind of devil-may-care smile that Errol Flynn had grown rich on. "Does it matter?"

The parking lot lights suddenly flickered back to life, pausing long enough to reveal an old man stumbling past before dying again. As Maisie tossed her butt out the window, her body suddenly came alive.

"I have an idea!"

Janie looked up sleepily. "What?"

"Put the gearshift in neutral and release the brake."

Janie shook her head, staring down the long stripe of 14th Street, tracing a straight line to the Mall.

"I can't do that. We'd roll right down the hill."

Maisie's eyes reflected the mad glint of Janie's cigarette.

"Exactly, I know it's not much, but there's a bit of a slope. We can coast down to the Mall!"

"But the headlights don't work..."

"That's okay, we won't be going very fast. Just keep to the center."

Janie turned the wheel toward the center line, already feeling an onslaught of butterflies at the prospect of Camille coasting blindly downhill in the dark. The little car didn't want to move at first. It paused right at the edge of breaking free, tires squeaking against the asphalt. Maisie opened the door and jumped out.

"You steer. I'll push. We used to do this when I was a girl in La Crosse. We might even be able to get her to start if we go fast enough!"

"How do I do that?" Janie wanted to know.

There was anarchy in Maisie's laugh.

"I'll tell you in a bit. For now, let's just get her moving! Put it in neutral and keep the wheel turned to the left."

Maisie left the door open, bracing her heels against the curb as she pushed the Nash out to the middle of the street. The Metro wouldn't budge at first, but then slowly, the weight start to shift.

"Now turn back to the right!"

As Camille started forward, Maisie gave her one last push before jumping back into her seat. Then they were off, rolling down the hill at a rate that left both women wondering if it might not be quicker to walk.

But their speed had doubled by the time they crossed the third intersection, and Janie had to swerve to avoid a stalled Buick. She braked inadvertently when a saucer appeared from behind the line of buildings, but she lifted her foot off the pedal before they lost any real momentum. She swerved to avoid a military transport on Constitution and suddenly, they were free.

There was an enormous crash as they passed the transport and, as suddenly as they'd gone out, the lights came on. Maisie gawked at the sight of the saucer impaled upon the obelisk, then a man stepped off the curb to make Janie swerve.

Without turning the key, the Metro suddenly roared to life. Janie threw the clutch into second and wound it up until Camille whined for third.

The rejuvenated street lights revealed how completely blocked the road was ahead of them, so Janie took a hard left, sending the little car over the curb and barreling across the lawn toward the Capitol Dome a mile away. The headlights came on, showing the way, but even in third gear, Camille screamed in protest.

"Turn around!" Maisie yelled. "We're going the wrong way!"

"I can't!" Janie screamed right back. "She's got a mind of her own!"

"Put in the clutch!"

"I can't! The pedal's stuck!"

Janie pressed down on the pedal, but Camille wouldn't let her take the stick. But Janie was right about one thing. The little car did seem to have a mind of its own. Janie watched the speedometer climb to fifty as they jumped the curb at 7th, miraculously slaloming through a crooked gap in the line of stalled cars.

"What are you doing?" Maisie screamed, her panic rising to a crescendo.

"I don't know, but I sure as hell ain't driving!" Janie yelled right back.

The stick and clutch suddenly moved in perfect synchronicity as the car shifted into fourth without Janie having a thing to do with it.

The speedometer had just touched sixty when Camille hit the worm.

Chapter 52 - The Real Thing

Donald Keyhoe was tired of pacing the same seven foot circle in the sand. He might have extended the circle, but the holding chamber was only so tall and doing so would have forced him to duck. He also might've simply taken a seat, with his back up against one of the I-beams at the chamber's outer rim. He could have done any of those things, but the real Joe McAfee had warned him away from two of them and Keyhoe had decided to leave the third a mystery.

Beyond pacing, there was precious little to do. Like Hynek and Ruppelt, Keyhoe was peeved that the bug leader had taken the inscrutable Mister X with him. In the wake of X's departure, pacing was the only activity left, though doing so made him feel a bit like a gerbil that'd lost its wheel.

"Will you cut that out?" Joe McAfee scowled from his corner of the seven-sided room. "You're making me antsy."

"You talking to me?" Keyhoe asked without altering his stride.

"Ain't nobody else doing nothing," McAfee pointed out.

"You sure as hell aren't," Keyhoe retorted.

"You're darn right I'm not," McAfee replied, jabbing the air with his stubby index finger. "That's cause there ain't nothing I can do and I already know it."

"We could try to escape," Ed Ruppelt suggested.

"Waste of time," McAfee countered, shaking his head. "This whole ship is filled with sand. Even if you could get out of this...here, you'd suffocate before you made it out of this room. The damned bugs breathe the stuff. Right here is probably the only pocket of breathable air on the whole damned ship."

"You don't know that," Allen Hynek objected.

"Well, you figure it out, genius. They breathe silicon, not oxygen. They eat it, too. That's what all this sand is here for. They swim in this shit, probably crap in it, too. Personally, I can't figure out what the hell they want with Washington. They like a dry climate. You should see the looks they give me when I ask for a drink of water. You'd think I said I wanted to have sex with their mother...if they even have mothers."

Allen Hynek looked up, suddenly interested.

"What do you mean by that?"

"By what?" McAfee said sulkily.

"What they want with Washington."

McAfee shrugged. "Nothing much, just that they hate water and humidity."

"Everyone hates humidity," Lincoln La Paz pointed out.

Joseph McAfee shook his head.

"Not like these guys. They kept me down in that exit chamber at first, you remember where you came in? Every time I seen one of 'em come aboard after being outside, the first thing they do is roll around in the sand, like the moisture in the air is unclean or something. That's why I can't figure out what they want with Washington. It's humid as fuck here. They must hate it. They should go someplace dry."

"Like a desert," mused Lincoln La Paz.

"Exactly."

"What else have you learned about them?" Hynek asked.

McAfee was silent for a moment, then shook his head.

"Nothing really."

"No, don't give up, Senator," Donald Keyhoe urged, now understanding where the scientist was going. "Nobody else has had a chance to observe them long term. Just tell us anything you remember, no matter how trivial it seemed at the time."

"Trivial?" McAfee snorted in disgust. "You think there's something trivial about being abducted by a bunch of eight-foot bugs? This has been a real fucking joyride from the moment they grabbed me."

"Start there," Keyhoe prompted. "When did they grab you?"

McAfee looked irritated by the question, but this was the most stimulation he'd had in weeks. "It was a couple days after I got this new goddamned intern. He was a Wisconsin boy who came highly recommended. Tall kid, ash blond hair."

"Was his name Clarence by any chance?" Ed Ruppelt asked.

"Yeah, how did you know?"

Ruppelt shrugged with a remarkable air of mystery.

"Lucky guess."

McAfee stared back at the young captain.

"Well, anyway, about the third or fourth day after he starts, I'm working late."

"There wasn't a bottle of scotch involved, was there?" Keyhoe asked.

"Matter of fact, there was," McAfee retorted, a bit defensively. "What of it? What's wrong with a guy having a few belts to relax after a long day?"

"Nothing at all, Senator," Keyhoe said soothingly. "So you're having a few belts, then what happened?"

McAfee's features turned surly.

"Well, I got three assistants working with me, but two of 'em are these little rat bastard liberal arts kids from UW. Those two start eyeballing me after my third shot, looking at me, a full U. S. Senator, like I got something to be ashamed about. Finally, I ask 'em if there's anything wrong and one of the little pipsqueaks has the nerve to tell me he doesn't think I'm behaving in a manner befitting my office. He says this like he's the senator and I'm the dumb fuck intern who barely knows how to wipe his ass."

"And this upset you?"

"Goddamned right it upset me. I told him right then and there that if that's the way he felt, then he could go get himself a job with that cold fish Stevenson-"

"You're referring to Adlai Stevenson?"

"Goddamned right I'm referring to Adlai fucking Stevenson. So I tell the little runt to get the hell out of my sight and take his little pink lady with him-"

"You're referring to the other intern now?" Keyhoe asked.

"Goddamned right I am. So those two take off with their tails between their legs, which leaves me along with this Clarence fella. And since I'm sick of this shit by this time... you got any idea how irritating it is being judged by some little rat bastard-"

"I think I can imagine," Keyhoe said diplomatically.

"So I'm sick of this shit, so I tell this Clarence that if he plans to hang around, he's gonna have a drink with me whether he likes it or not."

"How did Clarence take that?" Hynek asked, growing interested in the story.

"Well, at first, he doesn't react much at all," McAfee said, "but then it's like something just occurs to him like he just remembered he's allergic to scotch. So he says, no thanks, but he doesn't say it like he's all superior, so I decide it's okay to let him stick around."

"Okay," Keyhoe said, nodding, "so this Clarence sticks around and-"

"And," Joe McAfee blushed, "I proceed to get completely stinko. I don't know how it happened. I sure as hell didn't drink no more than usual. But it don't matter 'cause next thing you know, I wake up in this big sand pit where they ain't never heard of bathrooms."

"So what happened once you were aboard?" Lincoln La Paz asked.

"Hell, you've seen as much of this place as me. At first, I don't see nobody but this Clarence fella, and him I'm pretty pissed at. So I yell and cuss him out, but he just smiles. See, I was too dumb to know it, but he was trying to keep me talking so they'd know how I act. And there was another reason-"

"I think we know what that reason was," Keyhoe interrupted.

"You do?"

"They needed you to be present so they could make a duplicate."

McAfee brightened suddenly. "Hey, that's pretty good! You're a smart guy. I didn't figure that out until I was talking to myself face to face. How did you guess?"

Keyhoe shrugged, lifted his bony shoulders up toward his cadaverous skull.

"Stands to reason. We have a bit of an advantage on you, senator. We all testified before your committee this morning. We spoke extensively with your doppelgänger."

"My dobblewhat?"

"Your doppelgänger, that is, your double."

"That son of a bitch is running my committee?"

McAfee's jaw fell open. Clearly the idea had never occurred to him.

"Apparently, the bugs replaced several members of the committee with their own...," La Paz paused, groping for the right word, "people."

"Sonovabitch," McAfee swore politely.

"Did they ever interrogate you?" Ruppelt asked, branching off topic.

"Goddamned right they interrogated me, but I didn't tell them a goddamned thing, at least," McAfee blushed again, "until they brought out the Chivas. After that, I probably sang like a canary. But I don't think I told 'em anything important."

The four witnesses looked at each other, each thinking the same thing.

Whatever else you could say about the bug who'd replaced Joe McAfee, he was a hell of a lot more likable than the real thing.

"Okay," McAfee said, "enough about me. Who the hell are you guys?"

The four exchanged glances, subliminally electing Ed Ruppelt as their spokesman.

"We represent," the commander of Project Blue Book said, "the most in-depth knowledge about UFOs the country has available."

"I'm going to disagree with that definition," Keyhoe interrupted, waving off Hynek who'd also put up his hand to object. "We're just the best the public knows about."

Ruppelt started to protest, then slumped in capitulation.

McAfee did his own objecting.

"Why the hell would HUAC be looking into some wild-ass shit like UFOs?"

The four witnesses stared at the senator until Hynek broke the spell by giggling.

"Okay," Joe McAfee said, "considering what we're going through right now, maybe that wasn't the best question I could ask."

"I've got a better one," said Ruppelt. "What the hell are we going to do about it?"

"Yeah," McAfee pointed out, "but I'd say it's more like what can we do? We can't leave this place without suffocating."

"The senator has a point," Hynek agreed. "We can't breathe sand, and that means we can't move beyond this little pocket of air."

"So maybe," Keyhoe said, catching Ruppelt's eye for support, "we get them to come to us. There's five of us here. If we could catch one of the Clarences alone, maybe we could take him hostage and force them to let us go."

Joe McAfee's explosive guffaw caught them all by surprise. McAfee was wiping tears from his eyes by the time he brought his laughter under control.

"That is the dumbest fucking idea I ever heard."

"Why?" Keyhoe asked. "Five to one seems like pretty good odds."

For the first time since being brought to their cell, Joe McAfee rose to standing.

"Has any of you ever seen what one of these bugs looks like in the flesh?"

The four witnesses shook their heads.

McAfee extended his hand to draw their attention, then paused for effect.

"Would you like to?"

For a moment, there was no response, then Allen Hynek shook his head.

"You know," Hynek said slowly, "I'm not sure that's necessary."

"Indulge me on this," McAfee said. "If you want to get out of here, this is what you'll have to go through."

Without waiting for a reply, the real McAfee began to change, his flesh acquiring a mottled texture as his limbs separated and proliferated. The suit vanished, absorbed into the expanding nightmare growing out of his torso. The nubs of vestigial wings appeared along its spine as the head vanished and a long bulbous abdomen appeared out of McAfee's ass.

"I suspect," Donald Keyhoe said acidly, "that our little revolution is already over."

He was right, of course, but the revolution was rendered unnecessary when an enormous impact rocked the saucer and threw all of them to the floor.

Chapter 53 - The Warak Shu

The *warak shu* hummed in Jakob Kleinemann's hand. It was a happy buzz, the kind made by a shut-in senior receiving an unexpected visitor. Its energy extend all the way up his arm, a power so intense he couldn't stifle his gasp of alarm.

Jim Maddox eyed him curiously. Maddox stepped back, gesturing with a nod at Kleinemann's coat pocket.

"You know your pocket is glowing, right?"

Jakob Kleinemann glanced down to verify this, but he wasn't surprised to find that the ATC man was right. His pocket was glowing a warm ruby red. He nodded to Rita, a note of urgency in his eyes.

"I suspect it would be best if we were to leave now, Mr Maddox. If you feel you have to report our visit to General Cranston, I ask only that you wait until we are gone."

Maddox shrugged.

"Well, I'd like to know how I'd do that, even if I wanted to. The power's out and the phones are dead. Short of running over to Andrews and delivering the message personally, I don't even know how I could make it happen. Your secret's safe with me, at least until you're out of here. I'll tell my men to keep it zipped. You have my word on that."

Jakob Kleinemann reached his right hand into the dark and was surprised to find Maddox's waiting. The two men shook.

"We thank you for your help, Mr Maddox-"

"Call me Jim."

"We thank you, Jim. I wish I could tell you my name, but it is not allowed. Perhaps, one day, if we meet under better circumstances."

Maddox laughed sourly. "The end of the world is right outside our window. If we meet again, the circumstances could hardly be worse."

Rita Mae Marshaux, who'd had some experience in this arena, returned a reassuring smile that wasn't lit well enough for Maddox to see. Her reply, when he examined it later, was cryptic.

"I hope that will always be true, Mr Maddox."

The glow in Jakob's pocket grew more insistent.

"We must go."

"Just one last thing."

"Yes?"

"How'd you know my name is Maddox?"

The mysterious couple shuffled away from Maddox, moving toward the back of the room where an unlit exit sign marked the door to the stairs.

The woman's voice came back to Maddox as the door closed behind her.

"It's on your name tag, Mr Maddox."

After that, all he had left to do was wait for the lights to come back or the sun to rise. Jim Maddox put his money on the sure thing.

***

With the Ffaeyn sight making itself useful once again, neither Jakob nor Rita had any difficulty seeing in the dark. They made their way down the stairs into the lobby easily enough, but once inside the terminal the sight that met their eyes made them feel like they'd travelled back in time.

It was already late when the saucers were sighted, and the airport wasn't as full as it'd been earlier in the evening. It was later still when the power went out, stranding the skeleton staff and about a hundred passengers waiting for flights, with most seated at their gates, a considerable distance from any exit. Those who were close to an exit quickly made their way outside to gather on the sidewalk, but most of these retreated back inside once the threat was known.

Of those who remained inside, many were too far from the windows to see the fireballs streaking by. In their isolation, they huddled together for safety and companionship. With no other options available, they accepted the dark for the unalterable situation it was, until a man with a pack of matches came upon an unattended newsstand. The newsstand had been locked up for the night, but it wasn't hard to force the plywood door.

The stolen loot from the newsstand was burning bright as Jakob and Rita picked their way through the terminal. In some places, the flames drove back the dark, and as fire had done since time immemorial, its light drew the lost and hopeless.

The scene they found in those corridors was prophetic and inevitable. It was a declaration on the futility of human culture, the dwindling remains of its written language being used to cast prehistoric shadows on the stark walls of a civilization that was rapidly returning to a state of barbarism. The stunted figures hunched around the fires seemed like primitive things with their rounded spines and ducked heads. With the abdication of human culture, they were no better than cavemen, or hunter-gatherers returned to an earlier stage of human evolution.

Rita moved quickly around the edge of the circle, with Jakob close behind. If anyone noticed these additional shadows, no one was curious enough to seek their origin. The *warak shu* was a live pulsing thing now, its power driving Jakob forward like a drug. It was a compressed euphoria that spiraled through his arms and legs. He felt he would surely explode if he didn't get out into the open air.

Once outside, Jakob almost cried with relief, but the *warak shu* wasn't finished with him. Now, with his hand frozen around its shell, the strange device tugged

327

him onward, toward the corner of the building. Rita followed behind him with growing concern. A frisson of fear crawled up her spine threatening to engulf her. At the end of the drop-off lanes, Jakob found an alley that ran between the buildings before turning toward the darkened runway. He followed the alley, the *warak shu* now bright enough to throw distorted shadows up the walls.

He saw a light ahead and the warak shu drew him toward it, leading him out the end of the alley into one of the wide lanes where the planes parked to disgorge passengers. There were three planes there now, all dark and dead. The warak shu led him on, out to the runway where he finally found the source of the light.

The origin of the light lay a quarter mile down the runway, and he brought his hand up to shield his eyes against it. The light was a staggering display of magnetic energy that snaked across the empty tarmac like an electric dragon. Rita Mae froze at the sight, releasing Jakob's hand as visible bands of that energy coiled and snapped strange fire at their approach. When she tried to reclaim his hand, Jakob pushed her away. His eyes were shadowed, black points on his face where the light could not penetrate.

"The *warak shu* says I must go the rest of the way alone," he said.

Rita stopped, unable to process his words, then clutched at him with frantic strength. "No! I'm coming with you!"

"You can't," he said, his eyes on the dragon, a vision veiled to un-Ffaeyned sight. "It says that only I can do this. It can only protect one of us at a time."

"No!" She said again, her voice harsh and cracked.

Jakob drew the *warak shu* from his pocket, to show her the glowing ruby sphere of what had once been his hand.

"It says I must go alone," he repeated. "It would be dangerous, and I would not want to save a world that does not have you in it."

"You better come back to me," Rita cried, as sudden tears streamed down her face. "If I'm pregnant with your child-"

"I swear I pulled out in time," Jakob assured her, wondering if he really had. "We will be married on Saturday, I promise."

"The hell with that," Rita retorted. "If we survive, the wedding is tomorrow."

With that, Jakob seemed to glide away from her, as if his shoes were skates and the ground had turned to ice. Halfway across the tarmac, the dragon turned to face him, its spine arcing high over the battered asphalt.

A deafening crash came to them from across the river, an event that sent a trio of fireballs running toward them in retreat. Out over the Mall, a beam of cobalt blue split the night to strike at the blackened globe of the moon.

As if in answer, the electric dragon struck at the hand that held the *warak shu*. The *warak shu* responded in kind, sending a bolt of ruby light up to meet the blue from across the river. Both beams struck their targets, then split into a kaleidoscope of red and blue, each line seeking a saucer with laser-like accuracy.

Not having expected so spirited a response from such a backward planet, the bug saucers turned tail and ran, streaming upward toward the anonymity of deep space, the laser bolts hot behind them.

The *warak shu* in Jakob's hand turned cold and died with its dragon.

By then, the bug saucers were out of sight, leaving behind a sky empty of orange fireballs, but filled with streaks of burnt umber smoke that continued to shine with their own infernal light. The smoke lingered like any reluctant demon. Then, being lighter than the air around it, the smoke ascended to die in the high winds of the troposphere.

Chapter 54 - Help From Unexpected Sources

Wally Sands felt like shit.

After cracking his head open like a pterodactyl egg, after having the gall to gorge himself on soldiers like a glutton at his first smörgåsbord, Shff had come crawling back to Wally Sands like the blind, belly-crawling, worm he was.

And it was all so his worm could deal with a half-wit motorcycle cop that Wally could've easily handled on his own. In scarfing down such a heavy meal, Shff had exceeded the capacity of his many stomachs by a factor of five. By the time the worm shrank back to normal size, Shff was suffering from an almost legendary case of Antarean indigestion.

Or to define the truth more accurately, by the time he tried to shrink back to normal size. Watching from outside, Dexter Wye may have been puzzled by where the mass of the five devoured men could go, but Wally Sands knew it'd only been compressed. While the worm may have been able to approach its previous width, its weight had gone up a hundredfold.

"You just had to eat the whole thing," Wally scolded.

"*Shut up,*" the worm said.

"Why did you have to make such a pig of yourself?"

Wally staggered to his feet, his balance thrown off by the extra weight in his head.

"You wouldn't feel so bad if you just let me deal with that cop. You didn't have to eat him. And you really didn't have to eat those–"

"*Shut up,*" Shff said sullenly.

"You didn't have to eat those soldiers at all," Sands pointed out, finishing his thought. "You could've just let them run away. Just getting a good look at you scared the shit out of those boys. Now you're so fat, you're giving me a migraine."

Shff let out a worm's version of a belch. Sands' skull filled with the decaying stench of rotting soldier. Sands staggered again.

"Jesus! I guess they don't make breath mints for worms."

"*Get up,*" Shff ordered, "*we have to meet up with the others.*"

"Did you just fart in my head?"

"*Shut up and get moving.*"

Sands got back to his feet, his head bent forward like a heavy piece of fruit at the end of branch too skinny to support it. He took one step forward and then another, both times staggering sideways under the unbalanced load.

"Do you even know where we're going?"

"That way," said Shff, taking control so he could guide Wally's eyes in the direction he wanted to go.

"Corbett is over there."

***

Predictably, Perseus Grady had no intention of getting in touch with the bugs, even though he'd promised Allen Dulles. He left CIA headquarters just as Detlev Bronk arrived. He walked to the corner, and after a five minute wait, gave up any hope of finding a taxi. Like everyone else in the downtown area, he could see the saucers and he could hear the bleating horns of a thousand cars, all protesting the forced evacuation. He heard the shouts of angry men and women, unfairly rousted from their beds for no perceivable purpose.

Everyone was cranky and no one was going anywhere.

Through Phault's connection with every other worm on the planet, he learned of Corbett's order to convene in front of the Washington Monument. Grady paused at the miraculously empty street corner, looked off in all four directions, and didn't see a single cab in sight.

There was a reason for this, of course. Though he still wasn't fully aware of it, the Antarean damping field had gone into full effect while he was inside talking to Dulles. Under the blanket of the damping field, the only cars he could see were dead, dark, and immobile.

So Grady started walking, grateful that it was night and that the temperature had dropped to something closer to the worm's body heat. He didn't particularly like walking, but it wasn't all that far to the Mall, and he was closer to the center where the Monument stood than he was to either end. He turned south on 17th, then using the general confusion to his advantage, slipped past the Army barricade. It was readily apparent that the soldiers didn't know which way they were supposed to direct the cars, though that failure didn't matter so much with everyone stalled.

Now that he was out in the open, Grady finally saw what all the chaos was about. Dropping as low as fifty feet above him, the orange fireballs darted and hovered overhead, but never stopped moving for very long. He wondered why the bugs weren't landing and simply taking over. That was what he would have done.

As he passed the barricade, he heard dozens of voices, men shouting, women wailing, children crying. He saw brief glimpses of faces, front lit by the rusty glow of the saucers, that umber radiance giving their features a hellish aspect that seemed drawn from a lake of fire. Though the fall of Man wasn't described in any Bible Grady knew, the bugs' arrival felt like a prophecy fulfilled.

"Lordy," Grady said, marveling at the chaos, "what a mess!"

"It is nothing compared to the glory of Nemertea," Phault replied with her usual arrogance. *"If our ship was not destroyed, this world would already be under the command of our thang, Kraall the Indomitable! Now we must wait for our numbers to grow strong."*

"Yeah," Grady smirked, "you've said that often enough, but how would the world be any different under you worms?"

"We would be in control!"

Phault overemphasized the 'we' a bit too much for Grady's liking.

"But what would you do differently? I mean, humans have been top dog for thousands of years, and I know we've made a few mistakes, but we've prospered enough to control the planet. I know we have wars, and our resources aren't exactly divided up equally, but I think we've done a pretty good job so far."

Phault scoffed so loudly that Grady jerked his head to one side, though there was no hope of getting further away from the worm.

"You are weak, and you are so weak that you don't know how weak you are."

"We're not as weak as that argument," Grady retorted. "And you couldn't even survive here without us, so I don't see how you worms are so great. You need us."

"This world would prosper under a great thang such as Kraall!"

"Oh, please, Kraall wasn't even *thang* until your previous *thang* crashed your spaceship coming through the first wormhole he'd ever encountered. The only thing of substance Kraall ever did was telling your lot to abandon ship."

"How do you know that? Who told you?"

"You did, you persnickety little social climber. Your mind is as open to me as mine is to you. Or had you forgotten?"

"Z'Ang was a great thang!"

"Does 'great' mean something different in your language? I think the word you want is incompetent. He sure wasn't no Buck Rogers."

"Buck Rogers is a fictional character."

"Buck Rogers never crashed his spaceship coming through a wormhole."

"Buck Rogers is make-believe, much like your ability to defend yourselves."

"I am not having this conversation with you."

"Buck Rogers is like every man. You are all legends in your own minds."

"Well, I don't need to be a legend in my own mind! I've got you for that!"

Phault tried but failed to find the implied insult.

"Do you really mean that?"

"Ah, sweetie," Grady purred, "I can never stay mad at you."

***

"Do we really have to go?" Winthrop Walton Russell III asked.

"We'd better," Mudduk replied. *"You know how he gets."*

"Yes, I suppose," Russell said, "but I wish we could say goodbye to Doctor Ångström. I like him."

"I do, too." Mudduk said. *"He's very handsome."*

There was a moment of awkward silence before Mudduk added.

"For a human."

***

While Abel Corbett rejoiced at the unexpected arrival of his quarry, Wally Sands strode across the lawn, resurrected and whole. It wasn't all skittles and beer, though. Sands was fuming to high heaven at getting his head blown open to deal with a bunch of yokels from Fort McNair. His headache had grown steadily worse as Shff transferred his bloated discomfort onto his host.

As a result of his own difficulties, Sands didn't share Corbett's joy in locating the elusive Ångström. He barely glanced at the Swede as the third sister slipped inside the field of her father's protection. Once she was safe, Molly poked her head out from behind her father's thigh and stuck out her tongue. It was a childish gesture, but for Wally Sands, it was the last straw in a night full of them.

"I don't know about you," Sands snarled upon reaching Corbett, "but I've taken about as much crap from these trained monkeys as I'm gonna take."

"*Bring your host under control at once!*" Kraall broadcast directly to Shff.

"You may be *thang*, whatever the hell that it is, but you can shut up, too," said Wally Sands. "When are you imbeciles going to figure out that you don't have to do everything yourselves?"

"*He's upset,*" Shff explained. "*He gets cranky sometimes.*"

Overhead, two saucers zipped across the sky, then separated to hover at the far ends of the Mall.

"We've got weapons, we've got guns and we've got blasters," Sands went on, his diatribe growing into a full-on rant. "There's ways to deal with this shit that don't involve blowing a guy's head open. You worms need to learn to delegate responsibility."

Winthrop Walton Russell seemed to appear out of nowhere, something he was prone to do because the other worms rarely paid attention to him.

"*Hi guys, what's up?*" Mudduk asked cheerily.

"*Shut up!*" Kraall and Shff roared in unison.

"And I'll tell you another thing," Wally Sands continued. "I'm sick of all this fumbling around in the dark and I'm sick of these damn bugs and their fucking damping field!"

"Aw, settle down," said Abel Corbett. "You're gonna scare the little girls."

"Go fuck yourself," said Wally Sands. "I'm settling this shit now."

Lars Ångström coughed politely with the intention of drawing Corbett's attention. Corbett turned away from Sands to his less pressing problem.

"What the hell do you want?"

"I was wondering if you could ask your friend to refrain from using such coarse language. It sets a bad example for the girls."

Wally Sands sneered at the sheer prissiness of this rebuke, but Corbett only laughed. "A bad example for the girls? Doc, you're not gonna live long enough to worry about how your little brats behave in church."

Lars Ångström placed a protective restraint on Molly's shoulder.

"Are you threatening my daughters?"

Wally Sands started to say something, then stopped to stare at the bluish glow emanating from Lars Ångström's coat pocket. His brutish eyes narrowed as his forehead pinched into three tense rows of parallel lines.

"Hey...you got something in your pocket, doc?"

Lars Ångström didn't have to look down to know what was happening. He glanced over at Russell and was surprised to see the normally demoralized young man actually smiling. Grady noticed the smile, too.

"Hey," Grady said, putting two and two together, "what's going on here?"

What Grady was first to figure it out, Wally Sands was first to put into words. Recalling that Ångström had been left in Russell's custody, Sands turned on the unfortunate boy.

"Why you little-"

Winthrop Walton Russell didn't let him finish. With the beaming smile of a proud parent, he acknowledged his guilt.

"The best part is that it actually works for him."

The dawn came slowly for Corbett and Kraall, but it did come.

"You gave him our *warak shu!*"

Russell's smile grew wider. "And he can use it against us."

Turning to Lars, Russell suggested, "Perhaps you should demonstrate the *warak shu's* capabilities, Dr Ångström. They've never seen a working one."

"Have you lost your mind?" Corbett screamed. "You gave the most powerful weapon in our possession to a *human!*"

"He's a traitor!" Wally Sands shouted. "I always said he couldn't be trusted!"

"Doctor?" Winthrop Walton Russell arched one black eyebrow.

Lars Ångström let go of Molly to reach into his pocket. His hand found the *warak shu* or the *warak shu* found his hand. It was hard to say who initiated the action. The blue glow grew brighter, spilling out of his pocket like liquid light. A sphere of blue energy formed around his hand.

"What do you have in your pocket, Father?" Bubbles asked.

Inquiring minds always want to know these things.

"To tell the truth, I'm not sure," Lars admitted.

"Show them," urged Winthrop Walton Russell III.

"What should I do?" Lars asked.

Russell looked around for a target. Then, spotting the bug saucer hovering over the Washington Monument, he pointed at the rusty fireball.

"Your planet will fall prey to the Antareans if you don't do something about them. I'm not suggesting you destroy it, but..."

Lars Ångström removed the *warak shu* from his pocket and held it in his open palm. The *warak shu* twinkled like a captured star.

"Oooh, it's pretty, Father," Stormy cooed.

Like a gold digger getting her first look at a really big diamond, Stormy was unable to tear her eyes away from the flickering blue light.

"Can we play with it when you're done?"

"Golly," said Bubbles, sliding a thumb between her teeth to stifle a yawn.

It was way the heck past her bedtime.

334

"What should I do?" Lars asked again. "And how does it work?"

"Don't tell him!" Abel Corbett ordered on Kraall's behalf.

"Just tell it what you want," Russell suggested slyly. "From what I understand, the *warak shu* will do the rest."

Lars turned the device toward the fireball hovering over the obelisk, closed his fingers over it, and squeezed. A beam of blue light shot out of his palm to score a direct hit on the rusty disc. As soon as the light hit the disc, it shattered into a hundred separate streams, each shooting off to find its own disc amongst the thousands in the sky.

Not everyone was shocked to see what happened next.

It certainly didn't surprise the worms.

The disc hovering over the Monument died abruptly, and fell like the heavy stone it was, crashing down to be impaled on the point of the pyramidion. After that, the usual relationships between mass, weight, and gravity got involved.

The granite spike stabbed deep into the core of the ship, penetrating its hull until it broke through the other side. Pierced to the heart, its amber glow died with abrupt finality.

Seeing the fate of the flagship, the saucer over the Capitol Building rose like an untethered balloon. It shuddered when the fragmented beam of the *warak shu* struck it a glancing blow, but continued to rise until it vanished into the far reaches of the upper atmosphere, leaving a trail of umber smoke.

From across the river, where the airport lay dark on its island in the Potomac, a beam of ruby light answered the cobalt blue of Lars Ångström's *warak shu*.

Suddenly, it was all over.

From every part of the city, every bug saucer reached the same conclusion. As if controlled by a single intelligence, the saucers immediately broke away from whatever they were doing. In full retreat, they rose into the heavens, creating a cathedral spire of orange trails in their wake.

The smoke lingered until the wind tore it apart.

Wally Sands sneered contemptuously at the abrupt capitulation.

"Damn bugs never did have any fight in 'em."

***

As the bug saucers fled, the million muted lights of the capital city came roaring back, driving away the shadows that had crept down from the sky. All across the city, street lamps flickered to life and engines turned over and caught. Headlights burned phoenix bright, creating rivers of light along the major arteries.

But the *warak shu* wasn't done.

Without uttering another word, Wally Sands vanished from the world of July 1952. He left in much the same way the Cheshire Cat had disappeared from *Alice in Wonderland*, the only difference being that Wally Sands didn't have a smile to leave. The last of him to vanish were his angry potato eyes. These were the stigmata that lingered, glaring at Abel Corbett, long after the rest was gone.

Abel Corbett watched his lieutenant disappear, his face a mask of impotent disbelief. He went on staring at the spot where he'd vanished long after there was any reason to. But when he turned back to Lars Ångström and the girls, Corbett didn't appear to be at all distressed by the loss of Sands.

If anything, he seemed relieved.

"Not that I care," Corbett commented, with a nod toward the section of lawn where Sands had vanished, "but where the hell did you put him?"

Lars was busy asking his *warak shu* the same thing.

"No animals were harmed," was the *warak shu's* cryptic remark.

"I think he's been sent back to where I met you." Lars lied.

"Sure, I guess I could do that," said the *warak shu.*

"Doesn't matter to me," Corbett said, "now we can do this without that little prick's interference."

Then Kraall spoke, though only Corbett could hear.

"You've bungled this from the start," Kraall said, *"I believe I'll handle this myself."*

Abel Corbett was well aware of what this threat implied.

"Stay out of it, damn you!" Corbett screamed. "I can handle this!"

Ten yards away, the terrified girls pressed so hard against Lars Ångström's legs that he was pushed forward, though this was the last direction he wanted to go.

"You're an oaf, Corbett," said Kraall. *"This calls for delicacy and better judgment than you possess. I want that warak shu!"*

Corbett stopped, his hands flying to his head.

"No! Stop! You don't have to—"

Whatever Corbett had intended to say, it was destined to remain unheard.

Abel Corbett's head exploded, showering the lawn with tiny flecks of meat as the worm erupted in all its glory.

***

Many things seemed to happen at once, separate events that Lars Ångström experienced as one long braided thread. But however many the instances of cause and effect, one could follow any of the entwined strands back to a common origin, the terrified plea of Abel Corbett.

As the first event in the series, Lars Ångström mused that he would likely hear the hysterical squeals of his daughters for the rest of his life. He wished that something might be done to spare them the sight of the worm's emergence. He didn't know that this was the second time they had witnessed the sight in under an hour.

In this, he also felt regret for his future absences, knowing that Maisie would be the one to bear the brunt of his daughters' interrupted school nights, when this awful vision returned in the form of nightmares.

But he wasn't given time to voice those regrets. As his palm closed again over the blue glowing thing in his hand, he realized that the *warak shu* had been speaking to him for quite some time.

"on a more personal note, I'd like to say that I'm very grateful for this opportunity and will strive to provide the best service possible on all occasions."

"With that said, I see that you've become embroiled in what I can only characterize as a critically dangerous situation. We haven't been paired long enough for me to protect you directly, so I am pursuing an alternate course that I hope will prove satisfactory."

Even if he'd understood what the device was talking about, Lars didn't have time to say thank you.

Materializing as if out of nowhere, a creamsicle orange Nash Metropolitan jumped the curb at the 7th Street crossover and roared across the lawn to catch Kraall from behind, crushing the worm under its tires. The worm rose up to a fearsome height, then swayed back and forth before keeling over like a stunned python. Kraall reared up again as a shudder ran through his long pale length. The worm made a choking sound, then collapsed onto the grass and lay still.

"Is it dead?" Lars asked, forgetting who was around to hear.

"It sure looks dead," said Molly, peering out from behind his thigh.

The Metro continued on for a short distance, before wheeling around and sliding to a stop.

"It's not dead," said the warak shu, "but it won't bother anyone for a while."

Winthrop Walton Russell III walked over to the fallen Kraall, then waved for Perseus Grady to join him. "Give me a hand, Percy. I think he'll be okay once we get him back inside his host."

The two hosts each took an end of the groggy worm and carried Kraall over to Corbett's busted corpse.

"What are they doing, Daddy?" Bubbles asked, tugging on her father's sleeve.

"Don't worry about this one, Dr Ångström," Russell called, waving cheerily to the girls. "He'll be fine once we get him home."

For the first few moments, Russell's optimism seemed unlikely. Though his long frame was enormous, Kraall was limper than the overcooked asparagus that Molly turned her nose up at dinner.

But sensing that sanctuary was at hand, the worm began to shrink. It didn't do this as smoothly as Shff had when re-entering Wally Sands. Kraall would shrink a bit, then he would get stuck and thrash around for a bit. Then he would rest a while with Grady and Russell kneeling beside him, saying the kind of encouraging things one says to help a sick friend into bed. Once inside, the reconstruction began.

Lars was beginning to think this wasn't the kind of thing the girls should see when Maisie came up behind him. He turned at the sound of her shoes brushing the tops of the browning grass. He looked at his wife as if seeing her for the first time, her face lit up by the street lamps along the avenues bordering the Mall.

He thought she looked marvelous, though there was something about the loose way her clothes fit and her shiny cosmetic-free face that told him her night had been no less eventful than his. She had a glow about her that he hadn't seen in quite some time.

"I can explain," Lars began, intending to relate the story he'd come up with to explain why he'd failed to meet her at the airport.

Maisie looked across the lawn to where Russell and Grady had finally coaxed a fully shrunken Kraall back inside Corbett's shattered skull. The senator's daughter turned her nose up in disgust as the worm began to reconstruct its shattered home.

Maisie shook her head. "Don't you dare."

"As long as the girls are safe, I don't want to know."

***

Stormy, Molly, and Bubbles all ran toward the brave little Metro as soon as the car skidded to a stop. When they reached Camille, they first ran around to the driver's side to slap their hands against the window and shout excitedly at Janie Gently who hadn't budged since running over the worm. It was the girls singular focus that allowed Maisie to join her husband.

When she was able to shoo the girls far enough away from the door to get out, Janie Gently glanced over at the reunion of the Ångström parents with a complex expression that the girls were too young to read. After half a minute of their enthusiastic shouting, Janie gave in and began to write the story of Camille's heroism, adding several embellishments of her own. Nobody saw Abel Corbett get to his feet, and no one watched as Russell and Grady helped him across the lawn.

It took several minutes for the full reunion to take place, but eventually Maisie led her absent husband over to the Nash so she could introduce her old lover to her new one, and reclaim her lost brood in the process.

"Lars," Maisie said with hooded eyes, "I'd like you to meet Janie Gently. Janie gave us a ride home from the airport."

That was all she managed to get out before her daughters swarmed over her like hungry ants. Exhausted by all the excitement, Bubbles was particularly needy.

Maisie yielded to her youngest's insistence that she be held, turning her sideways to carry her on one hip. The feel of her baby's weight brought back a sense of normalcy that'd been profoundly lacking for most of the night.

"So," she asked Stormy, the usual spokesperson for all the girls' activities, "what happened to you three?"

Stormy opened her mouth to answer, but Molly butted in so animatedly that she never got a word out.

"We got kidnapped by gangsters!" Molly crowed.

"Is that true?" Maisie asked, turning to Bubbles for confirmation.

But Bubbles was already asleep.

***

As the sun broke over the eastern horizon, long shadows caught the upper branches of the elms and stretched out across the lawn. Lars yawned and stretched, realizing, though not for the first time, what a long night it had been.

"We should get the girls to bed. They must be exhausted."

Maisie nodded, her thoughts clearly on other things.

"Lars, we need to talk."

Lars Ångström looked down at his wife, but her eyes were turned away. As part of his research, he'd heard this tone of voice described by other men, but he'd never heard it from his wife.

"Yes?"

Maisie took a breath, surprised by her sudden burst of nerves.

Then she saw the way out.

"Would you mind so very much if we didn't go to Sweden? I know you had your heart set on the Olympics, but couldn't we just stay here instead? We could have a nice week in Washington, take the girls to the museums, and...I don't know, just show them the sights?"

Lars looked up into the sky, his eyes following the trajectory of something small and bright as it disappeared over the horizon. He turned toward the far end of the Mall where the great obelisk still stood proud and unbroken, standing guard over the city that was built to be the Paris of America. The bug saucer had departed, leaving a visible scar near its peak.

"Yes," he said softly, reaching around his wife to tickle his youngest, "I think that would be nice."

Bubbles stirred from her nap to lay her head on Maisie's shoulder, her hands exploring her mother's back. Sensing that something was different, she yawned and murmured.

"How come you don't have any underwear, Mommy?"

Maisie shifted her daughter's weight to the other hip, an embarrassed smile playing at the corners of her mouth. She directed the smile up at her husband's dawning look of comprehension. Then turning her back, she started toward the car, calling to him over her shoulder.

"I don't think we have room for you, Lars. Would you mind finding your own way back to the hotel? I can't thank Janie enough for all she's done tonight."

Chapter 55 - The Return of Arthur Ecks

With the display of his prisoner complete, Clarence pulled Arthur Ecks back from the viewport and dimmed the lights.

"What was that about?" Ecks asked.

McAfee waved Clarence away with another silent instruction. There was a creepy quality to how they did it that irritated Ecks no end. Clarence sank into the floor, this time going through the full transition before descending. For the first time, Arthur Ecks got a good long look at an Antarean.

Viewed dispassionately, which wasn't easy under the circumstances, the bug was a marvel of exoskeletal engineering. Clarence thinned considerably as he changed, the sections of his body growing longer and more slender. His limbs lengthened and narrowed as the positions of the major joints changed.

It was the most inhuman thing that Ecks had ever seen.

But it was the eyeless head that got to him.

How could these things perceive the world without eyes? He wished he had one of his eggheads around. Ångström would be useful, though there was no problem communicating with the bugs, but it might be interesting to hear Kleinemann's thoughts on the bugs' physiology.

It was strange to think that their natural environment was sand, not just to walk upon, but as something they could eat, breathe, and move through in much the same way that fish moved through water.

McAfee turned from the window, apparently satisfied with the present state of the offensive. He shook suddenly, a rippling action that had no analog in human musculature. The movement made Ecks realize something. The bugs weren't making changes to their underlying form when they made themselves look like human beings.

"How do you do it?" He wanted to know.

"Do what?"

"You know," Ecks waved, outlining his frame, "make your body look human."

McAfee's smile was genuine for once. "It's good of you to ask, Major. It stems from an early period in our development. We developed the ability as a hunting mechanism. Those changes allow us to make complex changes to our frame, including color, texture, shape, pretty much everything humans are able to perceive through their sense of sight. Other species aren't as easily fooled. We still have a bitch of a time with dogs."

Ecks nodded. This was interesting.

"So, nothing really changes inside your body?"

McAfee pursed his plump, fleshy lips. "No, there are internal changes, too. We have to survive in your environment after all. We have no need of oxygen and our respiratory systems don't deal with it. We derive our sustenance from silicon dioxide, as you might have guessed from the inside of this craft."

Ecks smiled for the first time in ages.

"So you literally swim in your food?"

McAfee laughed heartily. "I can see how you might interpret it that way, but the sand, and the silicon in it, is really more like your air. We process the silicon. The rest is discarded as waste."

Ecks frowned, then surreptitiously checked the sole of his shoes to see if anything was sticking to the bottom.

"That's actually worse. It means you're swimming in your own shit."

Ecks was pleased to see the insult didn't go unnoticed.

"Our waste is not biological, so there's no decomposition the way you think of it. Consequently, we have none of the negative connotations you associate with your own excrement. I think, once we're living among you, you'll find we're very clean neighbors. Of course..."

The faux Senator paused, apparently unsure whether to proceed.

Ecks prompted him to continue. "What?"

McAfee's expression was almost apologetic.

"Well, it's just that to make this world livable for us, we're going to have to make some serious changes. Some of them you won't like."

"Such as?"

McAfee shook his head mournfully.

"It's just awful how damp this planet is. We'll want to get rid of the water."

Ecks was understandably shocked by the idea.

"But human beings are made of water! We need water to live! Most of the planet is covered with water!"

"I agree, it's a problem. Maybe we could set part of the planet aside for your use, like all those nice reservations you set up for the indigenous people your forefathers displaced. Clearly, you don't have any problem with those."

Arthur Ecks was already shaking his head. He'd grown up near an Indian reservation in Oklahoma. They were depressing places at the best of times.

"Thanks, but I don't think so. Actually, I have a better idea. Why don't you just take over the parts of the world that we can't use because there's no water?"

McAfee cocked his head to one side.

"You have places like that? Places that don't have any water at all?"

Ecks continued to shake his head.

"Didn't you do any research before deciding to colonize us? What kind of slipshod operation are you running, Senator?"

"We knew there'd be a problem when we saw how much water you had, so we made our plans accordingly. It's probably silly, but as I've said before, we're really more administrators than conquerors. You can't administer anything if there isn't someone around to administer. We never even looked at the parts of the planet that didn't have people. Our primary concerns were with blending into the governments of the more powerful countries. We figured if we could knock off the big ones, we could take our time with the rest."

"But, you interest me. Tell me about the dry spots? Where do we find them?"

Ecks considered the dry places he knew.

"Well, there's the Sahara. Virtually no rainfall, over three million square miles of nothing but sand and rock. The temperature is always over a hundred degrees and, on top of that, large parts of it are virtually uninhabited."

By the time Ecks finished, McAfee's mouth was hanging open in shock.

"Well, this is embarrassing. We had no idea you had such an idyllic spot. Where can we find this paradise?"

Ecks made fists inside the pockets of his trousers. There had to be some way to make use of this interest. "Well, I'd need a map, or a globe of the Earth..."

McAfee waved his hand, summoning Clarence from the sandy depths.

"Clarence, stop the ship, we need to use the navigational controls."

Ecks laughed at this unexpected flaw.

"You need to stop the ship to figure out where you're going?"

McAfee's blush was of genuine embarrassment.

"Terrestrial navigation is new to us. We're still developing the technology. At present, we have to stop the ship when we want to get a positional reading or set a specific destination. It's inconvenient, but we'll have it licked soon enough."

The ship came to a stop and hovered in place while the positional reading was taken. When the reading was complete, an insubstantial blue globe flecked by wisps of cottony white took shape before them. McAfee approached the globe, inspecting the continents between the great sheets of blue ocean.

"Show me the area you're talking about."

Ecks approached the globe tentatively.

"Go ahead, it's just a projection."

"It's amazing," said Ecks, truly impressed. He strode around the globe until he found the great swath of the Sahara. He pointed to it.

McAfee pushed him aside greedily, his eyes widening hungrily when he saw the full expanse of this Promised Land. After a long moment, he gazed at Ecks with the most sincere expression he'd worn since they met.

"Thank you, Major. This gives us an environmental model to bio-engineer the rest of the planet. Using your Sahara as a template, we can establish the same conditions everywhere. It will save a great deal of time."

"But that's not what I meant at all!" Ecks protested. "I was thinking of this as a way we could peacefully coexist!"

The false McAfee shook his borrowed head sadly.

"Maybe I wasn't clear enough, Major. We're administrators, not explorers, and certainly not developers. We built our own civilization from the ground up, but doing it all over again would be like reinventing the wheel, to use a human expression. There's no real reason to start over from scratch when so much has already been done."

McAfee made a gesture to another of the Clarences, imparting a command the Clarence set off to fulfill.

"I think I'm going to bring the others up here to join us. You should all have a front row seat for what's about to happen."

Ecks was immediately suspicious.

"Why? What are you planning to do?"

In answering, the false McAfee turned away from Ecks to stare down at the dark expanse of the National Mall.

"Do you know one of the best ways to destroy a nation's morale?"

"I know a few, actually," Ecks admitted.

McAfee pointed out the viewport, where far off to the east, the first rays of dawn were breaking over the horizon.

"You do it by destroying its symbols. And I must say, Washington is just chock full of symbols, any number of which would be appropriate for the purpose. The best part is, you can destroy a nation's symbols without hurting anyone. We discovered long ago that killing our subjects creates resentment in the long run. The best coups are bloodless. I think we can agree on that much."

"What are you going to do?" Ecks asked again. He was pretty sure he already knew, what with the tip of the Washington Monument only a few yards below.

McAfee shook his head at Ecks' less than candid response.

"Please, Major, I'm sure you've put the pieces together. I'm just waiting for sunrise. That way, more of your tired sleepless refugees will witness it firsthand. That way, they'll be able to report the destruction to the rest of the population. We'll have thousands of eyewitnesses. News spreads faster when you have more people to disseminate it."

As if the bug's words were another signal, four Clarences appeared out of the sand, each carrying a struggling human in its limbs. All four were released as soon as the bugs surfaced, and each went through his own version of shaking himself clean.

"Well," Keyhoe demanded, "what the hell do you want with us now?"

Ecks answered before McAfee could butt in.

"They're going to destroy the Washington Monument."

"But that's insane!", Ed Ruppelt complained. "What could they possibly hope to gain?"

"They're trying to break our spirit," Ecks explained. "You know, the way the Nazis did with London, only without the bombs and the killing."

Allen Hynek looked like he wanted to say something, but whatever it was would forever remain a mystery. Without warning, the Antarean ship was rocked by a sudden jolt. An ocean of blue light washed in through the viewport. There was a creaking sound as if the strange metal that made up the better part of the ship's structural integrity had suddenly taken on the weight of the sand flooding its interior. An instant later, the bug ship dropped out of the sky like a stone.

It didn't fall very far though, just far enough to impale itself on the tip of the very monument it had sought to destroy. The ship shuddered with the weight of the impact, throwing everyone to the floor. The hull cracked with a deafening shriek of torn metal as the ship tilted, settled, and tilted again. The chamber around the humans, with its tiny pocket of oxygenated air, collapsed and began to fill with sand.

Ecks took a deep breath as he sank below the surface, hoping that the others had the same presence of mind.

Falling into sand with no earthly support was surprisingly like falling into deep water. All around him, the grains parted to allow him to pass, and for a time, there was nothing else to catch him.

***

Robert Ely Early would never know the fate of his younger brother. If he had known, it might have been one of the few things to have any kind of emotional impact on him. After the war, Early had returned from Europe as just another one of thousands of damaged men. He was far from the only one who wasn't able to return fully intact after the United State government rented his body for violent purposes. But even though he was damaged, Early was one of the lucky ones because he hadn't lost any body parts. The Army had returned him to the States with all his limbs functioning and intact.

All Bob Early lost in the war were a few marbles and the origin of that loss was pretty simple to track down.

It was the bombs. He just couldn't stand the bombs.

During his version of the war, Bob Early had been a magnet for explosive devices of every imaginable variety. He was already serving his country when the Army assigned him as a liaison to the United Kingdom. As fate would have it, he arrived just in time for the Blitz. For the next eight months, he joined his British compatriots as they ran for the shelters every time a German air armada was sighted. It became a form of daily exercise. Huddled in the cellars of London, he cowered with everybody else as the bombs rained down like a recently Anglicized form of bad weather.

He wasn't injured, in fact, he was able to make it through the entire war with no more than a few scratches, bumps, and bruises. But over the years that followed, the bombs always seemed to find him, no matter how well he hid. It didn't matter where he went, just as it didn't matter who was responsible for any of the dozens of explosives and incendiaries that fell close enough to kill.

Most of the bombs were German, but so many weren't that country of origin ceased making much of a difference. Friendly fire was every bit as dangerous and every bit as deadly. There was a time, when he was out on a tour of air bases, that a Stuka dive bomber nailed an ammunition dump near the air field. The bomb was far enough away not to be a threat, but the ammo dump went up like a Fourth of July celebration. Remarkably, he came out of that one without so much as a paper cut.

He was a little deaf in one ear, but the real problem was that, by the time he returned, Early was more than a little shaky around loud noises. Ambulance sirens made him break out in cold sweats, a car horn at a traffic light could trigger a panic attack, and just driving past an airport could precipitate a week's worth of nightmares.

Coming home with shattered nerves, he screwed up his first job interview by diving under the table. His reaction was triggered when someone pulled the fire alarm, but even after the cause was explained, he refused to budge. Three more bad interviews and a failed psychological evaluation ensured that, at least for the postwar years in question, he was no longer fit for his former profession.

Unable to serve as a police officer, Early found work as a night watchman for a company called Capitol Security Systems. In working for CSS, he was moved around between a bakers dozen of federal posting sites. It was quiet work for the most part, especially when he had the night shift. The work didn't pay very well, but the company was well aware of his condition and scheduled his assignments accordingly. As fate would have it, on the night of July 19, Bob Early was assigned to guard the Washington Monument.

Early wasn't the only guard, of course. He just happened to be the one who was doing rounds when the saucers attacked. The Monument wasn't even open. The doors were locked at sunset, leaving Bob Early and Darnell White inside for the night. From their posts inside 90,000 tons of marble, granite, and bluestone gneiss, neither man heard a whisper of the chaos that gripped the city from midnight onward. They didn't hear the arrival of the military, they didn't hear the screams of the terrified and frustrated populace. As the hours passed, both White and Early had good reason to be bored and frankly, they liked it that way.

Unfortunately, their blessed boredom was about to end.

As fate would also have it, it was Early's turn to do the rounds. Doing the rounds involved taking the elevator up to the observation deck and having a quick look around. The interior of the monument was well lit, and this included the long spiraling staircase as well as the observation deck. Bob Early was up on the observation deck when the power went out.

As the city was plunged into total chaos, courtesy of the Antarean damping field, a similar fate befell the interior of the Washington Monument. Without power, there was no light and more importantly, no elevator. Without the elevator, Bob Early was trapped on the observation deck, five hundred-fifty feet above the

Mall, his exit further impeded by the nine hundred stairs he would traverse in the dark if he wanted to make his way down to the ground.

Isolated at the top of the structure, Bob Early went into a predictable panic. His response to that panic was to lie on the floor and curl up in as tight a ball as he could manage. For the next hour, he would be beset by aural hallucinations of falling bombs, and harried by visions of dust and gravel raining down from above. Within seconds, he was back in the Blitz, shivering in cold terror as the bombs rained down from above.

But as time passed and nothing further happened, Early was able to calm himself. So it was dark. That was all right, he had his flashlight. He would survive.

But when his flashlight died an hour later, Early felt like some great bird had taken his heart in its talons.

He felt his way to the exit, only to be faced with a more imposing obstacle once he found it. With the elevator not working, the only way down was the stairs, and as Early stared down into this stygian pit of despair, he realized another truth. There was no way in Hell that he was going to walk down eight hundred and ninety-seven steps using a staircase he couldn't even see.

So Early felt his way back inside the observation deck and waited. There was a closed system phone he could use to communicate with Darnell White at the bottom, but the phone had failed sometime after the lights went out. With the phone out, and the lights not functioning, there was nothing to entertain him. He couldn't talk to Darnell to find out what happened, and he couldn't read the *Tales from the Crypt* comic book he kept stashed behind the water cooler.

After a while, to relieve the tedium as well as his claustrophobia, he took turns looking out each of the observation deck's eight windows. There were two to a side, with each giving over a view of the city in the four cardinal directions. Set into each wall, the windows were about two feet high by four feet wide. Early stood at each post for the same amount of time, peering out at the stars as well as the sights offered by each of the Monument's four faces. The silhouette of the Capitol Dome was particularly calming. It meant that life was still going on out there, even when the night sky was lit up by all those orange fireballs.

Early really didn't want to think about what those might be. As a result, he remained unaware of the one over his head right up until it came crashing down on top of him.

The glass of all eight windows was shattered by the impact. Within seconds, a veritable river of sand came pouring through. Early didn't have time to think about the incongruity of so much sand at such an altitude. He didn't had time to consider what had hit the great obelisk in his care. The noise was deafening. It was the groaning of a whale with digestive issues and the whole massive structure shuddered under the impact.

Since there wasn't anyone to hear or anything else to do, Early screamed and then he screamed again. The great edifice rocked and creaked as if it'd been struck by a bomb, groaning all the way to its base where Darnell White was fumbling with the keys to the door, desperate to get outside.

The Monument groaned as it strained to absorb the weight of something enormous. The river of sand continued to flow like a living thing, pushing Early back against the wall and pinning him there like a dead butterfly. He tried to swim against the tide, back toward the door to the stairwell that didn't seem like such a bad option now. But it was hopeless, and he knew it. He fought in vain to keep his head above the rising sand, but with the weight of a small beach holding him down, he could barely move.

And just when he thought his terror could rise no higher; he felt something move past him, sliding through the sand like an eel in still water.

Early screamed and instantly regretted it as his mouth filled with grit and drowned his cry.

Suddenly, they were all over him, the rough sides of their shells catching on his clothes and tugging him along to God knew where. He thrashed about, a slave to panic until one flailing arm was caught in an iron grip.

***

Dexter Wye would never know what impulse prompted him to pursue the reconstituted Wally Sands. Sands had given him the creeps from the moment they'd first met in 1947, and that was before the worm took up residence. Even then, there was an aura of violence about the man.

So what the hell did he think he was doing now that the worm had crawled back inside Sands' shattered skull? It wasn't the brightest thing he'd ever done, and even as he hung back at what he hoped was a safe distance, he couldn't come up with any reason to support the action.

He would never know where he found the courage, but he knew where his motivation was coming from. The man with the worm simply seemed like the most logical way to find Artie. After all, Sands was controlled by an alien, and Artie had been taken by aliens. As of yet, Dex was still unaware that there were two groups with designs on earthly sovereignty rather than one.

In following Sands so cautiously, Dex was too far away to be more than a distant spectator to Lars Ångström's confrontation with Major Corbett. He didn't see Sands actually disappear, but it was impossible to miss the beam of blue light shooting from Ångström's palm to knock a saucer out of the sky.

Dex started running as soon as the saucer came crashing down. He shot right past the Ångström family, entirely missing the sight of the creamsicle Nash Metro as it charged across the lawn to run over Corbett's worm. He was busy with a greater issue that had nothin to do with worms.

In his mind, he was sure that the downed saucer now balanced on the point of the obelisk must contain his friend. It was a crazy idea, but Dex trusted the intuition that told him it was so. He trusted that intuition even though he'd seen a dozen saucers that all looked exactly the same.

***

The great saucer, impaled on the tip of the Monument, would become the icon of its own defeat. Though its hull had been grievously wounded, its power wasn't shattered. Mere minutes after the crash, the ship repaired itself, and in rising up to join those that'd already fled, it came free with a shriek that nearly matched the volume of the impact.

When the saucer pulled away, it left behind its human hostages, and as if some ransom had been arranged, it recalled the lost particles of its environment, drawing them back inside through a process far superior to any vacuum cleaner ever designed by human or worm. With the extraction complete, the rent in the hull was repaired with a temporary patch, and those select few who were still paying attention, could only watch in awe as the amber flagship disappeared over the eastern horizon.

Feeling a bit like an Olympian god, Arthur Ecks looked out through the shattered windows. He looked out on the capital as the lights came back and the city returned to life. His flesh felt a need to brush away the last bits of sand, but surprisingly, there weren't any. He turned at a cry behind him, but it was the night watchman scrambling into the elevator car.

As the elevator descended, Ecks took note of the other men around him. Donald Keyhoe, Lincoln La Paz, Allen Hynek, and Ed Ruppelt joined him at the window to look out into the rising dawn, all eyes following the tangled skeins of the saucers' retreat. They shared a moment of silence at the unexpected victory and watched until the last streaks were gone.

When they came down out of the tower, all five men eschewed the elevator in favor of the stairs.

Arthur Ecks was the last to descend and he reveled in all eight hundred and ninety-seven steps.

And, he was positively delighted to find Dexter Wye waiting when he reached the bottom.

Chapter 56 - Majestic-Plus One Minus Three

It wasn't possible to convene a full meeting of the Majestic group until Monday morning. Several members were still out of town, and Sunday was a difficult time to reach any of them. Some were busy with church services, others with picnics and family gatherings, and even though the calls were made, it was nearly impossible to break existing commitments on such short notice. For most of the men, their wives wouldn't hear of it and that was all anyone needed to say about the issue.

As host, Allen Dulles was the first to arrive. The meeting was held in the same room where he'd met with Bronk, Vandenberg, and Menzel only two days prior. He arrived first for reasons both practical and intentional.

For one, the conference room was right down the hall from his office, and after the events of the past weekend, Dulles was impatient to discuss Majestic's poor response to the bug invasion.

Another reason he arrived early was to prevent the door being closed in his face. The CIA membership in Majestic was generally restricted to whoever held the Directorship. Three of its members were past Directors whose membership wouldn't terminate until retirement or death, whichever came first.

Dulles had been actively campaigning for the Directorship since long before his current boss, Walter Bedell Smith, accepted the post. Though he'd failed in that effort, Dulles had received assurances that the job would finally be his upon Smith's retirement, which was scheduled for early next year.

With that promise as leverage, Dulles had strong-armed his way into Majestic membership, using the argument that he might as well get up to speed before his new position became official. Naturally, he was shocked when he learned the true purpose of the group.

But his administrative arm-twisting hadn't gone over well with the other members, and as a consequence, Dulles still worried about the door being closed in his face on important issues. His early arrival, as well as his personal involvement in the weekend's events, averted that humiliation.

Next to arrive was General Nathan Twining. Twining was one of the three who'd openly opposed Dulles' candidacy. Twining greeted him with a curt nod and took a seat at the far end of the table. He was followed in quick succession by Bronk, Vandenberg, and Menzel, who'd shared the same cab. Dulles' greeting to the men who were already in on the secret, was even more restrained.

After that, there were the apologies from members who couldn't make the trip. These came from General Robert Montague who was in Europe, and Lloyd Berkner who was attending a funeral in Michigan. Admiral Sidney Souers, the CIA's first Director, also sent apologies, but gave no reason for his absence.

Gordon Gray had taken the train up from North Carolina the night before and looked like he hadn't slept very well. Jerome Hunsaker was chipper and greeted everyone, except Dulles, by first name. He addressed Dulles as 'Champ,' leaving the impression that he still didn't know the Deputy Director's first name. Hunsaker was the second man who'd voted against him.

The remaining trio of Admiral Roscoe Hillenkoetter, Dr Vannevar Bush, and General Walter Bedell Smith arrived in a group, already talking among themselves. It was Bush, as chairman, who called the meeting to order. After preliminary matters were dealt with, he got right to the point.

"All right, I will expect those of who were present to summarize and elaborate, but my initial understanding is that on Saturday night, between midnight and dawn, the city of Washington was visited by flying saucers."

"Not just visited, Van," interrupted Detlev Bronk. "We were attacked!"

"We'll get into that soon enough, Dee," Vannevar Bush purred. "As we will with who saw what and when. We've also heard reports from Washington National that corroborate the visual sightings as well as providing radar confirmation."

"Dammit, Bush," Vandenberg said forcefully, "these weren't just a bunch of goddamned lights in the sky. We saw extraterrestrials right here on the ground. Not only that, these aliens are shapeshifters who look convincingly human and can behave accordingly. They've already infiltrated human society."

Vannevar Bush wasn't fond of using the gavel bequeathed to him upon James Forrestal's death, but sometimes it was unavoidable.

"That will be enough, General. As I said, we'll get into particulars in due time. As I have often stated, any information that comes before the group needs to be kept compartmentalized. It isn't enough that we simply keep it within these walls. We have a workable relationship with these creatures and I don't believe any of us are willing to jeopardize that."

But Vandenberg wasn't willing to give up the floor yet.

"My aide was one of them, Bush. My own aide! They've infiltrated Congress, the armed forces, and God knows what else!"

As always, Bush pursed his lips at such public displays of emotion.

"Hysteria serves no purpose here, General. I'm sure we will find a reasonable explanation for everything that occurred."

"Reasonable explanations be damned! You weren't here," Donald Menzel said quietly. "The four of us who were have spoken separately and it is impossible to overemphasize this threat to our nation and to the world in general."

"We have a treaty with these creatures," General Twining reminded the group. "It is to our advantage to maintain the treaty. I'm sure."

"With all due respect, General," Detlev Bronk interjected, "we beg you to listen more closely. The aliens who attacked us on Saturday-"

"This deliberate use of misleading and inflammatory language is getting us nowhere," Bush interrupted, again applying the gavel.

"Please, Van, this is important!" Bronk insisted. "You mustn't try to minimize what happened, or worse yet, provide an explanation for events you haven't even heard about. General Cranston verified the sightings on radar and sent jets to engage the enemy. Those pilots confirmed the identification and got close enough to see the ships clearly. The enemy then proceeded to outperform the best flyers this nation has to offer. They had a weapon that was able to suppress every form of electrical energy known to us. Not only were our power plants affected, but so too were our individual generators, motor vehicle engines, and even car headlights that run on batteries."

"A high level attack response was issued to deal with the threat. Operating under Defense Plan Z, the entire city was roused from its beds and ordered to evacuate. The Army came in to direct traffic, and if you'll pardon my vulgarity, turned a bad situation into a real cluster-"

"This is all patently ridiculous," Nathan Twining growled. "We have a-"

"We all know we have a treaty, General!" Donald Menzel shouted. "Don't you understand? Whoever it was that attacked us on Saturday night...," Menzel's voice dropped by twenty decibels. "Whoever or whatever was behind the attack, they weren't the same creatures that we have the treaty with."

A sudden hush fell over the room.

"I saw them," Menzel continued, his voice barely above a whisper, "I saw them, gentlemen, and I saw them in their natural form. General Vandenberg is perfectly correct. They are capable of mimicking human form and speech. In fact, they do it so well that I would challenge any man in this room to detect them. I suspect, though I have no proof, that they've already infiltrated the offices of this government-"

"I'm sorry, Doctor Menzel," Gordon Gray interrupted, "but a statement like that does require some form of proof."

"Frankly," said Jerome Hunsaker, "this conversation is jumping around too much for my taste. Can't we just pick a topic to explore and stick to it?"

"I think that's an excellent suggestion, Jerry," Vannevar Bush agreed, lowering his gavel. "Is this amenable to everyone?"

After a pause, there were nods all around the table. They were, after all, men of science and service.

"Good," Bush nodded. "Now, if I may suggest a course of action, we should start with a summary of the events as they unfolded. When we reach a point where more details are required, we'll stop and explore that point. Will that be acceptable to everyone?"

Menzel, Bronk, and Vandenberg shared a questioning look before nodding in unison. Nobody looked at Dulles, who'd remained silent during the early volleys, apparently content to suck at the stem of his pipe.

351

"Excellent," said Bush. "Now, as General Vandenberg was on duty, perhaps he would care to begin."

All eyes turned to Vandenberg. In response, the general bit his lower lip as he considered how to begin. Finally, he sighed.

"I don't know if I'm the best place to begin," Vandenberg admitted, "but I'll tell my story and we'll see where it takes us." He paused to take a breath. "I assume that everyone is aware of the special HUAC session that took place on Saturday morning. I say it was special because, for the first time in recent memory, HUAC turned its attention away from its search for communists to explore the question of UFOs."

A rumble of dissension swept through the room, turning Vandenberg's story into fragments and random comments. Vannevar Bush applied his gavel once again.

"I can see that this is news to most of you," Vandenberg observed. "If you wish to go into further detail on this subject, Doctor Menzel can provide a summary. He volunteered to testify when word reached him about the subject matter. Doctor Menzel did his best to scotch the investigation, though it's hard to say whether he was successful or not. When the hearing concluded, he contacted this group to call a meeting. Doctor Bronk, Deputy Director Dulles, and I were the only members available, so we convened here in this very room."

"After that meeting, I returned to my office at the Pentagon. I was catching up on some paperwork when the lights went out. My aide, Lieutenant Clarence was with me, though he wasn't in the office at the time of the blackout. It was still late afternoon, probably about five o'clock, so there was still light outside, though very little reached into the inner corridors. Apparently, someone gave the order to evacuate, and that action was already in process when I left my office to see what was happening."

"When I returned, I found Lieutenant Clarence sitting in my chair with his feet on my desk. Naturally, I asked what the hell he thought he was doing. At that point, he pulled my own gun on me and directed me to take a seat. He then proceeded to hold me prisoner for several hours. It was well after sunset when he directed me to look out the window-"

"Why did he want you to look out the window?" Bush asked.

"He wanted to show me something. I didn't see anything at first, but after a moment, I saw that there was a great deal of movement in the night sky."

"Movement?" This query came from Hunsaker. "What kind of movement?"

"There were a large number of orange lights moving around, most no bigger than stars," Vandenberg replied. "They clearly weren't stars, of course, but at first, I didn't understand what I was seeing. I needed Lieutenant Clarence to enlighten me."

"What were they?" Gordon Gray asked. "I mean, what did this Clarence say they were? Who is this Clarence anyway? What level is his clearance?"

Vandenberg's voice was level and almost calm.

"He said they were the vanguard of an invading fleet."

"Preposterous!" Twining erupted, unable to stand for any more. "That is complete poppycock! The conditions of our treaty specify that there will be no discernible alien presence in areas where human density is above fifty persons per square mile!"

"Again, General," Detlev Bronk interjected, "the Greys are only one race, and to the best of our knowledge, they have done nothing to break the treaty."

The penny finally dropped for Nathan Twining. His next words were barely a whisper. "You mean, there's someone else out there?"

"Yes, that's what we've been trying to tell you."

"Still, it means nothing," Twining insisted. "this Clarence might have been pulling your leg."

"Nathan," Vandenberg said slowly, "when I tried to escape, he turned into a giant eight-foot bug. He did it right in front of me. I saw him change."

"You must have been mistaken."

"Right in front of me," Vandenberg repeated. "There was no mistake."

"So how did you escape?"

"I didn't. Hours later, once the attack was underway and he'd seen how little affect our weapons were having, he let me go."

Twining scowled, but voiced no further objections.

"So, did anyone else see these bugs?"

"I did, General," Menzel said, raising his hand. "I returned to the Senate building later that night. I'd hoped to confront Senator McAfee, but instead, I found the building overrun by bugs. I didn't see a lot of them, but I saw enough. And," he said significantly, "I met my own Clarence."

"Your own Clarence? What the devil do you mean by that?"

This came from Dulles' boss, Walter Bedell Smith.

"From what we've been able to ascertain," Bronk interjected, "the Clarence is a template used by the bugs when a nonspecific human form is needed."

"So," Bedell Smith said slowly, not sure he was grasping the concept, "these Clarences all look alike?"

Brink nodded, then shook his head as if qualifying his affirmation.

"There are individual modifications, based on need. The difference is usually in their clothing, based on the occupation being simulated. Most of the Clarences were dressed in tan suits, but General Vandenberg's Clarence wore a lieutenant's uniform. Doctor Menzel had a cab driver who was a Clarence."

"You realize you all sound like complete lunatics?" Nathan Twining pointed out as he rolled his chair away from the table. "Virtually everything you've just described is physically impossible. How could something completely change its physical form?"

"We've haven't the slightest idea," Menzel said flatly. "It just seems to be something this species is capable of."

A silence permeated the room for almost half a minute before Allen Dulles coughed for attention. Vannevar Bush pointed his gavel at the Deputy Director.

"The chair recognizes Mr Dulles. Do you have something to add, Allen?"

"I do," Dulles said, taking his pipe from between his lips. "I wanted to ask if anyone here is familiar with Project Nemesis?"

"Nemesis?" The name floated around the room, trampolining from one pair of lips to the next.

Twining frowned. "Yes," he said after a while, "I remember something by that name, back around the time this all began. Nemesis was one of the teams that was supposed to investigate first contacts. Why do you ask?"

Dulles nodded. "Good, that fits in with what the man told me."

Jerome Hunsaker looked from Dulles to the other men who'd been in town. "What man?"

"Yes," said Menzel, annoyed by Dulles' exclusionary tactics, "what man?"

Dulles replaced the pipe, then shifted it over to the other side of his mouth.

"While this was going on, I was visited by a man who claimed to be part of Project Nemesis."

Dulles' revelation was greeted by a long silence, but the silence was only a prelude to chaos.

"Why didn't you tell us about this man?" Vandenberg complained, on his way to more detailed protests.

"Wasn't Nemesis was canceled three years ago?" Twining asked.

"You should have told us at once," said Vannevar Bush.

"It was canceled," Roscoe Hillenkoetter claimed. "I signed the order!"

Again, Bush had to apply his gavel.

When the pandemonium had run its course, Gordon Gray asked, "What was this man's name and what did he say?"

Dulles smiled thinly, pleased that Gray had forgotten to call him Champ.

"We generally don't use names in my business, Mr Gray. I will say that, in approaching me directly, he ignored protocol, but I was satisfied that he was who he said he was. His primary reason for such a direct approach was to inform me that we were under attack. And though that would become obvious over the course of the next few hours, I believe he had sufficient cause to ignore the proper channels, in view of the nature of the emergency."

Given the magnitude of the previous revelations, Dulles' information seemed a trifle anticlimactic.

"Why are you bringing this up, Allen?" Walter Bedell Smith asked.

Dulles finished lighting his pipe, sending a thin cloud of white smoke up to the ceiling. "I was simply curious. I saw nothing regarding this Project Nemesis in the briefing papers I was given. Based on what Admiral Hillenkoetter just said, I believe my suspicion was justified. Now I wonder if he was one of ours at all."

"Could you provide us with a description?" Smith asked.

Twining was already shaking his head.

"It would be useless," he informed them. "Nemesis, and another group called...just a second, another group called Stall, were given a higher clearance than any we now use. But both groups were disbanded quite some time ago."

"Only officially," Hillenkoetter said. "Both were released from active reporting, as I recall. This was done to limit accountability and give the groups greater freedom of action. I believe both still exist, however."

Jerome Hunsaker laughed. "I should say they do."

Vannevar Bush frowned. "Explain."

Hunsaker shook his head in amazement at what he was about to reveal.

"As it happens, I have an old friend on the DC police force. He told me something I wouldn't have connected to any of this." Hunsaker came forward to rest his elbows on the table. "He told me that two men were booked on Saturday night for assaulting a woman and her children at the airport."

Gordon Gray frowned. "You're right. I don't see—"

Hunsaker smiled. "Both men had government IDs, and when the police contacted their superiors, those superiors sent a man to bail them out. Would anyone care to guess who employed these two men?"

Gray got there first. "It can't be possible."

Hunsaker's smile widened a notch.

"I'm afraid it's true, Gordon. Both are employed by Project Nemesis, as was the man who bailed them out."

"As was the man who visited me," murmured Allen Dulles.

"That's a rather startling coincidence, Jerry," Gordon Gray said after a stunned silence. The silence returned after Gray's observation, then extended to a length that grew uncomfortable for all concerned.

"Wait a minute," Hillenkoetter said, breaking the spell. "Allen, this man who came to you, how did he know we were about to be attacked?"

For a long shimmering moment, the question seemed to hang in mid-air.

Then, the entire room seemed to shift. It was an odd thing, like an eye blink that altered the perceptions of every man in the room. A shiver ran around the table, like a wave washing up on the beach.

Everything went out of focus, then realigned.

Vannevar Bush raised his gavel, then realized that there was no need for it. With the gavel still poised, Bush looked around the table, finding the same expressions on every face. Each expression was remarkably similar to his own.

When he could stand it no longer, Vannevar Bush asked in a shaky voice.

"Does anyone remember why we're here?"

The breakfast buffet at the Ambassador Hotel was uncommonly crowded for a Monday morning. Generally, Mondays were when weekend visitors checked out, with most leaving early to catch flights or trains. The business travelers that made up the Ambassador's bread and butter, wouldn't begin to arrive until later in the afternoon. As a consequence, Monday was usually the one day of the week when it was relatively easy to get a table.

Andre Domergue wasn't the *maître d'hotel* at the Ambassador Cafe, but that was only because the Ambassador didn't have a *maître d'hotel*, at least not in any official capacity. This apparent oversight was largely due to the hotel's reluctance to be characterized as anything less that 100% American. In the aftermath of the war, the position of *maître d'hotel* was viewed as a European affection, leaving Andre to pay the price for this occupational jingoism.

Despite his lack of official title, Andre was the man responsible for overseeing the waitstaff, taking reservations, and parceling out the cafe's limited number of tables. As he'd been tasked with these responsibilities for the better part of the last decade, Andre was well acquainted with the ebb and flow of business as it pertained to the cafe. And as he looked out over the packed dining room, he couldn't help but be disturbed by the fact that it was the second atypical day in a row.

The first atypical day had been day before. Sunday brunch was usually packed to the gunnels, and on most Sundays, he was forced to turn away almost everyone who didn't have a reservation. On most Sundays, those who elected to wait were generally looking at a forty-five minute delay.

But this Sunday, the 20th, had been exceptionally dull, as virtually no one had left their room before noon. The reason was entirely understandable, given the previous night's military emergency. What with the botched evacuation, the threat of invasion by air, a threat brought closer to home when the hotel was strafed by enemy aircraft, it was no wonder that most guests had elected to sleep in. The same scenario was being played out in almost every residence in the greater DC area. The lack of customers resulted in breakfast closing early and lunch being extended by an hour.

But Monday was quickly making up for any lost business. The moment the cafe opened, guests started streaming out of the elevators and stairwells, and not a one had reservations. Andre commented on this to the graveyard shift desk clerk who was just going off duty. The clerk informed Andre that he'd been bombarded with last minute requests by guests who wanted to stay another night.

It was curious, but in the first two hours of the rush, Andre was too busy to place the unusual activity in any useful perspective. It wasn't until every table was full, and he could relax into taking names, that Andre was able to indulge the only real pleasure he took from his job, listening in on table gossip as he made his way around the room.

Predictably, the talk revolved around Saturday night's alien invasion. There were peripheral issues under discussion as well as the predictable speculation as to who the visitors might be, what they looked like, and how they compared to the latest slew of monsters coming out of Hollywood.

There were complaints about the Army's handling of the attempted evacuation, its lack of preparation, and the futile response out of Andrews. There were individual stories of guests who'd fled the hotel, only to get caught up in the melee outside.

Andre smiled, feeling some sympathy for his friend on the night desk, imagining the anger they must have faced for the hotel's inability to protect its patrons from the invasion from space.

His rounds complete, Andre returned to his podium to review the list. Finding that a table for four had just come free, he waved to the group of men at the top of the list and escorted them to their table. As he was able to overhear their conversation, Andre was intrigued by how their experience compared to the others around them.

***

The four men were Lincoln La Paz, Josef Allen Hynek, Edward Ruppelt, and Donald Keyhoe. Upon their release from the impaled saucer, all four had returned to their rooms at the Ambassador, and all four had extended their stay to recover from their sleepless Saturday. Now with Monday having arrived, they decided to get together for breakfast before returning home. As the four took seats, the conversation that had started during their wait for a table continued unabated.

"So," Keyhoe said, addressing Ed Ruppelt, "I imagine Project Blue Book will be better funded for the foreseeable future."

The reporter's thin lips were twisted into a wry smile that, given his usual deadpan expression, represented the only evidence that he was making a joke.

Ruppelt laughed a little nervously. "You'd think so, though you can never tell with Congress and appropriations. One thing I'm sure of, is that we'll be able to expect Senator McAfee's full support in the future."

He paused before adding, "That is, if the real one managed to escape."

This comment represented all the enticement Andre Domergue needed. Domergue continued to hover nearby, his attention arrested by the mention of

Joe McAfee. Andre had a younger brother who actually was a card-carrying communist, and Andre like to keep an eye out for the kid.

"His committee is in for a rude awakening," Lincoln La Paz said, showing a previously unexposed gift for understatement.

"Frankly, I think the bug was a better person. The real McAfee is going to be in a bad mood when he gets back. I hope State survives the coming purge."

"He's just another a publicity seeker," Hynek pointed out. "I'm sure he'll do whatever it takes to keep his name in the papers."

"Just as long as he doesn't run for president," Keyhoe grumbled. "Can you imagine that sourpuss in charge of the country? Nixon would be bad enough."

All four men shared a collective shiver at the idea.

"So...," La Paz said finally, hesitant but determined to broach the next topic, "I guess it all comes down to what we're going to do now that we have the definitive UFO evidence we've all been searching for."

"What do you mean?" Allen Hynek asked.

La Paz sighed. "Just this. One way or another, we've all been searching for the truth behind the UFO question. We've all expended considerable effort in pursuing this question. I've managed to limit myself to the subject of the green fireballs, but that seems to have run its course now. I was being a bit disingenuous with the Senator when he asked if I had an interest in the subject beyond the fireballs. I do, but so far there hasn't been much I could do without inviting public ridicule."

Hynek nodded. "I see what you mean. My role has been to provide explanations for the unexplainable, and up until now, no one seems to mind if those explanations don't make sense. Personally, I'd like someone to undertake a more scientific study of the subject, especially now that we have such excellent first hand knowledge."

Ed Ruppelt winced.

"Actually, Dr Hynek, I'm not sure our information is all that good."

Hynek's jaw dropped with an audible click.

Ruppelt held up a hand to forestall any protest.

"Hear me out, Allen. Everything we've seen over the last few days, it's all subjective. We have no real verification-"

"There must've been some corroboration," Keyhoe pointed out. "Maybe on radar, from the airport or Andrews."

Ruppelt nodded. "That would be a start, but it's hardly conclusive. Most of it would come down to what people saw on Saturday night and then we're right back in the pool, going by people's individual testimony. And that testimony is going to sound crazy."

"I have something," Lincoln La Paz said quietly. "The broken windows on the observation deck of the Washington Monument."

"Hey! That's good," Hynek agreed.

"There are probably scrapes along the upper part of the pyramidion where it went through the saucer." Ruppelt mused.

"Now we're getting somewhere!" Keyhoe agreed. "What do you say to that, Ed?"

Ed Ruppelt considered this, and finally nodded.

"Yeah, that'll be good enough to get things started...if we can verify the scratches. That may be easier said than done. I don't know how the devil we'll be able to get up there."

"There's the windows," said Lincoln La Paz. "If we can get to them before they're fixed."

"It's unfortunate that we were being held captive while most of this was going on," Ruppelt mused. "I wonder what it was like for the people on the ground."

"It was quite terrifying," Andre Domergue assured them in his heavily accented English. "The Army tried to evacuate the city. There were road-blocks everywhere. The power went out and even batteries wouldn't work. Two saucers attacked this very hotel!"

The four men looked at Andre Domergue long enough to make the maître d' feel rude for butting into a private conversation.

"Pleases forgive my interrupting," Andre apologized, "I could not help but overhear."

When the silence went on, Andre turned to go.

"You will have to excuse me. I have patrons to attend."

When the maître d' had gone, Keyhoe leaned whispered exultantly.

"Did you hear that? Maybe this won't be such a tough sell after all! It sounds like everybody saw the saucers! I wonder what happened in other cities!"

"There's an easy way to find out," said Allen Hynek.

The professor caught the attention of a passing waiter, requesting that the morning editions of the New York Times and the Washington Post be brought to their table. While they waited for his return, the four turned their attention to other matters.

"The real question," said Hynek, "is what we can do to get the word out. Surely, there will be more willingness to share information. The existence of UFOs is out of the closet now. It stands to reason that the government will have to share that information to avoid a panic."

"But that's the very reason they gave for withholding it," Ruppelt said.

"But that can't possibly continue now," Keyhoe hissed. "The saucers were seen by thousands! They can't possibly keep the lid on it now!"

The dining room around them suddenly paused, turning into a frozen tableau, like a length of film sliding off the teeth of the projector. A wave of energy ran through the diners, cresting and falling like ripples in a pond.

***

Perhaps anticipating the Monday morning flood of customers, Lars Ångström was one to the few to reserve a table, but the table he reserved was only for five. The plan was to have the table available when Maisie and the girls came down to join him. Sunday had been an odd day, starting with their return to the Ambassador, a journey that Lars had undertaken on foot.

The walk didn't bother him that much. Even though he was exhausted by his exertions, Lars had serious doubts about his ability to fit inside Janie's Nash. Besides, it was a fine morning, with the sun rising orange and hot over the eastern horizon. As he was accompanied by the rest of Project Stall, everyone had a great deal to talk about and the walk gave them time to do just that.

The female Ångströms were back at the hotel by seven, and in their beds a few minutes later. The girls were exhausted by their adventure, and Maisie had them tucked in before anyone could even mention breakfast. Bubbles fell asleep before she got into the car and was a dead weight as Maisie carted her up to their room.

After the rush of excitement following her beaning of Abel Corbett, Molly had steadily faded. By the time she found her way into Camille's back seat, she was little better than Bubbles. Stormy, determined to show that she was more mature than her sisters, forced herself to stay awake, but even she was sound asleep by the time Maisie got around to tucking her in.

Saying goodbye to Janie was another matter. Both women knew that Lars was bound to arrive any minute, but somehow their rather chaste kiss turned into some serious fooling around. When Lars arrived twenty minutes later, he found a locked door with a 'Do Not Disturb' sign dangling from the knob.

Most husbands would have knocked or simply entered, but Lars had picked up on the chemistry between his wife and her new acquaintance. Unlike most men of his era, Lars Ångström didn't have a jealous bone in his body. His response to the situation was to take the elevator back to the lobby where he proceeded to rent a third room. Once inside this private domicile, he took off his clothes, showered, and fell asleep as soon as his head touched the pillow.

The sign was still on the door when he awoke that afternoon, so he left a note for his wife, gathered up the girls, and took them out for a day on the town, the only regret being that so many of the usual attractions were unaccountably closed. The girls didn't mind a bit. For one of the rare times they could remember, they had their father all to themselves, and that cancelled out all of the many problems they encountered.

Lars made his breakfast reservation with a stuffy Frenchman in a workingman's tuxedo. Andre Domergue noticed the name, and only his Continental reserve prevented doing a double take when he recognized the author from his photo on the inside jacket of his copy of *Sex!* Andre said there would be a twenty minute wait and invited Ångström to take a seat in the bar, with a promise that he would come for him as soon as a table became available.

Lars did as the *maître d'* suggested, and spent his time sipping a Bloody Mary while indulging in a promising flirtation with a cocktail waitress who said she was a matriculating junior at the Dunbarton College of the Holy Cross. It was due to this distraction that his attention was engaged in other matters when Maisie and the girls came down to claim his reservation for their own. The issue was further complicated when Janie Gently, his wife having failed to inform him that the reporter would be joining them for breakfast, arrived to claim the remaining seat.

***

Janie Gently arrived with a breathless urgency, her haste being a byproduct of her clandestine departure and a quick dash to her apartment for a change of clothes.

Andre Domergue raised a discerning eyebrow when the plain young woman requested the table of the notorious sex doctor, but politely guided Janie to the booth he'd assigned to the Ångström clan.

"Can I sit next to Janie?" Bubbles asked as soon as the reporter came into view. On the basis of their airport conversation, Bubbles had already taken a proprietary interest in Janie Gently.

"No, dear," Maisie said firmly, rising to let Janie take the booth's inner seat. "Janie will be sitting next to me. But you can sit across the table from her."

"What about Father?" Stormy asked, glaring at the intruder who'd usurped such a prominent role in the family hierarchy. Stormy supposed she liked Janie well enough, but she still couldn't imagine why her mother would want her around when their father was available.

"Your father has other friends staying at the hotel," Maisie said. "I'm sure he'll be having breakfast with them."

"How come we're not going to Sweden?" Molly asked, surreptitiously dipping her finger into the sugar bowl, an act that Maisie swatted her for before she could bring it up to her mouth.

"Well, dear," her mother explained, "we missed our flight when your father didn't show up, so now we'd have to buy new tickets, and tickets to Sweden are very expensive. Besides, I've never had a chance to show you girls around Washington. I spent my teenage years here, you know."

"But Father already showed us around yesterday," Stormy said sourly.

Maisie restrained her grimace, but just barely.

"Oh, I'm sure he didn't show you everything, dear."

"Yes, he did," Molly added, taking her sister's side. "Everything was closed."

"Well, I'm sure it won't be closed today. I'm hoping Janie can come with us, too. Won't that be fun?"

"Yay!" Bubbles crowed, unable to contain her joy.

"I do have to go to work every once in a while," Janie muttered, too low for the girls to hear. "I can't take every day off."

Maisie's hand disappeared under the table. The unexpected contact made Janie straighten in alarm. The hand remained in place until the waiter arrived to take their order. By the time the waiter left, Maisie had her rebellious subjects under control, and by the time he returned with pancakes all around, Janie had ceded the day to her new mistress.

"Can we go see the Monnament?" Bubbles asked.

"It's a monument, dear," Maisie corrected her. "Of course," she added after a moment of reflection, "that might even be a good place to start our adventure."

Molly snorted at the very idea that any afternoon with their mother could be considered an adventure. It certainly didn't compare to being kidnapped by gangsters and menaced by a giant worm. After a moment of rare reflection, she decided she was fine without the giant worm.

"Couldn't we-," Stormy began. She stopped upon realizing she didn't really know what she wanted. It was just that going back to where they were attacked by a giant worm didn't seem like the best idea in the world. As the eldest, she didn't like admitting it to her mother, but she'd already had three nightmares about the worms the last night alone.

On the other hand, she thought, reconsidering her stance, it might be fun to see if she could spot the scratch marks left by the bug saucer.

"That sounds lovely," she concluded so lamely that Molly punched her under the table. "I mean, it would be lovely if Janie wants to go," Stormy said, punching back.

It took Janie a moment to realize that someone had said her name, and a response was expected. "Oh, anything's fine with me," Janie said, squirming a little at the effect Maisie's hand was having.

It was then that the waiter returned with the pancakes. Feeling very mature for having thought of it, Stormy asked, "Are you going to write a story about the saucers, Janie?"

It was a measure of how distracted she'd been that Janie hadn't even thought about doing so. She forgot about what Maisie's hand was doing long enough to stare back at the oldest girl in open-mouthed surprise.

"I didn't even think of it," Janie admitted.

When Stormy's zeal faded a notch, Janie added, "But I think it's a great idea!"

The instant after that she wondered what her other colleagues were doing. She hadn't even looked at the morning papers, an oversight that, given her profession, had to border on criminal negligence. It certainly wasn't a mistake that Bertie or Fast Johnny would make.

"I gotta get a paper!" Janie blurted as she started to rise.

Maisie did something with her hand that took Janie's breath away.

"Just stay put, darling," Maisie urged her, "I'm sure the waiter can bring you one."

"I'm sure you're right," Janie gasped, drawing looks from the girls across the table.

Maisie signaled for the waiter, attracting his attention in a way Janie didn't think she'd ever master.

"We'd like copies of all the morning papers," Maisie commanded before the waiter could even ask what she wanted. "Will that do?"

"Yes!" Janie gasped again, her voice rising to a squeak.

"Oh, good," Maisie purred, taking a sip of coffee. "I hoped it would. You know, if you're ever allowed a vacation, we'd love to have you come visit us in Madison. Have you ever been to Wisconsin? "

The idea of visiting Wisconsin was just one of many things Janie Gently had never considered. "Yes, I'd like that," Janie said. "And no, I've never been."

The papers arrived shortly thereafter and, after Maisie released her to peruse them, Janie immersed herself in the headlines before delving into the back pages. Several minutes later, Janie looked up in frustrated confusion.

"There isn't anything in here about the saucers."

"Maybe it was in yesterday's edition," Maisie suggested.

"There weren't no papers yesterday," Bubbles said, gamely holding her milk in both hands to prevent spilling.

"Father looked everywhere," Stormy added.

"Of course," Janie said after a moment of consideration, "there couldn't be any thing in the Sunday editions. Most of the paper gets printed on Friday, before anything happened. And Saturday, there wasn't any power to run the presses."

But this topic of conversation went no further, as a wave of chronokinetic energy swept through the room, erasing almost every memory it touched.

***

Lars Ångström traded his spot at the family table for the phone number to the Dunbarton girl's rooming house. The waitress was a slight brunette with a good figure and an unflattering perm that Lars chose to ignore in light of her better features. The only negatives to this flirtation were that she had a boyfriend in Chevy Chase and didn't get off work till after six o'clock. Lars felt he could be patient about the one and oblique about the other.

He was rescued from what would've been a long wait by the arrival of Rita Mae Marshaux and Jakob Kleinemann. As a researcher experienced in both human relations and sexual behavior, it was obvious to Lars that the pair had been busy consummating their nuptials from the day before. In the aftermath of their union, Rita Mae vacated Mrs Kelley's rooming house to move into Jakob's hotel room. The glow radiating from both told him that the newlyweds were already becoming proficient in their new endeavor. Lars smiled benignly at his colleagues.

"I see you have no regrets about your decision."

"None at all," said Rita, taking the seat to his left. Though it was still early, the bar was already full of patrons waiting for tables. Acting with foresight, Lars had commandeered a small table within the Dunbarton girl's area of responsibility.

"After what we went through, I didn't think I could wait a week."

Rita reached for her husband's hand, but had to wait for Jakob to hop up onto his chair.

"You don't regret not having your family present?" Lars asked.

Rita Mae shrugged. "Not enough to wait. Anyway, it's better for Jakob to meet my brothers after the deed is done."

"I got nothin' to fear from you brothers," Jakob scoffed in an abysmal imitation of Cajun accent. "I got me a *warak shu* now."

"Well, you just keep that thing in your pants, mister," Rita scolded. "I don't want trouble with my brothers or anyone else in my family. Anyhow, I sent 'em a wire. That should be good enough for now. "

Lars reconsidered his own *warak shu*, using the Dunbarton girl and others like her for context. Perhaps he hadn't yet scratched the surface of its utility.

"How about you, Jakob? Are you sorry your aunts weren't there to see you get married?"

"*Ach*, no," Jakob replied before returning to his normal accent. "I have no regrets, You do not know my aunts. I can well imagine what they will say. She's not Jewish. Was there a rabbi? You might have hurt yourself stepping on the wine glass. I would never hear the end of it."

"Sometimes, a man must do what he wants to do without worrying about everyone else. But what about you? We thought you'd be on your way to Sweden by now."

Lars Ångström shook his head ruefully.

"My family rebelled after our adventure on Saturday. Now it appears that we'll stay in Washington for the week, then fly home. Complicating matters, my wife has made a new friend. So, for the moment at least, I am at loose ends."

"I wish there was some way we could help you," Jakob said, making googly eyes at his new bride. "But our itinerary is quite full."

"Yes," Rita confirmed, grinning back, "quite full indeed."

"There they are." A familiar voice called from over by the entrance.

"I just want breakfast," a grumpy voice replied. "I really don't feel like talking to anyone."

Rita Mae, as the only member of their table facing the entrance, waved the new arrivals over to join them.

"Aw, come on, Artie," said Dexter Wye, "it's only the docs and Rita. I'm sure they'll let you eat in peace." Dex smiled genially as he stepped aside to let Artie chose his seat.

"No one would dare get in your way, Arthur," Rita smirked, "unless they're willing to lose a limb."

Arthur Ecks reluctantly allowed himself to be led over to the table. Dex grabbed an extra chair from another table while Lars went off to inform Andre Domergue that there would be an additional Ångström quintet whenever a table became available.

Outwardly, Arthur Ecks appeared to be freshly shaved and scrubbed. His brush-cut hair was still damp from the shower and his forehead was freshly sprinkled with tiny beads of sweat that the humidity of the coming day would do nothing to curb.

Lars returned an instant later, with the news that a table for six had become available. This triggered a migration into the dining room where their positions were re-established at the new location. Menus were passed out and meals ordered before conversation resumed. The discussion that followed was the sort that was usually conducted in a sealed room, far from prying ears. Instead, the ongoing tumult around them, coupled with the unearthly topic of conversation, made the restaurant an acceptable locale for their debriefing.

"I guess everybody's heard the reports about last night," Dex ventured as soon as the waiter departed.

"I can't say *we* have," Jakob said, pouring connubial oil on an already blazing fire.

"Nor have I," added Lars Ångström, realizing that he might have been the only member of the team who hadn't gotten laid over the weekend, a very odd outcome indeed.

"Well," Dex said, glancing over at Artie who was busy polishing off a chicken fried steak and the half dozen eggs that accompanied it, "there were more saucers sighted last night, mostly on radar. Obviously, it wasn't as many as on Saturday-"

"I sure as hell hope not," Arthur Ecks said around a mouthful of scrambled egg.

"-but both Andrews and Washington National picked them up. They stayed high in the atmosphere and nothing came low enough to interfere with commercial flights."

Arthur Ecks swallowed and reloaded his fork.

"The interesting thing is that, after hovering for about three minutes, every one of them headed southeast."

"Does that have any significance?" Lars Ångström asked.

"It does," Ecks said before taking his next bite. Upon swallowing, he added, "I think our bug friends acted on a suggestion I made just before we crashed."

Between bites, Ecks related the story of his recommendation that the bugs check out the Sahara.

Jakob Kleinemann tore his eyes away from his new wife long enough to praise Ecks' ingenuity.

"That was an excellent suggestion. Whatever made you think of it?"

Arthur Ecks paused, a forkful of hash browns poised for entry.

"Just putting two and two together, I guess. It occurred to me that if the bugs were as dependent on sand as they appeared to be, a desert would be the best place for them. The other thing was that McAfee said they'd have to alter the Earth's climate to make the planet habitable. I figured if they weren't going to leave, the Sahara would keep them out of everyone's hair until we can figure out what to do."

"Well, I applaud your inspiration," Jakob said, surreptitiously sliding his hand up Rita's skirt.

"I agree," said Lars. "So the Sahara will be our solution to the bug problem."

"For the next few years," Arthur Ecks said, thrusting a large mass of gooey steak into his mouth, "now could everyone just let me eat in peace."

"But what about the worms?" Dex asked. The image of Wally Sands' worm consuming a motorcycle cop and an infantry quartet was an image he'd been unable to get out of his head. "I just hope no kids saw it. That's the kind of thing that'd give anyone nightmares for months."

The Ångström girls had seen both worms, though they closed their eyes when Wally Sands' worm was feeding.

"My daughters don't seem to have been overly affected," Lars said.

This wasn't remotely true, but he didn't want to admit that his room wasn't even on the same floor as his daughters.

"That's right," Dex said. "Your girls saw them up close and personal."

"Where do you think the worms are now?" Jakob asked.

The question was meant to be rhetorical, but Lars had an answer.

"I believe the first one, the one belonging to Captain Sands, was sent back to the lair where I was captured. I'd wager that's where Major Corbett was taken as well."

"Those guys are going to be a problem," Dex pointed out. "It's just like the bugs. Both the bugs and the worms can look like anyone you meet on the street."

"We got a bigger problem," Arthur Ecks said, putting down his fork.

"What's that, Artie?"

"We gotta figure out a way to cover this whole thing up."

The table fell into a numb silence that was broken when the newly minted Rita Mae Kleinemann said, "Oh, yeah. That."

***

Rita rarely said much on the occasions when Project Stall assembled for a full meeting, but this time there was good reason for her silence. Though she'd tried to relay the information several times, she'd been thwarted on each occasion by a restriction she'd been unable to get around. It was frustrating, even if it wasn't unexpected.

After all, the Ffaeyn had warned her.

She couldn't tell anyone about the Word.

She would only be able to use it, and even that was a one time deal.

So what was it to be?

If she used the Word, she could do what Arthur Ecks had requested which was to keep the Earth in a state of innocence for just a little while longer. If she used the Word now...

She could undo the chaos and the physical damage done to the city.

She could undo the memories of every person who had seen the bug saucers, of every person who'd witnessed the futility of the human effort to combat the menace from the stars.

The question was, was it worth it?

But if she only had one chance to use the Word, that also meant it wouldn't be available when the next threat came along. The Ffaeyn had warned her that she wouldn't remember their gift once it was gone. As relatively few had been hurt in all the chaos, was it worth the loss of the Word to put things back to normal.

Her first instinct was to say no. There was so much else that could happen, so many other threats that might require it as a last resort. She'd thought about asking Jakob if this might be something the *warak shu* could be used for, but whatever mechanism governed her stewardship of this gift, it was one that required her to make the decision alone, without benefit of counsel.

And who was she to make such a monumental decision?

A Cajun girl whose only real education had come in the years since she left home?

Checking out of the conversation at her table, Rita listened in on the tables around her where everyone was talking about Saturday night.

She heard the fear in their accounts, the unsettled apprehension that went hand in hand with the knowledge that humanity was no longer top dog on its home planet. There were other intelligent beings out there, with capabilities and technology far beyond anything Man could muster.

How long had Man been top dog?

A few thousand years?

Nobody knew for sure, but all indications pointed to it not being very long. In any case, it wasn't going to be true much longer, and an even bigger question remained.

As flawed as humanity was, would the world be any better under alien rule?

Her ears returned to the other tables where stunned families spoke of the things in the sky, things, that before Saturday night, seemed as unknowable as the nature of God.

She heard the worry in their voices, the trepidation of an uncertain future.

She heard their awe of the unseen beings who were able to traverse the stars.

She even heard something that sounded like hope, a release from the decision-making of flawed men. There were benefits, it seemed, to no longer being in charge, but were those benefits sufficient that mankind could afford to relinquish control?

The questions were complex, but it didn't take her long to decide.

She made her decision, knowing she was one of those flawed beings, but also knowing that it wasn't yet time to give up on human autonomy.

She spoke the Word in a whisper.

And the World was changed in ways that few would remember.

Chapter 58 - Loose Ends

The bug who'd taken the place of Joe McAfee during the first half of 1952 never came back from summer recess. If any regretted his absence, it was most likely the civil service employees of the State Department, many of whom were called to testify on the flimsiest evidence imaginable. This elder version of McAfee swept away all memories of the affable bug as he rained holy terror on civil servants performing relatively unimportant jobs.

But Joe McAfee wasn't the only returnee. Also returning were several well-placed members of the House Un-American Activities Committee, as well as a few dozen congressmen and senators who hadn't attracted as much attention. Not one of these men was returned with any memory of where they'd been or what had been going on in their absence, but with the bar for congressional awareness set as low as it was, their ignorance upon returning aroused very little suspicion.

By the time the government ended its summer recess, everything had pretty much returned to normal, which in the end, is just one more way of saying that it's a miracle humanity survives a single day.

***

Bertie Stein, after getting a firsthand look at what happens when a good Jew fails to observe the Sabbath, slept through Sunday and called in sick on Monday morning. He thought about retirement all through that day, ultimately deciding against it. There was no way he could sit around the house listening to Sadie yacking with her friends on the phone.

But when he returned to work on Tuesday, he discovered that his heart just wasn't in it anymore. He called his wife in California, where she was visiting the son from her previous marriage and gave her the news. They were moving to Florida, whether she liked it or not. It was one of the rare times he'd ever put his foot down with her, and he was surprised to see how readily she agreed to the move.

Bertie took Sadie and his retirement, and moved into a nice apartment in downtown Fort Lauderdale. He still complained about the various ways his body let him down, but from that day forward, he did it mostly from the comfort of a chaise lounge.

***

While so many of the principals in this story were having breakfast at the Ambassador, John Haste and Desiree Blythe were being married in a civil service at the District of Columbia Municipal Courthouse. It was a simple ceremony, attended by only the justice of the peace and a paid witness. Desiree cried tears of joy all through the ceremony, ruining her mascara in the process. When John Haste kissed her at the end, he had to curl his question mark spine down a full foot to reach her.

His discomfort was eased when Desiree whispered that it was all right to lift her. Haste wrapped his arms around his petite amour, lifting her so high that her toes brushed his kneecaps and his spine gave a great crack that startled everyone. He left the courthouse a much taller man than when he arrived.

In the wake of their pending morals charge, the newlyweds decided they'd had enough of Washington. Calling in a favor, Haste found a job with the Fort Worth Star-Telegram, reporting on a local circus known as the Texas legislature, while Desiree talked her way into penning a lonely hearts column on the basis of a truly spectacular interview.

***

Due to the overall effectiveness of Rita Mae's Word of power, General Neal Cranston was never called to answer for his decision to evacuate the city. In the aftermath of all that happened, there was an unspoken agreement by the powers-that-be to pretty much ignore the events of July 19-20. Nonetheless, Cranston found his career stalled from that night forward. When his assignment at Andrews ended, he was persuaded by General Hoyt Vandenberg, among others, to retire.

Long before that came to pass, he was surprised to learn that his mistress of three years had vacated the apartment he kept for her, leaving behind most of the gifts he'd bought. One notable exception was that ridiculous dog. Desiree also left a short note, explaining that she'd gotten married and was moving to Texas. Try as he might, Cranston didn't know what to make of that.

His initial reaction was one of mild euphoria. After all, the relationship had ended without having to endure the unpleasantness of informing his paramour that she'd grown old and fat and was being replaced. But as the days went by, the fact that she'd left so much when she absconded began to rankle him. It was as if their years together had meant nothing to her.

He began to consider ways of tracking her down just to tell her it was over, imagining that by making the decision his, he'd be able to sooth his discomfort. In the end he did nothing, and when the sun set on his career a few months later, he returned to Geraldine and Richmond in the belief that that at least he still had a wife, six children, and a reconstructed abode with national heritage status.

He soon discovered that his retirement was just one of many things he should've discussed with his wife. Upon learning of his intent, she served papers for divorce.

And naturally, she kept the house.

***

The worms inhabiting the skulls of Abel Corbett, Wally Sands, Perseus Grady, and Winthrop Walton Russell III, returned to their lair under the Senate building. They returned to lick their wounds, but also to regroup.

Kraall took an exceptionally long time to heal and the lengthy convalescence did nothing to improve his mood. It was one of the worms' limitations that while they were quite capable of healing a host, it took quite a bit longer to heal themselves. In some ways, Kraall never completely recovered, one being that he would harbor an irrational fear of subcompact cars for the rest of his days.

Not all of Wally Sands made the transit from the lawn of the National Mall back to their subterranean hideout. Lars Ångström's *warak shu* did an admirable job of getting him there in one piece, but it left a few parts behind along the way, specifically, every bit of body hair he had on his head, chest, back, and genitals. Sands hated the new look and cursed Shhf for his inability to grow it back.

Nothing really changed for Perseus Grady. He was third in the hierarchy when he started and still third at the end of the episode. The only thing that differed between his worm before and after was a newfound love for making crank phone calls. The calls all went to the same number and were answered by the same man. Oddly, that man never took any action to stop the calls, and over time, even came to look forward to them. For years after the events of July 19-20, the other members of Majestic-12 would wonder where the devil Allen Dulles was getting his information.

As Kraall had promised, Mudduk and Winthrop Walton Russell III were severely punished for their role in the worms' defeat. The punishment went on for about three hours and only ended when the device used to meet out their penalty failed, requiring Russell's service to fix it. By the time the drive was up and running again, Kraall had forgotten about the whole incident and moved onto other schemes.

In the end, the *thang* had to accept the fact that the worms weren't quite ready to conquer the Earth just yet.

***

The flying saucers that came to Washington after that first weekend were following a homing beacon that'd been set up to attract them to North America.

But once they entered the atmosphere, these late arrivals found that the beacon had been diverted, and was now directing them to a new homeland on the other side of the Atlantic.

Some of the bugs felt betrayed by the change of plans, and turned around to go back to where they came from.

But those who went to Africa found that all the promises were true.

August in the Sahara was a paradise on Earth.

Over the course of the next week, dozens of flying saucers were sighted over the District of Columbia. But though the reports would taper off by the end of the second week, they would remain significantly higher than they'd been in the months leading up to July 19th.

After the second weekend, President Harry Truman would meet with the head of Project Blue Book to ask for an explanation. It is assumed that some explanation was provided, but whatever Captain Ruppelt told the outgoing leader of the free world, it wasn't recorded for posterity.

After breakfast at the Ambassador, Arthur Ecks proceeded to his final task alone, leaving the other members of Project Stall to their own whims. The newlyweds, Jakob Kleinemann and the former Rita Mae Marshaux, checked out of the hotel and loaded up Rita's Ford for the drive back to Dayton.

Lars Ångström would be initially rebuffed in his attempt to join his family for their day's outing, but somehow wound up with custody of the girls for the second day in a row. Later that evening, he consoled himself by licking his emotional wounds and other things with the Dumbarton girl.

Dex drove Artie to his appointment, but stayed with the car.

The old man had aged significantly since the last time Arthur Ecks had seen him. For one thing, he wasn't playing golf anymore. If asked, Colonel Bee would claim that his abandonment of the game was due to arthritic joints, but Ecks suspected that the real culprits were the twenty-yard tee shots he'd been hitting since the previous fall. The falloff in his game had shamed him and that shame had taken a lot of the fun out of their briefings. With the fairways of the East Potomac golf course now an untenable location, Colonel Bee chose a park bench on the same side of the river, with a similar view of the Pentagon.

The old man arrived in a cranky mood. He took his seat beside Ecks, his weight heavy on the armrest as he lowered himself onto its weathered planks. He was already complaining by the time he made himself comfortable.

"What was all that racket the other night? I had a devil of a time getting to sleep."

Ecks watched a two-story houseboat drift by on the river. The houseboat was being drawn behind an ancient tug that was spitting salvos of oily black smoke.

"That's what I'm here to discuss, sir."

"I could swear that someone knocked on my door, well after midnight if you can believe it. Wanted me to get up. You can bet I told him where to go."

Three children, two boys and a girl, waved from the lower deck of the houseboat. The younger boy was playing a harmonica.

Ecks waved back.

"It was probably the Army. They tried to evacuate the city, you know."

The old man looked at Ecks as if he'd just said men had gone to the moon, then returned to report that it was made of an aged dairy product. The old man peered myopically out over the river to where the Pentagon rose above the shore like a grey edifice robbed of all color.

"You don't say," Bee replied. "Why on earth would they do that?"

Ecks smiled at the old man, realizing that the moment he'd been fearing the last two years might have finally arrived. This would probably be his last debriefing. Ecks used the old man's former rank for the first time since the war.

"Well, Colonel, on Saturday night, the capital was attacked by flying saucers from another world. For many of the reasons we've discussed over the years, the military was completely unprepared. The Air Force was ineffective and the Army tried to evacuate the city. The aliens brought us to a standstill. They had a weapon that projects a kind of damping field that renders any electrical device unusable. The result was a total blackout and thousands of stalled cars."

The old man shook his head, his chin dropping to his chest in shame.

"I just started wearing hearing aids, you know." He tapped the side of his head, pointing out the devices protruding from both ears. "Can't hear a damn thing without 'em. I take 'em out at night."

Ecks patted the old man on the shoulder.

"With the damping field, they probably wouldn't have worked anyway."

"So what happened? I assume you figured out something 'cause I didn't see any little green men on the drive over. How did you get rid of 'em?"

Arthur Ecks told him everything he knew about Saturday night. The colonel listened in rapt fascination, only interrupting when he sensed that Ecks was reaching the end.

"They actually took you prisoner?"

Ecks nodded. "Yeah, but it was only for a few hours. I had an interesting chat with the bug that was pretending to be Joe McAfee."

The old man stared back in disbelief.

"That part surprises me. You mean to tell me that Joe McAfee is a bug?"

Ecks nodded again. "He had some interesting things to say. He wasn't a bad sort, especially when you consider that he was here to conquer the Earth. All in all, I think we could have done a whole lot worse."

The old man scratched his chin meditatively.

"Conquer the Earth...you don't say."

The old man got a faraway look in his eyes, but offered no comment.

"He was quite affable," Ecks said, "at least until I said one thing that still puzzles me. For the life of me, I can't figure out why it upset him so much."

The old man sniffed.

"What did you say?"

Ecks peered closely at the old man. It'd been twelve years since he'd gone to work for the colonel, but he'd never been very good at reading the man. Whatever the reason, the colonel had always been a closed book.

"I said he'd be in a heap of trouble if he went through with the attack."

The colonel didn't look up. As far as Ecks could tell, he didn't react at all.

"You said that?"

"I did. What's more, I said it right after they'd trounced our Air Force, so he knew I wasn't saying it out of a position of strength."

"How did he take it?"

Ecks paused, recalling the startling change that had come over the bug.

"It was the only time I saw him really upset. He acted pissed off at me when I refused to testify at the hearing, but I think that was just play acting. I don't think he ever expected me to say anything of substance in front of the reporters."

"Upset, huh?"

"Yeah, then he said something really interesting. He assumed that since I'd said that, it meant I was working for some Council. You know anything about that?"

"Me?" Bee said, a little startled. "Why would I know anything about-"

"He referred to you by name. Said that I'd finally given myself away, and that I must be working for this Council because you work for the Council and I work for you. Is it true? Is there some Council we've been working for all these years? What do you think he meant?"

But Colonel Bee had recovered from his initial shock and now seemed unfazed by Ecks' revelation.

"I haven't the foggiest idea, dear boy."

"He said you were as old as Council itself."

"He did, did he? I don't know if that's flattering or not."

Ecks turned away from the old man to stare out across the river.

"I need you to answer a question, Colonel. Can you do that for me?"

The old man seemed uncomfortable.

"I suppose it depends on the question, dear boy."

"It's just..., I always thought we were working for the government."

"Is that your question? Because I don't hear one."

"Yes," Ecks said. "Are we working for the government?"

"Of course," the old man said, now visibly relaxing.

374

"The government of the United States?"

The old man tensed up again, then turned away. For the longest time, he said nothing. When Ecks saw that his eyes were closed, he feared the old man had gone to sleep. He didn't open his eyes when he gave his answer.

"Does it really matter so much?"

"I would just like to know," Ecks said softly, "if I'm a traitor."

When the colonel finally opened his eyes, they were as clear and blue as they'd been when he first pulled Ecks out his first assignment as an officer, setting him on the course that would guide the rest of his life.

"Arthur," the colonel said slowly, lingering over the two syllables of his name, "you and I may be the only men on this planet who aren't traitors."

Not knowing what to make of this comment, Ecks was quiet after that.

The clarity faded from the colonel's eyes.

After a long pause, he said, "I still can't believe Joe McAfee is a bug."

Ecks let out his breath, knowing this was as much as he was going to get.

"He was a bug. I think they returned the real McAfee when they took off. The thing that makes it worse is that McAfee wasn't the only politician they replaced. Apparently a third of the House of Representatives and a good part of the Senate was made up of alien shapeshifters. They're all gone now and the real politicians should be returning to work when they come back from recess."

The old man nodded as if this confirmed something he'd suspected.

"That explains a lot. There's been some mighty strange stuff coming out of the House this year. I was wondering why McAfee went soft."

"He did go soft," Ecks agreed. "But I gotta say, the bug wasn't such a bad guy once you got to know him."

The old man coughed, then cleared his throat.

"But what about the bugs? From what you said, they're gone for now, but they must have traveled light years to get here. That's an awfully long way, no matter how you slice it. Did they just go back to where they came from?"

Ecks thought about it, then frowned.

"No, I shouldn't think so. As you said, it is an awfully long way. Maybe it's just a feeling, but I think they're still here. I think they've just given up on the idea of conquering the world. McAfee said something I found very interesting just before the saucer crashed."

"What was that?"

"He said they were administrators, not explorers. He said they don't look for empty planets. They prefer planets with existing civilizations, where they can just slide into place at the top of the power structure. They came here in great numbers and, for the life of me, I can't see them just turning around and heading back to where they came from."

The colonel nodded.

"That makes a kind of sense."

Ecks continued. "I'm sorry to bring up the Council again, but from what I gleaned from McAfee, I suspect their presence here isn't sanctioned by the Council."

The colonel's face hooded over at the mention of the Council.

"So, where do you think they are then?"

Ecks looked out over the sluggish river, assembling the pieces of what he'd learned. He thought about mentioning the *warak shu*, the strange devices now in the hands of Lars Ångström and Jakob Kleinemann, but decided against it. If the colonel wanted to keep secrets from him, it was only fair that he held something back himself.

"For reasons I still don't understand, the bugs weren't able to take over on Saturday. But since it's so far back to their homes, and there are so many of them here, I don't think they've left. Nonetheless, I don't think they're going to be a problem, at least not for a while."

"Why's that?"

"One of the last things McAfee revealed to me was their plan to turn the entire world into a desert. Their natural environment is sand. They live in it and eat it and breathe it. They hate humid places like Washington and cold places like the poles. They hate the oceans here and the moisture that pervades most of the planet."

"So why come here at all?"

Ecks chuckled. "Well, part of the reason is they didn't do their homework before they arrived. For example, they didn't even realize that there's a large part of the world that's already perfectly set up for them. You should have seen how excited McAfee was when I made my suggestion."

Colonel Bee's eyes narrowed suspiciously.

"What exactly did you suggest?"

"I suggested that they try a friendlier climate."

"Where would that be?"

Ecks leaned back against the bench, staring out at the immobile face of the Pentagon across the river. There were thousands of men and women going about their business inside the building, but you'd never know from outside.

"I think they're headed for the Sahara."

The old man's eyes bulged open in shock.

"The Sahara? Why there? It's so blessed hot!"

Arthur Ecks smiled as he turned to look off toward the airport.

"Yeah, but it's a dry heat."

About the Author

I am not an alien, nor have I ever knowingly met one. I've never been abducted by Greys or probed by CIA operatives pretending to be Greys. For that matter, beyond a couple of weird childhood dreams, I've never seen anything that might be a flying saucer (except once, but that turned out to a weather balloon filled with swamp gas masquerading as the planet Venus).

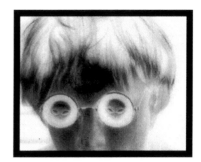

Frankly, I'm not much of a researcher. As a result, I make up a lot of the stuff I write about. However, I am incredibly indebted to the men and women who press forward on the UFO issue despite the skepticism they meet on a daily basis. This series does not intend to ridicule or parody those efforts, but rather to inject a little levity into a world that has grown far too serious.

If I can get anything across with these books, let it be to shine a light on the staggering amount of evidence one must ignore and the ridiculous explanations one must accept in order to believe that UFOs are NOT both extraterrestrial and real. It's hard to open the mind, but not impossible.

Each book in the UFO Sex Comedy series is based on actual UFO events or events that might be synchronous. They are populated by characters of my own creation or thinly veiled recreations of historical figures who shouldn't be mistaken for the real thing.

I can't claim that this work as science fiction and I doubt science fiction would ever want to embrace me as one of its own. Within these pages, there's very little accepted science. But science, like all human endeavors, changes over time. Contrast what we believe now with what our great-grandparents believed a hundred years ago. Who's to say what the world will look like in a hundred years? In many ways, this series is more about the past than it is about the future. Only the last book, should I live to complete it, is set past the current day.

I've tried to make the Sex part of these books fun (and maybe a bit enlightening) without getting too perverse (ie-going into horrifying detail). The books are occasionally salacious, but never hardcore, so don't come in expecting (or fearing) that. As to the Comedy..., you'll have to make up your own mind about that.

The author lives in Sonoma, California with his wife, Lee, and far too many spiders. He has public Facebook pages for Rhyscary Wade and the UFO Sex Comedy series where he can be contacted.

Made in the USA
San Bernardino, CA
28 March 2019